John Masefield

The Midnight Folk

The BOX of Delights

EGMONT

First published in Great Britain in two separate volumes:

The Midnight Folk
First published in Great Britain 1927
by William Heinemann Ltd
Published 1994 by Mammoth

The Box of Delights
First published in Great Britain 1935
by William Heinemann Ltd
Published 1994 by Mammoth

This omnibus edition first published 2001 by Egmont Books Ltd,
239 Kensington High Street
London W8 6SA

ISBN 0 7497 4872 9

3 5 7 9 10 8 6 4 2

A CIP catalogue record for this title is available from the British Library

Typeset by Dorchester Typesetting Group Ltd, Dorchester, Dorset
Printed and bound in Great Britain by Cox & Wyman Ltd, Reading, Berkshire

The Midnight Folk

For J. & L.

THE MIDNIGHT FOLK

It had been an unhappy day for little Kay Harker. To begin with, at breakfast time the governess had received a letter from his guardian, Sir Theopompus, the chemical powder merchant, to say that he would be there for lunch, but would like lunch at 2 p.m., as the trains did not suit. This made the governess cross, or, as she called it, 'put out.' On giving the order to Jane, the cook, for a very good lunch at two o'clock, instead of one, Jane was put out, for it was her afternoon off and she did not like to be put upon. Ellen, the maid, was also put out, because if you have lunch so late, it is tea-time before you have finished washing up. Jane and Ellen between them put the governess much further out, and then it was lesson time: Divinity, French, History and Latin.

Divinity was easy, as it was about Noah's Ark. French was fairly easy, as it was about the cats of the daughter of the gardener. History was not at all easy, as it was all about beastly Odo. He longed for Odo to come into the room, saying, 'I'm Odo,' so that he could jolly well shut him up with: 'Well, O, don't.' He got knapped on the knuckles rather tartly over history; then came Latin. That morning it was all adjectives, especially a loathsome adjective called Acer, acris, acre, sharp or piercing. It was that that put *him* out.

It came right at the end of lessons; that was the worst of it. As he was longing to be out of doors, he was always looking out of the window, watching the pigeons. He had to repeat acer line by line, in a sort of catechism.

The Governess: What is sharp?
Kay: Acer.
The Governess: Feminine?
Kay: Acris.
The Governess: Neuter?
Kay: Acre.
The Governess: Now the nominative; all genders.
Kay: Acer, acris, acre.
The Governess: Meaning?
Kay: Sharp.
The Governess: Or? What else can it mean?
Kay: Piercing.
The Governess: Accusative?
Kay: Acrem . . . Acris, acre.

Here the governess scowled rather, and would not say if he were right. Instead, she said: 'Genitive?' But how was he to leap at the genitive when he could not tell if his taking-off point, the accusative, were sound? Besides, had it a genitive? Could you say 'Of sharp'? What would be the genitive? Could it be acrae, acri, acri? That didn't sound right. What did sound right? Not quite acrorum, acrarum, acrorum.

'Well,' the governess said, 'what is the genitive?'

'Acrostic, acrostic, acrostic?'

'What?'

'Acrumpet, acrumpet, acrumpet.'

'You're a very idle, impertinent little boy,' the governess said. 'You will write it all out five times, and I shall tell your guardian, Sir Theopompus, when he comes. Now go and have your milk, but not your biscuit; you haven't deserved one; and mind you come to lunch with washed hands.'

The governess's Christian names were Sylvia and Daisy. Kay had read a poem about Sylvia, and had decided that it was not swains who commended this one, but Mrs. Tattle and Mrs. Gossip. He loved daisies because the closer one looked at them the more beautiful they seemed: yet this daisy was like a rhododendron. She was big, handsome and with something of a flaunting manner, which turned into a flounce when she was put out.

She left the schoolroom with something of a flounce after passing this sentence about the 'no biscuit with his milk.' He had had his biscuit stopped before, more than once. He had invented a dodge for making up for the loss of biscuit. He used to go to the kitchen cupboard, where the raisins were kept, and get a handful of raisins instead. Ellen was his devoted friend, and Jane thought that raisins were very good for him.

But this morning, alas, things had gone badly in the house, and Ellen and Jane were cross. When he put his hand into the blue paper bag for the raisins, Jane stopped him.

'Now, Master Kay,' she said, 'you put down those raisins, or I shall tell your governess about you. You go taking those raisins and then it's put down to me. You've got plenty of good plain food without going stuffing yourself. That's how little boys get a stoppage. And I don't want you bothering about in my kitchen when I'm as busy as I am. I've put your milk in the dining-room long ago.'

There was nothing for it but to go.

In the dining-room another trouble showed. There, on the sideboard, with his head in the tumbler of milk, which was tilted so that he was lapping the last remnants of it, was Blackmalkin, one of the three cats. Kay shooed him away, but three-quarters of the milk had gone, and Kay would not drink what was left, because the cat had breathed in it, and Kay had heard that a cat's breath always gave you consumption.

He went into the garden without milk or biscuit. Before he could settle down to any game, he was called indoors to wash his hands and then to put on a Sunday collar ready for Sir Theopompus. He loathed Sir Theopompus, a stout, red-faced man with eyes staring out of his head, as though he were at the point of choking. The worst of Sir Theopompus's coming was that there was always a lovely dinner, but 'no contentment therewith,' only the scowl of Sylvia Daisy if he did anything wrong.

Presently Sir Theopompus arrived in his fluttery way, with his gold-rimmed spectacles, his umbrella with the gold band and his gold watch and chain. The governess presented her reports, but mercifully never said anything about the Latin adjective. Sir Theopompus didn't say much to Kay, happily, but from time to time would ask some question, such as 'Are you enjoying your history? Got as far as the first Reform Bill yet? And what is your opinion of Lord Palmerston as a statesman, hey?' Then, after some more talk and another helping of goose, he would switch on to geography. 'Know all about latitude and longitude, hey? What latitude are you in now, do you suppose?'

Towards the end of dinner, when he was shiny with his lunch, Sir Theopompus asked: 'And what are you going to be, my young man? Got any plans yet?'

'I was rather hoping that I could be a jockey,' Kay said timidly.

A look of displeasure came upon Miss Sylvia Daisy's face.

'Not thinking of being a sailor, like your great-grandpapa?' Sir Theopompus said. 'Do you know about your great-grandpapa?'

'Yes, I know something,' Kay said.

'Oh! and what do you know?' said the governess very sweetly.

'He was a sea captain,' Kay said, 'and went a lot to the West Indies and Santa Barbara.'

'Yes,' Sir Theopompus broke in; 'and he took away the Santa Barbara treasure worth about a million pounds, as some think, and his crew mutinied, put him ashore and ran away with it. Pretty pickings for a crew of seamen. Of course, some say,' Sir Theopompus added as he rose from his chair, 'some say that your great-grandpapa brought that treasure home with him and hid it somewhere. Have you come upon any treasure in your grubbings?'

'No,' Kay said.

'Well, I'll tell you what I'll do,' Sir Theopompus said. 'If you'll find that treasure and tell me where it is, I'll go an honest halves with you.'

'But it wouldn't be an honest halves,' Kay said, 'because you'd have done none of the work and all the treasure belongs to the Santa Barbara priests.'

'Oh, so that's the line you're going on,' Sir Theopompus said. 'Now, you cut, for I've got to talk business here.'

Kay went out into the garden and amused himself until tea-time, wondering what the two could find to talk about, though he supposed that it was mostly about himself. Tea was very early, although lunch had been so late, because Sir Theopompus had to catch the 4.30.

Tea, with Sir Theopompus there, was a dismal function in the drawing-room, with the tea-set known as the Lowestoft and the stiff rosewood chairs which Kay was to be sure not to scratch.

'Well, have you found the treasure, hey?' Sir Theopompus asked.

Kay said that he had not.

'It seems to me,' Sir Theopompus said, 'that you're making this young man something of a moony. When I was a young fellow, by George, the thought of treasure would have set me going, I know. Don't you want to find it, hey?'

'Everybody says that it was never here, sir,' Kay said.

'Oh no,' Sir Theopompus answered. 'But a good many say that it was here and is here somewhere. Those West India merchants were a pretty odd lot of fellows, if you ask me. A lot of piracy and slaving going on there. I dare

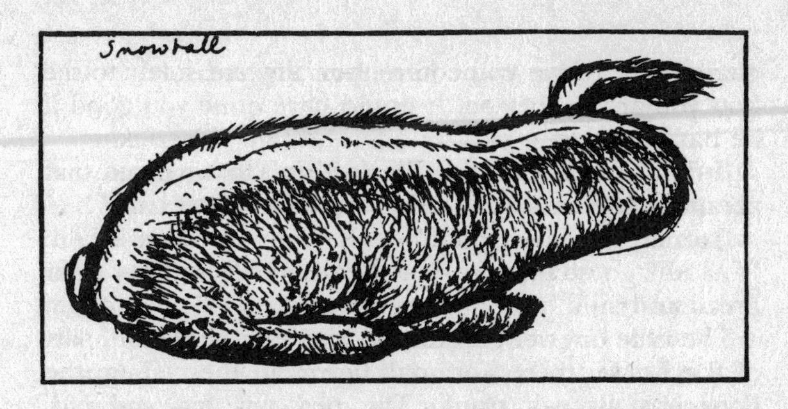

say your great-grandpapa was no better than his time, and a million pounds is a big temptation in the path of a man who's been just a merchant skipper.'

'Sir, he was a very good man,' Kay said. 'His portrait is in the schoolroom.'

'Well, he was a very good man, was he?' Sir Theopompus said. 'He didn't bring back the treasure that he was trusted with. We know what to call men of that stamp in the City, by George!'

The day had been full of contrariety. Now something in the day and in Sir Theopompus combined to Kay's ruin.

'Well, I don't care,' he said. 'You oughtn't to condemn a man who isn't here to answer.'

'By George,' Sir Theopompus said, 'we shall have to put you into Parliament.'

He went rather turkey-cocky about the gills, snorted, and said that he had to catch his train. When the wheels of the fly had scrunched along the gravel out of the gate, the governess turned upon him.

'What a very impertinent little boy you are, Kay,' she said; 'not only to me this morning, but to your kind guardian, who has come here specially and solely to see how you are getting on. It would have done you good if he had boxed your ears soundly and sent you packing.'

'I don't care,' Kay said. 'He oughtn't to have said that about great-grandpapa Harker, because it isn't true.'

'You are a wicked little boy, Kay,' the governess said: 'You will go straight to bed this minute, without your bread and milk.'

The little boy went upstairs to his room, in the old part of the house: there were oak beams in the ceiling; the floor was all oak plank. The bed was big and old, valanced to the floor, and topped by a canopy. Kay was very much afraid of it at going-to-bed-time because so many tigers could get underneath it, to wait till he was asleep; but tonight he did not mind, because it was still only sunset. He had two windows in his room. One looked out on a garden, where Nibbins, the black cat, was watching some birds; the other looked out over a field, where there was a sheep-trough. He did not like the look of the trough in the long grass, because it

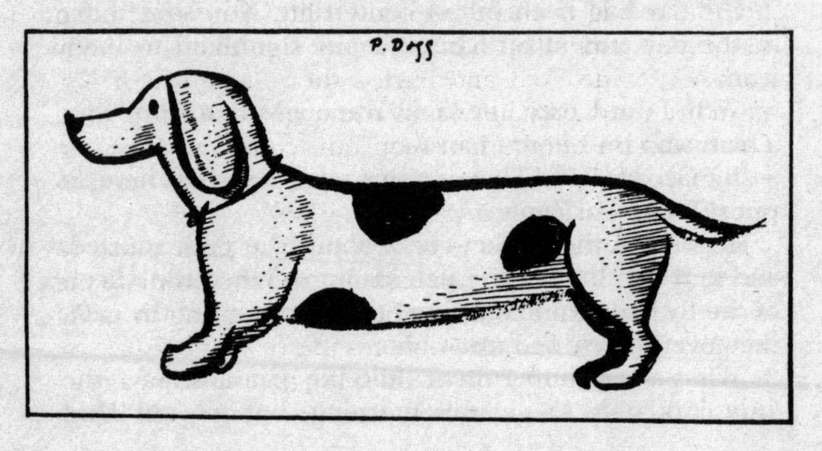

looked so like a puma, with its ears cocked. Beyond the field, he could see the stable, where Benjamin, the highwayman, had once lived.

Now in his room there were two doors, leading to different passages, which was terrible after dark, because of footsteps. On the wall were two coloured prints, The Meet and Full Cry, one on each side of the fireplace. Over the wash-hand-stand, as it was called, were two old pistols wired to nails. They were called 'Great-grandpapa Harker's Pistols,' and Kay was to be sure never to touch them, because they might go off. Then, on the other side of the room, there was the dressing-table, valanced to the floor, which made a very good secret room, where nobody ever looked for you. In the corner, near this, on a shelf on the wall, stood an old model of a ship, which Kay was never to touch, because boys are so destructive. This was the model of 'great-grandpapa Harker's ship,' the *Plunderer*, which had disappeared with the missing treasure so long before.

A very terrible thing about the fireplace was the stone hearth, 'as big as three men could lift,' Jane said. Ellen said that a stone like that was a sure sign that somebody had been murdered and buried there, and that if Kay wasn't a good boy, he would come out and warn him. Cook said once, 'she had seen him come out' and 'he was all in black,' which was a sure sign; 'and he wanted to speak,' she said, 'only it wasn't his time.'

This night the rooks were very noisy at their going to roost; the peacocks were screaming, and the brook at the end of the garden could be heard. 'It is going to rain,' Kay thought. He lingered over his undressing because he hoped that Ellen or Jane would smuggle him some bread and milk when the governess went to supper; but it was

Ellen's evening alone, when she always did her ironing, and Jane was out.

By and by the sun went down behind the wooded camp, known as King Arthur's Round Table, where King Arthur was supposed to ride at full moon. When the sun had gone, all the world glowed for a while; but it was not wise to wait till the glow had gone, because so soon the dusk began, when the owls would come, and the footsteps would begin, and the tigers would stir under the bed and put out their paws, and the scratchings would scrape under the floor. He knew that he had not been good and that 'he' might 'come out and warn him.' He got into the bed with a leap, because then you dodged the paws. He got well under the clothes for a minute, to make sure that he was not pursued. Luckily none of the tigers had heard him. The worst of it was that tigers look out for wicked little boys. When Kay came from under the bed-clothes he could not be sure that there was not a tiger lying in the canopy above him. It was sagged down, just as though a tiger were there. If it were to give way, the tiger would fall right on top of him. Or very likely it was not a tiger but a python, for that is what pythons do.

Now it became darker, so that he could see a few stars. Footsteps passed in the house, sometimes close to his door, so that gleams of candlelight crossed the ceiling.

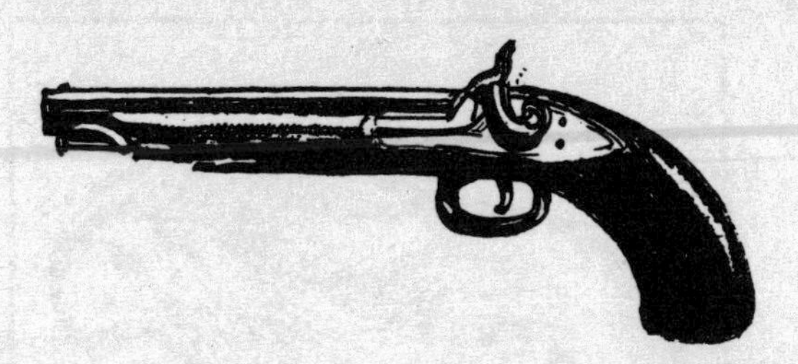

Very strange creakings sounded in the house; there were scutterings to and fro, and scraping scratchings. By and by he heard the governess, who had finished her supper, come to the room beneath him, the library, as she usually did in the evenings. He was cross with her for stopping his bread and milk, but glad that she was there. She opened the piano and began to play. Usually she played things without any tune, which she said he couldn't understand yet because they were classical. This night she played something that had a sort of tune, and then began to sing to it in a very beautiful voice, so that he was rapt away at once into joy: there were not any more tigers, nor pythons; only a mouse gnawing in the wainscot; or was it someone playing on a guitar and humming some song about a treasure?

After a time, he did not think that it was a guitar, but a voice calling to him: 'Kay, Kay, wake up.' Waking up, he rubbed his eyes: it was broad daylight; but no one was there. Someone was scraping and calling inside the wainscot, just below where the pistols hung. There was something odd about the daylight; it was brighter than usual; all things looked more real than usual. 'Can't you open the door, Kay?' the voice asked. There never had been a door there; but now that Kay looked, there was a little door, all studded with knops of iron. Just as he got

down to it, it opened towards him; there was Nibbins, the black cat.

'Come along, Kay,' Nibbins said, 'we can just do it while they're at the banquet; but don't make more noise than you must.'

Kay peeped through the door. It opened from a little narrow passage in the thickness of the wall.

'Where does it lead to?' he asked.

'Come and see,' Nibbins said.

Kay slipped on his slippers and followed Nibbins into the little passage: Nibbins closed the door behind him and bolted it.

'I'll lead the way,' he said. 'Mind the stairs: they're a bit worn; for the smugglers used to use these passages. But there's lots of light. Take my paw, as we go up.'

They went up some stairs in the thickness of the wall; then a panel slid up in front of them and they came out on to the top landing. Nibbins closed the panel behind them. It was dark night there on the landing, except for

a little moonlight. The house was very still, but looking down over the banisters into the hall, Kay thought that

he saw a shadow, wearing a ruff and a long sword, standing in the moonlight. The cuckoo-clock in the nursery struck twelve.

'All the house is sound asleep,' Nibbins said. 'Jane and Ellen are in there in those two rooms. They little know what goes on among us midnight folk. Give us a hand with this ringbolt, will you?'

In the oak planks of the floor there was a trap-door, which Kay had never seen before. Together they pulled it up: beneath was a ladder leading down into a passage brightly lit like the other.

'Close the trap after you,' Nibbins said, as he went down.

They went along a passage into a little room, all hung with swords and banners.

'This is the guard-room,' Nibbins said. 'Some of the swords are still here. The guards went away a long time ago. Least said, soonest mended; it's not for me to blame anybody. There are their names cut on the wall.'

Kay read some of the names:

Robin Pointnose.	Dogg.	Petter Horse.	
Eduardo da Vinci.	P. Dogg.	Tom.	Ernest.
Salado da Vinci.	Jack.	John.	Jemima.
Bruno Bree.	Peterkin.	Lenda.	Maria.
Snowball.	James.	Peter Gillian.	Susan.
G. L. Brown Bear.	Squirrel.	Wm. Brown.	Peter.

Alas, Kay knew those names only too well: they were the names of his beloved companions of old, before there had been any governess or Sir Theopompus. They had been his toys, of bears, dogs, rabbits, cats, horses and boys. They had all been packed away long ago, when the governess came, because, as he had heard her tell Ellen, 'they will only remind him of the past.' They were locked up somewhere, he thought; yet he often feared that they had been given away to other children, who would not know them or be kind to them.

'Why do you call them the guards, Nibs?' he asked.

'Why, because they were the guards,' Nibbins said. 'I told them they ought not to go, but Edward said that he had got a clue and had to follow it up.'

'What had he got a clue to?' Kay asked.

'The Harker treasure,' he said. 'I begged him to leave half the guards, but he said: 'No; I'll only be away a week or two.' So away they went, with the horse and cart, the big tent that takes to pieces, and all the hammocks and guns. Edward had his sword, the cocked hat, the coat with the piping, and his striped trousers, so you can see that he thought it important. But as to his being away only a week, he has been away a year or more; and not a word has come from any of them.'

'I'm afraid they are all dead,' Kay said. 'I wish they weren't.'

'Things have gone to wrack and ruin without them,' Nibbins said. 'What with witchcraft and that. Of course I'm only a cat, but I've got eyes, and a cat can look at a king. Still, least said, soonest mended. Now, come along, this way, down these steps. Now, do you see these eye-holes? They are cut in the portraits on the walls of one of the rooms. You can look down, if you like.'

Kay looked down through the eye-holes of Grand mamma Harker's portrait into the drawing-room, which was shuttered dark, except for some moonlight coming from the upper panes. This moonlight fell upon the table, where the red and white ivory chessmen were playing chess by themselves. They had come out of the box and ranged themselves. The kings called out the moves, but generally they asked the queens first. The pieces and pawns which had been taken stood beside the board, giving cheers for their own sides, and uttering little cries of warning.

'Well played, Red.'

'Now, White Knight, why don't you take him?'

'O, your Majesty, look out for the Bishop.'

'O well played, Your Grace; well played indeed.'

'That'll be Mate in three moves, if you do that, Red.'

'Will it really? Yes, my dear, I suppose it will. I'd better not do it then. What would you suggest?' etc.

While Kay was watching, Nibbins put a paw on his arm.

'Don't speak,' he said, 'Mrs. Pouncer is going to sing. Come along quietly, you'll enjoy this.'

He led Kay along a narrow corridor to another passage, where there were more eyelet holes. Kay looked

through the eyes of Great-grandmamma Siskin's portrait into the dining-room; but what did he see?

There were seven old witches in tall black hats and long scarlet cloaks sitting round the table at a very good supper: the cold goose and chine which had been hot at middle-day dinner, and the plum cake which had been new for tea. They were very piggy in their eating (picking the bones with their fingers, etc.) and they had almost finished the Marsala. The old witch who sat at the head of the table tapped with her crooked-headed stick and removed her tall, pointed hat. She had a hooky nose and chin, and very bright eyes.

'Dear Pouncer is going to sing to us,' another witch said.

'Hear, hear,' the other witches said. 'Dear Pouncer, sing.'

'But you must join in the chorus, sisters. Shall it be the old song, Dear Nightshade?'

'Yes, yes; the old song.'

Mrs. Pouncer cleared her throat and began:

'When the midnight strikes in the belfry dark
And the white goose quakes at the fox's bark,
We saddle the horse that is hayless, oatless,
Hoofless and pranceless, kickless and coatless,
We canter off for a midnight prowl . . .'

Chorus, dear sisters . . .

'Whoo-hoo-hoo, says the hook-eared owl.'

All the witches put back their heads to sing the chorus:

'Whoo-hoo-hoo, says the hook-eared owl.'

It seemed to Kay that they were looking straight at him. Nibbins' eyes gleamed with joy.

Petter Horse

'I can't resist this song,' he said, 'I never could. It was this song, really, that got me into this way of life.'

'But I don't know what it means. What is the horse that is hayless?'

'Aha,' Nibbins said. 'Well, we've time while they're at this song: it has nine times nine verses; but you ought to stay for some more Whoo-hoos. Doesn't it give you the feel of the moon in the tree-tops: "Whoo-hoo-hoo, says the hook-eared owl?" Come along quietly.'

Nibbins led the way up some more stairs, till he came to an open door, through which Kay saw the stars. 'Why, this is the roof,' he said. He saw how strange the roof was, close to, like this, with the twisted brick chimneys standing guard, with their cowls still spinning. He seemed very far from the ground.

'This is what they mean,' Nibbins said. 'Just open that middle chimney, will you?'

'But it is a chimney; it won't open.'

'No, it isn't. There's a bobbin on it; pull that; it's their stable.'

Kay scrambled up to the middle chimney of the three nearest to him. Sure enough, there was a bobbin on it. He pulled it, the latch came up, the chimney opened like a door; there inside was a cupboard in which stood one besom, one stable broom, one straw broom, one broom broom, and three kitchen brooms, each with a red headstall marked with magic.

'Take the besom and the broom broom,' Nibbins said, 'and pitch the others over the gutter.'

Kay pitched the five over the gutter; they whinnied as they fell on to the garden path, but nobody seemed to notice.

'Now let us mount and ride,' Nibbins said. 'But first, we'll shut the door.'

He was going to shut the door into the house, when the noise of the song suddenly became much louder. Somebody at the banquet said '*Hush*' suddenly; the singing stopped; the witches were holding their door open, listening.

'They've heard us,' Nibbins said. 'Mount, Kay, and ride. Mount, catch him by the bridle, say *Sessa,* and point him where you want to go. Watch me.'

Nibbins mounted the besom, Kay the broom broom. Just as he was mounted, he heard the sharp voice of Mrs. Pouncer calling from the foot of the stairs.

> 'Night-glider, tell . . .
> Are ill things well?'

Kay saw the besom toss up its head; it began to say:

> 'Save, mistress, save,
> From white thief and black knave.'

but before he could finish, both Nibbins and Kay said *Sessa* and pointed their horses toward the wood. Kay heard the witches clattering up the stairs on their high-heeled shoes. Looking back, he saw them all clustered on the roof shaking their fists and sticks, but already they were far away, for the two broom horses were rushing through the air so fast, that soon the house was out of sight. As they went over the elm boughs, they came so close to the top twigs, that some young rooks woke in the rookery and cried 'Kaa' at them.

It was merry to be so high in the air. Kay could see the village, with hardly a light in it, and the flashing of the brook where it went over the fall. Near the ponds, many little lights were twinkling. Kay wondered what they could be. A couple of white owls drifted up alongside Kay like moths; he could see their burning yellow eyes.

'We'll race you to the upper wood,' they said.

'All right,' Kay said. 'Come up, horse.'

The brooms were much faster than the owls: soon they were well ahead.

'You keep clear of Wicked Hill,' the owls cried. They said something more, but the brooms were too far in front for the riders to hear.

'We'll land here, if you don't mind,' Nibbins said. 'I'd like to speak with a friend, if he's anywhere about. Point his head down to the quarry there.'

When they had landed in the quarry, they tied the brooms to two spindle trees. 'It must be spindle trees,' Nibbins said. The quarry was bright in the moonlight and much over-grown with hazels and gorse.

'What is Wicked Hill?' Kay asked, 'that we are to keep clear of?'

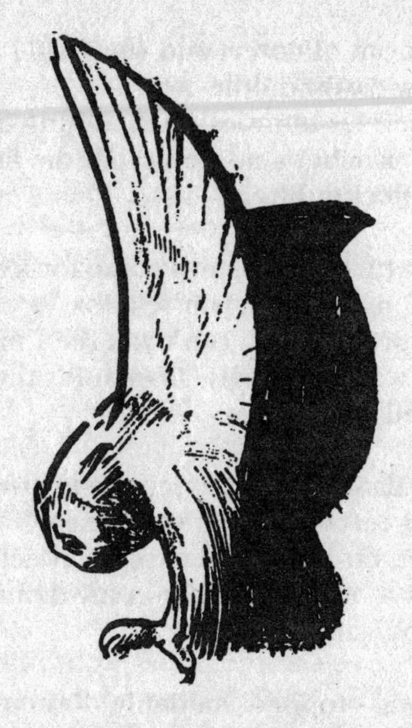

'They told us to keep clear of it, did they?' Nibbins said. 'That shows that there is something on. . . . However, this is where my friend lives, if he's not on his rounds.' He led the way towards the quarry end, where there was much tumbled stone worn into a track by feet. A warm strong scent was blowing about the place, more like a taste than a smell. The ground was white with little bones. Something that looked like washing hung upon the gorse bushes; it was not washing, though; it was rabbit skins hung up to dry. Someone with a most unpleasant voice was doing something with the rabbit skins, and singing as he worked; he was either folding the dry ones or hanging more fresh.

His song was not a nice one.

'I crept out of covert and what did I see?
Ow-ow-ow-diddle-ow!
But seven fat bunnies, each waiting for me.
With a poacher's noosey, catch the fat goosey, Ho says
Rollicum Bitem.

' "O pretty bunnies, let's come for a stroll."
"O no, no, no; you're a fox."
"A fox pretty dears; can't you see I'm a mole?"
With a weaselly, stoaty, snap at his throaty, Ho says
Rollicum Bitem.

' "Let's dance, one by one, arm-in-arm, as dear friends."
"O certainly, sir, if you please."
So seven fat bunnies had seven sweet ends . . .
Hay for a hennerel, snug in my dennerel, Ho says
Rollicum Bitem.'

The song stopped suddenly. Kay heard no sound of foot-steps, but suddenly two very bright green eyes were shining at him above some glittering teeth.

'It's all right, Bitem old boy,' Nibbins said. 'It's only Nibs. This is my friend, Kay. Mr. Kay, Mr. Lightfoot, Mr. Rollicum Bitem Lightfoot.'

'Oh, it's you, Nibs! Pleased to meet you, Mr. Kay. Come in, won't you? Sorry I didn't recognise you at once. This way.' He led the way to what looked like the mouth of a cave in the quarry face. 'It will be dark for you,' he said to Kay. 'You'll find some glow-worms on the shelf there, if you want a light.'

Kay took a glow-worm from the shelf; by the light of this he was able to see where he was going. The two others went down the passage in front of him. It was a

rough, dark, narrow passage, with many twists in it. Everywhere there was this strong, rich scent, so like a taste. There were many rabbit skins about, as well as feathers.

'Mr. Bitem deals in game,' Nibbins said. 'I have to consult him about some rabbiting.'

Mr. Bitem led them into his study, which was also his bedroom and larder. 'Bachelor's quarters,' he said. 'A bit rough-and-ready; but then I'm only here in the winter, really. Would you care to pick a wing or anything? No? I've some nice fowl, cold; and there's a bit of duck under the floor there. No? Well, what do you want with me, Nibs?'

'About our rabbiting to-morrow night, Bitem. Of course, you can speak freely before Mr. Kay. . . . I rather

think my cousin Blackmalkin has betrayed us to the keeper. I happened to see him come from the keeper's cottage; I was up in a tree among some ivy. He came out, licking his lips, for he'd been having milk. He didn't see me; he passed just underneath me; but I heard him chuckle to himself and say: "Keeper will get the lot of them." You see, Kay, my two cousins, Blackmalkin and Greymalkin, and myself, have been in this midnight business together for quite a long time. Well, lately we've been helping Bitem in the game industry, on quiet nights, after new moon, and so on; and we had planned a big hunt for to-morrow, out Coneycop Spinney way: a really big hunt; ourselves, Bitem and some of his relatives. . . . Now Blackmalkin has not been dependable for a long time. This magic business is very bad for a fellow, and he is in it deeply, with a very bad set, all the Pouncer Seven. You mark my words, he has been put up by the Seven to betray us to the keeper.

'When he had gone, I crept down from my tree, got into Keeper's cottage, and upstairs under the bed. Presently Keeper came in with those nasty dogs of his, and put his gun on the rack. "I've got some news for you, my dear," his wife said. "Here's Blackmalkin just come in to say that there's a big rabbit drive arranged for Friday night in the Spinney; that Bitem lot and his cousins are in it."

‘ “I’ll rabbit ’em,” Keeper said. You know his coarse, red way, “I’ll rabbit ’em.”

‘ “Yes, my dear,” his wife said, “Blackmalkin said you’d get the lot of them. Of course, after what he’d told me, I gave him some milk and that bit of sardine that there was.”

‘ “Quite right,” Keeper said. “If I get the lot of them, he shall have more than milk and sardine. He shall have Long Tail’s Wing.”

‘ “O hush, my dear,” his wife said; “somebody might hear you.”

‘ “Tut! nobody can hear me,” Keeper said; blowing out his big lips. “But I’ll rabbit ’em. Let ’em come on Friday, I’ll ask no better.” Then he went out and began oiling his gun; I could hear him singing:

> ‘ “I’ll get him oiled for Friday,
> So it shall be their die-day,
> And Satter-day
> Shall be Batter-day,
> And Sunday hot rabbit-pie day.” ’

‘I had to wait in the room for hours, because his nasty dogs were in the room below; but at last I could stand it no longer; I made a dart for the chimney, and was over the roof and into the pines before the dogs were upstairs. I heard Keeper ask, “What’s the matter with the dogs?” and his wife said: “It sounded like a young jackdaw got down the chimney again.” “I’ll jackdaw them jackdaws one of these days,” he said, “if they keep on jackdawing me.” “That’s that,” she said. So that was that, and here I am.’

‘Ha,’ Bitem said, ‘so that’s that for to-morrow’s hunt.

Now what can we do for Blackmalkin? Of all the traitors I ever did hear of! But we'll pretend we're going, up to the last. Keeper and the beaters will all be at Coneycop, waiting for us. And we'll send Blackmalkin there. But we, ourselves, will go off and draw out Brady Ride way: there's pretty toothing in the rabbit there, especially in the South Warren. And keeper and beaters will wait all night for us at Coneycop; and when they learn that we've been at Brady, they'll pretty well have it out of Blackmalkin for misleading them. They'll toss him in a game-bag, and serve him right.'

'I say, you have got a brain, Bitem,' Nibbins said. 'I knew you'd have a plan at once. That's the advantage of working with you; never at a loss: I never saw such a fellow.'

'A fellow had need to be never at a loss,' Bitem said. 'The huntsmen are bad enough, in their red coats, but at least you do expect a keeper to stand your friend.'

'If you wouldn't mind just moving to the door, Kay,' Nibbins said, 'Bitem and I could plan out our hunt a bit, using the floor as a map.'

Kay moved to the door. He watched them as they put rabbit-skins and feathers on the ground to mark places in the wood. He listened to them for a few minutes.

'This hen's head is the big yew. That rabbit-skin is the boggy patch; you know the place. Then here is where we got the partridge chicks. I'll put this pheasant's tail to mark the end of the South Warren. Hob Ferret'll join in here, and Jill will come if we want her. Then you will steal up here . . . and I will steal up there. . . . Yes, and then Greymalkin is awfully good at a drop-pounce. Then we'll all go over the down to North Warren. . . .'

Kay grew weary of all this talk, because he had never

been to Brady Ride Wood; he strolled quietly along the passage towards its mouth in the quarry face. He put back the glow-worm on the ledge, and peeped out of the entrance.

He drew back at once, because there, in the quarry, not far from the cave, was a man at work among the stones. He was kneeling in a patch of shadow, but his face came up into the moonlight from time to time. Kay saw from his velveteen coat that it was the Keeper. 'What on earth is he doing?' Kay wondered.

Presently the Keeper stood up to stretch his back. He was wearing gloves. He drew from a sack a big iron snap-trap, which he opened and set among the stones in the middle of the path leading to Bitem's earth. When it was set, he very cleverly and cautiously strewed it over with moss, dead grass, leaves, and earth.

'That will catch your light feet, Mr. Lightfoot,' he said; 'and then, with my good gun, I'll put an end to your snibbing of my rabbits. Many a young hunter will give a pound for that mask of yourn, and your brush shall be a cobweb cleaner before you're a week older. I'll get up my tree, my master, and watch till you walk click into it. You'll be coming home within an hour. I know your ways.'

Kay saw him move into the wood above the quarry, where he began to climb a tree. As soon as he was climbing, Kay hurried back to tell the others what he had seen.

'A trap?' Bitem said; 'and Keeper watching from a tree? I am very much obliged to you, Mr. Kay. I must be gone from here by the secret door. I'll move off to my place Wicked Hill way.'

'There's something on at Wicked Hill, the owls said,' Nibbins said. 'Do you think it would be safe?'

'A lot safer than this,' Bitem said.

'Yes, for you,' Nibbins said. 'But I meant for us.'

'They don't harm anyone who keeps outside the magic circle.'

'I'd love to go, just to look on,' Nibbins said. 'It's probably a big magic night, Kay, when they have a bonfire; and oh, I do love to see them at magic. It's terrifying, but I can't resist it.'

'Well, come along,' Bitem said.

'We can steal round to our horses and give you a lift, Bitem.'

The fox led the way out of his study into a narrow passage, where Kay had to crawl on hands and knees. This led into a biggish room from which several passages branched, water was dripping in one of them.

'Very convenient in here,' Bitem said. 'Lots of ways out and plenty of water; but this is the way we'll take to-night.'

In a few minutes they scrambled out among some gorse roots (at least a hundred yards from the Keeper) near the spindle trees where the brooms were tethered.

'You mount with me, Bitem,' Nibbins said; 'and you, Kay, just follow us. There are spindles where we can tether; lots of them.'

In a moment the brooms were sweeping through the air over the tree-tops. Kay saw a few white houses here and there below him, and many gleaming ponds and brooks. Far ahead, among the hills, was the glow of a bonfire. Soon they could see people dancing round it. Kay came to ground with Nibbins and Bitem beside a spinney on the hill. There were many spindle bushes in the spinney, but to many of them brooms were already tethered.

'I'll be off to my place,' Bitem said, 'over there among the Old Ones. You'll find the Night Folk up at the top. Good night.'

Wicked Hill was a big round lump with a hollow top. The lower slopes grew bracken and bramble, but near the top nothing grew except a short-bladed grass. The stump of an old gibbet stood at one end of it. An earthwork with two gates ringed the top of the hill. On the top of this earthwork the magic circle was burning in a narrow line of blue fire, which was being fed by little black cats who walked round the ring dropping herbs on it.

'That used to be my job when I did this kind of thing,' Nibbins whispered.

The bonfire, which had now sunk to a glow, was in the midst of the circle. The people who had danced about it were now drawn together in a group. They were listening to a wizard, in a long scarlet gown, who seemed to be their king or chief.

'That's Abner Brown,' Nibbins whispered. 'He's always the head of these big parties.'

'Hush,' Kay said. 'Let's hear what he's saying.'

'So, my brothers and sisters,' Abner was saying, 'we have had our evening's frolic; now let us come to our evening's business. The great task before us is to find the Harker Treasure.' (Here there were cries of '*Hear, hear!*') 'We all know what that was: it was the treasure of the great South American cathedral of Santa Barbara. It was a barge-load of gold, silver and precious stones, wrought and unwrought, but worth, so the records prove, at least one million seven hundred thousand pounds. There are seven times seven of us. If we find it, the share of each one of us will be some thirty-five thousand pounds. I ask you, is it worth trying to find?'

(There were loud cries of '*Yes!*')

'You say "yes," and you may mean "yes," but will you all work for "yes"?'

(There were shouts of '*Yes, to the death!*')

'Very well, then,' he said, 'I am glad that we are all resolved. We will now break up our party. Let all the Sevens leave the hill except the Pouncer Seven.'

When most of the party had gone, Kay saw that Mrs. Pouncer, Sister Nightshade and the rest of the Seven, drew near to Abner.

'Sister Pouncer,' Abner said, 'why are you vexed?'

'Enemies are at work,' she said. 'They took my broom and Nightshade's broom, so that we had to walk.'

'Do not be vexed, my Pouncer,' Abner said, 'because I am far from vexed. I have discovered something very important about the treasure.'

'Oh! what, dear Abner?'

'You are quite wrong about it. It is not in the Harker home, but Somewhere Near Here.'

At this there came cries of 'No! It cannot be. How can it be? Where do you suppose it is? Why is it not in the Harker house? Where is it?'

'We will find out that presently,' he said, 'of WHERE it is. Listen to what I have to say of WHEREABOUTS it is.'

The Seven drew nearer, intently listening.

'You know,' Abner went on, 'that when I was little, I helped my father and grandfather (both of them Abner Browns like myself) to look for the treasure. I might say I was at this quest from birth.' (Here there were remarks of '*Hear, hear!*')

'As you know, my grandfather once had the treasure, but lost it. For more than twenty years he and my father dug for it where they thought it would be. One of my earliest recollections is of helping them to dig for it in a hot country of very red mud.

'Then my grandpop disappeared, and within a week my pop died of the yellow fever. I had the harsh world to wrestle with before I could take up the quest.

'When I took it up, just thirty years after those two laid it down, it wasn't easy to pick up the threads at that place in the red mud. The yellow fever had killed 'most everyone who had lived there when my pop and grandpop dug there. But I met an old negro who knew just why my grandpop gave up digging and disappeared.

'He gave up digging, *because someone found the treasure and carried it off to sea.*

'He disappeared, *so as to settle matters with that finder.* The finder was an Englishman, named Benito Trigger.

'That is not much to go upon, is it? Thirty-five years ago, an Englishman gets to sea with the stuff three thousand miles away and disappears. My grandpop goes after him and disappears. At first I thought that this Benito Trigger might be Captain Harker himself, for, as we know, he lived for many years in quest of the treasure.'

'Or pretended to, so as to lull suspicion, while he lived on it,' Mrs. Pouncer said under her breath.

'But it was not Captain Harker,' Abner continued. 'For when I came here to make enquiries, I found that Captain Harker was at that time upon his deathbed.

'I need not tell you how interesting it was to see the very house in which old Captain Harker lived, and to see his tomb, and to stand within just a few feet of those bones which, when they were alive, had started all this treasure hunt.

'For the moment I ruled him out. "You didn't get the treasure, brother," I said. "You were in your tomb before

For more than twenty years he and my father dug for it —

it could have reached England, if it ever did reach England." '

'It was in his secret den before he ever sickened,' Mrs.

Pouncer muttered. 'Of course he had it; had it all the time.'

'But,' Abner continued, 'I fell right plumb in love with this green countryside, so full of real old buildings; so I just didn't rest till I'd taken Russell's Dene, that Queen Anne mansion, in the oak wood, where tradition says the Druids once practised their rites. There, as you know, we have been able to establish our Magic Circle, for the Quest of the Treasure, upon the Lines of the Ancient Knowledge.

'And there are red birds that come out of the wilderness with Knowledge. One of them came to me this spring, just after I was settled in Russell's Dene. He led me to visit a certain church, not many miles from here. And what did I find there?'

Here some of the Seven said 'The treasure? Some of the candlesticks? The church vessels in use again?'

'No, none of those things,' he answered. 'I found the tomb of my long-lost grandpop, Abner Brown. He had been drowned in the Great Flood here in February, 1850: February Fill-Dyke, as you call it.

'Was not that wonderful?

'I have now raked out something of his end. He was last seen alive at the Condicote Inn, the Ring of Bells, on the last night of January, 1850. He was then heard quarrelling, with whom?

'With Sir Piney Trigger, a rich Honduras merchant, who had just returned from two years' absence in the West. That Piney Trigger was the Trigger who had found the treasure and carried it off to sea: my grandpop had run him down.

'That night, after their quarrel, both my grandpop and Sir Piney disappeared. What happened, do you suppose?

Many asked that at the time. I answer it. I say that Sir Piney had the treasure here; that my grandpop had discovered so much and asked for a share. They quarrelled. I say that Sir Piney flung my grandpop into the flood and then fled the country. Left the country, left the treasure, and never dared come back for it because of blood-guiltiness.

'The case is reported in the *Condicote Remembrancer* for February, 1850: they knew nothing of any treasure, of course; only enquired into the disappearance. The coroner's jury supposed him to have been washed out to sea by the great Flood.

'Now Sir Piney was a well-known sportsman, mixed up in many shady matters. His daughter is still alive; I have seen her; there's no getting anything out of her.

'What I have tried to find out is: what brought him to Condicote that night? In the coroner's notes I found this: that it was supposed that he had come to look after a big barge of his which had come up the river some days before. It was a sea-going barge, fitted like a yacht: he had been in her in the West.

'I say that he brought the treasure in her. He hid it somewhere not far from Condicote, and had come to see to it, or to remove it, when my grandpop interfered.'

Here, as Abner paused as though for applause, Sister Nightshade asked: 'May he not have taken all the treasure away in the barge when he took himself away?'

'No,' Abner said. 'Because the barge (dead empty) had been washed ashore and stove in in the floods two days before he disappeared.

'No, my sweet Seven; depend upon it, the treasure is near here; and somewhere here, probably near the river, we'll find it.'

Here there was a sensation among the company: all were much impressed and excited. Sister Pouncer said: 'Was there ever such a Mind as our Abner's? Like crystal from the spring.' But after saying this, she moved nearer to Kay and muttered: 'This is all pure surmise. You have a Bee in your Bonnet, my good sir. I, too, have my views of where the treasure is, and we shall see who is right. Magic is a surer guide than a grandpop or a little-pop. For all your Tingo and Tango, Sister Pouncer holds the silken clew.'

'And now, my dear Seven,' Abner continued, 'we will have one short dance more, and then away, for the stars are dim and the cocks are stirring on their perches. Join hands and dance.'

A strange music began from somewhere in the air; the Witches and Wizards at once swept into a dance.

Nibbins was very uneasy. 'I can't keep out of a dance like this,' he said. 'Oh, it goes right through my marrow; and then in a minute they will all join hands and swing round and round, till they see all sorts of things.'

'You come away,' Kay said, pulling him down the hill. 'You always were one for getting into scrapes. Let's get back home, before they all come hurrying for their horses. If Mrs. Pouncer catches us at the spindle trees, we shall be in a mess.'

He made Nibbins run, keeping one hand on the scruff of his neck all the way lest the sound of the dance should prove too exciting. In a few minutes they were high in the air again upon their horses, sailing far from the hill.

'It's just as well we started when we did,' Nibbins said, 'for there's the dawn beginning.'

Sure enough, the sky behind them was showing colour: the two horses began to droop down towards the ground. Presently they were dragging along the ground, and at last they collapsed.

'We left it till too late,' Nibbins said. 'However, we're almost at home. Come along; the gate's locked, but we can get over the wall by the ivy.'

They left their horses in the road, scrambled up the ivy, over the wall, and then along behind the laurustinus till they were near the house.

'This is the place,' Nibbins said. They were within thirty yards of the house, in a thick shrubbery, but Nibbins must have touched a spring, for the ground gave way beneath them, and down they went into a secret passage. In another minute Nibbins was gone, and Kay was in his own room.

'What a night I have had,' he thought. His slippers were muddy from the soil in the garden. 'I shall catch it,' he thought.

The cuckoo clock struck five; the room was quite light. He popped into bed at once. He did not stay long awake, you may be sure. Just before he fell asleep, however, he heard a curious noise on the wall of the house, not far away, as though the jasmine had broken away and were scraping as the wind blew it. 'I suppose it's the jasmine,' he muttered drowsily, 'but it may be Ellen up already, sweeping the stairs.'

When he came downstairs to breakfast the governess was not down. She entered just as he was at the sideboard, helping himself to pork pie. She looked a little cross, as though she had not slept very well.

'You know,' she said, 'that you're never allowed to help yourself to pork pie. It's a very bilious, rich food; and then you won't be able to do your French. You must have an egg like any other boy. And you don't mean to say,

Kay, after all the many times that I've spoken to you, that you've been in the garden again in your slippers, and on the beds too! And then you wonder if you catch your death of cold!'

'But I haven't caught a cold,' he said.

'Don't answer me back, sir,' she said. 'You're a very naughty, disobedient little boy, and I have a very good mind not to let you have an egg. I wouldn't let you have an egg, only I had to stop your supper last night. Take off one of those slippers and let me feel it. Come here.'

Kay went up rather gingerly, having been caught in this way more than once. He took off one slipper and tendered it for inspection.

'Just as I thought,' she said. 'The damp has come right through the lining, and that's the way your stockings get worn out.'

In a very pouncing way she spanked at his knuckles with the slipper. He had expected a blow of the sort, and by drawing his hands swiftly aside, the slipper struck the spoons on the table and made them dance.

'Now, you naughty boy, put that slipper on, and you'll learn the whole of "pouvoir" before you go out this morning. What were you muttering under your breath, Kay?'

'I was just wondering if this was a duck egg or a hen egg.'

'Use the subjunctive and the genitive,' she said. '*Were* a duck's egg, not *was a duck* egg. And it's a hen's egg. Ducks' eggs are a great deal too rich.' At any other time Kay would have boasted that it was a double-yolker, but refrained, thinking that this would probably lead to confiscation, as too much for a young stomach. He ate his egg, but his mind was intent upon many other things.

Ellen came in.

'If you please, ma'am,' Ellen said, 'would you mind speaking to Jane.'

Jane was at the door behind her.

'If you please, ma'am,' Jane said, 'would you please to look at this.'

This was the dish on which the cold goose had lain, but, alas, now nothing remained but a few picked bones and a skeleton almost bare.

'The cats have been in again, ma'am. I don't know how they get in; and the chine's gone the same way, and there's two more brooms gone.'

'Did you lock the larder door, Jane?'

'Yes, ma'am, and I took the key and had it under my pillow. And if it isn't cats—and I don't know how cats get in—then somebody must have a key and come in in the night, and I don't like it.'

'I'll look into this after breakfast, Jane,' the governess said, 'and I'll speak to Wiggins.'

Kay stared at the bones of the goose. He knew how that goose and chine had disappeared. Almost immediately Jane reappeared.

'If you please, ma'am, Wiggins has found the two brooms, the besom and the broom. They were in the road outside, near the spring.'

'Well, how on earth could they have got there?' the governess said.

'I don't know how they got there,' Jane said, 'but I don't like it.'

The governess did not talk during breakfast, but seemed to be considering this question of the brooms and the goose. Kay's thoughts were far away with Nibbins, Mr. Bitem and that gathering of witches on the hill.

'Of all the dreamy boys,' the governess said suddenly,

'going off into day-dreams. It's my belief that you need a dose. It's my belief you eat too much. You'll put on your boots before you come to lessons, and ask Ellen to dry those shoes in the oven.'

'Please can't I wear my slippers during lessons?'

'No, you won't wear your slippers during lessons. For one thing, they're not dry and you'll catch your death wearing them; and, for another, you fidget me distracted, by rubbing one slipper off and then the other, just as though you were playing a game with them.'

This was a cruel thrust, because Kay did play games with them. When he had scraped off a slipper, he could push it about with his toes, and imagine that it was a canoe full of Redskins on the warpath, going down the rapids; or a diving bell at Tobermory, bringing up treasure from one of the ships of the Armada; or great-grandpapa Harker's ship, the *Plunderer*, engaging seven French privateers; or that famous horse Lottery, at various stages of the steeplechase, the prints of which hung in the study. But the boots were laced-up things that gave no solace. There they were, and there you were.

The governess stalked out of the room to investigate the larder door. Ellen came in to clear away. Kay looked up at the portrait of great-grandmamma Siskin. Her eyes seemed all right. 'This is the loveliest time that I've ever had,' Kay thought, 'and anything may happen.' He walked slowly round the room, tapping the panelling.

'What are you doing, Master Kay?' Ellen asked.

'I was just seeing if there were any secret passages,' he said.

'Oh, there's no secret passages in here, Master Kay. What should there be secret passages for?'

'Oh,' Kay said, 'when people were doing murders, they

always used to have them. And then smugglers had them.'

'The smugglers were never here,' Ellen said. 'Not in this house. Down by the river the smugglers were, so my father said. They had the Mill at Seven Hatches. Oh! and by Drowned-Man's-Copse way they'd a place, and at the Springs another; but they never could have come here; your great-grandfather would never have allowed them.'

'No,' Kay said. 'But he would never have known. They could have crept in at night and made the passages.'

'I don't think they could, Master Kay, not in stone walls.'

After he had put on his boots Kay went out among the laurustinus to look for that secret place where the trap-door had opened beneath his feet. Ten o'clock struck while he was still searching, but by great good fortune he got to the school-room before the governess arrived. It was French morning. He struggled through an exercise in Ollendorf and a little translation from Chardenal. Unfortunately, the governess would not let him translate what had seemed (at private readings) a very promising passage about an axe and skull, with a war-cry of 'Hailul-li.' She said that it was not fit for a little boy to read. Then came the dreaded moment.

'And now, Kay, since you were a very naughty little boy last night, and were most disobedient and dreamy this morning, you will learn "pouvoir," while I go to look at the larder again, now that Wiggins is there.'

'What do you think it was that did it in the larder?' he asked.

'You learn your lessons,' she said. 'Never mind about what I think it was.'

She left him with 'pouvoir.' Kay had a special prejudice

against 'pouvoir.' It wasn't a good, straightforward word like 'aimer.' It was a mean and ugly word, which went into 'peux' and 'pu.' It didn't seem to have any sense in it. He wrestled with it with each boot twisted round a leg of his chair, scraping up and down. Then, looking up, he saw great-grandpapa Harker looking down at him from his portrait over the mantelpiece.

The portrait was one that he had looked at during lessons ever since lessons began. It was just 'great-grandpapa Harker's portrait,' though it was labelled Baxter. When people were shown the schoolroom, the governess always said 'That is a Baxter,' and then people said 'Really!' or 'Fancy that!' or 'How interesting!' It was the full-length portrait of a man in old-fashioned clothes. There was a sort of shrubbery behind him and a sort of blueness behind the shrubbery. It was said to be the only full-length Baxter, as generally Baxter only did down to the knees. But now, as Kay looked, great-grandpapa Harker distinctly took a step forward, and as he did so, the wind ruffled the skirt of his coat and shook the shrubs behind him. A couple of blue butterflies which had been upon the shrubs for seventy odd years, flew out into the room. Great-grandpapa Harker took another step forward, and smiled. Now Kay could see into the shrubbery: it was just where Kay's fort now was, but the box trees had grown enormously since then, although the bullfinches were already there. Great-grandpapa Harker held out his hand and smiled again. His face, which had seemed such an old-portrait-kind of a face, became alive and full of welcome. He seemed a fine fellow, not at all old, and very kind and good.

'Well, great-grandson Kay,' he said, 'ne pouvez vous pas come into the jardin avec moi?'

Kay thought it odd, but it was a perfect excuse for not doing 'pouvoir': 'I would have learned it, but great grandpapa Harker asked me to come into the jardin avec him, so of course I thought you wouldn't mind.' He smiled back at great-grandpapa Harker and said, 'Oui, grand-grand-pere, thank you; je serai very glad.'

Great-grandpapa Harker held out both hands, and Kay jumped on to the table; from there, with a step of run, he leaped on to the top of the fender and caught the mantelpiece. Great-grandpapa Harker caught him and helped him up into the picture. Instantly the schoolroom disappeared. Kay was out of doors standing beside his great-grandfather, looking at the house as it was in the pencil drawing in the study, with cows in the field close to the house on what was now the lawn, the church, unchanged, beyond, and, near by some standard yellow roses, long since vanished, but now seemingly in full bloom.

Kay did not know quite what to say, so he said: 'Did the cows really come so close to the house?'

'Yes, indeed. This is Sweetlips; that one is Rosemary; and the brindle is Colinette.'

Kay was looking at the cows, who were all in the rich grass, grazing and swishing away the flies. An amiable-looking man, with a fat, pale face, a sun hat and big green spectacles, rose up from behind an easel among the roses. 'That will be all that I can do for to-day, Harker,' he said, as he packed his things. 'Come to think of it, you're the first full-length I've done.'

Kay knew somehow that this was Baxter. He watched him move off, across the grass, to the gate, which was not a drive gate, as now, but a farm field gate, overshadowed by trees long since cut down. Kay was alone with great-grandpapa Harker in a place that was his home, but yet strangely different; so much of it was not there at all, not yet built.

'Is that all the house?' he asked.

'Yes. Come in, great-grandson, and see it.'

He led the way along a cobblestone path to a door—'somewhere near where the dining-room door is,' as Kay thought. Pear trees grew up the house here. The porch was supported by the snouts of two carven wooden dolphins standing on their tails. 'I brought those from Sainte Eustasie,' great-grandpapa Harker said. 'They came off the stern of a Dutch ship that was wrecked there in the great storm of 1782, the year I was born. They must have blunted some chisels to carve them; feel how tough the wood is.'

Kay felt the hard, dark wood, as close-grained as African oak. Great-grandpapa Harker opened the door into a long, rather dark panelled room, now completely gone. There were some portraits on the wall; the man in the blue coat, with white stockings, now in the best bedroom; the man in the long brown coat with the red belt, now in the hall; and the lady that looked so like a camel. As they entered, a white cockatoo, which had been sitting quietly upon her perch, rose in excitement, with an open bill. An old, old lady was asleep in a chair. Something told Kay that when she had been younger she had looked like a camel. The only other things that Kay recognised were the arms in coloured glass; these were in a window, whereas Kay saw them daily now in the fanlight of a door: three oreilles couped, for Harker; two siskins proper, for Siskin; seven abeilles, grommelees or, for Colway; and three alms spirty, for Mynd.

Great-grandpapa Harker led the way out of the dining-room, which was dark, into the study, which was still darker—too dark, as Kay thought, for anybody to read in comfort in it. It was panelled up to the ceiling and lined with books, nearly all of them little volumes bound in calfskin. They had been arranged according to size. When he looked round, having entered the room, he found that there were folios behind him.

'You see, great-grandson,' he said, 'these books are not really books, but a shutter.'

He moved something in the wall and a shelf of books swung away and let in a flood of light. Over the mantel was the portrait of the man in the puce coat, who was now in the hall. There was a blunderbuss up in one corner, wired to some nails, and an old harpsichord, which was now up in the box-room with so many other mouldering wrecks.

'Now, my little great-grandson,' great-grandpapa Harker said, 'let me look at you and talk with you. Do they still think that I stole the treasure?'

'I'm sure you didn't,' Kay said.

'Many thought that I did, and that I hid it somewhere—perhaps in the floor above this room. For years I had letters from people (who dared not sign their names) accusing me of stealing it. I lost it. It was trusted to me and I lost it; and what became of it, no one knows; though I think it must be sunk or scattered.'

A black cat, with white throat and paws, which had been ashes for forty years, rubbed up against great-grandpapa Harker's legs, and then, springing on the arm of his chair, watched the long dead sparrows in the plum tree which had been firewood a quarter of a century ago.

'You ought to know about the treasure, Kay,' great-grandpapa Harker said; 'for until it is restored or traced, no man of our name ought to rest. Your grandfather would not move in the matter; your father could not; there is only you.'

'I'd love to hear all about it, if you'd tell me,' Kay said.

'It was in the year 1811,' Captain Harker began. 'I was then in the *Plunderer*, West Indiaman, which I commanded and partly owned, in the port of Santa Barbara, loading sugar. War was raging all over the world. We in the *Plunderer* were very short-handed. The Admiral on the station had impressed all our best men, and we had lost some by fever. We had a crew of twenty-one, all told, to load, sail and defend the ship, and of all of them only Hollings, my mate, was a man to trust in trouble.

'Nearly all the South American States were then breaking loose from Spain. A revolution broke out in Santa Barbara. The rebels marched upon the capital, which had only a hundred soldiers in the garrison. The people expected the city to be sacked.

'The Archbishop with his Priors came off to the *Plunderer* to ask me if they might lodge the treasures of the churches on board my ship for safety. I said that I had a very weak crew, that I was in an undefended port, and that French privateers were known to be on the coast. They said that as the rebels were in sight, they had no other chance of saving the things. So at this, I consented.

'They brought it aboard at once, and I had it stricken down into the after-hold. It consisted of church ornaments, images, lamps, candlesticks, reliquaries, chalices and crosses, of gold, silver, and precious stones. Most of it was packed in grass matting, but in the hurry some was bare. I had never seen such wealth; certainly my crew never had.

'In a way I saved it, for two hours later the rebels

entered the city and sacked every church within the walls.

'Then my troubles began, but not from the rebels. Seven ships were seen approaching the port. From the whiteness of their sails I judged them to be French. Hollings, my mate, agreed with me. Roper Bilges, my gunner, a drunken and careless man, thought that they

were Brazilians. Twiney Pricker, my sailmaker, a sinister person, with a great deal in him, said that they were French privateers. I gave the word to lower the boats and tow the ship out to sea, there being then a dead calm in shore.

'By the time that we were clear of the headland, the squadron was within shot. They were four French corvettes, two brigs, and a schooner, all full of men and well armed. In the first shots exchanged between us they wounded poor Hollings. They continued in chase till dark, driving us to the westward, but not gaining on us.

'I was more than anxious, having now only eighteen unwounded men on board, to sail the ship and defend this great wealth.

'After seeking guidance, I determined to make for our naval station at Puerto Recife, to hand over the treasure to the British Admiral commanding there, and ask him to re-return it in a ship of war when the civil troubles had ceased.

'Having set down this determination in writing, I read it to poor Hollings, to the gunner, Roper Bilges, and to the sailmaker, who all approved it. Going on deck, I read it to the ship's company.

'It was then dark, but the enemy ships' signals were still visible astern, perhaps two miles away. The wind was freshening from the north, which made the land a lee coast to us. Our rigging had been somewhat cut by shot, and with poor Hollings dying, the enemy near, the rocks close, night upon us, two wounded men to dress, and the whole navigation of the ship depending on me, I had my hands full. I have blamed myself bitterly for being taken unawares. I had no thought that what afterwards happened would occur.

'Poor Hollings died at midnight. With the wind freshening, I could not be present to minister to him. I stayed on deck till about three o'clock in the morning, when it was light enough to see the enemy ships far astern. That danger being past, for the moment, and the ship holding her course well, I left the deck in charge of the sailmaker, intending to lie down in my clothes for an hour. I was

gravely uneasy at my position, but did not doubt that I had decided rightly, both in receiving the treasure on board and in making for our squadron at Puerto Recife.

'I had not been long asleep when I was awakened by Roper Bilges bursting into my cabin with some of the crew, who seized me and bound me, threatening to kill me with their pistols, etc., and saying that the ship was now theirs. On my trying to reason with them, they put a gag in my mouth, and gave three cheers "for Roper Bilges and the Bishop's treasure." They said that they were now going to be gentlemen, and "on the account"—that is, pirates. Whether the first thought of this came from Bilges or the sailmaker, I cannot say; certainly Bilges was now their captain.

'After five days of standing to the West, they put me ashore on the coast three hundred miles from any settlement of white men, with no weapon but a knife and no means of livelihood but that and a fishing-line, which my negro seaman had the humanity to slip into my hand. They left me on the coast and sailed away upon a north-westerly course, as though for the Gulf. What became of them, no man knows.

'I was made prisoner by the Indians, who took me with them far into the forest, to their camp by the falls. I was with the Indians, as a slave, for more than five years. Being a slave is bad; it makes a man think too much of his own misery.

'Still, in the end I escaped, which few slaves do, and returned to a home of love and beauty, such as few slaves have ever had. I had been given up for dead by many; some supposed that I had run away with the treasure. I am glad to say that the Archbishop, who knew me, never thought that. He had caused the ships of our Navy to search for us. The Admiral in his Report said that the *Plunderer* had left Santa Barbara fighting an enemy squadron, and that although she had not been captured (as the men of the squadron confessed, when they were afterwards taken), she had probably received grave injuries and had sunk.

'When I made the truth known, the members of the crew were described and posted as pirates throughout the western seaports. I visited all the possible ports myself, and sought among the receivers of stolen goods for some trace of the treasure; I searched among hospitals, prisons, hulks and galleys for some of the crew. I found no trace whatever, nor could I find any ship, lighthouse-keeper, or signalman who had seen the *Plunderer* after me, when I saw her heading north-west as though for the Gulf. I do not know what became of her. Sometimes I think that she sank with all on board. Sometimes I think that she reached some port in the Gulf, where the crew settled and lived at ease. The treasure was trusted to me, my little great-grandson; I cannot tell you how the loss of it weighed upon me. I could not go back to my profession of merchant trader. My remaining days were passed in hunting for clues of it. For months I would say to myself, "No, the *Plunderer* sank with all on board." Then I would read that pirates had been captured in such-and-such a place, and after that I would know no rest till I had examined the confessions of the crew, what ships they had taken, and whether any could have been the *Plunderer*. Then after more months of thinking that she had sunk, I would say to myself: "No; Roper Bilges probably sailed her to Europe, to a port of France or Spain. He may now be a great man in either land." When such thoughts came, away I would go for months, to either land, or to Holland or Denmark, or further still to Italy and the Levant, to ask in the ports, till my heart sickened. I was known in many ports as "the mad Englishman." No one had ever seen the *Plunderer* except an Italian in Genoa, who had been my steward in her for a year.

'One of my griefs was this: that my wife and son (your grandfather) longed for me to give up the quest. They were sure that the *Plunderer* had sunk, and thought me mad to persist.

'Another grief was the knowledge that many people here believed that I had run away with the ship and stolen the treasure. It is said that listeners hear no good of themselves. I sometimes heard people say: "Ah, old Harker! They do say that he was a pirate and ran away with all the cathedral money." Or: "Yes, he says that they took the ship from him with all that treasure on board. I daresay he wasn't very unwilling. Why didn't he shoot them? he had his pistols." Or: "A very likely tale, that he was among the Indians for five years. Much more likely he was spending the treasure somewhere." Once I heard a man say: "It's my belief he's got the treasure hidden in his house. Everybody says so. Besides, if he hasn't, what is it that he's got hidden under the hearthstone in his bedroom?"

'My bedroom is now yours, Kay; the room over this.'

'What is underneath that big hearthstone?' Kay asked.

'Underneath that big hearthstone,' great-grandpapa Harker repeated. 'Of course, some say the treasure; then some think that somebody has been murdered and hidden there.'

'And what is there?' Kay asked.

'Would you like to see, my little great-grandson?' great-grandpapa Harker answered. 'There is not much to see. What is it, Rover?'

As he spoke, the door of the library was thrust open, a pointer came shambling, wagging and cringing all at once to his master's feet. The library changed and blurred at his coming. He seemed to have let a lot of light into the room. Indeed, even as Kay looked, it was not a room, but the field where the cows were grazing. But the cows were blurring all together, into one. They were, in fact, not cows, they were bushes, browner than bushes ought to be, with a blueness above them which he knew was meant to be the sky. He saw great-grandpapa Harker standing there, but something dark and oblong surrounded him and shut him away. 'Why, he's gone back into the picture,' Kay thought. The glass of the picture shut the old man still further away. The picture was over the mantelpiece, and there was he, Kay, on the other side of the table; bent over the French verb 'pouvoir.' Baxter's portrait of great-grandpapa Harker was staring down unmoving.

The governess entered.

'Put away your "pouvoir" now, Kay,' she said. 'It's time for writing lesson. Take a piece of paper and write a nice letter to yourself while I do my books.'

Kay began his letter.

My dear Kay,
I hop you are quite well.
I hop your friends, the cats, are quite well.
I am quite well.
Please give my love to Ellen. I hop she is quite well. We have a nice dog here, but he is norty.

He sucked the end of his pen for a long time, but could think of nothing more to say, except that the norty dog was quite well.

'Haven't you finished yet?' the governess said. 'How many more times am I to tell you not to suck your pen like that? You are a disobedient child. Let me see what you have written. Really, Kay,' she said, having read the letter, 'I forbid you to mention the words "quite well!" in any other letter that you write. You learn a phrase and then repeat it just like a little parrot. And then how do you spell naughty? N-A-U-G-H-T spells naught. N-A-U-G-H-T-Y spells—what does it spell?'

'I don't know quite what it would spell.'

'Yes, you do, sir. Think. Now what does it spell?'

'Think.'

'No, it doesn't spell think. It spells what you are, naughty. Now you'll write out N-A-U-G-H-T-Y twenty-five times. And look at your writing, all slopping and sliding. You will not put both your fingers on the pen. You never see me with my finger under the pen in that way. You'll never be able to write unless you get both your fingers on to the pen. Now put them on the proper way.'

• • • • •

Usually after lessons he played by himself in the garden—in the shrubberies if it were dry, and on the paths if it were wet. To-day he went out of the garden, to walk by the brook which ran beside it, to watch the minnows in the shallows, and to see his friend, the water-rat, coming from his cool swim to nibble a cress.

The water was clear, with green weeds swaying in it like fishes' tails. The water-rat slid into it with a little fall of earth and swam downstream to his hole.

'I do wish I could be a water-rat,' he thought.

He wandered into a lane and then away across the fields to the church, where he found old Bert the sexton going up the tower to wind the clock.

'Mr. Bert,' he said, 'did you ever know my great-grandfather Harker?'

'Why, Master Kay, I've known all of you. I've known your father, Mr. Harker, and your grandfather, old Mr. Harker, afore him; and yes, I knew old, old Mr. Harker, but he was an old man when I came on to be a boy. That is, he wasn't an old man, but he seemed old; and he *was* old, beside old Mr. Harker.'

'Will you tell me about him?'

'Why, I don't know that I can. Let me see, now: old, old Mr. Harker. He'd been a savage Indian, so they did use to say. Ah! old, old Mr. Harker. Yes; things were very different in those days. They'd no railways in those days; nothing but the coach up and down. And they'd the old gallows up on the hill. Let me see about old, old Mr. Harker, then, whether I can tell you anything. He lived where you live, only it wasn't built on to then, the new part; that was your grandfather built that, old Mr. George. I remember old, old Mr. Harker had a stick he used to walk with, a foreign stick all carved by the savages. They used to say he had a lot of foreign treasures all buried away, all gold and that; but I never believed that; for my father once heard him say to old Mr. Robert, that used to live in the Dingles' old place, but they made him Bishop after, "Robert," he said, "if I could only find that treasure, it would be a load off my mind." So I never believed he had treasure.

'But about him, Master Kay. I used to see him stumping about with his stick: he had the rheumatic complaint from being wet through so often. He gave me some of these foreign fruits once, done up in sugar, because I took a letter for him. They did say he oughtn't to have died when he did, for he wasn't what you would call old, but they did use to say that he had something on his mind, if you understand me. He had his tomb done out very pretty in the south aisle, though it seems old-fashioned now. There it is, by the pew where they Pengas sit, just this side of where they put your grandfather.'

Kay stood upon the stone which covered great-grandpapa Harker. On the wall, above the pews near it, was a memorial tablet carved with a small lady in high relief mourning beside a very big urn. A ship showed in the distance, part of an anchor stuck out of the urn; underneath the design was an inscription:

'Beside this Stone
Lie the mortal remains of
ASTON TIRROLD HARKER,
son of Charles Tirrold Harker, Esquire,
late of Seekings House, in this Parish.
Born 17th August, 1782. Died 13th January, 1850.

'He was constant in Affection, spotless in Integrity, a useful Magistrate, eminent in his Calling, manly in Fortitude, womanly in Tenderness. He combined the graces of a Scholar with the Virtues of a good Citizen. Reader, canst thou say as much? If not, forbear to judge.

'This Stone was erected 1850 by his sorrowing Widow, Jemima Siskin Harker, eldest daughter of Sir Brambling Siskin, of Siskin Hall, whom he married in 1811.'

A stone to Jemima Siskin Harker, erected by her sorrowing son, George Tirrold Siskin Harker, lay a little to the east of this tablet on the same south wall.

Kay spent some few minutes looking at these and other tablets in the aisle. He then tried to make out the subject of a stained glass window, which he had puzzled over at a distance during many a dreary sermon. He could not get it clear: there were bits of heads, glories, horses and old writing; what he had decided was a yellow, half-lop rabbit seemed to be a hat with spikes. This was a blow, for the rabbit, named Bunkin, had beguiled even the litany.

'Mr. Bert,' he said, 'could you tell me the name of the gamekeeper who looks after Coneycop Spinney?'

'Why, yes,' the sexton said. 'That's the Squire's covert. His keeper lives by they pine trees, out by Rye Meadows. Roper Bilges is his name, and Bilges in his nature, they do say.'

'Roper Bilges!' Kay cried. 'Roper Bilges? Were his ancestors gunners?'

'No,' Bert answered, 'not so far as I know, unless shot-gunners.'

'Did they come from these parts, do you know?'

'No, they came from up Salop way somewhere; not so long since. That Roper's brother is footman to Sir Hassle.'

'Were there ever many smugglers here when you were a boy, Mr. Bert?' Kay asked.

'You mean what they used to call the Night Hawks? Why, no, those were done before I began; they took to killing people. No; but there was something like them going on, bringing brandy and tea and that: not so very many years ago. I knew some who were concerned in it, though it's best not to speak of it. Only it was a blessing to poor folk in those dear times. Dreadful the prices were. I don't know who the head of it was, except that he was a gentleman; and he worked it very cleverly, no one quite know how. No, they never caught him, but it came to an end.'

'Was there anyone called Brown, or Trigger, doing it, do you know?' Kay asked.

Mr. Bert's face changed at the two names; he looked hard at Kay.

'The name I always heard tell was Mr. Galloway,' he said. 'But it may not have been his real name.'

'I suppose all the things were brought up the river?'

'Yes, all these fellows, the Night Hawks as well, brought their things up the river. And a very queer thing, now that we're talking of this, was what happened at the time of the great flood. There were some barges that had come up with corn to the old mill that was: he's gone now, but you can see where the wheels used to be—Condicote Old Mill, they called it; a very big mill he used to be; you'll have been to the place.'

'Yes,' Kay said. 'I went there to a picnic once, and

afterwards we all fished, but never caught anything.'

'Well, that's where Condicote Old Mill was,' Mr. Bert said. 'And about these barges that had come up: they'd come to what they called the wharf just below the lock in very rough rainy weather. You'll remember the wharf, maybe; it is just at the Mill. Then there came the Great Flood, when all those barges were washed away and stove in about Cold Comfort Bridge. My father was a carpenter and builder, and as the barges were stove, he offered for the wood, to break up the wrecks and carry them away. Now when he came to break up those barges, he found that every one had a false bottom; there was a secret place in each one, where quite a lot of things could be put; and in two of them he found packs of tobacco, only the flood had got at it. So that shows you, doesn't it, how the stuff came and where it came to. My father never mentioned it to people; but it was queer, come to think of it, wasn't it?'

'Yes, indeed,' Kay said. 'And do you remember the Great Flood?'

'Why yes, Master Kay; no people who saw it will forget it. There was a week of storm in January after a very wet season—oh, dreadful it had been, with the corn all lying out as late as October, all sprouting in the stooks. Then in this week it rained very hard, and the river rose; and then at full moon the spring tides came up and stopped the head of water from getting out. So it was like a sea all the way from Up-waters to Seven Hatches and beyond; bridges broken, all except the old one; cows, pigs and sheep carried away: no getting across the river anywhere for days and days; and the weirs—oh, they were terrible, they would turn a man's mind to look at them, with all bits of cow-byres, haystacks, pigtroughs, trees, hencoops, bee-skeps, everything just going tumbling down. I saw a cradle go over at Condicote Old Mill, and if there had been even twins in it, no man could have saved them. And nearly all the boats were gone, too. It was all like a big sea as far as one could see, with hedges and trees standing out of it, and sometimes a sort of island, with a few cows on it mooing to be milked, poor things, or a poor horse, running round, half-starved.'

'Did you ever hear of a Mr. Brown who was drowned in the flood?'

Again Mr. Bert's face changed. 'You mentioned that name before,' he said, 'as well as another name. There was a lot of talk about those two: that that Sir Trigger—for he was a Sir—murdered Mr. Brown, and flung him in the water and then fled.'

'Do you think he did?' Kay asked.

'No, Master Kay, I don't. It's my belief that they both fell into the flood at Condicote Old Mill, and were drowned, only the Sir Trigger was washed into a mudbank and buried, whereas Mr. Brown was carried to Seven Hatches and found. Three or four people disappeared in the flood and were never heard of again. I believe Sir Trigger was one of them. If not, Master Kay, I would say that it was the other way about: that the Brown man murdered *him* and was drowned while escaping.'

'What makes you think that, Mr. Bert?'

'It's a long while ago,' Mr. Bert said, 'and everybody concerned is dead. But that Pimply Whatto's father, who was a bad one, when he was dying, told my father that on the last night those two were seen, he saw them both at the "Ring of Bells," so as to know them. And at midnight that night he saw them both again, near the Mill, and the Brown man was threatening the Trigger man, saying,

"I've warned you twice: you'll get no third time." And the Trigger man said, "If I lay hands on you again, I'll mark you. Get out!" And the Brown man did get out; but when the Trigger man moved on, Whatto saw the Brown man creep after him and take out a pistol; and no man ever saw them again alive. They both went on towards the flood. Whatto never came forward with this story at the Enquiry, because he was afraid he might be charged with murdering them himself. Besides, he wasn't there himself for any good, you may be sure. And maybe his story isn't true, for he wasn't always quite the one for the truth. It's best to give them both the benefit. The Great Flood was more than enough to drown them without either of them doing murder. Still, that was the tale he told.

'They put a tablet to that Brown in Little Zennor Church, if ever you go there.

' "To the memory of ABNER BROWN, Esq., a stranger,
A victim of the Great Flood."

'But there, I'm rambling on past dinner time.'

He had moved away, after dusting the knees of his trousers, when he stopped.

'That Mr. Brown was a western gentleman, it was thought,' he said. 'No one knew where he came from. He had twenty-five pounds in his bag at the Inn, and no clue to where his home and people were. A white-haired man, he was. I've often thought of his people, far away, never knowing; though they'll have done sorrowing by now, poor souls.'

• • • • •

That night Kay had not been long asleep before he woke up to find the room brightly lit as before, although it was dark night outside. In the passages near his room there were whisperings and footsteps, as though people were pausing at his door to mutter some password. He sat up, expecting them to come in, but they passed on. When they had gone, he quietly opened his door an inch or two and peeped out. Some people in scarlet cloaks were just passing through a door at the end of the corridor, but one of them had paused. She was a young, very handsome witch, with long ear-rings. 'Come along, sweet Belladonna,' her companion said, 'we shall be late for our Chapter.'

'Wait,' Belladonna said; 'I must just see what is in here.'

'No, come along; we must not keep Abner Brown waiting.'

Saying this, the witch pulled Belladonna away, and in a moment the door closed behind them. Whether it was the closing of the door or the sudden movement, Kay could not tell, but at the instant something fell on to the carpet from Belladonna's sleeve or pocket. Kay crept out to see what it was. It was a little red glass bottle, with a cut-glass stopper.

'I expect it's her scent-bottle,' he thought. He tried to open the door through which she had gone, so that he could give it back to her, but the door was fast closed, and what was worse, the handle gave him pins and needles when he touched it. And another strange thing was that all this part of the house was unlit, while his own room was brighter than a summer day. The cuckoo clock, inside the closed room, cuckooed for eleven o'clock.

When he was back in his room, he looked at the little glass bottle. 'Witches' scent,' he thought. 'I wonder what it smells like.' But it was not scent; it was labelled like a physic bottle:

'INVISIBLE MIXTURE.

Take 3 drops upon a lump of sugar. Night Dose.
" 6 " " " Day Dose.

Repeat dose if necessary.

'I believe it's the stuff they take to make themselves invisible,' he thought. 'I'll try it; and then I'll go out to the gamekeeper's cottage to see how they behave when they find that the hunters aren't at Coneycop Spinney at all.'

He had some old lumps of sugar put away under the carpet. He took out one of these and carefully opened the bottle. The mixture had a warm, rich smell, like the smell of green bracken on a very hot day. 'I must be very careful of this,' he thought. He dropped three drops on to a lump, popped it into his mouth, and re-stoppered the phial. A glow went through him, as though he were sucking the loveliest peppermint ever made. He hid the phial in a mouse-hole in the skirting-board behind the valance, and then stood up. He felt a pepperminty feeling go tingling along his toes, and lo, he looked at his toes and could not see them, nor his legs, nor his pyjamas; and though he looked at himself in the glass, he was not there; he was invisible. 'I say, what fun,' he said. He put on his slippers and went down into the hall, where a mouse was eating a crumb in the centre of a patch of moonlight. The mouse did not see him, but went on grinding and nibbling at the crumb till it was finished. He pushed the chair against the garden door, clambered up it, drew the bolts, turned the key, undid the chain, took off the burglar alarm bell, and opened a way for himself. In a minute he was over the wall and away to the pinewood out by Rye Meadows.

It was thrilling to walk up to rabbits in the grassy places, and to stroke them, while they thought that his touch was either a grass-blade or the wind. An owl blundered right into him, bounced off, hovered, tried to make out what it was that it had hit, and then sheered off, much puzzled. At Peter's Patch the keeper's dogs came out barking at him, with the keeper after them.

'What are Sol and Jo barking at?' his wife asked.

'Sounded like a footstep to me; but there's no one here.'

'I expect it was only a rabbit.'

'I'll rabbit them rabbits. Come in, dogs.'

When they had gone into the cottage, Kay crept a little nearer. Some friends of Mr. Bilges were there. Kay peeped in at the open door. The dogs snarled, and their hair stood on end with terror.

'Quiet dogs, will you?' Mr. Bilges said, kicking them in the ribs. 'Now we'll have a little drop of our nice spirit, which nobody knows about.' He produced a bottle, some sugar and a lemon, while his wife brought a kettle of hot water and a bowl; then they began to brew a punch. Kay could see the keeper's friends: they were Brassy Cop and the Pimply Whatto, as they were called; the two worst poachers and fighters in the district. The other was the young Bilges, who was footman to Sir Hassle Gassle. They drank the punch when it was made; then they began to boast.

'It must be nearly time to move off to the Spinney,' Brassy said. 'I heard the clock go one.'

'They'll not be finished before two or three, we hear,' the keeper said. 'What I want to do is to come in among them with my good gun, just as they're packing up my rabbits. I'll soon settle their hunting.'

'Ah!' his brother said. 'What I want is to get their rabbits and get the money for them. I reckon to get four times drunk out of what we get to-night.'

'What I'm for,' Whatto said, 'is to bang them black and blue with my knoppy blackthorn.'

'Ah!' Brassy said, 'a few good bangs on the heads with that, and they'll not poach so gamesome another time. But I've got my nice brass knuckle-dusters. That's what I'll dust them with.'

'Why, mercy me,' the Keeper's wife said, 'if we haven't left the game-bags down at the Hall! Whatever shall we bring their rabbits home in, when we've beaten them?'

'Ah!' the keeper said, 'why, whatever shall we?'

'We shall want a big thing. There'll be a hundred rabbits, they said.'

'A hundred rabbits,' Brassy said. 'They'll kill and we'll eat, and bang 'em into the bargain.'

'But what shall we bring the rabbits home in?'

'I don't know. Except we each carry twenty.'

'I know what we can pack the rabbits in,' the keeper cried. 'My old grandfather's sea trunk, or chest, as he called it. That will hold the rabbits. I'll fetch it down.'

Kay heard him go upstairs. Soon he came down, trundling the chest after him. It was a big black wooden chest, bound with iron at the corners. It had the name 'R. Bilges' painted in dirty white letters on the side. There were rope beckets or shackles curiously wrought, instead of the usual handles to lift it by.

'He might be your grandfather's coffin,' Brassy said.

'He was a seaman gunner, my grandfather was,' the keeper said; 'and a fine old drunken boy he was. It's my belief he had something on his conscience. There's some of his things still in here.'

On opening the box to empty it, he pulled out some old bottles covered with wickerwork, an old leather kneeboot, a patched pair of shoes from which the buckles had been cut, and some books. 'That's my old grandfather to the life,' the keeper said. 'Just some empty bottles that you can't drink, and old leather that you can't wear. Into the woods with you!'

Kay had just time to slip aside before bottles, boots and books were flung out past him into the wood.

'Now, Brassy,' the keeper said, 'if you'll take that end, I'll take this, and we'll move off to the Spinney. We won't take the dogs.'

'Come on, then.'

The three men moved off towards the Spinney.

'Make an end of them all, my Bilges,' the keeper's wife cried.

'Never you fear,' the keeper answered, beginning to sing:

> 'My name it is Roper and Willem,
> And I do intend for to killem,
> With my good gun-and-cartridging
> I'll finish their partridging,
> For I'll shootem and deadem and stillem.'

As they moved into the pine-wood, Kay saw the black figure of Blackmalkin step from the hedge to join them. 'They'll be at work in the Spinney now,' he said. 'You'll catch them just as they're packing up the spoils and planning what they'll do with them. Oh, what fun it will be to see their faces! But I say, keeper, what is that by the gate that your dogs are barking at?'

The dogs had come out to bark at Kay, whom they could scent but not see.

'I'll dog those dogs,' the keeper said, turning back a little. 'Get you back into kennel, or I'll give you one. Keep the dogs in; don't let 'em make that outlandish row, as though a basket of wild cats was turned loose.'

The keeper's wife called in the dogs and shut the door on them.

'Now, Blackmalkin,' Keeper said, 'and what are *you* gawping at there? Are you going to bark too?'

'No,' Blackmalkin said. 'I suppose it is all right.'

'Suppose what is all right?'

'That path there, from your house to the wood.'

'What could be wrong with it?'

'Look at it,' Blackmalkin said. 'Didn't you see the twigs stir on the path, just as though somebody trod on them?'

'Can't you see that nobody trod on them?'

'Yes,' Blackmalkin said. 'But they moved as though someone trod on them.'

'It was the wind,' Brassy said.

'Or a mouse running across.'

'I know when a mouse runs across,' Blackmalkin said. 'This wasn't a mouse.'

'Well, then, it was the shadow of a leaf or a moth, or a bat.'

'It looked like a person's footstep.'

'Well, there isn't a person, so it can't have been.'

'Look here,' Pimply Whatto said, 'how much more time are we to waste? Nice fools we'll look if they've gone with the rabbits before ever we get there.'

'Yes, come on,' the keeper said. 'You go in front, Blackmalkin, and forget all about what you thought you saw.'

They all moved off after this, growling at Blackmalkin, who kept looking back suspiciously at where Kay stood. He had seen the earth and twigs displaced by Kay's feet. Kay saw him looking back until the party was so far downhill that he could look no more.

When they were all out of sight, Kay looked at the things which the keeper had flung away. The bottles and leather seemed useless to him; but he looked at the books with interest. They were:

Mother Shipton's Prophecies Explain'd.

Zimmerman on Solitude.

The Execrable Life and Death of Scarlat Blackbones, the Barbadoes Pyrat.

A Book to Reckon Tides.
The Sea-Gunner's Reckoner.
Tom Maggot's Fifty Merry Jests.
The Sea-Gunner's Practice.

All of these books, except the last, were dirty, tattered, dog's-eared pamphlets without covers. Kay left them where they lay, but took *The Sea-Gunner's Practice* to look at later. He did not think that this could be wrong, since the keeper had flung it away.

He was not sure of the way to Coneycop Spinney. He went down the hill as the others had gone. The path led over a brook in to the valley below two rolls of down. He went on till he came in sight of Coneycop Hill, which there was no mistaking. A strip of wood in a bottom below the hill seemed likely to be the Spinney. It was a still, moonlit night, with nothing stirring except himself. He could not see the keeper's party. He went cautiously. Soon he caught sight of Brassy Cop staring into the Spinney from behind a tree; Blackmalkin was beside him. Coneycop church clock, which was just beyond Coneycop, struck four. Kay marvelled that the time had gone so quickly; but every instant had been lovely, being out there alone in the moonlight, seeing everything, but not being seen. Suddenly, quite silently, two figures crept past him, peering at the Spinney. They were so intent on what they were doing that they never scented him. Both were very muddy and shaking with excitement. One was Nibbins, the other was Bitem.

'There's the keeper,' Nibbins whispered. 'He's got no dogs now, hush!'

Kay saw the two Bilges, followed by Pimply, come up to Brassy.

'Not much good waiting any longer,' the keeper growled. 'Here it is beginning to be light. Not a sign of any hunt, nor of any rabbit.'

'I suppose they got the alarm and didn't come,' Pimply said.

'How could they have got the alarm? And here we've waited hours in the cold and have to drag that empty trunk back.'

'Where's the hundred rabbits you promised?' Brassy asked.

'I'll hundred rabbits you if you ask that again,' the keeper said. 'Of all the withering watches I've ever watched, this has been the witheringest and the watchiest. Here, you Blackmalkin, if that's your name, where's your friends that were to come, eh? Where are they?'

'Well, they *said* they were going to come,' Blackmalkin said.

'Ah, they *said* did they? And on what you said we've suffered.'

'Are you sure you didn't get the night wrong?' Pimply asked.

'I'll bet they said Friday next week and he mistook it,' Brassy said.

'No, I didn't mistake it.'

'Well, if you didn't mistake it, where are they, then?' young Bilges asked.

'I don't know.'

'Nor we don't know.'

'Wait a minute,' Pimply said. 'Here's people coming. Perhaps it's them, after all.'

Kay saw a woman and a man coming hurriedly towards them.

'It's your wife, Bilges,' Brassy said. 'With that young

Artful Artie.'

'Is Bilges there?' Mrs. Bilges asked.

'Yes, I'm here; of course I'm here. What is it?'

'It's about Brady Ride Wood, Bilges. Here's Artful just come from there. While you've been watching here, that Bitem and his friends have cleaned out all the rabbits from the whole south warren.'

'Not a scut left white in the whole boiling,' Artie said.

'They've been and cleaned out South Warren?'

'Yes.'

'That's why they never came here, then. The whole thing was a blind to bring us here, so that they could hunt in peace.'

'Seems like it.'

'How many rabbits would there be in South Warren?'

'A hundred and fifty, if there was one.'

'You've been made a fool of, Bilges.'

'Yes,' Bilges said, 'I've been made a fool of. We've all been made fools of. And this sneaking, prying Blackmalkin that told us all the story, is the one that made us the fools. Don't you try to sneak away, you Black, sneakin' sneak, for I've got you by the scruff.'

'I didn't make you a fool. I told you the truth. Oh, please let me go, you're almost choking me,' Blackmalkin said.

'I've a very good mind to quite choke you. You were in the plot with them. You knew they were going to Brady Ride Wood.'

'Oh, please, sir, I didn't, sir!'

'Yes, you did,' Pimply said. 'Don't you dare deny it.'

'Of course he knew it,' Brassy said.

'And we gave you milk and the bit of sardine,' Mrs. Bilges said.

'Oh, please, ma'am, they disagreed, ma'am, indeed, indeed, they disagreed.'

'Yes, and we're going to disagree,' Bilges said, swinging him up by the scruff. 'He's led us all here for the whole night, and his friends have robbed our rabbits. I vote we fling him into Sousepig Pond.'

'Yes, with a stone round his neck.'

'Oh, no, please! Not into a pond: I shall catch my death. I can't stand water, indeed I can't.'

'Who's going to put you into water, to poison what's good drink (when mixed with gin)? No. Sousepig Pond is mud, and mud is what you're fittest for. Take his tail, Pimply, and twist it if he tries to escape.'

Kay saw them carry Blackmalkin away down the hill. He followed them at a little distance to see what they would do. Not very far from the end of the Spinney was a big shallow pan fed by a spring, and full of water in the winter, but now full of soft pale mud in which Farmer Fattenham's pigs loved to wallow as a protection against the flies. It was a most filthy, messy place.

At the brink of this hollow the party paused.

'Now, Blackmalkin,' the keeper said. 'This is Sousepig Pond, and as you're a dirty little pig, you're going to souse in it: once for sneaking and once for squeaking and once for telling us lies, oh.' As he sang these lines he swung Blackmalkin round his head and pitched him SWOOSH into the mud. They all laughed at him and mocked him as he tried to clamber out.

'There. Now we'll go home,' the keeper said. 'Another time perhaps he'll be careful who he tries to make an April fool of.'

The party moved off for home in a very bad temper. Kay heard them growl as they passed.

'And we've got to drag that sea-chest up the hill!' 'And all those rabbits, which we could have got sixpence apiece for; let alone the soup and the skins . . .'

'If I'd shot that Blackmalkin with my good gun, I'd only have given him some of what he deserved,' etc., etc.

Kay saw Nibbins and Bitem peering from behind the hedge, both of them shaking with laughter. When the keeper's party had passed out of sight, Nibbins and Bitem hopped over the hedge to the brink of the pond. Kay heard them call out:

'I say, I say! how did . . . how on earth . . . Here, there's someone in the mud. Get a stick, quick. Here, give us a paw. Stick out your brush, Bitem. Poor fellow, he's pretty nearly smothered. Catch hold, now. Pull now, Bitem; pull; he's coming . . . I say, he's nearly stuck past saving. Heave together now. There he comes! Why if it isn't poor old Blackmalkin! Why, Blackmalkin, whatever brings you here?'

'Whatever brings you here?' Blackmalkin growled. 'This is a pretty sort of time to come hunting, just as it's getting light. You're nice people to arrange to go hunting with. I turned up, according to the plan; Keeper catches me and souses me in the mud; you two silly asses go gallivanting somewhere, and turn up grinning, hours too late to do anything. Oh, for pity's sake stop grinning in that insane way; it's nothing to laugh at, that I can see.'

'No, we're really ever so sorry,' Bitem said. 'But we'd better be off to our beds; it's too late to do any hunting now.'

'Perhaps at least you'll explain where you two grinning idiots have been passing the night, while I've been waiting for you.'

'We got into a bit of fun out Brady Ride Wood way,' Bitem said, 'and the time slipped away just like magic; we'd no idea it was so late. But we mustn't keep you talking here, old man; you'll be taking cold.'

'Yes,' Nibbins said, 'you must hop off home, old man; have a good rub in the bracken shed: nothing like

bracken for mud; and then have a good stiff bowl of hot milk, with a sardine to it, if you can get one.'

With this they set off to their homes.

Kay followed at a little distance, and let himself in just as the blackbirds were stirring. He was visible by this time, but very dim and blurred. As he climbed into bed, the thought occurred to him, 'Suppose I'm invisible at breakfast time. What on earth shall I do then? I'll give Ellen a jolly good scare, that's one good thing.' At this he fell fast asleep, till Ellen called him for the second time, by shaking him hard.

'You'll be late again, Master Kay, and then you'll be punished.'

He sat up in bed, blinking, not knowing quite where he was. He stayed there blinking long after Ellen had gone. He was not quite sure that he had not dreamed all his adventures; he was no longer invisible, that was very sure. Then as he sat blinking, a nibbling, scrunching noise came from the dressing-table. Something there was grinding and eating one of his lumps of sugar. He sat very still, staring at it. He could see nothing, but the lump was being turned about and becoming smaller. Presently it was all gone, and the scrunching ceased. Then a queer thing happened. There was a little odd flickering sort of a noise upon the dressing-table. One of the other lumps of sugar moved in a most odd way to the edge and toppled over to the floor. After lying there for a few seconds, it began to move again, along the edge of the skirting board, behind the dressing-table, where he could no longer see it. Soon after this, the scrunching noise sounded from somewhere in the wainscot. 'I know what it is,' he thought, 'the mice have been licking the Invisible Mixture.'

He hopped out of bed and pulled the phial from the mouse hole. Alas, they had been more than licking it. They had contrived to pull or to knock out the stopper, or perhaps he had not fixed it in properly, and the precious mixture was gone, either drunken by the mice or evaporated. Even the smell of green bracken and the flavour of peppermint had gone from it. It was just a tiny empty phial of red cut-glass. In his grief and disappointment, he flung it through the open window into the bushes. 'I'll never be able to be invisible again,' he thought. 'Just as I'd set my heart on it!'

As he entered the dining-room he noticed Nibbins curled up on his chair with his chin twisted up underneath his paw, sound asleep. The governess asked for Blackmalkin.

'Oh, I can't let him in, ma'am,' Ellen said, 'he's in such a pickle. He's plastered with mud or something, just as if he'd been down a rabbit hole.'

Blackmalkin was brought in plastered with the mud of the hog-wallow.

'He'd better be bathed,' Kay said, 'because that mud is like tarring and feathering. It closes all the pores of the skin, and he may die.'

A big pan of hot water was brought and, although Blackmalkin objected very strongly, he was soaked, scrubbed, rinsed and dried.

'Another time,' Ellen said, 'you keep out of those rabbit holes, you foolish thing. You get enough food here without crawling down rabbit holes which don't belong to you. Another time the rabbit hole will fall right in on you, and then where will you be?'

After lessons that morning Kay went to his bedroom to the cool, pink secret cave made by the valance of his bed. 'I don't suppose the book will be here,' he thought; 'that was probably only a dream, though it was a jolly one.'

When he turned back the flap of rappy carpet, the book *was* there. He turned over on his stomach with a sigh of pleasure, to examine it in peace.

'The Sea-Gunner's Practice,' he read to himself, 'With

a Description of Captain Shotgun's Murdering Piece with the improved Breech Action for use upon Salvage Coasts; Together with Tables and Proportions for all Pieces usual to that Service, by B. Blastem, Master Gunner.' On the flyleaf, in a neat handwriting, with a clove-hitch flourish below it, was the name of the owner:

'Aston Harker, Seekings House, 1804.'

'Why,' he said to himself, 'it is my great-grandfather's book. How very strange!' The book had been the property of other men before it had come to Captain Harker, for other names and earlier dates were written in it. He settled to read. 'The Sea-Gunner's Practice' was stiff reading for a little boy, though there were thrilling pages in it. One page was labelled:

'To make the fine mealed Gun-Powder, for Priming.'

Another had the heading:

'To make the coarse corned Gun-Powder.'

Another began:

'To make Coloured Flares and other Artificial Fire Works.'

'Some day,' he thought, 'I'll make gun-powder by the help of this. Then I'll fire off great-grandpapa's pistols that are on the wall, and I'll have fireworks every night.'

At the end of the book some twenty blank pages had been left by the publishers, so that sea-gunners might make notes and accounts of their stores according to the tables printed for their guidance. Captain Harker had made notes upon the first of these pages; the rest had been scrawled upon in a clumsy, coarse, untidy writing, by someone who did not know how to spell. In the cover of the book, at the end, was a pocket, which had once contained an engraving of Captain Shotgun's Murdering Piece. The engraving was gone; in its stead was a very old brittle yellow piece of newspaper, headed:

'—EW YORK, December 1811.
Strange Rescue in Gulf.'

He read on. 'Great interest was roused in West Street last evening by the arrival of the ship *Seamen's Rights,* Captain Isaac Winterbourne, with a cargo of logwood from Campeachy. Captain Winterbourne reports that while in the Gulf he saw smoke rising apparently from the sea. Thinking that some ship might be on fire or assailed by pirates, he stood towards the smoke, and was soon rewarded by raising the Cranes Reefs, or rocky islets mentioned by Narvaez in his "Gulf Pilot." The smoke proceeded from a fire of driftwood kindled by a solitary castaway, whom they found to be too crazed by his misfortunes to give a clear account of himself. No doubt he was the survivor of some merchantman wrecked in one of the great hurricanes, of which the last season was so fruitful. He seemed accustomed to a seafaring life, but neither his clothing nor his speech gave any clue as to who or what he was, the hardships to which he had been subject having destroyed his reason.

'On arrival in West Street, Captain Winterbourne sent him to a well-known doctor in Bleecker Street, from whose house he escaped in the course of last evening. Though he is certainly harmless, his manner may perplex or even frighten people, and the following description of him is issued to the public:

'A strong-built man of five foot seven or eight inches in height, brown hair and eyes, short sandy beard, nose broken as though by a blow, and the lips somewhat slobber. When found on the rocks, he was dressed only in a suit of thread-bare cottons. He left the *Seamen's Rights* in a costume supplied by Captain Winterbourne, tarred trousers, a tarred hat, blue shirt and jacket. He had no property but an old Bible, a Prayer-book and a pamphlet on gunnery, to all of which the demented creature appeared equally attached. All these volumes had had several possessors and gave no clue to his identity.

'Captain Winterbourne in his passage home was twice assailed by the tyrants of the waves, but by his vessel's speed was on both occasions able to uphold the challenge of her name.'

Kay wondered if the story could refer to some survivor of the *Plunderer*. Captain Harker had said that the *Plunderer* was last seen sailing towards the Gulf. Here was Captain Harker's book taken from a rock in the Gulf at about the time of the *Plunderer's* disappearance. And then the strange thing was that the book had been in the possession of this gamekeeper, whose name was Roper Bilges.

'Yes,' Kay thought, 'the gamekeeper is the descendant of my great-grandfather's Roper Bilges, and probably the man taken off the reef was Roper Bilges himself. I'm jolly glad that he did have some hardships. But wait a minute. There's all this writing at the end. Perhaps that will tell me more.'

Turning to the writing at the end, he read as follows:

'The true statement of Roper Bilges, gunner in the ship *Plunderer*, Captain Harker, master.

'Since I have been spared to see that honesty is the best policy, I, Roper Bilges, set down the truth, so that justice may be done on villains. After I took charge of the *Plunderer*, to prevent her falling into bad hands, I had words with Twiney Pricker, the sailmaker, as he called himself, though he was nothing better than a pirate, having been one often, as I will swear. On my giving him orders as captain, he gave me low words, which I passed by, thinking that they would wait till we was ashore. In the night he came to my cot with three others, with Jake and the coffin-maker (having been such in Bristol), and English Joe, that deserted the *Blanche* frigate and had her on his stomach in blue. They said, "——, we'll no more Bilges for captain. Get down into the boat!"

'They put me ashore on some rocks, where there was nothing but birds and a kind of rat what lived on shell-fish and the rain. They give me nothing but Bible and Prayer and one about gunnery. Pricker was against giving me fire, but the men stood out for me to have that. When they pulled back to the ship, she filled and stood off, and I never heard of her again: she was going, as they said, to the French settlements.

'On being left alone, I collected driftwood for a dozen fires which I always kept well heaped up so as not to lose my fire. I ate on rats, shell-fish and sea-birds, and the fish in the pools. At first I thought the crew was doing it for a pretend and would come back and take me off, but my fine Scoundrel Pricker saw to that.

'I reflected what my lot would be when the rains ceased on those hot rocks, with no shade, and whether I would go mad, etc.

'My main fear was of an hurricane which might whelm me out of this wicked world, which is but a snare. My one hope was, I had good books by me.

'On the eleventh day, or it may be the twelfth, for my mind was not very correct, being crazed with horror at T. Pricker's monstrous ingratitude, I was took off by the ship *Seaman's Rights*, Captain Winterbourne, master, with whom I returned to New York, tho' not recovered in my brains. So fearing to be had into the mad-house to be cut open by the doctors, I thought it best to avoid into the country parts, where little by little my reason, which parts me from the brutes, came back as good as ever it was, tho' no thanks to T. Pricker, the mad-house being my dread as well he knew.

'Coming back to England, I see in the newspapers that Captain Harker is not dead, of which I am heartily glad, for I never meant him harm, and I am glad not to have his blood on my soul, it lying all on Twiney Pricker, who, I doubt not, has reaped his judgement according. It was he had the treasure. Whether it profited him I leave all to judge, for from that day to this no one has ever heard what came to him and them. One thing is sure, the ship is sank, for else we'd have heard of their folly, spending their ill-gotten gains, etc.

'If she was not sunk in a squall, she was cast away, and her crew and fine sailmaker captain made examples of as pirates, as I heartily hope. But having suffered according to his deserts, I forgive him the dirty turn he done me, but, if this should come after my death into the hands of the police, let them know that Twiney Pricker was from the northern parts, a sailmaker by profession and speaks in the northern way, lobster-eyed and blue of both eyes, wears his beard in the Newgate fringe fashion, has two teeth missing from the upper jaw on left side, being hit with a pot in a dispute about the victuals. He has also a lady's heart transfixed with arrow on chest in gunpowder, also the fat ox of Bedford on his right arm. He speaks somewhat thick, owing to the teeth being gone, stands a short fellow but very thick. His hair which we call Twiney, is of a fair colour, like sea-twine. Anyone laying such by the heels would be entitled to the reward against pirates; though for my part, not being wishful to testify against an old shipmate, as well as being of a Xtian Turn and having forgiven him, would like to be kept out of it, not to come into court, if I could have the half reward for him; my one wish in this, being for justice on bloody-minded villians. If he be now dead (as I sadly fear) guvvanment should hang his bones up as a warning what comes to these fine sailmakers that puts their betters upon rocks and would not give them even fire until forced to by some as would have shot them if they'd refused, it being only bullets as such Dogs have brains to understand, being very ignorant Fellows, for all they sit so high, as these Northern Parts men do.

'But I have now done with these wicked men, and took back my own name of R.B., and no harm can come now, Capt. H. being now dead: so I live at peace; only write this so as Truth may prevail and justice be done. The half reward might be left for Roper Bilges, at the Post Office, Shrewsbury, and would consent to a third. R.B.'

Kay read this story through three times. 'It served him jolly well right,' he thought, 'to be served as he served my great-grandfather. I'm jolly glad that he was put ashore. It is hard luck that all the treasure was lost, but anyhow I'd rather that than for Twiney Pricker, and the others to have the benefit of it. It is exciting fun, piecing out the story.'

He went to the library, where with some trouble he pulled out the Atlas, which had belonged to his grandfather. It was a big, heavy book; he lugged it to the table, turned up the Western maps, and tried to find the Cranes Reefs. After some time he found them, as little black specks in the midst of the pale blue Gulf, not very far from the lagoons of the French Settlements. 'That is where they left Roper Bilges,' Kay thought: 'and somewhere between those specks and the coast is where the *Plunderer* sank. I expect she is all covered with coral now, or fallen all to bits.'

He left the Atlas open on the library table and returned to his lair above. When he had read the tale again, he left the 'Sea-Gunner's Practice' on his dressing-table.

'That is what happened to the treasure,' he thought; 'Pricker took it from Bilges and then it was sunk. I wish that I could tell great-grandpapa Harker, for that would be a load off his mind. No one could call that his fault.'

• • • • •

That afternoon the governess took him into the village, where he had to wait in the milliner's shop while she matched a reel of silk; to wait outside the butcher's (and not to play in the water of the gutter there, because there was blood in it) while she complained of last Sunday's joint, which had been tough even when minced; then to wait outside the stationer's, and not to go staring at the sweets next door because she would only be a minute, whereas she took eleven, because she met Mrs. Gossip there changing her novel; then in the last torment to wait in the sitting-room of Mrs. Tattle, looking at her case of wax fruits while 'they' talked about Mr. Holyport's sermon, and the sermon before that, and whether bugles were going to be much worn that year. The mention of bugles roused him for an instant, but it was soon plain that it wasn't his kind of bugle, and that neither the governess nor Mrs. Tattle would come rousing the forest like Robin Hood: far from it. Then there was talk of the butcher, whose meat was so tough, and of the new butcher, down in the River Road, who had supplied a piece of veal that really, Mrs. Tattle was usually afraid of veal, because Dr. Gubbins says that you must be careful about veal, especially at night, but that this piece of veal, really it wasn't like veal at all, but just like young lamb, so crisp when hot and delicious cold. Then there was all this talk about this and that in the newspapers that it was really dreadful what people were coming to, especially young people. . . . Here there came a home-thrust at Kay, who wasn't at all 'what we were when we were girls,' which was very likely true.

However, this visit, like so many others, came to an end at last. He was walked home to tea at home with a lecture about not fidgeting when he was paying a call, and especially of not twisting his hat-elastic round and round, and then letting it untwist, just as he'd been told not to at the swing, because it made everybody sick.

He was undressing for bed that night when the governess, who was preparing to play the piano, called to him from the study: 'Kay, was it you who had out the big Atlas and left it open here?'

'Yes, it was, please.'

'What did you have it out for?'

‘Please I wanted to look out a place.’

‘Yes, but why didn’t you ask me or Ellen to put it back when you had done with it? You must get into the way of being tidy and not leave great books about when other people want to use the table.’

It was just this interruption which kept him from putting the ‘Sea-Gunner’s Practice’ into the secret nook. It was lying there on the dressing-table, just as he had left it; he had almost picked it up to put it away, when she asked that question: then it went out of his mind. He got into bed, making up his mind to keep awake; he was quite sure that he would not go to sleep. He half thought that he would get out of bed to hide away the book, but he did not see the use of it. One of the mice was scrunching away at the wainscot; he wondered if it were still invisible. It went scrunch and scrunch, as though grinding at the wood sideways. The scrunching mingled with the singing of the governess at last in a very drowsy noise which made the room dimmer, dimmer, and dimmer, until . . .

He woke up suddenly, wide awake and still with terror from the knowledge that someone was in the room. He rolled under the clothes at once, waited terrified there for a minute, and then peeped out.

The room was brightly lit, as before, by no apparent light. It was dark night out of doors still, as he could see. An old woman in a poke-bonnet was standing close to his bed looking about her. ‘Our young friend is fast asleep, Blackmalkin,’ she said, ‘but tread quietly. I must have a look about here.’

He knew that sharp voice at once, and the next instant saw her face; it was Mrs. Pouncer.

‘Yes,’ Mrs. Pouncer said, moving to the book upon the

dressing-table, 'what have we here? Aha, a very interesting book; very interesting. No wonder, Blackmalkin, that we pull down big Atlases, to see where Gulfs and places are. A very interesting pretty little book, Blackmalkin dear, but not at all the sort of reading for a nice young gentleman who ought to be giving his mind to pouvoir. I think, my dear Blackmalkin, I will remove this little book.'

At this she put it into her handbag, which shut with a snap. The odious Blackmalkin sidled against her ankles, purring.

When she had taken the little book, she said, 'I will just look round the room, Blackmalkin dear, in case there should be any other things of interest.' She lifted up a pair of glasses upon a handle, and began her search. She looked under the valance of the dressing-table. 'Sugar, I see,' she said. 'Our young friend's private lunch, I presume; rather dirty sugar; unwholesome, I should say. Something of a smell of peppermint, too, isn't there; or am I wrong about the peppermint; not quite peppermint, either, though; but I've lost the scent now.' She stared at the prints and at the model of the *Plunderer*. 'The sports of our dear fathers,' she said, 'and the toy . . . ah . . . *Plunderer*, I see . . . Ah, *Plunderer*; the name of the ship . . .'

She paused for a minute over the ship; then she pulled a chair to the wall, stood upon it, fixed a magic lens upon the handle of her glasses, and stared through the model fixedly. 'Nothing there,' she said, 'nothing hidden there: no clue.'

She carried the chair across the room, again stood upon it, and examined the pistols in the same way. 'Useless,' she said, 'no clue there. But let us now look at the hearthstone.'

She rolled back the carpet so as to expose the slab. It was a big, clean block, six feet by four, apparently mortared and leaded into brickwork. She knelt down upon it, tried several magic lenses in her glasses, but seemed unable to see through it with any. She tapped it with a little hammer which she had in her bag. She pressed the knobs in the planks near it, as though hoping to press a secret spring. Nothing happened.

'I don't think that there is anything there,' she said. 'But there may be a hollow space. . . . It is a very big stone for an upstairs fireplace. There seems to be nothing more to examine here.' She tapped the window-seats and the wainscotings, looked under the bed, pulled the sofa to one side.

'I think, my dear Blackmalkin,' she said, 'we might go. There is nothing of any interest. We will go back to the library, where books like this seem to be found.' As she moved past the dressing-table on her way to the door, she paused again. 'It is odd,' she said. 'I really distinctly caught that smell of peppermint, or not quite peppermint. Perhaps it is a little the smell of mice, my dear young friend. You really ought between the three of you to be able to control the mice.'

The odious Blackmalkin sidled against her ankles, purring.

'He's a regular little sucking up sneak,' Kay thought; 'I'm jolly glad the keeper soused him.'

Mrs. Pouncer looked at Kay for a moment; he rolled slowly over drowsily. 'How soundly our young friend sleeps,' she said. 'Well, the sounder the better; we don't want young friends prying about the house while we're at work.'

Saying this, she moved out of the room, followed by Blackmalkin. When the door was closed upon her, Kay sat up to make sure that she had gone.

'I'll know her again if ever I see her,' he said to himself. 'She has a hooky nose, a hooky chin, very bright black eyes, long dingle-dangle ear-rings which click, a poke-bonnet, a red cloak, a stick with a hooky handle, and pointy, black shiny shoes. And although in a way she looks old, in another way she looks very young. And she has bagged my book. . . . I'll see if I can't follow her, to get it back.'

It was all very well to make this resolve from a warm bed; but when out of bed, and about to open the door on to what might be a dark passage full of witches, it did not seem so wise. 'And yet,' he thought, 'Roper Bilges' name is in the book. If she finds out, somehow, that I got it from the Keeper instead of from the library, she'll probably tell the governess, I shall be asked how I got it, and then there'll be a row. It will all be discovered then: my going out and everything. I must get the book.'

He looked out into the passage, which was now all dark and still: the house was asleep. He could not see Mrs. Pouncer nor her cat. 'They'll be in the magic room,' he thought, 'and the magic room is in this direction: it's in the wall, here.'

But although it was in the wall he could not find it, nor any door nor window to it: there was nothing but the bare wall, papered over. 'I believe I'm only dreaming this,' he said.

He was about to go back to his room, when he heard a door open in the northern corridor: a light appeared. He shrank back into the powdering-chamber, as it was called, near which he was standing: lying down on the floor he could see fairly well.

Blackmalkin appeared, bearing a red light. After him came Mrs. Pouncer, crowned and wearing a long robe covered with magic signs; she bore a staff or wand. After her came Greymalkin, bearing a smoking dish. They did not see him; they went straight down the stairs into the hall. The smoke from Greymalkin's dish was sweet to smell and gave one an excited feeling.

'I do believe,' Kay said to himself, 'that they are going to practise magic in the hall. I'll jolly well watch what they do, and see if I can't do it myself.'

He gave up the thought of the book: that did not seem nearly so interesting as watching magic.

Unfortunately, although he climbed to a place from which he could see into the hall, he could not see where Mrs. Pouncer stood, nor what she did. He saw Greymalkin coming round from time to time with the smoking dish, and he could hear Mrs. Pouncer's voice making the incantation.

'I know what she is doing,' Kay thought. 'Witches make incantations to call their familiar friends, who tell them all that they want to know. I do wish that I could hear what she said. . . . And I wonder what Blackmalkin is doing all this time.'

He tried creeping down the stairs, so as to see, but the old stairs creaked, and the noise of the incantation, growing louder, frightened him. There came a rushing noise, the hall-door opened with a clang; Kay felt the cool night air in a blast about him. Looking down at the hall, he saw a glittering child enter from the garden. The child strode up to the circle in which Greymalkin had been moving.

'I am here,' he said, 'why have you called me?'

Mrs. Pouncer's voice replied: 'Tell me, if you know, what became of the ship *Plunderer*, after Roper Bilges was put on the island.'

'I do not know,' the child answered. He moved back to the door, growing less bright as he receded: he seemed to fade away. The incantation went on for a minute, then there came another rushing noise; a glittering girl came into the hall and strode up to the circle.

'I am here,' she said. 'Why have you called me?'

Mrs. Pouncer repeated her command; but the girl did not know what had become of the ship. When she, too, had faded away, other figures appeared one by one, as the incantation went on: an old man, an old woman, a youth crowned with ivy-leaves, and a woman riding a black mare. Mrs. Pouncer ordered the old man, the old woman and the youth, each in turn, to tell what became of the *Plunderer*; each said 'I do not know' and faded away; but when the woman on the black mare rode in, Mrs. Pouncer did not mention the ship; instead of that she strode up to the circle, and said in an angry voice: 'Why do you come? You are not called.'

'I am here,' the woman said; 'and I will not go without reason.'

'I charge you to be begone,' Mrs. Pouncer cried.

Kay saw Blackmalkin and Greymalkin run up beside Mrs. Pouncer; Blackmalkin shook his red light, Greymalkin his dish of burning gums; Mrs. Pouncer uttered charms and threatened with her wand. The woman seemed angry, but backed her black mare out of the door, out of sight.

'The bold-faced thing, to front me so,' Mrs. Pouncer said, as she went back to her incantation. Somehow, the woman's riding in had upset the spells: it was a long time before another person appeared. When he did appear, he was a stern-looking man all dressed in red.

'I am here,' he said; 'why have you called me?'

'Tell me, if you know what became of the ship *Plunderer* after Roper Bilges was put on the island.'

'She sank.'

'With all the treasure on board?'

'Yes.'

'With all her crew on board?'

'Yes.'

'Can I get at the wreck, or where the wreck was?'

'No.'

'Nor take the treasure from her?'

'No.'

'Where is the wreck, then?'

'Where you cannot find her.'

'Answer me, where is she?'

'Gone.'

'Where was the wreck; I charge you, tell me.'

'I will not be charged. Beware, you, how you order me.'

He spoke these last words angrily, so that Kay, who was frightened, slipped back into his bedroom. He heard them talk angrily at each other for some minutes, making more and more noise, till Kay wondered that the governess did not wake. Mrs. Pouncer seemed to be getting rather the worst of it.

'Kay,' said a sweet voice at the window.

Kay hopped round with a start. A light was shining in at the window; someone had opened it. It was the woman on the black mare. They were floating there beside the window, while she looked in to call him. There were golden wings on the mare's shoulders and hooves: he had not noticed these before. The hooves were treading the air much as a swimmer will tread water.

'Will you come to ride with me?' she asked. She was a somewhat fierce but smiling lady, with keen grey eyes full of courage, and a face tanned by the wind; her cheeks were a rosy brown and her smile most winning.

'There's room on the saddle in front of me,' she said: indeed there was, a most lovely little blue saddle with golden stirrups and a bar in front to hold on by.

'Won't you come?' she said.

'May I, really?'

She held out her hands to him and helped him into the saddle. One thing troubled him. 'Suppose Mrs. Pouncer comes back into my room and finds me gone?' he said.

'That will be arranged for,' she said. 'Look. There's Nibbins in your bed, so curled up that anybody would think it was you.'

Indeed, there was Nibbins wrapped in the bedclothes, curled well down into the pillow. It was great cheek of him, Kay thought, not asking leave.

'How do you know about Nibbins?' he asked.

'Oh, I know about a great many things.'

He heard the quarrel downstairs in the hall become very noisy indeed, as though Mrs. Pouncer and the man were flinging things at each other.

'We will come away from all that,' the woman said, as she touched up the mare. Instantly she had swung away from the house towards the hills, flying high and very swiftly through the cool summer night, so warm in patches above bare ground. They passed quite close to the church tower with its four gold weather-cocks.

'Oh, do let me look at the weather-cocks close to,' Kay said.

'You shall give them some golden corn out of my mare's nosebag,' the woman said. And then, lo, the mare sidled up to each weather-cock in turn, and Kay was able to offer golden corn-grains from the nosebag to each. The weather-cocks were old-fashioned and somewhat battered birds, rather stiff upon their perches and blind from the weather. Each, on eating the grains, flapped his heavy golden wings and crowed a little. When all had been fed, they went on with their song, which they hummed together to pass the time.

The North-West cock sang:

> 'I watch the common people live and die
> Between the hard earth and the windy sky.'

The North-East cock sang:

> 'I watch the great ones ruling, in their pride,
> That cannot last, the life that cannot bide.'

The South-East cock sang:

> 'I watch the wild life stirring in the wood
> The green sap and the hungering for blood.'

The South-West cock sang:

> 'I watch the Mind that seeks and will declare
> The meaning and the purpose everywhere.'

Then they all sang together:

'We keep the watch and face the wind that blows,
While under us the heavy hour goes.'

The wind shifted a little as they sang, so that each of the four creaked a little as they came round to face it.

'Good-bye, weather-cocks,' Kay called, as the mare galloped away. 'I should think they loved it up there, up in the wind, with the jackdaws and the pigeons, and the bells chiming every third hour.'

'You wonder what became of the *Plunderer*,' the woman said.

'The man said that she sank, with all the treasure on board, and all her crew.'

'Well, perhaps we shall know more about that presently. . . . Come up, mare.'

They were now going so fast that the rivers and ponds streaked away far beneath them like flashes of light.

'It is true,' the woman said, 'that the *Plunderer* sank with all her treasure, as well as with all of her crew who were in her at the time; but one of her crew was not in her at the time; he had been put ashore on an island before the ship was wrecked.'

'Yes, I know,' Kay said, 'Roper Bilges, the mutineer, who put great-grandpapa Harker on shore.'

'Ah, how clever we are!' the woman said with a strange smile. 'But we will not talk now, for we have to come down here.'

'Where are we?' Kay asked. 'How far have we come?'

'We are in the North,' she said, 'at Trigger Court. We have come some hundreds of miles.'

The mare slackened pace as she glided gently down to the end of a lake, from which a grass slope led to a big house. It was still dark night everywhere. Owls were

cruising along the woods near the water; fish were leaping in the lake and rabbits hopping about on the lawn. The mare steadied near the front of the house, which had many blank windows, and one wide-open French window, brightly lit, on the second floor.

The woman stopped the mare beside this window. 'We get down here, Kay,' she said. She leaped from the saddle into the balcony, and then taking Kay's hands, she jumped him down beside her, and at once drew him with her into the lighted room.

It was a big, bright, pretty bedroom, hung with white chintzes which were patterned with pink roses tied with pale blue ribbon. The furniture was old and very shiny from polish, lacquer and brass. A fire was burning in the grate, although it was a summer night. To their left, as they entered, about fifteen feet from the window, was a big double bed, hung with chintz like the rest of the room. In this bed, propped up by pillows, a wicked old woman in a very gay dressing-gown was reading a sprightly story, at which she was laughing. Beside her, on a table, was a bottle of champagne: she sipped a glass of the wine from time to time. In her mouth was a long cigarette-holder containing a lighted cigarette.

'He, he,' she chuckled, over one of the jests. 'He, he. Oh, dear, if I read any more of this, I shall crack my ribs to matchsticks!'

'Miss Susan Pricker,' the woman called.

The old lady sat up fiercely in her bed. 'Deuce take your impudence, ma'am,' she said, 'I'm not Miss Susan Pricker. My name is Piney Trigger, of Trigger Hall. And what are you doing, coming in at the window at this time of night?'

'Miss Twiney Pricker,' the woman said, 'don't think to bluster me, ma'am. Your name is not Trigger, but Pricker.'

'If I ring for my medical attendant,' the old lady said, 'you will be removed in custody.'

'You may ring for your medical attendant, ma'am, but he will not hear; because, in the first place, the bell will not ring, and in the second place, he has gone to a dance and will not be here until dawn.'

'Look at that boy,' the old lady replied, 'catching his mortal end in pyjamas.'

'His mortal grandmother!'

The old lady put down her cigarette: she clenched her fist at them, pulled off her cap and wig and hurled it at them.

'Take that for your impudence,' she said. 'If I rise from this bed, I'll make you eat it.'

'Miss Pricker,' the woman said, 'a great many years ago your father helped to do this child's great-grandfather a cruel wrong, which altered his life for him. Your father was swiftly punished for his share in the wrong, and got no benefit from it, but you can at least tell this child what became of the ship *Plunderer*, and how your father came to change his name. In the meantime, won't you put on your head-dress; the night air may otherwise strike chill.'

'Thank you, Miss Whoever-you-are. The night air certainly makes you sufficiently cool. I will put on my cap. And how do you know about Sir Piney Trigger?'

'He was not Piney Trigger, but Twiney Pricker.'

'Prove it,' the old lady said; 'as they say in the law courts, prove it.'

The young woman pointed at the wall. 'There, Kay,' she said, 'is a portrait of this lady's father, the Twiney Pricker about whom you have read. See if he be like the description.'

Kay looked as he was bid. The man in the picture had

cold blue eyes which stuck out like lobster's eyes. He had a wide mouth, which suddenly opened to show two teeth gone on the left side. The hair was just the colour of twine; it was twiney hair. The man looked 'sinister,' as Captain Harker had said, but with 'a great deal in him,' mostly evil, but not all; he was like the old lady in the bed. He wore good black broadcloth, a white stock, and a blue necktie about the stock. The portrait had a label beneath it:

'Sir Piney Trigger, Honduras Merchant. d 1850.'

'Twiney Pricker had that sort of hair,' Kay said, 'and those kind of lobster eyes, and two teeth gone on the left.'

'A great many thousands have all those marks,' the old lady said. 'Think again, child. And then perhaps you will remove yourselves.'

'He had a woman's heart transfixed with an arrow, done in gunpowder on his chest,' Kay said; 'and the fat ox of Bedford in the same on his right arm.'

'He had nothing of the kind,' the old lady said.

'Yes, he had,' the woman answered. 'Look there. Look at the portrait.'

As they looked at the portrait, Sir Piney Trigger, Honduras Merchant, stirred in his canvas. His hands, which were coarse, blunt and square-fingered, unbuttoned his waist-coat and rolled back his costly frilled shirt. There was the transfixed heart upon his chest, and the greater part of the ox of Bedford, fat beyond belief: he could not well show the beast as far as the tail without tearing his shirt.

The old lady poured herself a large glass of champagne and drank it quickly.

'Very well,' she said, 'he was Twiney Pricker. What of it?

He is not going to be bothered by that at this time of day, I think. I like to think that he was Twiney Pricker, and had a bit of go and a bit of fun as a young man. He did put his captain ashore, he, he! and ran away with the ship, with all the Bishop's candlesticks . . . ho, ho, ho! How we used to roar with laughter over it! . . . and then he rounded on the gunner who was giving himself airs . . . and put him ashore too. Let me see, what was his name? It was one of these marine names, Squilges or Dirges.'

'Bilges,' Kay said.

'Just as I was saying, Bilges. He put Squilges ashore. But the others did not like that so well; for the next night, or almost the next night, they put *him* ashore on a sandbank. But my father marked some of them first: pinked, they called it then. "Pinked them in the plexus" was the phrase. All these fine old phrases are gone out, since pinafores and temperance became the rage. My father pinked them to purpose; but they were too many for him.

'My father said that being on the sandbank was easily the hottest time he ever had; there being nothing whatever to drink, except the dew that collected at nights upon his tarpaulin hat. He used to lick this as it collected; and in the day he bathed in the sea. Food he had largely to do without, except a kind of marine worm which he found buried in the sand. Pa used to say that he never put in so much sleep as upon that sandbank. That, and thinking what he would have to eat and drink when he returned to civilisation, was how he passed the time: that and bathing, and getting into wet sand to avoid the hottest of the sun, and, of course, digging for these worms: quite the early bird.

'A man like my Pa is not easily to be quenched, any more than I am. My heart is no more use than a shifting backstay, but I can take my wine, I hope, and begone dull care. I'll sing till I die.

'I'll live to the age of a hundred and eight
And then I'll go courting to find me a mate;
I'll live to the age of a hundred-and-nine,
And finish my bottle whenever I dine:
I'll live to the age of a hundred-and-ten,
When I'll mount on my horse and go courting agen.'

'Deuce take these lily-livered times! I'll have a devilled bone to my breakfast as long as I've a gum in my mouth. Cheer up, my lads, there's shot in the locker still.

'What was I saying about my father? Oh yes . . . he was on the sandbank, wasn't he? How did he get off? Why, a chasse-marée came by, not looking where she was going. He saw someone on board her striking a light with a flint and steel; so he hailed her to keep off or she'd be ashore, and then begged them to take him off, which they did, though most of them thought he was a ghost.

'Who were they? Well, everybody is young at some time, I suppose; and I suppose everybody has to live: one may as well have one's fling. Besides, the rich of that time used to flaunt their wealth: it was the greatest temptation to the poor to come to take it. I suppose they cracked people's crowns to take it. Some crowns are exceedingly easily cracked; and a lot, which are cracked already, are better cracked. Deuce take me, I'd have been a pirate myself if I'd had the chance. Besides, these people who rescued my father weren't pirates, they were only on a pleasure cruise. Besides, it was legal in a sense, for they were at war at the time, or just had been, or would have been, or soon would be again. Besides, although my father said they had a lot of watches and necklaces in the chasse-marée, that proved nothing, rather the reverse, for one of the party, a very gentlemanly fellow, was a jeweller by profession, and another, who was said to have been a titled person, was a collector of such things, what they call a connoisseur. Lots of people do collect them. What more natural than that he should acquire some on a pleasure cruise? I should call it quite remarkable if he didn't.

'However, I find a lot of these squeamish, mealy-mouthed people of the pleasant present day, who live on pap and poppy-cock, are always ready to condemn anybody who lives in a way that is not their own way. Nothing shows a narrow mind like that. I'm glad to say I'm without prejudice. If a man says to me, "I'm a pirate, madam," I say to him, "I admire your pluck, sir. Do you want a mate, sir?" That is my opinion of pirates. But then I take after my father. Burn my wig and bonnet if this bottle isn't empty!

'These people, whoever they were, lived on the shores of one of the lagoons near there: I daresay they do still. Some were French, some Spanish, some Americans, a few of all sorts. They'd rather lost their way. My Pa directed them how to steer.

'That very evening, as they sailed, they sighted the masts of a wreck sticking out of the water, with the sails still set. My father knew the sails at once, from having made them and mended them. The wreck was the *Plunderer* lying in six or seven fathoms of water. She had been caught in a squall, when the men were drunk. You see what came of getting rid of my father, the one man who could have saved them.

'There wasn't a sign of the crew, my Pa said, but the sharks there had a well-fed sort of a look. Near by were the two boats floating bottom up. That was the end of them. Those that hadn't been drowned the sharks had eaten.

' "That's my old ship," my Pa said, "that I fell overboard from the other night."

' "She's fallen overboard herself now," they said. "What was in her? Anything worth diving for?"

' "No, only sugar; it will all be spoilt."

'So they left her there and sailed on; but my Pa took a very careful reckoning of where she was.

'If you will oblige me with a light to my cigarette, instead of gawping at me in that South country fashion, it will be a comfort and a change. Tobacco isn't ladylike, they say. Don't talk about these pinafore things to me: ladies, quotha!

'About my father. . . . He landed with the chasse-marée people, in a very pleasant French city; I name no names. Nice ironwork on the balconies, he said there was, altogether a change from the sandbank and the worms. But he was destitute. He could not set off at once by himself to fetch the treasure from the *Plunderer*, and for a long time he could not find anyone to be his partner. That is where respectable people fail: they won't gamble.

'My Pa had a hard year of it, and all the time that treasure was sinking deeper into the coral. Believe me, he was there a year before he met a sportsman.'

'Was the sportsman's name Abner Brown?' Kay asked.

'Yes, child, it was. Who was Abner Brown? He was a local gentleman who received things: that is, bought things from pedlars and people. My father dealt with him and at last persuaded him to come to look for the *Plunderer.* My Pa had no money. Abner had. Abner fitted out a yawl; then he and my Pa set out in her to whereabouts the *Plunderer* had been, and spent a month there dragging the bottom with grapnels, hoping to find the wreck. They sailed to and fro, to and fro; they found coral and seaweeds and squids with parrot-heads, but no *Plunderer.* Of course a year had passed; there had been storms, and sandbanks form quickly there; then she might have been struck by lightning and broken apart. Still, it was sad not to find any trace of her.

'After a month Abner said he would search no more; it was no good looking any longer. My Pa was all for searching for another month, but of course it was Abner's yawl, and then the stormy season was at hand; so there was nothing for it but to turn. My Pa spoke his mind though; he called Abner a lily-livered papgoose. He said Abner bore no malice for this, but on their coming ashore, gave him a sum of money, and sent him along the coast to a seaport where he could go into the hotel trade.

'You might think that this was handsome in Abner Brown, my mouselike Miss and Sir. Judge by results, I say.

'What was he like, this Abner Brown? He was like a white, sweet, sanctified horse-dealer, or a hymn-singing cutthroat, or any cherry-lipped poisoner who will drop a tear at your pain and put ratsbane in your beer at the same breath. Talk? He would talk the hind legs off a mule. Weep? He would weep at a word. He wept when my Pa called him a papgoose. He was always weeping: a crocodile was a drought to him.

'But how you two can expect me to speak of a man like that without rinsing my mouth to clear the taste away, is more than I can comprehend.

'What did my Pa do? He went into the refreshment trade, selling liquor to seamen. Then he did a little crimping, which is either needlework or keeping a sailors' home. With the profits of this he went into the industry business, getting negro servants from savage parts to places where they could go to school and wear proper trousers, instead of the fans and things, sometimes only pieces of sealing-wax, my Pa said, which they were accustomed to where they lived in their heathendom. He did very well in the industry business and brought many heathen savages into the advantages of civilisation. Sometimes they died, of course, but that was due to the fevers, that wasn't my Pa's doing. My Pa always gave them what he gave to a seaman, fifteen inches broad to lie upon, and always the very best plank and chain. He spared no expense in those ways, never: penny wise, pound foolish, was one of his mottoes.

'However, there were so many anxieties in the industry business, my Pa gave it up, and went to Honduras, where he became a merchant under the name of Trigger. Until then he had usually called himself Suarez—Benito Suarez—which means Blessed Suarez. Now that he was Trigger he prospered so that he gave up thinking of the *Plunderer*—put her out of his mind as lost, in fact.

'When he was very rich he came to these parts, where nobody knew him except as the rich Honduras merchant. He was knighted, too, Sir Piney. Very jovial we were. When people saw a yellow turn-out tooling down to Epsom behind two bits of blood, they sometimes asked: "By Jove, who is that extraordinarily handsome woman in the scarlet and fur, with the geraniums in her hat?" The answer always was: "That's Miss Trigger, the beautiful Miss Trigger, that the Begum offered a cool million for; that is

moonlight, right through a lock that the Queen herself was opening. That was a triumph for my Pa.

'But it was the beginning of the end in one way. If he'd not taken to the moonlight business, he might never have known that Captain Harker was still alive. The best place for his moonlight was on a river not five miles from where that Captain Harker lived, or moaned rather, for that Captain H. was a morbid man, mealy-faced, always mourning about the treasure. My Pa was doing his moonlight business right close to that man's home, and saw him again.

'When I consider the change that seeing that man made in Pa, I feel that I must open another bottle.

'Some of the change was due to liver, no doubt, but the rest was remorse. "It was I," he said, "made poor Captain Harker as he is. O woe, woe!"

'I did what I could to change his heart, but who can change the heart when the liver's all wrong? No one.

' "Piney," he used to say, "Piney, I have been a great sinner."

' "Nonsense, my Pa," I used to say. "And if you have, you ought to be proud of it."

' "No," he said, "I am not proud of it. It weighs in here," and then he would beat where his liver was.

'At last he said: "One thing I can do. I can get that treasure back to Captain Harker before I die, if two marks of the five are still above water."

' "Why, rubbish," I said. "What stuff and rubbish! I never heard the like." For I didn't want my Pa at his age, and with his liver, to go wandering about in all sorts of mud and climates, dredging in the sea and diving. Still he would go, and without me. There was nothing for it but to let my Pa have his own way, and he was away two years.

'And do you know what he found at the end of twenty months? Oh, the deceitfulness of false companions! Never shall I forget my sweet Pa's letter about it. My Pa found that one whom I sullied my lips over by calling him a gentleman had robbed him and deceived him. He found that Abner Brown had taken the treasure years before. This was how he discovered it: listen.

'After he had searched for twenty months and more, my Pa had to change his divers: he was advised to hire some Indian divers from the pearl-fisheries, because they stood the heat better. They were very nice men, these Indians; they always called him Massa. When he brought them to dive where the *Plunderer* had been, they said: "O, Massa, him no good. Mr. Blown he get the tleasure here long, long time ago; he take him all away, boxy and bundley and big piecee tandletick."

'That was what Abner Brown had done in return for my Pa's trusting him with the secret.

'When he took my father to look for the *Plunderer's* wreck that first time, long, long ago, he sighted the wreck, as it chanced, when Pa was asleep. Did he tell my Pa? No. Like a false knave he made a note of where she was, and told my Pa it was no good looking any longer. So back he sailed, waited till my Pa had moved elsewhere, then came back with his divers and took everything.

'But the divers were able to tell my Pa what had happened next, though.'

'Abner lost it,' Kay said.

'Yes, my little lovebird, he lost it. He was taking it back to that French city that I mentioned. He had it all, and he was only five miles from home. All seemed to favour his false heart. But lo, when he got near, the

Army and the Navy were there, rooting out all the Settlement and hanging a lot of them. Abner had to leave his boat full of treasure and fly for his life; and even so, though he was not hung, he had seven years in a chain-gang.

'But it is my Pa that I want to talk of, not Abners and treasures. When my Pa came home at the end of those two years, he did not talk about them, but about his liver. "Piney," he said, "my liver's like a shifting backstay. It takes me across the brisket instead of supporting my vital organs."

'He was a broken man on his return, my Pa. First he would say that about his liver. Then, once, he flashed out, just like his old self: "By goom, Piney, yon Abner was theer, digging and digging for t' brass and finding nowt." But that was only a rally. He told me nothing more than that about his last four months of search: only that yon Abner was there. What could one make of that?

'Then once, in a dreadful voice, he said: "Captain Harker is dead, Piney. After all, Captain Harker is dead. But I have been beside his tomb, Piney, and told him I did my best." Ah! after all my longing for him, to have him like that!'

Here the poor old lady shed a few tears, tried to fill her glass from the bottle, and finding it empty, sucked its neck instead. After a few puffs at her cigarette she went on:

'And he was only at home for two days. He went off again. No harm in that: he was always going off in the old days to see about his moonlight. But this time he went off muttering about the tomb. And this time he never came back to his poor little Tiney Piney, never, never, never, never, never: Shakespeare.

'Do you ask me "Was it liver?" No, I say, it wasn't liver. He went off in the fly, muttering about the tomb, and what became of him nobody knows.'

Here she sat up in bed and gripped the bottle by the neck as though it were a club.

'Ah! what happened? What happened?' she said. 'What happened in those last four months in the West? What happened when he went from here to Condicote? And what happened on that midnight after he left the "Ring of Bells" Inn? I ask what, and I ask why, and nobody answers.

'But if you ask me, I say that Abner Brown was at the bottom of it. However hard he was digging when Pa saw him, he certainly followed Pa here. Why?

'To try to get money from him, probably, by blackmail. He came to this house and my Pa kicked him out. Next day, my sweet Pa went away, forever and forever farewell, Cassius. He was traced to Condicote, and there he was seen talking to Abner Brown, for Abner followed him. "The gents were having words," the potboy said. "Sir Trigger kicked him out and told him to do his worst." It was the wettest season ever known, and the great floods were out. No one has ever learned what happened next. He went out very late, after dinner, to which he drank only barley-water, and he never came back, though the maid had put out his nightgown and laid the warming-pan in his bed. He was never seen by mortal eye from that day to this.

'Abner Brown was seen. They found my fine papgoose partly eaten by fish, but identified by his linen, at Seven Hatches Weir, having been drowned, the medical men said. Some said that my Pa had killed Abner, but with a liver like a shifting backstay my poor Pa was deprived of manly pleasures. To be killed by a man like my Pa, let him lay not that flattering unction to what he called his soul: Shakespeare. That he had a tooth knocked out by my Pa's hand is glory enough for him.

'Some said that Abner had killed my Pa. I say, bosh, both Miss and Sir. It was thought that my Pa fell into the floods while in a spasm from his backstay.

'What took him to Condicote? Did I mention the word moonlight ever?'

'You did,' Kay said.

'Then don't repeat it,' she said. 'Moonlight is a thing of the night, all these things beginning with M are: there's Moonlight, and Murder, and Mystery, and Missing the Midnight Train, and Mourning and Much-loved Pa; all dark, sorrowful things.

'However, a long life and a merry one is Piney Trigger's motto, and a very good one too.

'Miss Piney Tricker is a girl whose wisdom is most
weighty,
She never went to bed till three till she was over eighty.
When claret red is in her head, she carols from her
throttle,
Hurray, hurray, my jolly lads, let's have another bottle!
Tooral-loo.

At ninety-five her chief delight was going out to dances,
At ninety-nine she dazzled men by fire from her
glances;
And now that she's a hundred odd, she fills her glass
with liquor
And says hurray, my jolly lads, hurray for Piney Tricker!
Tooral-loo.

'I call myself Tricker in poetry, because Trigger has so few rhymes. There's bigger, and digger, and figger, and jigger, and pigger, and rigger, and wigger, and the man who goes zag-zig is a zagger-zigger. If he isn't, I don't know what he is, and I'm sure you don't. Where is that electric light switch?'

For some minutes Kay had been longing to speak, but the old lady had talked with such energy that he had had no chance. As she paused to grope for the light switch, he broke in:

'Miss Trigger-Pricker,' he said, 'your father found the treasure and I believe he brought it to somewhere near Condicote. And some think it may be there still. And Pimply Whatto's father said he saw Abner Brown, with a pistol in his hand, following your father towards the floods on the night they both disappeared.'

'I shall most certainly give Sophronia a piece of my mind,' the old lady answered. 'Not only is the stitching giving way in the seams, but the stuff itself shows signs of wear, which is not the wear for Piney Tricker, Man's True Blue TOAST.'

She said this very rapidly and at the same time seemed to recede. He could not see her so clearly, nor could he see the lobster eyes of Sir Piney staring out of the portrait. The fire in the grate had burned dim, all the room was dim, and far away, though he could hear Miss Piney's voice going on still like a mill-wheel. He felt the young woman with her fierce and smiling face pluck him towards the window, where the horse was, but he was so very, very sleepy that he really could not keep his eyes open. He managed to say, 'Do let's stop at the weathercocks,' but they were already rushing and rushing through miles of wind.

'Weather-cocks, Master Kay,' Ellen said, as she shook him awake from his bed. 'Do wake up, there's a good boy. Such a boy to wake I never did see. Now don't be late for breakfast, but get up at once, like a little moral. Why, you sleep like one of them things that curl up all winter! Now don't go to sleep again, or I don't know what she'll say.'

As it was Sunday, he had no lessons that morning, except the Collect for the day, which had to be learnt by heart. After this he was taken to church to a pew in the forward part of the nave, from which he could see the chancel through the hollow of the tower. He was much too young to understand or follow the service. He liked some of the hymns, and adored Miss Holyport, who played the organ. Apart from these joys, church had few solaces. Often in the summer a swallow would flit about: when there was no swallow, the only thing to do was to look at the walls, which were full of queer things. For instance, if you looked at the lines of mortar which held in the irregular stones on the walls, you could sometimes imagine that they made pictures. Close to him there was a very good portrait of Henry VIII, thus:

and a picture of a boat, thus:

which filled in a lot of time. Then, in some of the walls were the mouldings of windows and arches long since filled in: it was quite good fun to imagine the windows and arches as still there, and to go through them into some jollier place than church. He knew all the memorial tablets within sight by heart, from Captain Porkins, late of the 91st (Duke of Cumberland's) Light Horse, who was slain while doing staff duty at Hougomont on the Field of Waterloo to

> 'ANNABEL BETHESDA MEE, Spinster of this Parish.
> She rests in peace till Wars and Tumults end,
> We an Example mourn, the Poor a Friend.'

But the chief pleasure in church was to look at the carved and painted figures arranged along the wall-pieces of the chancel-roof. There were sixteen of these on each side. They had been put there, with the chancel roof, somewhere about the year 1500. No one knew quite what they represented, for only a few of them were winged. They were 'the busts and heads of men and angels,' so the guide-book said. Some tried to make up the sum of 32 thus:

12 Apostles.
7 Virtues.
9 Worthies.
4 Archangels.
—
32

To Kay they were all sorts of things at different times. Now they would be the Condicote and Muck Zennor

Rugby football teams (with an umpire each) all lined up for kick-off; anon they would be the Australian eleven, 1882, facing the team of Cambridge University, which beat them; then on another Sunday one side of them would be A False Start for the Derby, from a well-known print, while the other side would be the start for the Grand National Steeplechase, 1839, with Mr. Mason on Lottery, and Mr. Martin, in his pink sleeves, on Paulina. Sometimes they would be Britons and Romans, and sometimes they would be the House of Parliament, with the East window coming in on them as Oliver Cromwell.

After the service, people gathered outside the church in the broad walk near the porch. The governess was stopped by Mrs. Gossip, who had something to discuss with her. The two of them walked together deep in talk through the churchyard. A man whom Kay did not know, but who seemed to know him, clapped him on the shoulder and began conversation with, 'Well, Kay, have you found the Harker treasure yet?'

He started, because how could this man know how much the Harker treasure had been in his thoughts for these last few days?

'Oh, don't look so startled,' the man said. 'I won't peach if you've found it, but I'm afraid that there's no hope of that. But there is a treasure that I wonder you don't seek for.'

'What treasure is that?' Kay asked.

'Well, did you ever hear of Bendigo, the highwayman? Benjamin, as people called him.'

'I should think I had,' Kay answered. 'He used to live in our stable when it was a house. But had he any treasure?'

'Oh, I expect that he had a great deal of treasure,' the

man said, 'from robbing the stage coaches. I was reading an account of him in the Annual Register. He kept his mare Dowsabel, which is a French name, Douce et belle (meaning gentle and lovely), at the "Cock and Pye," the inn where you go to see the hounds meet. They searched for his property when they caught him, but they never found anything. You ought to look in your stable for it.'

'What sort of treasure would it be, please?' Kay asked.

'Oh, purses of guineas, and repeater watches (that is, watches which will *repeat*, that is, restrike, the last hour that struck whenever you press a spring). Then I expect he took gold rings and pocketbooks full of banknotes. Those were more worth having, don't you think, than pieces of eight, which were only worth four shillings when all is said?'

At this point the governess claimed Kay and led him back to dinner.

After dinner Kay thought, 'Well, why shouldn't I explore for Benjamin's treasure?' The governess always passed her Sunday afternoons in her study, which she called 'having some letters to write,' but he judged from her bitterness when he had been noisy in the garden on these occasions, that she really took a long nap.

All through his life he had dreaded exploring that side of the garden, where the stables, that had once been Benjamin's home, stood. In some undated past a man called The Tailor had been found killed in one of the outhouses there, 'stabbed right through the skull,' as Ellen said, 'which shows you the force that must have been used.' To-day The Tailor seemed very far away and treasure very much in the air. 'I'll go,' he said.

The stables (they were no longer used as stables) stood at the end of a long chain of buildings or ruins, which shut the garden from the road on that side. First was the barn, the thatch of which was green with moss and sunken into pits, which would presently be holes. Next to this was the dangerous brew-house, where cavernous old barrels stood falling asunder, as their hoops rusted through. The rotten floor was full of holes, through some of which you could hear the murmur of running water. Indeed the brew-house was a terrible place, which made one remember the worst that one had ever heard of Sweeny Todd.

When he entered it this afternoon, another tale came back to him, that one of his grandfather's workmen, who had worked in the brew-house, had so soaked himself with spirits that at last, as Ellen said, 'he took fire and burned all blue. There was nothing left of him but some black oil on the floor.' However, Dr. Gubbins had thrown doubts on this tale.

Beyond the brew-house was an open space, which had once been covered by the malting-house. It was now a jungle of giant heraclea, nettles, plantains, burdock and dandelion. Beyond this jungle was the pigeon-house built out like an apse from the wall of the stable. Both pigeon-house and stable were swathed more than a foot thick in ivy.

As Kay came into this wilderness, a big grey cat, which he had learned to call The Phantom from the swiftness with which he fled, leaped from his sleep in the sun and disappeared. This time Kay saw that he had darted into a hole below a projecting stone, which looked like a paving-stone. After poking and digging at the hole for half an hour, he found that there was a hollow beyond and below it. He fetched a trowel from the tool-shed, cleared out the entrance, and grovelled on the ground, trying to see. Yes, there was a room or cave.

Creeping into the house, he took some candle-ends and a box of matches from the pantry mantelshelf. By candle-end light he could make out masonry, slug-tracks and specks of quartz in the stone.

'It must be Benjamin's secret den,' he thought. 'I'll get down it to make sure.'

He fetched a newspaper, in which Joe, the gardener, who came once a week, had wrapped his lunch. He lit this, dropped it into the hollow, and saw it flame down, lighting up a little cellar about five feet deep. Within a minute he had squirmed down feet foremost into this cellar, to explore. The phantom cat had long since gone by another hole between the stones, through which he could see into the garden. He could find no other opening. Roots of ivy thrust into the ground among the masonry; tendrils of ivy with bright, pale leaves, had trailed in through the holes. There were slug-tracks on the floor and walls. A dead centipede was phosphorescent in a corner.

'What a lovely place,' Kay thought. 'I shall be able to come here always and have it for my cave. I'll bring bread and ham here. I'll keep a catapult here. Perhaps I'll run away some evening and sleep here. I wish I could get one of those lanterns with coloured lights; that would be just the thing for here.'

He lit two more candle-ends. By their light he found a recess in the wall, where the stones had been removed. In this lay a padlock with the key rusted into it, half-a-dozen links of rusty chain, the heel-grip and rowels of a spur, and part of a horse's headstall.

'These must be relics of Benjamin,' he thought. 'The spur that he spurred Dowsabel with. I shall call this place

Benjamin's Lair.'

Footsteps sounded outside. He saw Mrs. Scatternews coming down the path within a few feet of him on her way to call on the governess. He could hear her muttering, as was her way, 'The bombazine, ninepence three-farthings; two pennyworth of tape, eleven-three; a penny reel, a shilling-three; two packets of best assorted—but they're gone up: how much did Sarah say they came to?'

'I can be here,' Kay thought, 'and no one will ever suspect where I am. It's the loveliest place that I've ever found, and I'll spend all my time here always and have books and a clothes-brush, so that the dust won't show.'

He made another careful examination of the walls and then 'Terang, terang, terang!' it was the bell for tea.

When he came indoors he found that Mrs. Scatternews was more fun than Mrs. Tattle; she had been to Mr. Holyport's lecture, the night before, on 'My predecessors in this parish.'

'Imagine the things that went on here,' she said. 'The parish was honeycombed with crime. No sooner was the smuggling stopped, than the highwaymen broke out and stole Sir Hassle Gassle's repeater watch worth five hundred guineas. No sooner were the highwaymen hanged, than out came the rick-burners, holding meetings and setting fire to property. Oh, it was dreadful! And all in red nightcaps, too, just as in the Reign of Terror. No sooner were *they* all sent to transportation, than back came the smugglers, only this time they came secretly, and left the brandy and wines at the doors, just as though they were the milk, and so cheap. . . . Mr. Holyport read from the journal of the reverend gentleman who was rector here in the 'forties. He said that "although wages were lower than he had ever known them, hardly a man in the parish failed to find means for a Saturday intoxication." Then he went on to say how the parish now remembered only its criminals, Benjamin, the highwayman, and Mr. Galloway, the nickname of the smuggler, whereas in former times it remembered its saints, St. Alpig of St. Alpig's well, who is thought to have had a hermitage near the river; and St. Conda, to whom the church was dedicated. He said that this was because courageous energy is always valued and remembered, and that though the highwaymen and the others often used their energy wickedly, they still used it, and risked their lives to use it. We shall have half the boys in the parish to-morrow playing at highwaymen and knocking people's eyes out. I wonder that he did not tell the girls that they had better all take to being witches!'

'Do you mind,' the governess said, in her very sweetest voice, 'do you mind if we do not talk of witches? I am sure that we ought not to talk of them, because of course, well . . . really.'

This ended the talk of witches.

After tea Kay went back to the garden, thinking to explore the stable for some other relic of Benjamin. Usually the stable was locked, there being now no horses, but to-day, to his surprise, the door was open.

The reason for its being open lay within on the wheelbarrow. There, on some straw, with a crimson, drunken face, lay Joe the gardener, fast asleep, breathing heavily. He was a very drunken man, who had been in the Afghan War. When sober, he could set wires for rats (which never failed) and sing, 'As I was a-walking by the light of the moon.' He could also dance two or three steps of the step-dance.

Kay was afraid of him when he was drunk, because

Ellen and Jane were. He edged away from him cautiously.

Two stalls further down the line was the harness-room, which Kay could just remember, or thought that he could remember, in the warmth and glitter of use. A memory, so early that it might have been a dream, showed him that room all bright with a blazing fire, gleaming with bits, curb-chains, buckles and stirrups, and comfortable with the smell of saddle-soap and metal-polish. Two men, called Bob and Jay, had been there then, singing Twankydillo as they worked; and Bob had opened the marvellous carven corner cupboard, which had the arms of the Harkers, three oreilles couped proper, done above it between supporters. Inside there had been a blaze of shining things, the coach-lamps, and the silver turrets that old Mr. Harker had used when he drove four-in-hand.

The corner cupboard was still there, but frouzy and cobwebby. Rusty bits of harness still hung on the nails; the grate was broken. Starlings in the chimney had knocked soot, mortar and scalings down into the room. Cobwebs containing bits of fly, bluebottle, gnat, clegg, bee, wasp and moth, covered the window. There was a broken carriage clock still on the mantelpiece.

Kay pulled the rusty key of the corner cupboard so that the door swung slowly open, to show its blackness of decay. Dry-rot was at work upon it; spiders, earwigs, woodlice and centipedes all had their dwelling there. There was nothing within except a scrubbing brush and a horse-picker. Kay took the scrubbing brush to serve as a clothes-brush in Benjamin's lair. On second thoughts he took the horse-picker too.

In the next stall he found another treasure. Two years before, in the winter of the great frost, Joe had made him a toboggan by nailing battens across two runners. The toboggan had disappeared at the thaw; Kay had not seen it since; but now here it was, shoved aside, propped up against the manger; even the rope still on it. 'The very thing I've been panting for,' Kay thought. 'This will make a ladder down into the lair.'

Outside the stable, on the walls which seemed to be directly over his lair, he noticed the toadflax. It had little, mouthed flowers of palest purple touched with gold, which reminded him of snapdragons, violets, and sweet-peas; it had vivid green leaves and thrusters of purple. Noticing it for the first time on this exciting day in that place, he remembered it always, as something even more strangely beautiful than most flowers.

A solitary mushroom grew on the site of the manure-heap. He seemed to remember that Bob, in the old days, had grown many baskets full of mushrooms there. Now the giant burdock and the overgrown laurels had taken charge; all the garden was like that: weeded up.

As he was clambering down the toboggan rungs into his den, the runners gave way beneath him, so that he fell. He found that one of the runners had sunk into the floor, through the run of some rat, into what looked like the lid of a box. On groping with the horse-picker, he pulled out the remains of a wooden box, long rotted into touch in the ground. Within its shell was mouldy stuff, which may once have been cloth. Underneath the mouldy stuff was something hard, done up in what felt like a mummy rabbit, which had been tied with strips of leather now broken. The wrappings unrolled to display a tin box rather more than a foot long, also tied with leather. The hinges were decayed through. The lid came off as he opened it. Inside was a bundle tied with oil-skin, which contained a rather heavy net purse and a decaying mahogany box with battered metal corners. Kay opened the mahogany box first. It contained a pair of duelling pistols, by Turner, Milsom Street, Bath, 1803, so an engraved brass plate said. With these pistols, in little beds in the green baize, were wads, caps, a rammer and picker, and a neat carven horn with a stopper at the end. They were the real duelling pistols with the saw handles which he had read of in books. Rust had eaten deeply into their cocks and barrels, but they were still pistols, perhaps the very pistols with which Benjamin had made people stand and deliver. The purse, which was secured by sliding rings, contained six heavy bullets, a broken shilling of George III with a cross cut on it, a cameo ring, a monogram seal and a small pewter snuff-box embossed with a fox's mask. He knew that the broken shilling had been cut with a cross for use against ghosts. Ellen had told him of a farmer who had shot a ghost with such a bullet at the Wantways, where the suicides were buried. 'No ghost,' she said, 'can stand silver marked with a cross.'

In the bottom of the purse was a paper pulp, which seemed to be rotting Scottish bank-notes. On the inside of the lid of the pewter snuff-box someone had scratched with a sharp nail the following inscription:

S 100 yds frm. S.S.S.

J.G.Z. R.P.C.

What that meant Kay could not tell.

'It's where Benjamin's treasure is hidden,' he said to himself. 'South a hundred yards from S.S.S. What would

S.S.S. be? Might it be,' he thought, 'South of Seeking's Stable? This may have been called Seeking's Stable then. J.G.Z. and R.P.C.—I suppose that those are the initials of his gang. Now, a hundred yards south from here would take me into the Crowmarsh Estate.'

Going out from the lair, he began to measure. Eleven yards took him from his lair to the garden wall. Beyond the wall was the road, roughly eleven yards across, counting in the grassy strips. Beyond the road was a higher wall, topped with broken glass; beyond that was the Crowmarsh estate. Twenty-two yards from a hundred left seventy-eight yards. Seventy-eight yards into the estate would bring him across a piece of orchard into a spinney of scrub, in which some tall fir trees grew. 'It must be somewhere there,' he thought, 'but I shall catch it if I'm caught trespassing there.'

The bells began their lin-lan-lone to call people to the evening service. It was time for him to go indoors. The governess had walked off with Mrs. Scatternews. Ellen gave him his cup of bread-and-milk.

'Ellen,' he asked, 'how long ago did Benjamin live?'

'Oh, a long, long time ago,' Ellen said. 'In my grandfather's time, in the French wars.'

'Do you know if he had a gang, who went about with him?'

'Why no, Master Kay. I think he was all by himself. They do say that the man who had the "Cock" in those days, a man named Morgan, was in with him. The "Cock" was a coach-inn, where the coaches stopped. They do say that Morgan kept a spy on the people who came by coach, to see if they had money or necklaces. If they had, he used to tell Benjamin, or send out a little girl to him to say dinner was ready. And he used to water the guard's gun, too, so they said. And then Benjamin used to lie in wait for the coach and rob the people. He robbed Sir Hassle Gassle once as he was coming home from the races, near Gassle Court, and took his gold repeater watch worth ever so much that was given him by the hunters. That wasn't this Sir Hassle Gassle, but his grandfather.

'Benjamin had a mare called Dowsabell, that was trained to stop coach-horses; she would go right across the leaders and turn them into a ditch. They do say the coachmen were in with him.'

'Do you know any of their names?'

'Why, no. It was all so long ago.'

'Is it all written down in a book about him?'

'Why, no Master Kay, who would write a book about him?'

'I don't know, I thought they might.'

'Why, he was only a poor thief, Master Kay, who took what didn't belong to him by frightening people.'

'And he did really live up in the stables here?'

'Yes, that was like a house, then, opening on the road. He used to lodge there and let out he was a traveller for malt; or so they say, it may be only old tales.'

'Did your grandfather ever see him?'

'Why, yes, Master Kay, many a time; and he was at his taking. You see, he stopped a carriage out Rugby way, and took some rings and a watch from a gentleman. The gentleman said nothing while he was being robbed, but he recognised the mare, because he'd seen her, as it happened, just in the last day or two in the "Cock" stable. So the gentleman thought, "Probably you belong near there," so he had a watch set.

'By and by Benjamin came back to these parts. The watchers saw him riding to the "Cock" by the brook where they dip the sheep, so as to come to the back of the stable. They were all ready for him, in about the stables, and some were in the road hidden among the trees. Well, as he came down to the brook to jump it, he saw these people, for one of them raised his head to see the mare take the jump. Others say it wasn't that, but the little girl who used to say dinner was ready waved a red handkerchief, which was their danger signal. Anyway, he saw it wasn't safe, so he turned the mare and rode for here. But some of them were in the road, so that couldn't be either, and they all gave him chase across the Tump, and then past Barbara's, and along the Long Lane there, down past Hollings' Quarry, all shooting and shouting out "Stop, Thief," and lots of new people joining in; oh, they'd more than a hundred persons out.

'My grandfather was working then for old Mr. Pullean that lived at Ley Cop. He was digging in the flower-bed, he said, when Benjamin came over the hedge. He said the mare was nearly down, for she was a little thing, he said, and not fresh when she started, and she'd come five miles best pace and been hit too, for she was bleeding from the side, poor thing. So Benjamin said, "Come up, old girl. Tell them I went along the road," he said to grandfather. But they were too close on him for anything of that.

'So then Benjamin put the mare at the fence out of the garden. It was a big blind place with a stank of water the far side. The mare got over clear, but she didn't land clean, she fell back, and she couldn't get up. My grandfather said Benjamin gave a little cry, like he'd been shot through the heart. But he picked up his pistols and ran down the field along the stream to the little spinney. You will know the place well, Master Kay; it's the big foxes' lie where we saw what we called the shrike's larder. It was all full of scrub and stubbed stuff, and deep, on this side, from a fall of earth. Well, Benjamin got in there and tried to load his pistols, and they all came riding up shooting at him, shouting out to surrender; and young Mr. Dog-Face, as they always called him, who was

— So he turned the mare

and rode for here—

afterwards sent to Botany himself, shot him in the arm and broke it. So then they got a cord of old Mr. Pullean's, what had the washing on it, and tied poor Benjamin with that.

'My grandfather said he was all trembling from the fall and the ride, and the fight and from pain, but not at all from fear. He was not a big man, but middle size, and slight rather: very active, though: ran just like a hare. He'd black hair and eyes, altogether very black, yet clean-shaved, as people were then. Rather a slight, quick man, with a nice face, nothing bad in it, only bold. So then he was taken off and that was the end of him.'

'Did they ever find his treasure?'

'How you do run on about treasure. I believe it's all you ever think of. He never made much by it, to leave treasure. Just barely enough to pay his horse-meat, my grandfather said.'

'What happened to the mare?'

'O, she'd broken her back. She was taken to the kennels. Old Sir Hassle had the hounds then. He used to come in all hungry from hunting and take like a ladle-full of the hounds' broth, all dead horse and pony; but there, some men you can't make particular. And you'll be one of them, to judge from your stocking. Whatever have you been doing to get your stocking into that state?'

'I say, Ellen, thank you for telling me all about Benjamin. Did you ever go into the Crowmarsh Estate? Is it very dangerous?'

'Now don't you go going there, Master Kay; it's not allowed. It's preserved; and apart from the keepers it's full of mantraps and spring-guns; the one will blow your head off and the other will nip your ankles half in two, like they did to my Cousin Bob. He went in there, against the notice, and got caught in a mantrap; he didn't walk the same in a twelvemonth after. Then they've got their bloodhounds loose there some days, able to tear a child's head off; and always they've got their watchers just now, so soon before the shooting. You run off to bed now, like a good boy, and let me be sure you say your prayers; don't gibble-gabble them, but think what you're saying.'

When he got into bed, the sun was nearly down; a glow from it lit the wall opposite, so that the hunting men riding at the brook in Full Cry were made most vivid. A ray touched the model of the *Plunderer* so that she glowed, too, and the green stripe upon her forecastle and the scarlet rims of her tops looked beautiful against her brown and black. 'I have had a jolly day,' he thought. 'And to-morrow, I'll jolly well go into the Crowmarsh Estate to see if I can't find the J. G. Z.'

Just before he fell asleep he was almost sure that the water in the brook in Full Cry had eddies in it; eddies, and those little clouds of dissolving earth which the water-rat makes when scared from a bank. 'He must have been a jolly good painter,' he thought, 'to be able to do all that.' He fell asleep soon after this, thinking that if he were a painter, he would paint, well, he did not know what he would paint; so very much was happening.

As before, he woke up into what seemed like broad daylight, although he could see the stars through the window. He was aware at once that something very odd was happening in the print of Full Cry: the hunting men, whose red coats were flapping, were turning from the brook. And what was the matter with the brook? It was very, very full of water, and coming with such a strong current that it swished against the loose alder root. He could see not only eddies, but bright, hurrying, gleaming ripples which ran into bubbles, and yes, yes, it was coming into the room, it was running on both sides of the bed, clear, swift, rushing water, carrying down petals and leaves and bits of twig. Then there came the water-rats, who dived with a phlumphing noise when they caught sight of him. He was in an island in the midst of the stream; and the stream was so crystal clear that he could see the fish in the shallows, flapping like water-plant leaves, and filmy as dead weeds.

But what on earth was happening to the model of the *Plunderer*? He could see that the water had reached her on the wall: she was afloat. She seemed to be alive with little tiny men, all busy with ropes. No, they were not men, they were little mice, 'water-mice, I suppose,' he thought. Now she was coming across the stream to him; and how big she was, or, no, how little he was; he was no bigger than the water-mice. There she came slowly to the edge of the bed. She had flags flying, a Blue Peter at the fore, a house-flag, with three oreilles couped proper, on the main, and a red ensign at the peak. But lovelier than the flags were the decks, with the little doors, each with a shiny brass handle and real lock and key, opening to the cabins. Then there were real lifeboats ready for use. He could see the barrels and lockers in them marked 'Best Preserved Milk,' 'Corned Beef,' 'Ship's Bread,' 'Pemmican,' 'Raisins,' 'Chocolate Cream,' 'Turkish Delight,' 'Split Peas,' 'Currants,' 'Hundreds and Thousands,' 'Mixed Biscuits,' 'Dry Ginger Beer,' etc., etc. No fear of starving in lifeboats like those. Then all the little brass cannon were shining in the sun, ready for use, with the little powder tubs all handy, and little men standing by them ready to fire them off in salute. Then as the ship came alongside the bed, each little gunner blew puff upon his match, to make it glow (some of them had red-hot pokers instead of match), just as the *Sea-Gunner's Practice* described, and popped the glowing end on the touchholes. All the little brass cannon went bang together in salute.

Then Kay saw that the captain of the ship was his friend the Water Rat. He was standing on the poop, with his telescope in his hand, telling the mate to put the gangway over for Mr. Kay. Some of the little seamen at once thrust out a gangway on to the bed.

'Step on board, Mr. Kay,' the Captain said.

'May I really and truly?'

'Yes, we're waiting for you.'

Kay walked from his bed to the deck. He was amazed at the neatness of everything: all the rows of buckets, the sponges and rammers for the cannon, the capstans that worked, the compasses that pointed, the cask, painted red, for salt meat, and the other cask, painted blue, for fresh water; and all the rigging, with little ladders on it for going aloft. Then there was a ship's kitchen on the deck close to him, with a real little cook, with a wooden leg, making plum-duff for dinner at a real fire.

'Welcome on board, Mr. Kay,' the Captain said. 'I thought we might stand over to the westward to see what we can find of the old *Plunderer*. We've got a cabin prepared for you, with a hammock slung in it; and here are some nice long sea-boots to pull over your pyjamas, and a double-breasted pea-jacket to keep out the seas and keep in the plumduff. And now, my hearties, cast loose forward, let go aft. The tug has got her. Hurray, lads, for the westward.'

Kay noticed now, what he had not noticed before, that on the other side of the *Plunderer* was a tug-boat under steam. Long before, he had had a beautiful tug-boat with a scarlet funnel. She had gone by real steam made by methylated spirit, which you lit under the boiler in a little lamp. But after two voyages, she set forth across the Squire's pond on a windy day, and in the drought of the gale she caught fire, blazed for a few minutes from stem to stern, and then went down head first in deep water. Yet now here she was, repainted, and with powerful new engines in her, which were threshing the water as they towed the *Plunderer* clear of the bed.

Soon they had swung round clear of the sofa, and headed to the west, through the open window, into the night. Side lights and towing lights were lit; she plunged on beside her tug, casting streaks of coloured light upon the water. Soon she was in the stream where Kay had so often seen the Water Rat. Someone in the *Plunderer* turned a strong searchlight on to the water ahead. Look-out men went aloft to watch the water: they called to the helmsman from time to time to do this or that to dodge the rocks. 'A bit anxious, this reach of the stream,' the Water Rat said, 'but there's lots of water to-night.'

The ship went faster and faster over rapids and shallows: soon she was in the big, quiet pool where the stream entered the river. An otter looked out at them and wished them good luck. A moorhen came out and swam ahead of them to show them the best passage. Dawn was now breaking; but all the world of men was asleep. Kay saw the deserted quay of the river bank where he had so often watched people coming to hire skiffs. A light was burning there, although morning was growing everywhere. Kay saw the tug stand away from the *Plunderer*'s side and cast loose the tow-ropes. The *Plunderer*'s men ran aloft and cast loose the sails. When Kay next looked back, the river wharf was far astern; the ship was running swiftly down the river under a press of sail.

'But come, Master Kay,' the Captain said, 'breakfast is on the table. Step down the ladder with me to the cabin.'

He led the way down to a passage where there were a great many doors labelled First Mate, Second Mate, Third Mate, Captain's Stores, Instrument Room, Chart Room, Steward's Pantry, Bullion Room, warranted iron-lined, Captain's Bath, Mates' Bath, Jam Room, Sardine Room, etc., as well as one big open door leading to the cabin, where the table was set for breakfast. They had for breakfast all the things that Kay was fondest of: very hot, little, round loaves of new white bread baked in the embers of a wood-fire, very salt butter, a sardine with a lot of olive oil, some minced kidneys, a poached egg and frizzled bacon, a very fat sausage all bursting out of its skin, a home-made pork-pie, with cold jelly and yolk of egg beneath the crust, a bowl of strawberries and cream with sifted sugar, a bowl of raspberries and cream with blobs of sugar-candyish brown sugar that you could scrunch, some nice new mushrooms and chicken, part of a honeycomb with cream, a cup of coffee with crystals of white sugar candy for a change, a yellow plum, a greengage and then a ripe blue plum of Pershore to finish off with.

'That's the way, Master Kay,' the Captain said. 'I always believe in a good breakfast: something to do your work on and start the day with. And now, if you've finished, as you haven't had much sleep lately, perhaps you'd like to keep the next watch in your hammock. Come up on deck for a moment first, though, we are now in the open sea.'

The wonder of it was that they *were* in the open sea,

out of sight of land, with the ship under full sail flying westward. One or two of the water-mice were at work far aloft: others on deck were washing their clothes and hanging them out to dry on clothes-lines, or fishing with hooks and lines, or feeding the sparrows (which they kept for the eggs) in the hencoops, or polishing the brass on the ship's bells and railings. The sea was all blue and bright, the hot sun was shining, not a cloud could be seen. The ship was flying faster and faster.

Kay's cabin was a charming room, with mahogany lockers, and a porthole covered with red curtains. A telescope hung on a rack ready for use. A canvas hammock swung from hooks in the wall, it had a pillow, mattress, sheets and blankets. The Captain showed him how to get in and tuck himself up. In a minute he was fast asleep.

He was wakened half an hour later by the ship anchoring in calm water. On going on deck he found

that she was not far from a low, tropical shore, blindingly white, from the surf bursting on it. Palm trees grew here and there on the shore: there was no sign of man. The water, bright blue to seaward, with vivid green streaks, was clear as crystal.

'Now Master Kay,' the Captain said, 'we will get into the diving-bell and go down to see what we can see. We are now just over the wreck of the old *Plunderer*.'

'How do you know?' Kay asked.

'We can always get directions about wrecks, we under-water folk,' the Captain said. 'We ask the otters, and they get into touch with all sorts of sea-folk, mermaids and sirens, not to speak of dolphins and these other fellows. Some of them are very old and have astonishing memories. It was a mermaid who told Tom Otter about the *Plunderer*, and he told me.'

The diving-bell was a tight little room, just big enough for two nice comfortable arm-chairs. It was built of iron framing, with floor and side windows of strong clear glass. Air-pipes and speaking-tubes were let into the walls and through the roof. When Kay and the Captain had taken their seats in the arm-chairs, the crew closed the door very carefully so that no water could possibly squeeze in. Then they hoisted the bell up and began to lower it carefully into the water. Kay found that he could see quite clearly through the glass of the sides and the floor. The fish came to the windows and sucked at them with their mouths. Presently, when the Captain called through the speaking-tube to stop lowering, he turned on a searchlight which pointed through the floor. Kay could see the bottom of the sea, growing like a garden with white and red coral, weeds, anemones and sponges, all seeming to dilate in the light. Some gaily-coloured fish came poking to the light, to find if it were good to eat; a few big fish, some of them like shadows, others like round collapsing bags with suckers waving from them, drifted or finned by, all noiseless; there was no whisper of sound, except a drumming in the ears. 'There's what is left of the *Plunderer*,' the Captain said.

Lying on the bottom, partly on white sand, partly among coral and weed, was the wreck of an old wooden ship. All that remained in sight of her was her stern post, her nameplate, marked *Plunderer*, a part of her keel, and a few ribs fallen out of place. All these timbers had been blackened by years under the sea. White and blue barnacles were growing on them; sprays of red and white coral had thrust up among them. The sunlight made all these things so glorious suddenly that the Captain turned out the light. Kay could see even the eyes of the lobsters peering into the crannies of the coral.

A mermaid floated to the side of the diving-bell. She was young and merry-looking, with bright, big brown eyes and very white teeth. She wore a gold crown over her long brown hair. Her cheeks and lips were full of colour. She put her mouth to the glass and smiled at them. 'That's Sea-Flower,' the Captain said. 'Say good morning to her.'

'Good morning, Miss Sea-Flower,' Kay said. 'Can you tell us how this ship came here?'

'Yes,' she said. 'She was upset in a squall, long ago, and all her men were drowned. They were making merry at the time. You can still see one of them: that scarlet coral is he. But open the door and come with me.'

Three other mermaids had swum to the diving-bell, together they opened the door. In an instant, Kay was swimming with them in the warm water that was so like

green light. All the floor of the sea shone. Here and there were patches of a green plant which had flowers like flames, they were so bright. At first he thought that everything there was dead; but when he had been twenty seconds in that tingling water he knew that it was full of life. The white sand of the sea-floor was alive with tiny, scurrying, glittering creatures, little beings looked at him from the branches of the coral, flowers poked out eyes at him upon stalks like snails' horns, he could see the leaves of the seaweeds shine with joy at every good suck-in of light. All these living forms were swaying gently as the swell lifted and fell: all were glistening and tingling with joy; a kind of drowsy song of delight moved through the water, everything was singing, or murmuring or sighing because life was so good.

Kay went up to a big scarlet fish that had pale goggle-eyes and a collapsing mouth; he tickled its throat; and others knew that he was liking it, because they, too, came to have their throats tickled, till he was surrounded by fish of all colours and shapes, scaled and slimy, finned, or legged, or feelered, all noiseless, most of them strange, many of them most beautiful.

'Come away, Kay,' the mermaids said. 'But first look at the lovely golden lad.'

Lying among the coral, as though he were resting upon a bank of flowers, was a golden image of Saint George, still holding a white shield with a scarlet cross.

'We used to sing to him at first,' Sea-Flower said, 'hoping that he would wake. The ship was full of golden and silver people at one time. We loved them, they were so very beautiful; but they never answered when we spoke to them. Men came here searching for them in the old days, dragging anchors for them along the sea-floor. At last some Indian divers came down and carried them all away to a yacht, all except this one, which they would not touch, because we had so decked it with flowers.

'I see that you know who it was who took those lovely things. He was going to take them to a city of evil men near here. We followed his yacht on his way thither, for we were sad to lose our lovely people. But come, Kay, you shall come with us as far as we can go on the way those golden people went.'

They all set out together, Kay between Sea-Flower and Foam-Blossom, each of whom held one of his hands. Foam-Blossom was a golden-haired mermaid, with bright blue eyes and lovely rosy cheeks; she was always laughing. 'Is not this lovely?' she said, as they went swimming along.

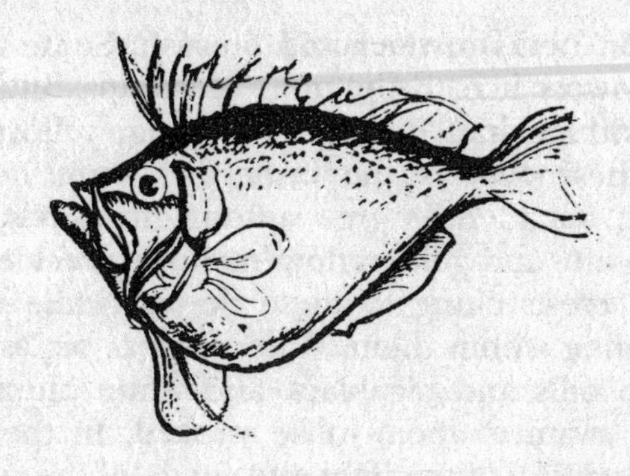

'O, it *is* lovely,' Kay said. Every stroke of their arms took them over some new kind of shell-fish, or past some new anemone or waving weed.

'Come,' Sea-Flower said, 'let us go in on the tide, at the surface.'

They rose up together to the air. There, on the shallow shore, long lines of rollers were always advancing to the beach, toppling as they went and at last shattering. A little river came out to the sea there; its little waves seemed to enjoy meeting the big waves.

'Come,' Foam-Blossom said, 'let us ride on this big roller that is just going in.'

Together they sat on the neck of the wave, with Kay between them. Kay felt the wave begin to run like a horse, and to gather speed and to lift. Soon the toppling water began to hiss and foam all about them; the shore seemed to rush nearer, and then they all rolled over and over in boiling bubbles into the cool pool of the river, where the sea-shells looked as though they were all made of pearl.

Soon they were swimming up a river which flowed

between ranks of reed and bulrush. Some of the reeds had flowers like the plumes of pampas grass, but pale blue; others had delicate, dangling, yellow tassels. All over these flowers the butterflies were hovering and settling. Giant flags grew among the reeds, with heavy blue, white and golden flowers. Little speckled birds with scarlet crests clung to these flowers while they pecked something within them. Water fowl as big as swans, with orange bills and big black and white plumes on their heads, swam to them to be stroked. In the gloom and zebra striping of the light and shade of the reeds Kay saw long-legged water birds standing ankle-deep, fishing. Here and there, when they passed mud-banks, he saw the turtles enjoying themselves in the cool ooze.

Presently they left the river and swam up a backwater, where the reeds on both sides gave place to quince-trees, which smelt like Arabia from the ripe fruit. At the end of the backwater there was a patch of red mud much poached by the feet of cows that had come to drink there. Beyond the cows was a little roll of grass-land.

'The man took the gold and silver things this way,' Sea-Flower said. 'In those days, the river ran this way, through all that grassy piece and for miles beyond it; we

often used to swim there. We followed his yacht for a long way, further than we can see from here. He was a rosy-faced man, not old, but his hair was already grey; his eyes were very bright; and his mouth, when one could see it through the beard, was most cruel and evil. He had three Indians with him, who were his divers and sailors, whom he used to beat.

'When he was in a narrow part of the river, he heard guns, for his city of wickedness was being destroyed. He poled his yacht far into the reeds against the mud, and sent one of his Indians to find out what was happening. As the Indian did not come back, he sent a second Indian; and when the second did not come back he sent a third; but the third did not come back, either.'

'What happened to the Indians?' Kay asked.

'They all went home to their village in the sea; they have houses there, built upon piles driven into the water. In the rainy seasons they keep very snug in their hammocks and tell each other stories.'

'And what happened to Abner Brown, please?'

'He waited for the Indians to bring him news. When

they did not come, he changed his yacht's hiding-place, by driving her still further into the reeds, and then he set out by himself to find out what was happening. He was captured as a pirate that same night and sent far away.

'Nobody found his boat, she was too well hidden, but there came great changes which hid her further. At first we used to play in the water near her, hoping that she might soon fall to pieces, so that we might have her gold and silver people again; but then there came the earthquake, which raised the river bed and buried the yacht in the mud. After the earthquake there came the great summer-floods, which made a new channel for the river and altered all the coast. When the floods went down, the place where the yacht lay was five miles from the water and covered deep with flowers, so the birds told us.

'The man came back presently to look for his yacht; but with the land so changed he hardly knew where to begin. We used to see him digging sometimes, when we went up the streams. But he was evil, do not let us think of him; let us go to the sea, to play in the rollers as they burst.'

In a few minutes they were in the shining shallow water across which the breaking rollers were marching.

At first, Kay was frightened of the waves as they curled and toppled high over his head. Very soon he was wading to meet them, so that they could break all over him or carry him in to the sands.

'And now,' the mermaids said, 'let us all go down to look at the city under the sea.'

They all swam for a few minutes; then Kay suddenly saw something very golden in the green of the under-water.

'Those are the walls,' Foam-Blossom said. 'And if you listen, you will hear the bells. Let us wait here.'

They had paused at what had been the harbour. Three or four little ships had sunken with the city; they were there, still secured to the walls. Sponges like big yellow mushrooms covered one; another was starred all over with tiny white shells; another was thickly grown with a weed like many coloured ribbons. The walls, which had once been of white marble, seemed golden in that dim light. As Kay looked he heard a sweet but muffled booming of the bells as the swell of the water surged and lapsed in the bell-tower.

'Come, Kay,' Sea-Flower said, 'the city gates have fallen open; we can go in.'

They passed through the gates, which now drooped upon their hinges from the weight of the shells which grew upon them. Inside the gates was a guard house, with a rack of spears still standing against the wall. Beyond that was a street, with shops open, and fish slowly finning from shop to shop. At the end of the street there was a temple with a bell tower. No one was in that city. Kay went into two of the houses; in one, the kitchen was set out with pots and pans for dinner; two eggs were in a bowl and the bone of a leg of mutton was on a dish;

in the other, the beds in the nursery were turned down ready for the children, and in one of the beds a child had set a doll, on which the little shells were growing. There were gaily painted carvings on some of the walls, showing the racing of children and romps and tugs-of-war.

'What is this city, please?' Kay asked, 'I would love to go all over it, into every house. What is it called?'

'We call it the Golden City. But look, here come the merchildren, playing Touch and Tag; let us play with them.'

At that instant, about twenty little merchildren came

darting down the street, at full speed, with streaming hair, bright eyes and laughter. They twisted about like eels, dived down chimneys and through windows, crying aloud from joy in the fun.

'I wonder,' Kay said, 'if we might play Hide and Seek? This would be such a lovely place for it.'

'Yes,' Foam-Blossom said, 'let us all play Hide and Seek; Sea-Flower shall be He. And Kay, you come with me, for I know a lovely place to hide.'

She took him through one of the houses into what had been a garden. The fruit trees still stood, but were now crusted over with shells. Sponges, anemones and corals, which were so covered with points of glitter that they seemed full of eyes, grew like mistletoe on the branches. There came a sort of cloud in swift movement across the golden light.

'Look,' Foam-Blossom said, 'there's a ship passing overhead. If you look up, you may see one of the crew looking down.'

'That reminds me,' Kay asked, 'I meant to ask you before. Did you ever see another man taking away those golden and silver people? He may have taken them away in a big barge.'

'Why, Kay,' she answered, 'that is the *Plunderer* passing. There is the Water Rat Captain looking down. You must be quick; and oh, do look at the flying fish.'

Kay felt a sort of swirl as he rushed past a lot of green bubbles into the light. The billows burst all about him suddenly and the sun made him blink. Foam-Blossom, the lovely merchildren, the city and its gardens, among which the beaked fishes had flitted like birds, were gone. He was sitting on the end of the *Plunderer*'s jib-boom in the clouds of spray flung up as she sailed. Sheets of spray, as bright as snow, soared and flashed all round him. Then he saw that it was not spray, but a flight of flying fish, skimming and falling like darts, all glittering and quivering. 'O, how lovely,' he cried.

As he cried, he heard his window creak; somebody rolled him into bed and the *Plunderer* went back to the wall. As for the sea, it was not there. When he opened his eyes, Ellen was there, but no water at all.

'Where did it all run to?' he asked.

'Where did what all run to? Wake up,' Ellen said. 'You are such a one to sleep as I never did.'

'Well, it was here a moment ago,' he said.

'I declare, you're dreaming still,' she said. 'Now don't go to sleep again. Breakfast will be in a quarter of an hour, and you're not to be late, she said: I was to tell you specially.'

• • • • •

When lessons were over, he went out to Benjamin's Lair with a little compass, which had been on the school-room shelves for years. With this he judged that a point a hundred yards south from the Seekings Stables would be in the Crowmarsh Estate, somewhere near a big fir tree in the spinney. All of the Crowmarsh Estate was an unknown world to him, where spring-guns banged, man-traps snapped, bloodhounds tore the heads off children and the Pimply Whatto had been shot in the leg. Yet it looked quiet enough in the hot summer morning; no bloodhounds and no keepers.

'I don't believe that anybody's there,' he thought. 'I'm sure that nobody's there.' He hovered about, unable to make up his mind to it, until the bell rang for dinner.

After dinner he wanted to go, but the thought of the blood-hounds daunted him. Then he thought, 'From the loft in the stables I may be able to see over into the estate beyond the spinney there.'

He scrambled into the stable through the harness-room window and then climbed the steps nailed to the wall. The loft was very dark. It was littered with musty straw, in which black walnutty things, which had once been apples, lay. Baskets, hives, a honey extractor, brood-frames, comb foundation, saddle-trees, decaying top-boots and the catcher of a mowing-machine lay in one corner. In the wall, showing light at the edges, was a big wooden shutter, through which the hay and straw had once been hoisted. Through just such a shutter, when he was drunk and wasn't minding what he was doing, Ellen's uncle had fallen at the Tuttocks and broken his huckle-bone. However, by being sober and very carefully minding what he was doing, Kay reached the little glazed window at the side without mishap. He looked through over the road and the orchard.

Old Jarge came by with a pair of steps and a bag of tools on his way to see to Mrs. Tattle's dove-cot. He explained this to Mrs. Bucket, who was on her way to see her married daughter. They said that it was lovely weather for the crops, though a nice drop of rain would freshen things up a bit. When they had gone, pretty Polly Colway drove past in her dog-cart with a friend. When she had gone, Kay stared at the Crowmarsh Estate. It was all peaceful. In the orchard the grey trees were growing barer of leaves, as the fruit ripened. The birds were moving without alarm, rabbits humped themselves about, nibbling grass at the spinney edge. Somewhere just a hundred yards away was

$$\frac{\text{S.S.S.}}{\text{J.G.Z. R.P.C.}}$$

'I'll try it,' he said. 'I believe it's safe.'

Within a minute he was flat on his stomach in the Crowmarsh spinney. 'It's all lies about the keepers being here,' he said to himself. 'Nobody ever comes into this spinney. The branches are all covered with that brittle stuff, which hasn't been brushed away.'

He looked back at the ruins of barn, brew-house and stable. A hundred years before, Benjamin had lived there; two hundred years before, people had died of the plague there, so Ellen said. There was a mark on one of the doors, which had once been a red cross to show the dead-cart man that a corpse was inside.

He reckoned up his distance. 'Two cricket-pitches still to go,' he thought. He crept through the spinney to look at the other side, there he saw that a hundred yards south from S.S.S. would take him to the middle of a pond in a cemented basin.

'That is where he put it,' he thought. 'People often buried their treasures in ponds. It's the safest place you can choose really, but I shan't be able to get it.'

He looked out in peace at the Crowmarsh Estate, which he had never before seen. Rabbits were nibbling the grass. Just beyond the pond was the old ruin of an elm tree swathed in ivy. Beyond that was a paddock, where hunters were being summered. Beyond the paddock was pasture, in which the Crowmarsh Guernseys were grazing; beyond that was grass, where someone was lunging a chestnut colt. 'Those young gentlemen care for nothing but horses,' Ellen had said.

A pheasant walked out of the spinney close to him. 'What lies people tell,' Kay thought. 'Of course, there can't be bloodhounds and spring-guns. The rabbits and pheasants would set them off at once. I'm going down to look at the pond.'

He crept to the water's edge to watch the insects and the spinning of grains of sand below the lip by which the water trickled away.

Looking up, his eyes were caught by a big hole in the ruined elm tree. It was a hole big enough for Kay to get into.

He was thrilled by holes in trees. Ellen had often told him how they had found the skeleton of a man inside a big hollow oak in Sir Hassle Gassle's wood. 'He was supposed to be a murderer or something, who had got in to hide and didn't think that it would be hollow all the way down; but it was, so there he was and he didn't dare to cry out, people thought, for then he would have been taken and hanged, so he just starved to death. Father said that his coat was still on him, hanging by the buttons, and bits of shoes with buckles.'

Then he had read of a skeleton in armour found inside another hollow tree near one of the battlefields of the Wars of the Roses. The man must have run away, climbed in, fallen down and died there. And other things were found in oak trees. The rector had half a dozen black iron barbed arrow-heads, which had been shot into an oak tree in the Butts in the reign of Henry VIII. He had found them when sawing up the logs for firewood. Old Mr. Colway had dug bullets from old trees at Naseby.

'Very likely,' Kay thought, 'Benjamin's treasure might be in the hollow of the tree, for of course I can't tell what S.S.S. is. It might be Stable's Southern Side. A hollow tree would be as good a place as a pond.'

At that moment, as he stared upwards, a white dumpy figure sidled into the centre of the hole, stared down at him with big fierce eyes and then, closing both eyes, stood still like a stump of decayed wood. 'A white owl,' Kay said. 'He's got a nest there. I'll climb up and peep in.'

He was wondering, how painful a peck from that hooked beak would be, when he heard the click of a gate-latch. 'It's the keepers,' he said, 'they've seen me.'

Peeping round the tree-trunk through the ivy, he found that it was worse than the keepers. It was young Mr. Crowmarsh and his mother, whom everybody called,

'The Tigress.' They were about a hundred yards away, coming slowly toward him, deep in talk. If he ran for home, they would recognise him or run him down. And then there was that terrible notice, 'Trespassers will be prosecuted.' What was he to do?

'Get up into my house,' the owl said. 'Look alive or they'll catch you. O, my mouse and sparrow, take hold of the ivy and pull yourself up. That's better. Now the other foot. Now catch a good grip of my claw. Now, oh hoo, a long pull. Up you come. Now here you are in my nice house; just step aside behind the ivy till they've gone by.'

Kay stepped aside behind the ivy as he was bidden. He found that he was in a snug room littered with moss, dead leaves and soft, rotten wood. He heard the two companions come to the foot of the tree.

'I thought I heard a squirrel, then,' young Mr. Crowmarsh said.

'I don't think it was a squirrel,' his mother said. 'I expect it was only Blinky flapping his wings. Our red squirrel has gone. I can't help thinking that that man Bilges shot him.'

'A regular scoundrel, Bilges, and his brother at the Gassles is as bad,' the young man said. 'But is this the old Blinky that used to roost in the ivy on the ruin?'

'It is,' old Blinky growled.

'There he is growling,' the young man said. 'It *is* old Blinky. Well, I'm glad he's alive still. I've half a mind to climb up, to look in on him.'

He had clambered up a foot or two when his mother stopped him. 'The tree really isn't safe,' she said. 'Besides, you will ruin your clothes.'

Probably he would have climbed up, but at that moment some of the bark gave way beneath his feet, which brought him slithering down.

'There, you see, it isn't safe,' his mother said. 'You must come along now. Look in on old Blinky some other time.'

When they had gone, old Blinky said, 'Well, Kay, have you been riding the hoofless horse lately?'

'No, I haven't.'

'Nor found the treasure yet?'

'No, not yet. But I found out where it went to, up to a point. It was swallowed up in an earthquake, and though some people say that it was afterwards dug up and taken away, others aren't so sure.'

'Well, why don't you make sure?'

'Please, I don't know how to.'

'Is it as good to eat as mouse and sparrow?' Blinky asked.

'It isn't good to eat at all.'

Blinky blinked at this and gurgled in his throat. After a long time he said, 'Do you want to find this stuff?'

'Yes, please, rather.'

'Well, I might find out for you, perhaps, if you tell me just whereabouts to begin.'

'The place was somewhere near the Golden City . . .'

'Not so loud, please,' old Blinky said.

'Why? There's nobody listening.'

'How do you know? There are a lot of these invisible people everywhere, and spies . . . well. It will be wiser to whisper.'

Kay whispered into Blinky's ear directions which he thought could help.

'Right,' Blinky said. 'Now I'll tell you what I'll do. I'll call my friend the Swift: he'll take the message to the stormy petrel, who is much the fastest bird there is. The petrel will be across ocean in no time . . . then he'll pass the word to a skua or something on the other side, and the skua or something will ask my cousins about it. I've a lot of cousins over there, very good sorts of creatures, but they have an odd habit of living in holes in the ground. I can't understand the habit myself; but each man to his taste; it will come in handy now, though, for of course they will know everything that is underground in those parts. By the way, here is Swift. He'll go at once; he'll have an answer by your bed-time. Hoo, there, Swift.'

The Swift paused on the ledge of Blinky's Lair. He was a fine bird, bright-eyed and eager.

'I say, Swift,' Blinky said, 'this is our friend, Kay. He

wants to find out about some treasure, so will you pass the word along to my foreign cousins? Put your head up to mine, will you, it had better be whispered. There are reasons why this should be kept secret, if it can be.'

As he whispered the directions to Swift, it seemed to Kay that something rustled in the ivy above them.

'Right,' the Swift said, 'I'll take the message and wait for an answer. It should reach me before roosting-time; if it doesn't, I'll send it by Bat. Anyhow, you will get it before you start your evening's hunting, and you can send it on to Kay. Good-bye, all.'

He slipped into the air and was gone before Kay could thank him. As he sped away, Kay was quite certain that somebody or something rustled in the ivy above.

'What was that?' he asked.

'What was what?'

'That noise in the ivy.'

'I didn't notice any noise.'

'There was a noise like someone climbing in the ivy.'

'I expect it was the wind,' Blinky said. 'The wind is always rustling this ivy. Time and again I keep thinking it's a mouse, but it never is; it's always the wind.

> 'A very queer thing is the wind
> I don't know how it beginn'd
> And nobody knows where it goes,
> It is wind, it beginn'd, and it blows.'

He uttered these last words very drowsily, and snapped out a snorey kind of grunt once or twice after he had finished. He blinked at Kay once or twice, then closed his eyes and fell fast asleep.

'It sounded liker someone climbing than the wind,'

Kay thought. 'But he was so drowsy he probably did not hear it.'

He would have climbed up to make sure, but at that moment the church bells began:

Ding dong, ding dong,
Dong dong, ding dong,
  Ding dong, ding dong,
Ding ding, dong dong.

And then struck the hour. He was sure that it would only be four o'clock: alas, it was five: the tea bell must have gone long ago; he would be late again; he would 'catch it' this time and very likely be sent to bed. And he was still up the tree in the Crowmarsh Estate.

Despair made him reckless; he slithered down the tree, ran to the spinney, dashed across to the road, scrambled over the gate and ran for home, not caring how many keepers caught him. He did not know who saw him, there were people in the road as he passed. He was ruined anyhow; what could one or two more witnesses add to his sentence? He tried to brush the green powder, dust, and ivy clips from his clothes as he ran; he was in a filthy mess. Then his right hand had one of those black resinous smears which you get from laurel or pine boughs. That would not come off, as he knew only too well, except with hot water, Ellen and pumice-stone. 'O, I shall catch it this time,' he moaned.

There was no question of making himself later by washing and brushing; he went straight in to the dining-room, and there, oh horror, horror of horrors . . .

There was the governess in her icy-sweet society manner sitting at the horrid little society tea-table, with the best tea-service, which everybody called the Lowestoft, pouring out tea for Lady Crowmarsh.

'She saw me after all,' he moaned to himself. 'And now she's come over to sneak.'

'Kay,' the governess said, 'you're very late. Say how do you do to Lady Crowmarsh, then come and have your tea.'

He said how do you do to Lady Crowmarsh, and was expecting the sword to fall on him for trespass, when the governess noticed the state of his hands and clothes. 'Where have you been, Kay?' she asked, 'to get yourself into that pickle? Go and wash your hands and brush your suit before you sit down.'

'O let me plead for him, won't you?' Lady Crowmarsh said. 'I don't like a little boy to come in to tea too tidy. Come and sit by me, Kay, and tell me all about your fossil collection. Have you found any more nice fossils lately?'

He had given up collecting fossils for more than a year, under orders from the governess, who found that grubbing in the quarries brought him into meals too muddy. Lady Crowmarsh had once seen him grubbing for fossils and had remembered it. He thought that it was nice of her to remember, but he still could not understand why she did not begin about the trespassing. Before he could answer, the governess broke in with: 'O don't ask about fossils, Lady Crowmarsh; the very thought of those quarries in the rains, and the state of his clothes when he comes in, is enough . . . and then lumps of stone under all the taps, and the taps left running . . .'

'I like men to get through the collection habit in childhood,' Lady Crowmarsh said, thinking of her son, who was still a collector of things and something of a disappointment to her. 'And now about the bazaar. Are you quite sure that you can take the Magic Peepshow?'

The words Magic Peepshow made Kay prick up his ears. He looked hard at the governess, who changed colour at the words, as though she did not quite like them. 'O yes, Lady Crowmarsh,' she said, 'I will do so gladly; but might it be called the Wonder Peepshow, as Magic Peepshow might give people such strange ideas . . . magic, you know . . . well really . . . in these days.'

'We've always called it Magic Peepshow in the past,' Lady Crowmarsh said. 'I don't think that anyone has minded, as it is only to amuse the children . . . still, call it Wonder Peepshow if you would really rather.'

'I think . . . perhaps . . . if you don't mind.'

Kay thought her a silly ass to object to the word Magic. 'Ah,' he thought, 'if you knew what goes on at midnight in this very room you would be less particular.'

Lady Crowmarsh was very nice to him during the rest of her stay. He could not think why she did not begin about the trespassing; his spirits began to rise as he thought: 'She may not have seen me after all. And Sylvia Daisy hasn't found out yet, either.' But he knew that his black hands and dusty clothes would be inquired into later, when Lady Crowmarsh was gone. 'I shall catch it, then,' he thought, so he ate as much tea as he could, because his chance of supper was slight. 'When Lady Crowmarsh goes,' he thought, 'as soon as she is outside the door, it will be "Kay, how dare you come to tea in that state. You will scrub your face and hands and go straight to bed." '

When Lady Crowmarsh rose to go, she said: 'This young man shall come with me, if you will spare him, to open the gates for me.' She clapped him on the shoulder and pinched his ear; but in such a kind way that he did not mind. 'She can't know,' he thought. 'She can't have seen me.'

As they walked to the gate together, he felt that he could not let her be ignorant of how he had trespassed on her estate.

'Lady Crowmarsh,' he said, 'I'm very, very sorry, but I went into your estate to-day, in spite of the notice. I climbed the tree with the owl's nest, and I was hiding there while you were just below, with Mr. Crowmarsh, just before tea.'

'Oh,' she said. 'Were you?'

'Yes, while you talked of old Blinky.'

'Well, why do you tell me this?'

'At first I thought you knew, and now I feel I ought to tell you.'

'Hm,' she said, in a very tigerish way, 'you are quite right to tell me. And what if I take you straight back to the governess and make you tell her?

'Don't look so lost, child. I'm not going to do any such thing. But tell me . . . had you climbed the tree after the cat?'

'No, Lady Crowmarsh; what cat?'

'There was a black cat in the ivy there. It is yours, I think. I have seen it go over your wall. A black cat with white paws and throat.'

'Yes, that's Blackmalkin. I didn't know that he was in the tree, though I did hear something rustle.'

'You'd better tell him not to touch old Blinky,' Lady Crowmarsh said. 'Blinky has been in that tree for years, and was in the ruin before that, until we pulled it down. Do you often come into my grounds, may I ask?'

'No. I never came before to-day.'

'What made you come to-day?'

'Please, I wanted to see where a hundred yards south of a place would bring me.'

'What a curious notion. And where did it bring you?'

'To the middle of your little pond. Could you tell me, please, when those little ponds were made?'

'They were made in 1782, when the formal garden was laid out. I suppose you are not interested in formal gardens.'

'Please, I don't quite know what they are.'

'Well, come in and see. Then, if you like them, you can come in to see them again whenever you like, as long as you don't disturb the birds. The gardens will bore you, but you may like to see my mice. I have a great many mice, for I'm interested in them.'

Kay spent a most happy hour looking at the mice. When he was dismissed to his home he was given a big bunch of Muscatel grapes for the governess. 'Give her these from me, with my compliments,' Lady Crowmarsh said. 'And say that it was all my fault if I've kept you from preparation or bed.'

Kay walked home with the grapes, fearing that he would 'catch it' for being there so long, as well as for the other matters.

'Please,' he said, 'Lady Crowmarsh took me to see her mice, and she sends you these grapes, with her compliments.'

'That is very kind of Lady Crowmarsh,' the governess said, with a greedy gleam in her eyes. 'Please put them on the sideboard; but let me be sure, first, that you haven't eaten any on the way. It was very kind of Lady Crowmarsh to take such notice of a dirty little boy who comes in late for tea; particularly as I hear you were seen climbing a tree in her estate this afternoon.'

She said these last words with slow relish, knowing that they would surprise him. They did. How could she have known? Who could have been and told? Could it possibly have been Blackmalkin? There he was, curled up on the armchair, pretending to be asleep, but Kay could see that he was listening with all his might, and grinning too, although he kept his face down.

'Don't try to keep things from *me*, Kay,' she said, 'for you see I get to know. Now don't let me hear of you climbing trees there again, or woe betide you. Now it's past your bed-time, go to bed at once. I know all about owls' nests, remember.'

Kay went up to his bedroom sorely perplexed. It was bad enough to be sneaked on. But supposing the sneak had heard the directions for finding the treasure? Supposing the treasure were still there under that red clay? Supposing the sneak lay in wait for Swift, Bat or Blinky as he brought the news from over sea? Suppose the sneak tortured the messenger until he told where the treasure was? Perhaps he had done that already . . . it was time for the message to be there; and it wasn't there.

He stood at his open window for a long time, hoping that the message would come. Some swifts were flying about; none of them was his Swift. Presently the sun went behind the wood, which at once became very black. It was said that in the camp in the wood, called King Arthur's Round Table, there was a door which led to the Table itself. Now the brown owl, which had nested in the hollow bough of the ruined pippin, flew out to look at the twilight. 'Perhaps he will have the message,' Kay thought. No, the brown owl cried his Tchakking cry and flew away.

Now that the swifts had gone to their roosts, the red in

the west grew clearer. In the middle heaven this red merged into a green in which a planet glowed. Soon bats began to flitter here and there across the green sky; he could hear their little shrill cries. 'Perhaps one of those is the bat with the message,' he thought, so he called: 'Bat, Mr. Bat, I am Kay, please.' It seemed that he had made a mistake; none of those was his Bat; he had no answer.

As it was now chilly near the window, Kay got into bed, where he sat up waiting for the message, which did not come. He heard the owls in the wood at their hunting. 'That settles it,' he thought. 'The message has been stopped. Swift told Blinky that he would have an answer before he began his evening's hunting. They have laid in wait for the messenger and caught him.'

Then, in his drowsiness, he began again to wonder: 'How did she find out all about owls' nests, remember? Did Blackmalkin sneak, or could she have overheard me telling Lady Crowmarsh? If she heard it from Blackmalkin, she must be a friend of the witches. But of course she can't be, that's absurd. I must have been watched by someone in the road who sneaked. All the same, it was Blackmalkin who has made them catch poor old Blinky.'

He worried over this, wondering what he could do, until he fell asleep. He woke up, or half woke up, about an hour later, when Abner's voice (he thought it was) rang out in the hall, saying: 'Well, if you won't speak, you shall very soon be made to speak. A little torture will soon change your mind. Down with him to the dungeons.'

He thought that he heard this. He thought that it was followed by a scuffling and dragging noise, with calls of 'Down you go.' 'Put him in the kennel.' 'We'll teach you.' He thought that he heard Blinky's voice giving a little hoo of pain. He was so very sleepy that he could not be sure that all this happened. It sounded like voices in a dream in the dark night. He heard some chain jangle, then a door slammed; after that he slept very heavily.

Presently there came a noise in the wainscot, and shuffling of feet on the carpet and someone clearing his throat. Kay sat up to see what this could be. He saw a strangely disreputable Rat, who was wiping his mouth with the back of a dirty paw. 'What is it?' Kay said. 'Have you come with a message from Blinky?'

'I'm Rat, I am,' the Rat said. 'I'm a cellarman, I am. I never done nothing against no young ducks; nor I didn't neither not against no chicks. I lives in a cellar, and I does a bit in the dustbin. But him as says I ducks and I chicks, he says what isn't it, because I never.'

'And what do you want now, Mr. Rat?' Kay asked.

'I don't want nothing,' Rat said. 'Him as thinks as Rat

wants anything for doing anything, he'd ought to have the cat after him, and he'd ought to have the dog after him.'

'Yes, yes,' Kay said, 'I'm sure he should.'

'Ah,' Rat said, 'that's what.'

'Is there anything that I can do for you, Mr. Rat?' Kay asked.

'Ah,' Rat said, 'there's many might have asked that question before now, what didn't. Because a fellow is a cellarman and does a bit in the dustbin, and comes a bit close to a old bone now and then (though even that he don't often), people thinks, why, I don't know what they don't think. But what I says it, a fellow is a fellow; you have to come back to that in the end, for all your Tirritts and flurts, and then where are you?'

'Yes, where?' Kay asked, because he didn't know where he was.

'Well, that's what I said, ain't it?' Rat answered in a surly tone. 'I thought I'd settled all that once for all.'

Kay could not think of anything more to say; he was silent.

'Ah,' Rat said, 'it's a cruel life is being a cellarman. If I'd my time again, I'd be, I don't know what I'd be, but rather than be a cellarman again, I'd have the cat after me, and I'd have the dog after me, and I'd have . . . I don't know what I wouldn't have after me.'

'Is it as bad as that?' Kay said.

'Ah, that's what,' Rat said.

'Look here, Mr. Rat,' Kay said, 'will you have a lump of sugar? It's a bit grubby, but I haven't sucked any of it.'

'Now there's talking,' Rat said. 'A lot of persons talks, and what good does it do? I ask you, what, and echo answers where. I eats your very good health, Master Kay, and as good a bit of sugar' (he called it shugger) 'as ever I grit my teeth on. That's Mr. Spiceman's sugar, that is . . . you won't tell me that that came from that old cove in the Jewry. He's a mean one, he is; he traps his basement . . . gah. He sick a terrier-dog on me once; he's a regular mean one. I suppose, Mr. Kay, you haven't got such a thing as a seedless raisin about you?'

'Yes, I have,' Kay said, 'in my waistcoat pocket. Here you are. I'm afraid they're a bit stuck together.'

'That don't matter, not for that,' the Rat said, taking the raisins. 'It's wonderful how a bit of squash brings out the plumminess. It's a real treat to one what lives in a cellar to taste a bit of plumminess. It takes him at once right out into the vineyards and that; like what I saw once when I went marine cellarman. But it don't do, not being a marine cellarman, because they light a stuff what smokes, and the smoke it goes creepy and creepy. You don't want to breathe none of it, neither, for it lays you dead; ah, many and many a fine marine cellarman has it cut short afore he'd gnawed through the flour barrel.'

'What a shame,' Kay said.

'Ah,' the Rat said, 'that's what.'

There was a pause after this while the Rat smeared his mouth with the back of his paw. 'I suppose,' he said at last, 'you don't carry no bit of bacon-rind upon you?'

'No,' Kay said, 'I'm afraid I don't.'

'Ah,' the Rat said. 'A bit of bacon-rind, what has been hung in the sun so as to take the crisp off, it's, why I don't rightly know what it's, but it's pretty picking of a morning, ah, and of a evening.'

'I could get you some to-morrow, perhaps,' Kay said.

'That's a fine day, to-morrow,' the Rat said. 'I never did hold with no to-morrow, but as for "to-morrow perhaps," that's when it's going to rain soup and the grass is going to grow spoons.'

'Here's a bit more sugar,' Kay said, 'it's a bit lead-pencilly, I'm afraid, from being in my pocket.'

'I'll chanst the lead,' the Rat said, taking the sugar, 'and I thank you kindly. But what I come here to see you about wasn't nothing to do with no sugar, what you're so fond of, nor about no raisins, what's plummy or not plummy, nor about no bacon-rind, what you've got mountains of and grudges a little bit; yes, even so much as a smell of. No; it wasn't about any of these things, as well I would have let you know, but for all my words being so snapped off short in a way as makes my blood boil. No; it was about our friend as I come to see you about . . . our friend as we needn't name the name of. There's been dark doings, that's what's what, and if you was to follow me, instead of talking quite such a lot, it would be thatter and whatter.'

He turned to go, still smearing his mouth with the back of his paw. Kay followed him out of the bedroom into the deserted corridor, and then down the stairs to the hall. Kay did not know what time it was; he thought that it could not be very late, because the governess was still at her music in the library. The Rat opened the hall cupboard door. 'It's in here, Master,' he said in a low voice.

When they were both inside the cupboard, the Rat closed the door upon them. He produced a piece of phosphorescent wood, which gave a faint light. 'It's in here, Master,' he said again. The panel at the back of the cupboard came out; behind it there was a gap in the wainscoting from which one could step on to the cellar stairs.

'They've got him down here,' the Rat said. 'Chronic, I call it, padlocked up in that old dog-kennel.'

'Old Blinky?' Kay asked. 'Is it old Blinky?'

'Ah,' said the Rat, 'that's what.'

He led the way down the cellar steps into the darkness of the cellar, which was only lit by a ray of moonlight from a grating and by a sort of dimness about two other gratings higher up. Kay could see the faint bulges of a line of barrels against the wall and smelled the stale beer in the saucer underneath the spiggot of the cask in use. It was a creepy place even in daylight.

'There's dark doings goes on down here,' the Rat said. 'Those cats comes down here and they makes a night of it, as they calls it. An honest cellarman can't get a wink at night sometimes, though they leaves pickings, too. This is where they put your friend.'

He led the way past the wine cellar to a corner, where, as Kay knew, an old dog-kennel had been stored.

'There's a place to put a fellow,' the Rat said. 'It gives one the thought of mange even to see. They've clapped a padlock on him, too. Trying to make him tell what he's got to tell.'

Kay heard the moaning of poor old Blinky inside the kennel.

'I say, Blinky,' he said, 'I'm most awfully sorry. Is there anything I can do?'

'Never you mind about me, Kay,' Blinky said. 'But you'd better know the truth about the treasure. I got the message and then the Pouncer and Abner and another of them came down upon me. It was Blackmalkin who betrayed us.'

'I thought it was,' Kay said.

'They're trying to get me to say what I know,' Blinky

went on, 'but they never will. Now, you bring your ear close to this hole in the kennel, and I'll tell you just the story that was brought to me.'

Kay did as he was bid and old Blinky began his tale.

'You were quite right about it being buried by an earthquake,' he said. 'The red mud-bank was toppled right over it and the river changed its course. It was under the ground for years and then somebody found it.'

'Was it Sir Piney Trigger who found it?' Kay asked.

'No, it was a farmer called Old Man John who found it. Old Man John found it while he was digging his cellar in the house he built right over where it lay. He didn't call it treasure though; he called it "Sin-and-heathen idols," and left it all propped up against the cellar-wall; it stood there for years.

'Then some people, two men and a little boy, all with the same name . . .'

'Abner Brown,' Kay said.

'That was the name . . . they came to the district to look for it; they dug for it for years without coming anywhere very near.'

'Yes,' Kay said, quoting the old lady, 'yon Abner was theer, digging for t'brass and finding nowt.'

'Then after a good many years there came that man whose name you just mentioned; please don't mention it again, for it is one of those gunny names which I can't abide . . . well, he, that gunny man, he found out where the treasure was, and oh, my goodness . . .'

'I say, how you made me jump,' Kay said. 'Whatever was the matter?'

'Kay,' Blinky asked, 'what was that footstep over there?'

'It was Rat, moving away, wasn't it? Is that you, Rat?'

There was no answer. 'What sort of a footstep was it, Blinky?'

'A sort of a stealthy footstep,' Blinky said, 'I shouldn't be surprised if that Blackmalkin had crept up in the dark and heard all that I was saying. O, if I could only get out and make sure.'

At this, he beat against the sides and roof of the kennel. Kay, who was peering into the darkness, heard someone hurry up the steps.

'Stop, you beast,' he cried; but the thing, whatever it was, had now gone.

'Kay,' Blinky said, 'we've been overheard. They'll kill me now that they know my story. Can you move the roof of this kennel? It seemed to give when I bumped against it.'

Kay thrust at the roof. 'Why, it lifts off,' he said. 'I believe I can shove it sideways. Mind, while I shove.' He gave a great heaving shove; the roof slid off and crashed upon the floor.

'Thank you, Kay,' old Blinky said, 'I can leave the cellar through the gratings which the cats use.' As he spoke, he floated down the cellar on his wings, and drifted through the grating into the night.

'And he hasn't told me half the story now,' Kay said. 'He stopped just where it was beginning to be thrilling. Well, he's safe, that's one good thing. I'd better get back to bed.'

He groped his way to the stairs, wishing that Nibbins might come to guide him; he stumbled over a cask stave, which surely had not been there when he came in with Rat; then he bumped into an empty barrel and sent it slowly rolling into the middle of the cellar. 'I'm making a fearful row,' he thought. 'And she hasn't gone to bed;

she'll hear me.'

However, he reached the stairs, climbed up them, and paused inside the hall cupboard. All was silent in the hall. Someone had left the kitchen door open so that he could hear the cricket chirping to the silent house. 'She's gone to bed,' he thought. 'I do believe she's gone to bed.'

He very cautiously peered out. All the lights were out, that was a sure sign that she had gone to bed. The moonlight was streaming into the hall through the windows. None of the midnight people was there; all was still. He crept out of the cupboard and up the stairs to his room.

He noticed that a light was burning in his room, but this did not surprise him, because for these last few nights a marvellous light had always burned there. He looked out carefully for Blackmalkin or a witch, neither seemed to be about. At last he plucked up his courage, made a dash for his room, and rushed straight into the governess who was standing there, waiting for him, just within.

'You've been in the cellar, you naughty little boy,' she said. 'You know as well as I do that that's forbidden.

Haven't I told you, I don't know how many times, that I won't have you in the cellar? And look at your pyjamas, sir, all cobwebbed and whitewashed. Now you'll have to put on a clean suit. What were you doing in the cellar, sir, to begin with?'

Kay did not quite know what to begin with, he was upset by being caught thus; luckily she did not give him any time; she went on:

'What did you do to the owl? Don't you dare to say you let him go.'

'I did let him go.'

'You *what*?'

'I let him go.'

'You . . . let . . . him . . . go?'

'Yes, he was down there in a dirty old dog-kennel that Joe's going to burn, and he was frightfully unhappy, so I let him go.'

'And how did you know he was there in the first place? You could only have learned that he was there by listening and prying. You've been at the keyholes, sir, don't tell me, instead of going to bed.'

'I haven't been at the keyholes.'

'Yes, you have been at the keyholes, sir, don't contradict me. You listened and you pried, and then you crept down to thwart us. I suppose you know what owl it was?'

'Yes, it was Lady Crowmarsh's; I was talking to her about it after tea.'

'Yes, it was Lady Crowmarsh's. And I suppose you know that Lady Crowmarsh would have given hundreds of pounds for that owl. We took it this evening out of the claws of the cat, and put it in the cellar because I knew that it would prefer the dark, intending to take it over to Lady Crowmarsh after breakfast. Now that you have let it go it will fly away and never come back, now that it has been frightened here. I shall tell Lady Crowmarsh whose fault it is that her pet is lost. Nicely you've repaid all her kindness to you, letting her pet go!'

'It was a wild owl; it wasn't a pet.'

'Yes it was a pet. It was her pet owl that she had had for years.'

'It was a wild owl,' Kay said.

'If you go contradicting me,' the governess said, 'I shall write a letter to the schoolmaster and ask him to bring his cane. Now here are your clean pyjamas; take off those you're wearing, and get into bed, but don't think for one moment that you've heard the last of this from me, because you haven't. You and I to-morrow will go through our accounts together, and if I find you've caught your death, going down to that cold cellar, woe-betide you.'

The light had long since dwindled into the light of the governess' candle. She now flounced out of the room with it, leaving Kay to change his pyjamas and get into bed in the dark.

'How on earth did she know that I was in the cellar?' he wondered. 'If she heard me, why didn't she come down to stop me? Those steps that we heard must have been Blackmalkin on the sneak again; he ran up and sneaked, that was it. But if she's in with Blackmalkin, she's in with the witches, too, that's certain. Listen!'

Down in the hall Blackmalkin was wailing under a spanking. 'Hark,' Kay said again, 'I believe she's spanking the little sneak; that's his voice, anyhow!'

The governess paused for breath in her spanking. 'Another time,' she said, 'when I send you down to listen' (Kay had now opened the door, so as to hear), 'when I send you to listen, you'll wait till the end of the story, and not come away with the best of it not told. You shall have no milk for a week.'

After Blackmalkin had gone away, whimpering and growling, saying, 'I'll be even with you before long, you'll see if I'm not,' Kay tried to sleep, but could not, because he felt sure that somebody was weeping just outside, in the garden. It was not Blackmalkin; it was somebody saying: 'O woe, woe, woe; I can't make anybody hear.'

Then he distinctly heard the voice of Miss Susan Pricker Trigger say: 'Drat my wig, my sweet Pa, that boy is in his bed there. Sing out to the horrid little toad, I mean the darling cherub, to buck his stumps and come and open the door. Wait, I'll do it for you. Boy, if you don't want to be skinned alive; I mean my pretty little love, if you want to be thought a little angel, will you jolly well, I mean most obligingly, open the door to my sweet and no longer livery Pa, and to me the pretty lady who loves little boys?'

Kay looked out of the window. It was very odd, but there were Miss Susan Pricker Trigger and a cloaked man. 'I believe it's Sir Piney,' Kay thought. 'If they go on making this noise the governess will hear them.'

'No, she won't then, my smart young sir,' Miss Piney said, as though she had read his thoughts, 'she will not hear, being at this moment elsewhere engaged. But bang my cannon, boy, don't keep a lady waiting.'

'All right,' Kay said, 'I'll come down and let you in.' So he did; he showed them into the drawing-room, and asked them to be seated. The room was brightly lit, though the clock said a quarter to one.

'My Pa and I have taken the liberty,' Miss Trigger said, 'so that you may know. The very first time my Pa and I have promenaded we come to see Mr. Harker; isn't that so, my pa-kin?'

'It is, ma poppet,' Sir Piney answered. 'Mr. Harker, tha is beset with Abners and evil. Mr. Harker, ah did my best to restore it; only ah coom too late.'

'Did you find the treasure then?' Kay asked.

'Why, as to that,' Sir Piney said, in his North Country speech, 'why as to that, it wasna so mooch me as t'other fellow. T'first thing ah see when ah coom there, was where t'Old Man John had doog oop t'earth. And t'first thing ah see was t'gunwale of t'yacht, with ma initials coot, wheer ah'd coot them when ah was droonk.

'So ah thinks, no need to look further. Old Man John has doog up t'boat, he'll have t'brass in his cellar.

'Old Man John was a foonny chap. So ah oop to him. "You've got t'brass," ah says.

' "'Tisn't brass," he says, "it's sin-and-heathen idols."

' "'Tisn't yours," ah says, "it's Captain Harker's."

' "'Tisn't Captain Anyone's," he says, "except Captain Belial's or my Colonel Mammon's."

' "Old Captain Harker is dying for this," ah says. "Let the poor old man have it."

' "Many die for the likes of this," he says, "so here it will stop, out of all harm's way."

'Ah hadna coom all that long way to be talkt to like yon, but, tha see, ah had to be coonning; ah did what foxy does to goosey. "That's talking," ah says. "Tha's got soom sense, lad, oonder tha cap," ah says, "as well as soom religion."

'But ah had to think quick. Tha see, yon old farmer was daft; he might take up t'brass any day and doomp it in t'sea. Then ah'd have been fair scooppered.

'Then yon papgoose Abner was in the land. He might

find oot aboot t'brass any day. He might shoot t'old farmer and take all t'brass to hissen. Then ah'd ha' been fair scooppered.

'Ah was vara weaselly. Ah wasna going home without yon stoof for Captain Harker. Vara coonning ah was.

• • • • •

'So when ah was all ready, with ma bonny wee dukey all ready for sea, ah call ma Indians. "Coom on," ah says, "ma lads, 'tis to glory we steer." So off we all go to t'Old Man John. Ah wasna going to hurt him, tha oonderstand, nobbut joost a bang and a bag.

'So when we coom oop to t'Old Man John, he says, "Art going to yon revival meeting?" he says. So ah walks roand him, to get t'soon into his eyes. "That's reet," ah says. "The revival meeting." Then ah oop with bang and ma we bonny Indians they oop with bag.'

'Now, my Pa,' Miss Trigger said, 'the first time we take a sweet evening walk, I am quite sure we ought not to remember unpleasantness. It's very nice to see this little cheraph, but I'm sure he wants to hear where the treasure is now, not what you may have done when provoked. It's the pepper in you again; when you feel inclined to give way to pepper you must fight it down. You must sing one of your nice songs now, about' (here she sang):

'As I was a-walking in the green month of May,
I met with my true love and thus did she say,
"O sweet grows the clover and blythe grows the corn,
And the nightingale sings in the bonny white thorn."

' "O true, love," I answered, "But what can I care

Since the . . ." Now join in with me and sing from there.'

'Ah was only telling Mr. Harker in ma own way, ma Piney,' Sir Piney said, 'Ah was nobbut beginning at t' beginning.'

'My sweet Pa,' Miss Piney said, 'that kind of beginning is over for you now for ever, it is ended. We are beginning such a lovely time; don't let us mix it with any bangs or brandy. Put it out of this little serub's mind with a song, begin at:

' "O true love," I answered.'

'Ah daresay tha's reet, ma Piney,' Sir Piney said.

Kay saw Sir Piney rise to his feet, draw breath, beat with his hand, and look at his daughter for the signal to start singing.

Somehow the song did not begin, though Miss Piney was nodding, and her father was beating with his hand. Something made Sir Piney flit rapidly over to the table; his daughter opened her mouth very wide.

Then both Triggers faded swiftly, the drawing-room faded; but, no, Sir Piney was shaking a book on the table, saying, 'Page 275'; he seemed angry about something, the book shook and shook, until it was as indistinct as the leaves of a tree all blown together on a windy day. 'All right,' Kay said, 'I'll remember the page.' At this, he rolled over, wide awake.

'It must all have been a dream,' he muttered, for the Triggers were gone; he was in his bed in the dark night, not in the drawing-room at all. 'He seems to have got the treasure,' he thought. The church clock struck one.

He was glad that it was not midnight. A cock, probably Mrs. Gossip's cock, roused in his roost by the booming of the bell, flapped on his perch and gave a half-hearted crow. A horse stamped on the path just below the window, someone reined up there, blew a horn with a flourish and cried in a clear voice:

> 'The harvest moon is rounding:
> King Arthur holds court this First Night.'

At the stamping of the horse, Kay had been afraid, lest it should be the Nightmare, which Ellen's father had seen, trotting on the road, not making a sound, but with a tongue of pale fire lolling over her teeth, and eyes of blue flame. At the sound of the voice all Kay's fear left him; he hopped out of bed and looked down.

There were two grey horses, one of them led; the rider of the other was a hatchet-faced man, clear in the moonlight, with rather long, yellow hair falling over his shoulders. He had a horn slung over his shoulder and a sword at his side.

'Are you for the Court, Master?' the man cried.

'May I?'

'The horse is sent for you.'

Kay ran downstairs, opened the door; the man helped him up into the saddle of the led horse. A sword was hanging from the saddle.

'You may need that,' the man said. 'If the Black Knight's at the ford, we'll have to fight our way.'

'Will it bend, if I chop with it?' Kay asked, thinking of the sixpenny swords which did bend.

'It's Gareth's sword,' the man said. 'It will cut through steel and the bone beyond it.'

'Could I chop off a person's head with it?'

'That's never an easy chop,' the man said. 'Your man's

shield is generally up to his ear.'

'Could I if it wasn't?'

'So many mails are double at the throat,' the man said.

'Could I if it were single?'

'Your man is generally looking out for a chop,' the man said. 'And a chop takes such a long time, you can see it coming.'

'But suppose he didn't see it coming?'

By this time they were in the broad, open green which ran between the lines of the houses of the village. The moonlight was very bright, and, lo, a marvellous thing, all the fronts of the houses were gone, just as though they were doll's houses; Kay could see the shops and the living-rooms laid bare, with all the people in bed: Mr. Spiceman, the grocer, and old Mr. Spectacle, the clock-maker; and Mrs. Sweetlips, who made such sugar-candy; there they all were, and floating about them as they slept were the loveliest people Kay had ever seen; they were like people made of light and of rainbows, and with exquisite faces and hands. They were soothing the sleep of all there; driving away little black Annoyances and Bothers, and giving Lovely Dreams instead.

'What are those people?' Kay asked.

'Those?' the man said. 'An old man called St. Alpig, down by the river, always sends those. They are quite real. They go about the world and help people. Now there's the ford, and . . . yes . . . there's the Black Knight. Take your sword in both hands, that's the way.'

'Halt there,' the Black Knight called. 'Come up one by one and render up your weapons.' Kay could see him in the blackness of the ford as a big black man on a black horse reined up in mid-stream. The steel gleamed on his lowered helmet and moving sword. He stood stock still.

The water gleamed as it flowed round the horse's fetlocks. It was all still, moonlit night, not a cock-crow, not an owl's cry, not a fox's bark, no whisper of wind, nothing but that grim form in front and the water tinkling away past the fetlocks.

Kay thought that he saw the black form incline forward in the saddle as though to urge up his horse.

'Charge him, Kay,' the messenger cried. 'Chop him on that side, I'll chop him on this.'

Kay felt his horse leap forward with a splash into the ford. He had long since dropped the reins, so as to have both hands on the sword. He trod down deep into his stirrups and leant against the back of his saddle . . . then . . . swoosh . . . he lashed out sideways at the Black Knight's head just as he lashed out to a ball on the leg side at cricket. He had a lovely feeling that he had made a magnificent hit. As his horse came out of the river on the other side, Sir Lancelot caught his rein. 'Well hit, Kay, well hit,' he said. 'There goes his pagan head; look.'

Turning round, Kay was just in time to see the Black Knight's head, spouting blue fire, rolling splash into the river; his black horse, carrying his body, galloped away into the night.

'He'll come back to put his head on again, presently,' the messenger said; 'Merlin ought to deal with him.'

'Merlin is going to deal with him,' Lancelot said. 'But meanwhile, Kay, that was a superb chop. You got in every ounce of your weight just in exactly the right spot; and, then, it was so perfectly timed. I never saw anything so neat. There was his head, and then . . . flash . . . there wasn't his head.'

'You ought to tell King Arthur about it, Sir Lancelot,' the messenger said. 'For a midnight chop there's been nothing like it since you fought that mad giant Ugg, the one with boar's tusks, in the thunderstorm. I'm used to midnight work, but I missed him altogether. I tell you, Sir Lancelot, this Kay will make a Knight, and oh, won't our present Kai be jealous.'

By this time they had ridden up the hill into the dark lane, overshadowed by yew trees, which was still called King Arthur's ride. The lane was a good place for wild Canterbury Bells, which were now in full bloom. Every Canterbury Bell was now lit with a glow-worm so that the lane glittered.

At the gate of the Round Table Camp it was as light as day; but inside the camp it was brighter than any day; all things seemed so soaked with light that they glowed.

'I see that King Arthur is over there, hearing petitions with Merlin,' Sir Lancelot said, as he dismounted. 'But in the meantime, Kay, you come along with me and see the camp.'

First, they put the horses into the stable which ran down one rampart. There were seven hundred horses, all white, cream-coloured, grey or piebald (none darker than that). They were picketed in long lines, eating grass from the Holy Meadow, which is always green; each one of the seven hundred was so gentle that Kay could feed him by hand, or slip between his legs, without any fear of a kick. Many of the horses knew Lancelot, for he had the gift of drawing beasts and birds to him. When he came into the lines, there was a general whinny of welcome.

'O, I wish that horses would whinny to me,' Kay said.

'But they do,' Lancelot said. 'They're saying Wh-wh-wh-whelcome Kay.'

'Please, what do you do here?' Kay asked.

'This is King Arthur's court, where all people come

who care. Many come, as you can see. It's hard work here all the time. Ah, there is the Queen . . .'

They were standing near a little covered well or trough of bright running water. A chariot drawn by two white, small, very fiery stallions, with harness of red enamel, drove rapidly up. There were two ladies in the chariot, one of them a sweet-faced, sad woman in a black dress. 'That's Brangwen,' Lancelot whispered. 'The Queen is driving.'

Queen Guinevere was standing to drive and urging her lovely horses like energy itself. She was a somewhat fierce-looking and splendid beauty, with the marvellous red-gold hair that gave light in the darkness. The fierceness of the drive had brought colour to her cheeks and made her eyes glow like violets. Her mouth was of an exquisite beauty, a little parted now from excitement.

'Guinevere's beauty has had peers
But none has matched her mouth and ears.'

Her hair was plaited, then heaped on her head and held there by what looked like a twisted strand of gold leaf. She wore a dress of rough green linen with a crystal neck-clasp.

'So you've brought Kay to us,' she cried, half reining in. 'I welcome you, Kay. Arthur and Merlin could see him now, Lancelot, if you would take him there. And some day will you drive with me, Kay?'

'O, I would love to,' Kay said.

She looked at him very earnestly and smiled. 'We will drive,' she said; 'we will drive the Holy Road next Midsummer Night, against Uther's Spirit Horses. He drives there against any who come, eleven miles on the grass.

You must not forget that you have promised the Queen.'

'Indeed I will not forget,' he said.

She smiled and drove on towards the end of the horse lines. Lancelot led him away towards the King. 'She is the queen of all horsewomen,' he said. 'She is the daughter of an old King in Shropshire.'

Indeed, everybody in the Court seemed happy. The people who had brought petitions were going joyfully away, some of them with parties of Knights who were going to see their grievances set right. All the troubled people had been comforted, and all the friendless little children were receiving the loveliest toys from the Lady Vivien; there were horses and chariots; but the little tiny horses were real; then there were tame bullfinches and linnets which perched on the children's fingers and sang to them; but the most beautiful of all were the Bird-Kites made by Merlin. These were like real big birds, which flew; on their backs were little boxes with seats in them in which the children sat as they flew. Some of these birds sang like skylarks when they were high in the air. Then near the gates of the camp, Kay saw parties of Knights returning from quests, with prisoners whom they had set free, or with evil Kings and tyrants whom they were bringing to judgment. Then in one place, there were most lovely people all shining with light and colours, some of them singing and all happy. 'Those are the best people of all,' Lancelot said. 'Remember, that if you call them ever, they will come to you.'

'Will they, really?' Kay said.

'They have promised that to the King. *All* those lovely people will come to you whenever you call.'

They were now drawing near to the central space of the camp where the King sat with his counsellor Merlin.

The King was unlike anybody Kay had ever seen; he could not see Merlin so well, because he was bent over a map which a very muddy traveller was showing to him. Something in the shape of the muddy traveller, or his attitude, seemed familiar to Kay. He was pointing out places on a map and asking Merlin about them. Merlin looked up suddenly and said something to the King. Kay saw Merlin clearly as he looked up; he had a strange, troubled, happy face as though he were always having very difficult puzzles set to him and always finding the answers. The King turned, spoke to the traveller and then told a couple of Knights: 'Go with him, will you, to see if you can find this treasure? It ought to be restored.'

He nodded (and Merlin smiled) to the traveller, who at once rolled up his map and turned away with the Knights to his horse, which was being held at a little distance.

'Now, Kay,' Lancelot said, 'it's your turn. Come along and speak to the King.'

He drew Kay forward through the crowd, and the body-guardsmen cleared a path for them. He saw King Arthur look at him with a smile of welcome . . . then, suddenly he heard his name called:

'Kay . . . Kay . . .'

Looking to the caller he saw that it was the muddy traveller who had now mounted his horse. The muddy traveller was Edward, his beloved Edward, Eduardo da Vinci, as he was called . . . and his horse was Peter Horse, the best of all horses . . . and with him was Robin Pointnose, on Horse . . . and they were all waving and calling and whinnying to him.

'Edward,' he cried, 'Edward . . . how are you?'

'Why, Master Kay,' Ellen said, rolling him awake.

'Don't you know my name's not Edward yet? Do wake up, there's a good boy: it's almost breakfast-time.'

'So that was only a dream, too,' he said, 'just as I made sure that it was Edward. But now it's real . . .

'And now I shall be simply frightfully punished, because of old Blinky last night.' He went down to breakfast, with his heart in his boots.

Presently the governess came down, glowered at him to show that she had not forgotten, said an awful grace in Latin, and . . . instead of speaking or eating, she became deeply interested in a letter which had come for her. It was a very queer letter written in green ink on yellow paper with very untidy writing: the governess read it through three times. She never ate much breakfast, to-day she ate none, though she sipped away three big cups of strong China tea, each with four lumps of sugar and a third of the cream. She said no word about Blinky. She never noticed when Kay ate the third egg. She never gave him his coffee.

Then, just before lessons, a very smart carriage came to the door. She was evidently expecting it, for there she was in the hall, all dressed for going out. 'There'll be no lessons to-day, Kay,' she said. 'And I shall be out for lunch. Mind I hear no bad reports of you when I come back.' Then out she sailed to the carriage, where a footman opened the door, and a lady who dangled and glittered (Kay could not see her face) welcomed her. Away they drove, with two very shiny grey horses, and the footman sticking out his elbows.

Blackmalkin came purring along the hall after Kay.

'Yes,' Kay thought, 'you're to give reports of me when she comes back, aren't you? You shall go into the stable, my son, and do an honest day's mousing for once.' So he popped Blackmalkin through the stable window into the harness-room and left him there with the mice and a saucer of rain-water. 'He is the sneak,' he thought. 'All the sneaking has been done by him.'

'And now,' he thought, 'I'll look at the book in the drawing-room which Sir Piney shook so hard.'

The book was on the table just as it had been when Sir Piney had shaken it. It was a fat, drawing-room sort of a book in a worn binding of imitation green leather. It was called 'Aunt Susan's Compendium of Pleasant Knowledge, 1841–2.' He looked at page 275; it seemed very dull, being directions how to make a pretty and useful pen-wiper out of scarlet flannel and a merry-thought bone. 'It was only a dream,' he said. He left the book on the hearth-rug.

'What I really want to know,' he thought, 'is what she has to do with the witches. I'll bet she is in with them. Of course she is in with them, she uses Blackmalkin as a spy. And of course she invites them here to supper.'

'Hoity, toity, child,' said Grandmamma Harker's portrait on the wall above him. 'If you think that, you should deal with her: search her room, bless us and save us. You must be the master in your own house. Don't let a witch take the charge of Seekings. This is a house where upright people have lived. Let's have no Endorings nor Jezebellings in Seekings. Bell her, Kay; Book her, boy; candle her, grandson; and lose no time: for time lost's done with, but must be paid for.'

He looked up at her portrait, which was that of a very shrewd old lady in a black silk dress. She was nodding her head at him so that her ringlets and ear-rings shook. 'Search the wicked creature's room,' she said, 'and if she *is*, send word to the Bishop at once. It's more than a

Rector's work to deal with an Endor.'

'All right,' Kay said, 'I'll go. I *will* search.'

To the west of Kay's room, up a small flight of stairs, there was a corridor, into which he never ventured, it was so dark and awful.

On both walls were dark old portraits and the doors of the rooms where their originals had lived and died. When these doors were shut, the corridor was as dark as the cellar. He knew that the doors to the right and left, at the farther end of the corridor, were the doors of her rooms; her bedroom to the left, her study opposite. His heart thumped and his mouth became very dry as he went up the flight of stairs, past the large scale old yellow chart of the Port and Bay of Santa Barbara, towards what might be a kind of dragon's den.

To his great joy, the corridor was light. Her study door was swinging open, with a bunch of keys dangling from the keyhole. And this was strange (and even awful), because he knew that Ellen had never seen the inside of the study since the governess had taken charge: it was always locked. Why was it open now? Could she have crept back unknown, unheard? Was she inside the room, like a spider in her web, waiting for him to appear? Would Greymalkin, that mysterious cat, who was so seldom seen, be on guard there, ready to fly at him? Would there be worse guards; fiery dogs or a python? Or would there be secret guards, who would watch him through portraits, say nothing to him, but report all his doings on her return?

Very timidly he tapped upon the door, half expecting that she would answer. No answer came, all was still within, save for the blind flapping near the open window, a cruising wasp, and a butterfly trying to get out. He took his fate in his hands and walked boldly in.

There was not any sign of Greymalkin; the room had no visible spies. There were no portraits on the walls for spies to look through. There were a good many books in the shelves, and some portfolios of drawings propped against the wall, for she was always sketching (rather well). On her writing-table was a round case full of coloured discs, which looked very odd and gave Kay a queer feeling; he was glad to turn away from them. Even then, he didn't like the look of them; he covered them with a cloth. On the desk was . . . what . . .?

On the desk was the handbag which Mrs. Pouncer had carried when she had come into his bedroom with Blackmalkin. He would have known that bag anywhere, because it was black, with steel moon and stars worked on it. Beside the bag lay the Roper Bilges' copy of the Sea-Gunner's Practice, but it had been tampered with; all the written pages at the end had been neatly removed; they were no longer there.

'I say,' he said to himself, 'how on earth did she get this from Mrs. Pouncer?'

How indeed? It was not so easy to say.

He stood in the middle of the room, staring round him. It looked innocent enough, but was it? There were some strange little woodcuts on the bookshelves. When he looked at these more closely they frightened him, much as the discs had. Then there were some most strange playing-cards with Latin underneath their figures; he did not like the look of these. Then the books were not quite all that they might be. He only opened one; it had hieroglyphics instead of print. He put it back in its place and opened one of the portfolios of drawings. He did not like that at all: the drawings were of strange black figures upon red paper. He began to be very much afraid.

Then he thought that it was not very nice of him to come spying on her, when her back was turned; so he went out of the room.

Then he thought that Grandmamma Harker was right, that he ought to make sure that his home was not being used for witchcraft; so he went back again. He had not yet looked into the cupboard.

The cupboard (as he knew from Ellen) was really a room, being what was called a powdering chamber.

'And supposing,' he said to himself, 'supposing Mrs. Pouncer is really her sister . . . and supposing she is in the powdering room, living there . . . that would account for the way the things go from the larder.' He looked through the cupboard keyhole; it was dark within; he could make out nothing. He flung the door wide open, crying 'Aroint thee, witch,' in case Mrs. P. should be there.

Mrs. P. was not there; no one was living there; the little room was in use as a clothes cupboard, but what were the clothes which hung from the pegs? Ah, what indeed?

There was a row of seven crooked pegs.

From each peg there hung a witch's complete outfit; thus:

1 long scarlet cloak.

1 black stick with a crooky handle.

1 tall, black pointed shiny hat.

And attached to each hat there was something . . . he had to turn up the nearest hat to see what it was. It was marked inside Sylvia Daisy. The outside was a marvellous wax face of Mrs. Pouncer.

'Now I know all about it,' he said. '*She* is Mrs. Pouncer;

this is her mask . . . and look at all her magic and witch things on the shelf. She is a queen witch; she'll take a whole Archbishop to settle . . .'

He looked at the magic things on the shelf. There was a magic lantern which lit the cupboard like daylight when he touched a button; there were magic baskets labelled *Wish*; there were magic ladders and ropes, which pulled out, and out, and out, to any length you pleased; there were fox-eye and cat's-eye spectacles for seeing in the dark (he pocketed a pair of these); there was a gallon tin of Invisible Mixture; there were seven pairs of one league shoes; seven pairs of seven league shoes; and seven pairs of forty-nine league boots (these last were screwed down to keep them still). Then there were green and scarlet and yellow bottles, labelled Snake Bite, Dragon's Blood, and Pouncer's Best Bewitching Mixture. Then there was an ivory box labelled 'Ointment for turning little boys into tom-tits' (Kay did not touch this). Then there were bowls of gums and herbs for incantations. Then there were books, oh, such books with such titles:

Broomsticks, or the Midnight Practice.
Spells and How to Bind Them.
The Beginner's Merlin.
Merlin's 100 Best Bewitchals.
Were-Wolves, by one of Them.
Shape-changing for all, by M. Le Fay.

And at the end of the shelf was a small red book: 'Why I am a Witch,' by Sylvia Daisy Pouncer.

'I say,' he thought, 'that is confession; she glories in it. I'll write to the Bishop. I don't care if it is sneaking. She has no business to be doing this kind of thing.

'All the same,' he thought, as he looked at the row of scarlet cloaks, 'it would be rather sport to try on Mrs. P.'s things.'

He hesitated for an instant, then he lifted the cloak from the peg; the outfit came down in one piece. He put it on before the mirror; the cloak was rather long; but when he said: 'I wish it were shorter,' it shrank to the right size. When he looked at himself in the glass, lo, he *was* Mrs. Pouncer, hooky nose, crooky chin, and wicked, black, piercing eyes which could see further into things than his own eyes, as he very soon found; they were eyes like gimlets.

'I say,' he said, 'I look exactly like her. Now I will just watch myself conjure.' And at this he put his left hand on his heart and struck the crooky stick downwards on the floor.

Instantly he felt himself lifted into the air, off his feet, and through the open window. He had not time to catch hold of the rose trellis, he was carried so quickly past. He

went floating along the drive, over the gate, over the Crowmarsh Estate, past Blinky's tree, over the manège where they were lunging the chestnut colt, then faster and faster, past the house where the poor mad lady lived, past the milestone on Racecourse Road, past the white rails of the course . . . on, on, on . . .

'O dear,' Kay cried, 'it's taking me straight to where all the witches are . . . and they'll turn me into a tom-tit. Stop, stop. I charge you to stop.'

It didn't stop, he didn't stop; he went faster and faster.

Soon the second milepost was passed; then the third, the stick began to point downwards towards a wooded hollow where the house called Russell's Dene stood. The stick was pointing towards the house; nothing that Kay could do seemed to have the slightest effect. 'I can't turn it or stop it,' he said. 'It's going straight to those windows.' The house was a big brick building of the time of Queen Anne. It had a gloomy, heavy look as though it were drunk and wore a wig.

'I'm going straight to where all the witches are,' Kay thought; 'they will bewitch me into a mouse and set the cat at me. O dear, O dear.'

The stick carried him swoop through one of the upper windows into a big, gloomy room, panelled to the ceiling. There were two open doors in this room, one on each side of Kay. People were talking just beyond one of these doors. Kay heard his governess' voice saying:

'What was that, that came through the window in the next room?'

'It was my cat, Jouncer,' the milky voice of Abner Brown replied. 'He always comes in that way.'

'Really?' the governess said. 'By the pricking in my toes I thought that it must be one of us.'

'No, dear Pouncer,' Sister Aconite said, 'my toes pricked, too; but I distinctly heard the cat's feet go patter-patter.'

'Jouncer *is* one of us,' Abner Brown said. 'He knows our moonlight games and loves them. But . . . more coffee, dear Brother Venom?'

'No, I thank you, Master Abner.'

'How time has slipped away, my dear Seven,' Abner Brown said, 'in listening to Sister Pouncer's thrilling story revealed by this Owl. What a pity that her faithful spy Blackmalkin did not wait for the end; it might have spared us so much trouble; we might have learned the whole truth. And this Harker child released the Owl, you say?'

'Yes, imagine it. I'd a very good mind to tom-tit him there and then.'

Here the other witches joined in with: 'It's a pity you didn't.' 'The idea of such impertinence.' 'Just as we might have learned the whole truth, too,' etc., etc.

'Wait,' Abner Brown said. 'Does this Harker child know more of the Owl's tale than we do?'

'He may. He may know the whole truth.'

'So I think,' Abner said. 'I am sure, or almost sure, that old Trigger got the treasure. What he did with it is the question. *I* think he gave it back to old Harker, who put it under that big hearthstone which you say is in his room. We'll look there this afternoon. But in the meantime I have been preparing a Peep Show into the Past. The spells for that must be almost working now. We *may* be able to see exactly what did happen. I *saw* it as a child, remember, but was too young to know, and neither my pop nor my lamented grand-pop ever explained it to me.'

At this instant, a gong began to beat in a room somewhere on the other side of the house.

'Hark,' said Abner Brown. The gong-beats changed to a voice which cried: 'The spells are working. The Past is laid bare. I charge you to come to see it.'

'There is the call,' Abner said. 'Now, if nothing blurs the picture, we may see what happened. Let us come along, then. Will you not wear your wrap, dear Pouncer?'

'No, thank you.'

'This way, then; through the door . . .'

'O, O,' Kay thought, 'they are coming here; they will catch me.'

He had no time to think what to do. Since the stick would not take him back through the window, his only possible way of escape was through the door beside him. He slipped through it into a corridor just as the witches entered the room where he had been.

The corridor was long and white, with doors on each side. Quite close to Kay was a small steel door standing ajar. It was very heavy. He slipped past it into a narrow passage and closed it behind him. He just had time to draw the heavy bolts before the witches were pushing at it from the other side. Kay went along the passage into a small room, brilliantly lit, although it had no window. There was a second steel door; when Kay had shut and bolted this, he could hear no sound of the outer world; not even the witches hammering on the steel outside.

'I am a prisoner now,' he thought.

The room had steel walls, some of which were hung with red velvet, all marked with magic. There were eight chairs in a row facing these red curtains. Kay sat down wondering what he was to do next. Suddenly fiery letters appeared one by one across the curtains, spelling out the words,

OPEN US.

'All right,' Kay said. 'I will.' So he walked across and opened the curtains. Behind them was a recess in which stood a tall red pedestal the height of a man. On the top of the pedestal was a man's head, made in gold or other bright metal. This head was fitted with spectacles and ear-pieces of a magic kind, so that it might see and hear the past.

'I have seen and heard,' the head said. 'Remove these trappings from me.'

Kay removed the spectacles and ear-pieces; as they pricked his fingers, he dropped them to the floor, against which they burst. After this there was a silence, till the head said, 'One minute is past, question me.'

'What have you seen and heard?' Kay asked.

'You shall see and hear,' the head answered.

The room became suddenly dark, except for a glimmering about the head.

'You are looking into the past and hearing it,' the head said.

Instantly Kay saw a tiny shining picture, of waves beating on a beach; but, no, it was not a picture, it was real; the waves broke and the trees beyond the sand were shaking. It grew larger, till it was like the scene itself; the surf was bursting, the sun glaring, and the hard leaves of the trees clacking on each other.

A man came out of the jungle on to the sand. He was dressed in grey cotton clothes, and wore a tall straw sun-hat. He was staring along the beach. Suddenly he turned

his head and looked straight at Kay, so that Kay saw his face. The words of Miss Pricker Trigger came into his mind at once, 'a white, sweet, sanctified horse-dealer . . . a cherry-lipped poisoner.' The man in front of him was so like those descriptions. He had long white hair and beard, a rosy face, and a smile. His eyes had a way of turning up, as though looking at heaven were his chief delight; his hands were plump and white, he smoothed down his beard with them. Yet when his eyes turned up, Kay felt that the man was watching out of the corners of them. His outside seemed all woolly white lamb, and the inside all bitey rough wolf. 'That is old Abner Brown,' Kay said. 'It could not be anybody else.'

Abner Brown poked into the sand for turtle eggs, found some and then sat down to suck them.

'Yes, my Benito Suarez,' he said, in his milky voice, when he had sucked the eggs. 'I thought I recognised you when you came by three days ago. I was sure that you were my Benito and so you are. And you are looking for what we looked for all those years ago . . . just as I am. Now, as no one seems to be about, I'll look at these papers of yours, which I made so bold as to pinch from your room at the inn this morning, while you were fishing.'

Here he settled himself comfortably, pulled out some letters and read:

'Oho,' he said, 'so your real name is Trigger, is it? Sir Piney Trigger, of Trigger Court, England. . . . You must be a rich man, yet you come looking for my property.

'Well, if I don't find my property soon, I'll see if I can't squeeze a little of your wealth out of you. I guess you'll be quite glad to pay little Abner not to tell what he knows about you. So.

'Though I guess we are on the brink of finding my property, now that we are digging that red clay. . . .'

At this point he stood up muttering, 'I may be Millionaire Brown even now.' Shading his eyes, he stared at a big, strong wooden ketch, with tanned sails, which had just swung into sight on her way to the sea.

'That's the wherry that was at Watford's Farm Landing,' Abner said. 'I wonder what she's doing. She was to have taken Watford's cotton, but not till next week. I may be wanting her myself if all things go as I hope. But she is laden and seems to be making for the sea.'

After this Abner picked some berries from the shrubs, as a dessert to the turtle eggs. 'Well, well,' he said at last, 'I have had my little walk; I'll be getting back to the great work. To-day may repay me for all my troubles.'

At this moment, there came a loud cry of 'Popper, popper, are you there, popper? Hey, pop, where are you?'

'I'm here, Ab,' Abner called. 'Don't make such a noise, boy, even if you have found it. What are you yelling murder for? Have you found it?'

A man of about thirty years of age appeared through the scrub, he was dragging by the hand a boy of about five. Both were like old Abner in the face, being plainly son and grandson; both were scarlet from running, and gasping for breath.

'Speak, can't you?' the old man said. 'Have you found it?' Young Abner panted and waved towards the wherry:

'He's got it . . . in the wherry.'

'Who's got it? Got what? What wherry?'

'The man Ben, all the treasure; he tied old farmer up in a bag and took the lot. He's taking it to sea in his barge there.'

At this old Abner boxed his son's ears. 'Don't bring me a crazy tale like that,' he said.

The son took out a pocket telescope, focused it, and handed it to his father. 'Take a see for yourself, pop,' he said. 'That's Ben steering.' 'And now little Ab, don't you stand there grinning as though this were something good to eat.' At this he boxed *his* son's ears, which set him howling.

Old Abner took one hasty glance at the steersman. 'It's he,' he said. 'It's Benito Trigger. There's only one chance, and that's a poor one. He's going about now, there are his head sails shaking. He will make one short tack almost to that little point. If we run there like smoke we'll get there as soon as he will. As he goes about, you hail him, Abner; he may not know you.'

'What am I to say?' Abner said.

'Yell out Danger, or Murder, or ask a passage, or say a snake's bit you, yell Help.'

'He won't pay no heed,' the son said.

'Anyway, he'll look at you. And while he looks I'll give him all the lead I've got in my shooter. Run, now, run. Let the brat stay here. Stay here, Ab, and eat berries. Pop and Grandpop are going in swimming.'

They left little Ab on the sand, while they ran as fast as they could towards the channel. Kay saw the barge leaning over, with all her sails wrinkling full, and a white streak spreading at her bows. She was making good speed, for the current in mid-channel helped her. Son Abner ran for the point, the old man ran more to the left. Kay saw his white hair blowing and saw him draw his revolver.

In a minute, Abner was crouched behind a shrub. Abner, the son, was hopping from rock to rock to the water's edge. He flapped the rocks with a bough to scare the snakes which were sunning there. His father, a much more poisonous snake, was now making a rest for his shooting arm.

The barge came rapidly nearer, her bows gleamed in the sun, her long, green wind-vane streamed away to the leeward. Kay saw an Indian crouched in her bows. The sails still hid the steersman, but Kay kept saying to himself, 'The steersman is Piney Trigger, or Twiney Pricker. I shall see him, for this is he alive, this is what happened.' Young Abner was now knee-deep in the creek, with his arms lifted as though pleading for help.

Something seemed to trouble the ketch; the white streak at her bow suddenly dimmed to grey; at the same instant the full, wrinkling, swelling bag of the foresail crumpled up, shook and banged. The wind went out of the mainsail an instant later, then her wet side swerved itself round and Kay saw the helmsman stoop as he pitched some gear across and let the boom gybe. The foresail flapped and filled on the other tack. Young Abner (just an instant too late) shouted, 'Hi, brother, for any's sake. Hi, hi, hi, give me a passage.' The steersman, whose eyes were on the sail, cast a glance at him; young Abner cried again, 'Hi, brother, take me down with you.' Then bang, bang, bang went the shots from the old man's revolver: a white streak suddenly appeared on the barge's side, where a splinter had been knocked off by a bullet.

A fourth shot followed (it flew wide somewhere), then the revolver jammed. By this time, the barge was moving fast away on the other tack. Piney Trigger shook his left hand at them as he swept far out of shot. The breeze was freshening, out there in the estuary; little bright splashes flew up on the barge's side as she hurried away. In less than a minute she was fairly out to the sea, heading away from the land.

The two Abners met together and watched her; they

said nothing till she was out of sight. The old man fidgeted with his revolver, and as he could not open the catch, flung it far out into the creek.

'There, he's gone,' he said at last. 'I'd have shot him full of holes, if the running hadn't made my arm shake; then just as I'd got the bead well on him the wheel jammed. Where's he making for?'

'England, I reckon.'

'Go on with our England; he's off for one of the islands.'

'Well, couldn't we tell the coastguard at Crab Point, and have him headed off?'

'He'll be twenty miles at sea before you get there, and what good would it do to us, if they did head him?'

'Well, at least, they would stop him having the stuff.'

Abner answered this with a snarl. After a pause, he said, 'Now that we're cooler, answer, How do you know he has the stuff?'

'I was digging in the new place,' his son replied, 'when I heard some waggons coming along; they were going along the pike to French-fellows Pier. I didn't look up till they'd passed. Then I thought they looked like old John's waggons, and I thought that one of the men in the second waggon was this Ben fellow. I just thought, "he's getting a lift to the pier to do a bit of fishing." I went on with my digging and dug quite a piece. I found one of these Indian arrow-heads.'

'Sit on it,' his father said. 'Get on.'

'I suppose an hour later, old farmer John came running up, pretty near out of his mind. "Did my waggons go past here?" he asked.

' "Sure," I said.

' "Was that man called Ben or Trigger in them?"

‘ “I guess so. What’s the matter, John?”

‘ “Matter?” he said. “That fellow and his Indians; you call him Ben, but his real name’s Trigger. He and they knocked me flat, tied me up, and took all the stuff I had outen of my cellar. It was that gold and silver which I guess you’ve been looking for. I had it and they’ve took it . . . loaded it up on to my own waggons and said they was going to the pier. But I’ll pier them yet,” he said. “I’ve sent to the Marshal. I’ve called Joe. I’ve got my gun. You call your pop, quick now, and we’ll get him at the pier before he can be off in that yawl of his.” He was pretty near dead with rage and running, but off he went for the pier and I came looking for you.’

Old Abner sat on the rock swaying from side to side. ‘When first we came here,’ he moaned, ‘I thought of trying out by John’s farm there, but them Indians put me wrong. And it was there all the time. And that fox, old John, had it in his cellar and watched us digging for it twenty years. I’ve gone harvesting there and drunk a horn or two with him a dozen times and he grinned and said nothing. He had us fooled at the time, the worst kind of fools. What was he planning to do with it?’

‘Keep it from doing harm, he said.’

‘He’s been fooled himself now, pretty good,’ old Abner said. ‘But he’ll answer to me for the fool he made of me . . .’

‘But how did the Trigger find where the stuff was?’ he asked after a pause.

‘John told me that,’ his son said. ‘He found bits of the boat in John’s yard. Found it first go off. He never had to dig nor nothing. He had us fooled all the time. Now he’s got it.’

‘He won’t have it for long,’ the old man said.

'I don't know for that,' his son said, 'old John won't stop him; old John, I reckon, will just let it go without a word, as soon as his dander goes down.'

'Well, I won't,' his father said. 'I'll get this Benito Trigger, sir, wherever he comes ashore. I'll have the stuff yet, or my fair half of it, or he shall squeal for it. I'll start this day. He ain't done with me yet, he's only begun.'

At this point, little Abner broke in upon them with:

'I guess I wanna go home.'

'Well get home. Walk,' his father said.

'I guess I don't wanna walk.'

'Well, I guess you'll just have to.'

'I guess I ain't gonna walk.'

'I guess you are. How else are you going to get.'

'I guess I wanna be carried.'

'Who's gonna carry you?'

'I guess you are.'

'I guess I'm not.'

'Then I guess Gran'pop's gonna carry me.'

'I guess he ain't,' Gran'pop said.

'Then I guess I'll stay here an' yell.' Saying this, he started to yell; his father boxed his ears, to give him, as he said, something to yell for. Old man Abner said, 'I'm off, for Trigger's home; when he gets there he'll find me waiting for him.' At this, the picture suddenly dimmed, the figures of the three Browns blurred into the background; Kay saw the surf and the waves of the sea, and then, lo, the shining head said, 'That is all,' and the picture vanished. Kay rose from his chair; at the same instant the scarlet cloak which he was wearing turned into a scarlet canoe; it floated him up from the floor, bored a big hole in the wall, floated him through, and then sped him home like a bird. In a minute the outfit was on its peg and Kay was in the drawing-room, looking at Aunt Susan's 'Compendium.'

The book was on the hearthrug, open, but somebody must have handled it since he had left it there. It was open in the middle to show him that there were two volumes of 'Pleasant Information' bound together (for 1841 and 1842), and that therefore the book contained two pages numbered 275, one of which he had not seen. He turned to page 275 for the 1842 volume. It bore a chapter heading:

Secret Writings.

It went on thus:

'Though in the enlightenment of modern times the need of secret methods of correspondence has become less frequent than in the past, it may still fall to the lot of our readers to want the knowledge of such methods. It may not be generally known that an effective secret writing can be made very simply, by using, instead of the letter needed, a letter some distance before or after it in the alphabet. Thus, instead of writing CAT, write BZS or DBU. With a little practice, people can become ready writers in these changed alphabets . . .'

'That's queer,' Kay thought. 'Perhaps Benjamin used a secret writing when he wrote those notes about the treasure.' He had not time to prove it at the moment, because Ellen carried him off to dinner, but after dinner he took an exercise book and a pencil to his lair below his dressing-table. Then with great care he made several alphabets in columns. After a little juggling with these, he found that the letters SSS
JGZ.RPC

might possibly represent not those letters, but two letters later in the alphabet: thus

U.U.U.
LIB TRE

It was very perplexing work, almost as troublesome as acer, and the result was odd; still LIB TRE did seem to spell something, whereas JGZ seemed like initials, and what English name began with Z?

He was about to try another combination of alphabets, when he heard a carriage in the drive. 'She's coming back,' he thought. An instant later he heard her in the hall, with others. 'She's brought the witches here, or is it only Mrs. Gossip?' he asked, as he listened. Abner's voice told the footman to wait.

'It is the witches,' he thought. 'What has she brought them here for?' He heard her bring them along the hall, up the stairs to the corridor outside his room. They did not seem to be more than five.

'Wait here a moment,' she said, 'I must just see if anyone has been in my room.' You may imagine how Kay felt when he heard her say this.

While she was gone the others muttered together. 'We must get to the bottom of it.' 'She had one of our cloaks, for I saw the red skirt flick past the door.' 'Well, we shall find who it was, and then . . . snip . . .'

The governess came back from her room. 'Come on in here,' she said, leading the way into Kay's room. 'It is safe in here, we can't be overheard in here. This is the child's room, where Captain Harker slept. Some of you must sit on the bed, there won't be room for you all on the sofa.' She made sure that both doors were shut.

When they were all seated, she said, 'It is true that I left my window open, but I have looked at the robes, they are all cool; it cannot have been anyone from here.'

'Then who was it?' Abner asked. 'Someone, in one of our robes, was listening to us while we lunched, and got before us to the image; and all our spells were wasted; worse than wasted, for the knowledge must have gone to an enemy. I ask, who was it?'

'Not one from here,' the governess said. 'We will make an incantation to-night to find out who it was . . . and then . . . short shrift.'

'Yes,' Abner said. 'If it won't then be too late for short shrift. However, this is the room, you say. Let us have a look at this hearthstone.'

At this, he pulled back the carpet so as to show the stone.

'No doubt about its being big enough,' he said. 'And it certainly hasn't been disturbed in recent years. We're in plenty of time if it's buried here. Off coat, Uncle Venom, and then we'll get the cold chisels at it.'

Kay heard the two men take off their coats and settle down to work.

'The stone's leaded in,' Abner explained. 'We will chip out the lead and prise the stone up with our crowbars.'

Kay heard them chip at the lead, while the three ladies said, 'How fast you're doing it.' 'It won't take long at this rate.' 'What can we bring you for refreshment?' etc., etc.

'This is only Quaker-leading,' Abner said, after they had chipped for some minutes. 'We'll have this up in no time. It is a thin melting of lead to cover the bolt-heads. I can prise the bolts out now with the jemmy, if you'll hand it to me, Sister.'

'Here's the jemmy, dear Master.'

'Thank you. Yes. It is as I said. Here come the bolts, they pull right up. It's a good deal easier than I'd expected. Now, Uncle Venom, if you'll take this crowbar, I'll take this one. It seems to me that one good heave will make her swing on her axis.'

Kay heard them heaving and panting. It wasn't quite so easy as they had expected. At last Kay heard them say, 'It's giving. There it is. Now then.' Kay heard the stone swing back. All five people were intent upon what was beneath. Kay could just see their bent bodies craning forward into the hollow.

'It's not just under the stone,' Abner said. 'The space seems to me to be right underneath the fireplace. There's a room of sorts.'

'Is there anything in it?' Sister Aconite asked.

'I'll soon see,' Abner said. 'It'll be something of a squeeze to get down.'

Kay could see him squirming down, legs first, into the opening. Presently his head disappeared.

'Is there anything there?' the two women asked.

'Nothing,' he said from below. 'It's an empty room. The stuff hasn't been here, at any rate not for many years. It's dry, empty and dusty; not a thing in it, except this.'

Kay could not see what 'this' was, but it was evidently a small thing. He heard it being passed about.

'It's only the handle of a sword,' Sister Aconite said.

'It's not even that,' Abner answered. 'It's the handle of a cutlass worth about ten shillings when new. Well, there's a disappointment. Or rather, one more false trail removed. We know that it isn't here at least. But what on earth was the room made for? That beats me. Is there any other place in this house where old Harker could have put it?'

'None, that I know of,' the governess said.

'Nothing in the cellar?'

'Nothing; I've searched.'

'Well, where did Trigger put it, if he didn't give it to Harker?'

'Where, indeed?'

'Well, we must go on with our incantations till we get another clue,' Abner said.

'We're spending a small treasure in gums and herbs,' Uncle Venom said. 'It's my belief that Miss Susan Pricker Trigger has it, all the time.'

'Maybe she has,' Abner said. 'But I don't think she has. Anyway, that will be easy to prove, as things turn out. It must be somewhere, and we must get it, and we will get it.'

Kay could see him sweeping the particles of lead and brick displaced by the work down into the opening. Presently the stone was rolled back, and the carpet replaced.

'Our young friend will notice that these two bolts have been unleaded,' Abner said.

'He won't,' the governess said. 'He's the most unobservant boy I've ever met.'

'The maids will notice, though,' Sister Aconite said.

'A very good imitation can be made,' Abner answered, 'with candle grease and soot from the chimney.'

In a few minutes he had covered the two bolts with melted grease and soot.

'They won't notice that,' he said. 'And now we'll be moving.'

He gathered up the crowbars.

'I suppose that there's no clue on the sword,' Sister

Aconite said.

'It's all rusted deep,' Abner answered. 'If anything ever has been scratched on it, it's rusted out now.'

'What shall we do with it?' Sister Aconite asked.

'Well, the young shaver might like it.'

'No, indeed,' the governess said, 'that might be giving him all sorts of ideas.'

'I'll take it with me, then,' Abner said; he put it in his pocket. They all left the room.

'Well,' Kay thought, as they went downstairs, 'they are just about cool enough.'

• • • • •

After tea Kay was sent to hold skeins of wool for Ellen, because the Women's Winter Knitting Club would soon be meeting and boys ought to make themselves useful. Ellen talked of old times as she balled off the wool.

'Things were very different in my father's time,' she said. 'They call them the good old times; but I don't know, I'm sure, what my father found good in them. Oh, the dreadful things he used to tell. For it wasn't then like it is now, Master Kay, with so many things done for poor people; no. Why the farmers used to beat the boys black and blue, and pinch their ears till the blood ran.

'And then there was the war time, fighting against that Boney. Oh, the money there used to be then. Never anyone sober in the parish on market nights; everybody had the French brandy, by what they called the Night Hawks. They used to bring the brandy by night right up the river, and then bring it about to people's houses, and so cheap. But the Night Hawks were bold ones; they killed poor Mr. Parminter. There was a lot of them hanged for that. They hung them up on the top of Cop in those days. My father used to show me the sort of like a hollow where the gallows was, but the boys have all altered it now, scrabbling about for poor people's bones and that, which they say keep you from drowning, but I don't know I'm sure.

'Then they put Boney on his island in the end; and then there wasn't any more French brandy, nor nothing else; oh, dreadful it was, and bread so dear, my father said; many's the time he was glad of a bite of oats out of the horse-bin. And then like men came down from the cities, my father said, to tell the young men not to stand it, because the French didn't. So then they got what they called the Liberty Tree out in the wood . . .'

'Liberty Tree,' Kay said, 'what was that?'

'It was that big beech-tree, Master Kay, in the middle of Corselaydead Wood, where the four big rides meet. We went past there with Rose and Will, if you remember, the day we walked to the Flower Show. They called it the Liberty Tree, my father said, because there's Liberty cut on it, and that's what they did in France. They put a red cap on it, and that made it Liberty, and then they took their oaths. The Liberty men were bold ones, too; they burned a lot of ricks and that, till they were sent to Botany. My father had the red cap that was on it, till mother wanted it for crawlers. There's not many knows about these things now, for the old ones are gone, and the young all go into the towns and never care.'

• • • • •

When Kay went to bed that night he knew that Benjamin's writing meant a hundred yards south of the

Liberty Tree; but he could not understand what the S.S.S. meant, even if the S.S.S. stood for U.U.U. Then, just as he was falling asleep, it came over him in a flash. 'Of course,' he cried, 'I see what it means. What an ass I was, not to see it before; it means a hundred yards south of the Liberty Tree under three big yews. That is it, of course. I wonder if there *are* three big yews, I cannot remember. But of course there will be.' His mind at once made pictures of enormous yews with interlocking boughs growing over 'the sort of like a hollow' where Benjamin's treasure lay. Soon they began to cover Kay with shadow, so that he fell asleep.

He had not slept for long before a shrill crying sounded in his ears. When he woke, the room had something in it that was fluttering and battering against the ceiling and the walls. When his eyes grew accustomed to the light he saw that there was a bat in the room. He had always loved bats, because of their bright eyes, cocked ears, and nice leathery umbrellary wings and the little hooks to them. He had always longed to be a bat, so that he could fly in the twilight and hook himself up head downwards somewhere high up in a steeple when he was tired. Now here was a bat actually crawling along his bed to him.

'Good evening, Kay,' the Bat said. 'I've come from my friend Tom Otter; we thought what fun it would be if we could persuade you to spend an evening with us. We live in an interesting old place which you might like to see, and I've brought you a suit of wings, in case you care to come.'

'I'd love to come,' Kay said, 'it is most frightfully kind of you to think of me.'

'Hurray, he's coming,' the Bat said. 'We hoped you

would. Now I'll help you to put on the wings.'

'Just try flying from the bed to the window-ledge,' he said, 'and then fly back once or twice. You'll soon get the hang of it. It's really very easy.'

Kay found that it was quite easy after the first attempt. 'Come on, then,' the Bat said. 'You keep by me. It isn't far, really, to our place. I generally go this way.'

Kay put on his pair of fox-eye spectacles and followed him. It was amusing to see his friends, the grocer and the carpenter, walking in their gardens, and to fly just over their heads. It was eerie to hear them say: 'The bats are very bold this year; that one nearly knocked my glasses off.' Then Mrs. Grocer said:

'When bats grow bold
We shall have cold.'

Mrs. Carpenter said:

'When bats fly low
It's going to blow.'

Both the husbands said the same thing: 'Well, I wouldn't be surprised if we did have it a bit cold, if we did have it a bit blowy.'

Presently they came in sight of the river, at a point which Kay longed to spend days at, exploring, but was never allowed, as it was dangerous.

Some twenty years before, there had been a mill there, with two wheels. The mill was now vanished to its foundations, but the mill-race head was still there in a quiet pool forty yards long, in which water lilies were spreading. The shoots of the wheels still dribbled water even in the hottest summer. Beyond the mill-shoots was a causeway or bridge, under which the main river ran over a lasher; at the further end of the lasher was the lock by which the barges had passed on their way up or down stream. The railway had now put an end to all this traffic.

Above the mill and bridge, the river was a shallow basin, a hundred yards broad, broken up by islands and withy plats, where there were swans, kingfishers, many moorhens, sometimes a heron, and now and then wild duck, or duck that had escaped (these were the ones that Kay loved to think of) and gone wild. Below the mill, there was a deep, turbulent, foaming pool from which the current sped away upon its course. There was a big idle back-eddy at one side of it, where bubbles, like glass tea-cups upside down, sauntered back towards the lasher, and then either ran at once into the current or were driven back to saunter round again.

The causeway was pleasant in calm weather. You could put in ships above the lasher, and watch them go down the falls and through the rapids, or round and round the wheel of the pool. But in times of flood it was wonderful, and terrible, when all the hatches were wide, and the roar of the weir could be heard for a quarter of a mile. Then you could imagine yourself beside the Maelstrom or Niagara, and the fountains of the great deep being broken up. It was there that he had seen Dr. Gubbins's pig swept past, a cut-throat corpse, in the great February flood of two years before. Jane had said, 'All pigs cut their throats in the water'; yet Kay could not understand how they could, as they never had any razors. Jane did not know how they could, either, but affirmed the melancholy fact.

The Bat swerved down towards those foundations of the mill which overlooked the eddy. 'Come in after me,

through that hole where the big stone has fallen,' he said.

The Bat led the way along the hole into what once might have been a part of the cellar of the mill. It was a rather damp, dark place, lit by a greenish glitter, which Kay did not understand. A hairy thing, which smelt very strongly of fish, rose up out of the gloom.

'Come in, Master Kay,' Tom Otter said, 'and welcome to our poor abode. Damp but pleasant, as we say. That greenish light that you see is the water. It comes right up here and the moon shines through it, which gives that effect. Would you like to taste a bit of fish? We've got very pretty trout. Or what you might prefer is to put on otter pads and a skin and come on down for a swim.'

'I'd love that,' Kay said.

The Otter produced an otter skin with pads attached. Kay put it on.

'There's really nothing like the water, is there?' the Otter said. 'I'll show you some queer things down there beneath the water. You'll find that you'll be able to see, when you get down.'

'I'll just take a cruise above the falls,' the Bat said. 'The gnats are at their best in this weather.'

After he had gone the Otter led Kay into the water. In a moment he found himself in the eddy, from which he could see the current of the stream running away in glittering streaks.

'Dive now,' the Otter said. 'There's nothing so lovely as the water at the foot of the fall, where it comes down all white and goes up as bubbles. And stuck there in the crevices of the hatches you'll find all sorts of odd things.'

Sure enough, Kay did see all sorts of odd things. The bones of Dr. Gubbins's pig, the skeleton of a pike with his teeth still fixed through the web-foot of the skeleton of a duck, two addled swan's eggs, bits of old branches as white as bone and the bow half of a tin gunboat, which had once been the joy of his heart, now sunk beneath the waves fast by her native shore.

'Of course, things are quiet now,' the Otter said. 'We don't get the fishing nor anything else that we used to have. The river used to be much wilder, but still in a flood it's wild enough for anyone. A thing that you'll like is to dive down here and come up in these little twists and eddies and then dive down again. Of course, we can't do that when the spates are on.'

When they were weary of this happy pastime, the Otter said, 'Now I'll show you another thing. Those beastly otter hounds have been after me more than once. They never can make out where I go to. I go to a place here, which they have never suspected. The entrance is a spring in the river-bed. Come on down with me.'

He dived down into the heart of the current into an upward eddy of water far colder than the water of the river. Kay could see a fissure in the rock of the river bed, from which this cold water gushed. Some little fish, which were tickling their bellies with the chill of the eddies, darted away as they drew near. Kay shuddered at the cold of the spring, and had to strike out hard against its force. It was pitch dark down there in spite of his glasses; Otter seemed to be taking him down a deep well. Suddenly he shot upwards into a glimmery cave, and clambered up on to rock strewn with river-drift.

'Here is a place,' the Otter said, 'which no hound yet has ever come near. There's light, if one feels the need of that, from the chink in the rock there. There's nearly always a fish or two where the spring comes up, at the place where we dived. I could live here all the year round, only that one misses the noise of the falls. Take a look about you, Master Kay. It's a snug little place. I've dodged the hounds here twenty times, if I've dodged them once.'

Kay saw that he was in a little cave or hollow among rocks. The floor of it sloped a good deal. A sort of glimmer showed from a fissure in the rock, but one could not see through the fissure from either side. At one end of the cave the wall seemed to have been cut or wrought by men; there was a sort of shelf in it. Over the shelf, fixed to the rock, was a very old broken bone cross. 'I know what this has been,' Kay thought; 'a hermitage. It's the cell where old St. Alpig lived. That is his bed or his altar; and then, I suppose, the steps or passage he used fell in. There seems to have been a fall of rock there. I say, Mr. Otter, did you ever come across any bones of men here?'

'No,' the Otter said, 'all men have been gone from here for years.'

At this moment they heard a strange scraping and scratching noise in one corner of the cave; it seemed to come from beyond the fall of rock. 'Someone digging,' Kay whispered. 'Is it a rabbit?'

'No, that's not a rabbit,' the Otter said, showing his teeth. 'No rabbit ever dug like that.'

'Can it be men?'

'No,' Otter growled. 'Men clink when they dig, and stop to talk, and then pass round a bottle and begin again. No . . . I don't know who this could be. It's big, whoever it is. It might be Stoat. I don't exactly want Stoat coming round here. He may be all very well; but he hasn't the name for it. Down here we often get blamed for things we'd never dream of taking. But Stoat never dug like that.'

'Could it be Badger?'

'Badger?' Otter said. 'Well, I hope not. But that isn't Badger's digging. Badger growls and grunts as he digs, and sings his beastly digging song.'

'What is that?' Kay asked.

'Mind, I say nothing against Badger. To see him go for a wasps' nest is to see real courage. Then his teeth are simply superb; there's no other word for them. But he is rather a joke. He growls down into the ground before he begins— "I'm as good a man as you are, and so I'll show you." Then he scuffles out the earth and sings to it.

'"First I'll dig a this way,
Then I'll dig a that way,
Then I'll dig a criss way,
Then I'll dig.
Then I'll dig a one way,
Then I'll dig a two way,
Then I'll dig a run way,
Then I'll dig."'

The scratching noise continued.

'Don't tell me that that's Badger,' the Otter said. 'Badger never dug like that. I don't at all like that snuffling noise, that sort of woofing noise.'

'Why, what do you think it is?' Kay asked.

'I hardly like to say,' the Otter whispered, 'but it's that beastly kind of woofing noise that the hounds make when they go blowing along at the holes on the river bank. If they find a way in from that side, which they never have before, this place won't be safe. He's coming nearer, too.'

Presently the unseen digger stopped from his scratching and scrabbling. He cleared the earth from his muzzle and began to sing in a most unmusical voice:

'When the afternoon's quiet brought peace to the soul
I spied a white duck on a pond,
I asked the sweet creature to come for a stroll,
And, though she did peck a bit,
I wrung her white neck a bit,
Ho says Rollickem Bitem.

'Then, strolling along in the field by the mill,
I spied a grey gosling at grass,
Who found me all hungry and left me all still,
For a goose in digestion
Solves every harsh question.
Ho says Rollickem Bitem.'

'It's Bitem,' Kay said. 'Is that you, Bitem?'

'Yes,' said Bitem on the other side of the stone.

'Is that you, Kay?' Nibbins's voice asked. 'What are you doing?'

'I'm in here with Otter,' Kay said.

'Well, look here, Kay,' Nibbins said. 'Do please shove this stone aside, if you can get at it from your side. We've been having adventures, Bitem and I, and we're dead beat. Can we get out your way?'

'You'll have to swim for it,' Kay said.

'Well, shove the stone aside, Kay, and let's have a look. Even a swim is better than what we've been having.'

With a good deal of trouble Kay managed to get the stone to one side; Bitem and Nibbins came pushing through into the cave. Both were out of breath and covered with earth. They lay down panting.

'They've turned poor old Bitem out of his quarry-earth,' Nibbins said. 'Roper Bilges sent the news of it to the hound master, who had it all stopped up for the season, just as poor old Bitem had got it all into order with all the bolt-holes bored. So I told him that I knew of a place near the old lime kiln here, a place that I've sometimes come mousing in. I did a bit of batting there too, when I was young, but we won't mention that to Bat. Well, we came along to look at it and prowled around in it. Then, while we were grubbing for a bolt-hole, suddenly, bang, the floor gave way beneath us and down we came. I never saw such a place. We fell fifty yards, I should think, by the feel. We couldn't get back through the hole that we fell from; we couldn't reach it, or near it. Then we both thought that our only chance would be to dig down to the river this way and then swim for it, but the stone was so hard that we'd almost—at least, I'd almost—given up hope. Of course, it takes a lot to make old Bitem give up hope.'

'You'd both be the better for a bit of fish,' the Otter said. 'Would you like it fresh or some that's been hung a bit?'

'I like it well hung,' Bitem said. 'But Nibbins here would like it fresh, I'm sure.'

'Well, I'll bring you a bit of both,' the Otter said.

While Otter was fetching the fish, which took a minute or two, Nibbins said, 'I'm not at all sure, Kay, that you oughtn't to have a look at what is beyond there. There's a very queer smell.'

'Do you think it's treasure?' Kay said.

'Well, it's a very rich smell,' Nibbins said, 'a cellary smell. You ought to smell it, anyway.'

'What sort of thing is it that smells?' Kay asked.

'There's round things and there's square things,' Bitem said. 'Neither is good to eat.'

'You've got things like that,' Nibbins said, 'in the cellar, Kay. Take a look.'

It was not so easy to take a look. Kay pushed through with Bitem and Nibbins into the cave, which was pitch dark, but very much more spacious than the one in which he had been sitting. He could see little there. There was hardly a ray of light. He groped with his hands and felt walls of rock. Groping downwards, he felt something like bales of sacking tied with strips of leather, further on were some small casks lying on their sides. A fragrance that was sweetish, heavy and rather sickly came upon him from these barrels. It was a little like the smell in the decanter cupboard of the side-board, when the stoppers had been left out.

'That's the kind of thing that we came down on,' Bitem said. 'However, Nibbins always falls on his feet, and I've been used to falling anyhow since those beasts in red first came after me.'

'But where did you fall from?' Kay asked. 'Do you mean to say that you fell through the roof?'

'I should think we did,' Bitem said.

Kay put up his hand, but could feel no roof above him.

'It's getting lighter, now,' Nibbins said. 'You'll be able to see in a minute. There. Perhaps you can see now. Yes, there's the hole we fell through.'

Far above their heads was a hole in the rock of the cave. Part of a broken and rotten ladder was still fixed to it: men must at one time have used the place as a cellar.

'It's a wonder you weren't both killed,' Kay said.

'I'd never suspected a place like this,' Nibbins said. 'It's just a little ordinary sort of place up above, that you have to squeeze through.'

By this time, Kay was able to see the cave; it was like a very dark old church, with stalactites dripping from the roof. In the lower end of the cave were tiers of barrels and cases.

'I know what this is,' Kay said. 'It's the cellar where the Moonlight People put their brandy and tobacco, and those are some which they never removed. Now Piney Trigger worked the Moonlight business; supposing he brought the treasure here . . . Supposing it isn't brandy but the treasure . . .?'

'I say,' Otter said, 'it's almost sunrise. You'd better be off, Kay, with Bat here. Slip off your otter skin and put on your bat's wings.'

Bat helped him to put on his wings. 'Come quickly,' he said. 'It's a great deal later than I thought.' As he led the way up, through the hole by which Nibbins had fallen, Kay called to him:

'How will Nibs and Bitem get out? They'll be drowned if they try to swim, and they can't climb.'

'Otter will manage something,' Bat said. 'Come on quickly, I've only got a few minutes left. Creep along this passage here. Now here we are in the ruined lime-kiln.'

They crept out over some fallen stones of the kiln (which still smelt of the warm, rank taint of Bitem's passing) into the overcast summer morning not yet light. The leaves of the trees hung heavily, occasionally dripping; there was a good deal of mist about. Not far up the road, as they flew, Kay caught sight of the backs of four labourers, with pickaxes over their shoulders, shambling drowsily to their work. They were going very slowly. Two of them carried lanterns, one of them had a coil of rope slung about his neck, all four were plastered with the rather pale clay of near the river.

'They're going early to work,' Kay said.

'They're going from work,' Bat said. 'They've been working by the river all night. Look how tired they all are.'

Indeed, as he spoke, the four exhausted men sat down on a heap of stones by the road, one of them seemed to fall asleep at once. The other three were dazed stupid with tiredness and nodded forward as they sat. Kay knew them as he flew over them. Two were the knights whom Arthur had sent with Edward 'to see if they could find the treasure,' only the night before; the third was Edward; the fourth, the sleeper, was poor little Brown Bear. Could they have been looking for the treasure in the river? They were sopping wet. They looked so utterly miserable and discouraged, that it was plain that they had found nothing. 'That's where the treasure will be,' Kay thought, 'sunk in the river, deep in the mud, where no one will ever find it. I never thought to ask Otter about it.'

'O, Edward,' he cried, 'cheer up. And do come home . . .'

Edward lifted his weary head and stared stupidly at him.

'I'm Kay, I'm not a bat,' Kay cried.

'Come on,' Bat said, tugging him with his hooked wing. 'We haven't got a weenit to weese.'

'But I must speak to Edward.'

'Queek, queek,' the Bat said, in his shrill way. But lo, it wasn't the Bat that said queek, queek. Kay was sitting up in his bed in full daylight. The curtain-rings were saying queek, queek as they clinked in the wind.

'A very good morning,' somebody was saying, 'for a dance round the Liberty Tree.' There was nobody there. The Bat, the heap of stones and the four dog-tired companions were all gone; yet somebody had said those words . . . 'dance round the Liberty Tree.'

'I don't know about dance,' Kay said. 'But I'll go to the Liberty Tree. I'll take a measuring tape, I'll see if there are three big yews, and I'll have a trowel to dig with, in case.'

• • • • •

It did not take him long to reach the Liberty Tree in Corselaydead Wood. As Ellen had said, 'There was Liberty cut on it,' though the bark had almost overgrown the cuts. Sure enough, a hundred yards south from the Liberty Tree brought him to the centre of a space between three big yew trees. Ten minutes of trowelling there brought him to . . . There in the earth among the yew roots was a roll of something much decayed and worm-eaten, containing something heavy. It was a mildewed, rotted leather, wrapped round mildewed, rotted tarpaulin, wrapped round something that had once been wood. Inside the wood was more leather, which might once have been a money-bag. Inside this was a tin box about the size of the saddle soap-box in the harness-room of the stable. Inside this was something done up in an old silk handkerchief. Inside this was something of a sort that he had seen in the clockmaker's shop, an old gold watch fatter than the governess's table clock. It was very big; it had a dial for the seconds as well as for the hours; there was an engraved inscription on the back:—

> 'Presented to Sir Hassle Gassle, Bart., by the members of the Condicote Hunt, as a small tribute to his manly Probity and truly British Sportsmanship, in which the Virtues of the Citizen and the Cheerfulness of the Companion have been signally united. April 17th, 1810. God Save the King.'

'I know what it is then,' Kay said. 'Of course, this is Benjamin's treasure. This is the repeater watch which he took from Sir Hassle Gassle, "that Sir Hassle mourned to his dying day," as Ellen said. I'll take it at once to the present Sir Hassle.'

The church clock was chiming for nine o'clock when he passed beneath the baronet's arms upon the gateway. The arms were three hassles gassle's, muzzly, and the supporters two gassles showing their teeth. Kay's heart sank when he heard the chimes; he would be at least an hour late for breakfast.

He crossed the flagged courtyard to the door, where a long bell handle of twisted iron, when vigorously pulled, made a faint ting to sound in the east wing of the house far away. Presently, after he had rung half a dozen times, a footman opened the door, and told him that there was no need to have rung so often, since people weren't deaf, and what did he want, ringing like that? Kay recognised the footman as Roper Bilges' brother, who had been at the ducking of Blackmalkin.

'Please,' Kay said, 'I was afraid the bell wasn't working properly. I want to see Sir Hassle Gassle on very important business.'

'Sir Hassle is at breakfast. What is your business?'

'It's private.'

'You'd best write to Sir Hassle, then,' the man said, 'and make an appointment when to see him. That's the rule with private business, you ought to know that.' He was about to close the door, when young Lady Gassle, dressed for riding, crossed the hall on her way to breakfast. She was a very beautiful young woman, with eyes so bright and teeth so white that she always seemed more alive than anybody in the room with her.

'Why, it's little Kay Harker,' she said. 'Don't shut the door, Bilges. What is it, Kay? Do you come to see me?'

'No, please, Lady Gassle. I wanted to speak to Sir Hassle.'

'Well, come in,' she said. 'We're breakfasting. Have you breakfasted?'

'No, not yet, Lady Gassle.'

'Come in, then, and breakfast. What a pickle you're in, though. Have you been taking a toss? Let me just mop you up a little and get some of the earth off.'

When she had tidied him a little, she took him into the big, bright breakfast-room, which had a red and blue Axminster carpet on the floor, shining red mahogany furniture, six big paintings of thoroughbred hunters, a gleaming globe of the world, and Sir Hassle at breakfast, with *The Times* propped against the coffee pot.

'You owe me that gold watch and chain, my Polly,' he said. 'Kem is in for the Grasslands.'

'What majority?'

'Sixty-seven, a very near thing. Hullo. Who's this? Kay Harker? Coming to breakfast? Right. Are you a pork-pie man or just an egg man?'

'Please, a pork-pie man; and, if you please, I've found your grandfather's gold watch, that Benjamin, the highway-man, took.'

'Well, I'm blest,' Sir Hassle said.

'That will just do for the gold watch and chain I owe you over the election,' his wife said.

'Of all the things I ever knew happen,' Sir Hassle said, when he had examined the watch, 'this is just about the neatest. It's the thing my grandfather worried over till he died; and it worried my father, too, and it's a great pleasure to me to get it back. And all the Hunt will be delighted, too. It has been very well preserved, too; it will be possible to get it to go again. I shall owe you a big debt, Kay. What can I do for you? You must think, and let me know.'

'Please,' Kay said, 'when you go hunting, will you please not hunt a fox, who is a good fox, really, and very nice, who may live somewhere down not far from where the old mill once stood.'

'Well, if he's a good fox and very nice and a friend of yours,' Sir Hassle said, 'and you tell him not to go goosing and henning among the farms down there, I dare say we shall be able to do without him.'

It was now half-past ten, an hour after lesson-time. He could not imagine what she would do to him. Lady Gassle guessed that he might be wanted for lessons. She asked her husband to take Kay in front of him on his hack, which he did. Kay rode all the way, and learned a lot about horses, how this one was called Old Joe, and how they remembered everything, and how clever they are and how nervy.

'But if you're so fond of horses,' Sir Hassle said, 'you ought to come up on Wednesday and Saturdays, at eleven, and ride with my little boy, Bill. Would you like that?'

'Oh, I should think I should.'

'Well, come along then on Saturday.'

'Please, I don't think I should be allowed.'

'That's all my eye and Betty Martin, you won't be allowed. I'll get my wife to write about it.'

• • • • •

When they reached Seekings House, Ellen was in a fine taking. 'Whatever have you been doing, Master Kay, going out like this without your breakfast and never a word?'

'He's been breakfasting with me,' Sir Hassle said. This was excuse enough for the moment, but when the Hassle Gassles had ridden away she turned on him again.

'It's lucky for you that your governess had to go off to Russell's Dene again,' she said. 'They sent the carriage for her just before breakfast, so she doesn't know about you; otherwise I don't know what she'd have said. And whatever have you done to your pyjama coat to get it all over fish scales?'

This came from wearing otter-skin, Kay thought, but before he could answer, Ellen went on: 'I couldn't let you wear it again in that state, I've had to wash it. And then, another thing, poor little Nibbins is missing; he wasn't in last night and he hasn't been in all morning. Jane and I think that Bilges the Keeper has shot him, for he always shoots cats, though he's got no business to. And I don't know what we'll do without little Nibbins.'

• • • • •

'Yes,' Kay thought, 'Abner has sent for her because he has found some clue. And the fish scales on the pyjamas show that last night wasn't a dream, but real. And the treasure is down in the cave by the mill, and poor little Nibs and old Bitem are down in the cave and can't get out, unless they try swimming and get drowned. And if Abner *has* got a clue by incantation, and goes to the cave for the treasure, he'll find them both there and shoot them. What am I to do?'

'Ah, that's what,' said a voice behind him. Rat, the cellar-man, was standing there, smearing his mouth with his paw. He looked much more seedy than formerly, having newly come from the dust-bin.

'Well,' he said sourly, 'and what are you looking at *me* for? *I* ain't done nothing; I never didn't; not never. It wasn't never Rat done it. You thinks acos I don't wear no pyjamas all over fish scales as I larders and I sculleries, but I don't; I only dust-bins; except sometimes I rubbish-heaps. And what's dust-bins? Glass bottles, mostly, what's empty. What's dust-heaps? Old tins what's been under the tap. And what's life? That's what.'

'I've saved a bit of bacon-rind for you,' Kay said. 'It's here, in my soap-dish.'

Rat took the bacon-rind without joy and without thanks; he ate it in a greasy sideways sort of way, with a good deal of bolting. However, when it was down he was a different being.

'As neat a bit of rind,' he said, 'as ever I stummikked. He put me in mind of a bit of rind as maybe you, what lives on such, may have forgotten, but what a pore cellar-man, what don't get, no not the smell of rind, not twist in a year, does dwell on down in the dark, ah, many a long day. He wasn't thrown out on no dust-bin, but took to the hens, and the sun cooked him beautiful, ah, he *was* a rind, he was. But what I says is a cellar's a cellar, ain't it, and a friend's a friend, ain't he?'

'Yes,' Kay said, 'certainly.'

'Ah, you admits it now,' Rat said, 'and nicely you shows it. You ain't stirred neither paw nor tooth for your friends, though you've been back hours. Here's Bat come digging at me, saying, "You go and see if he's gone to help them, acos they're down there and can't get out, unless they gets drownded trying." So I says, "But if he knows they're here, he'll help them." "No," Bat says. "He mayn't. He may be took by such. And *I* can't go," Bat says, "acos I can't see in this here flaming daylight that is my distraction. But Nibbins and Bitem," he said, "is down there in agonies, and what'll help 'em if Kay don't?" That's what.'

'But how can I help them?' Kay asked.

Rat didn't answer this, but walked to the door and beckoned to him to follow. Just outside the door, he shoved back the tread of a stair, and motioned to him to enter the opening. Kay found it fairly light inside. In the darker corners some bats hung, fast asleep.

'Them's them as bacon-rind is flung away on,' Rat said. 'They thinks scorn of rind. Gnats is their joy, and they're partial to a midge. But here's what . . .'

He had opened a panel in the wainscoting of a little

room which Kay recognised at once.

It was Mrs. Pouncer's cupboard; there were the magical books, the gums and unguents; the cloaks, masks and hats had been removed. 'They will be doing magic in them,' Kay thought.

'That's what,' Rat whispered.

'Of course it is,' Kay said.

He saw at once what to do; he took down from the shelf a pair of one league shoes, the magic lantern, a ladder, a rope and an extra pair of spectacles.

'And him,' Rat said, pointing to one of the baskets.

'You mean, to carry the things in?' Kay asked.

'No, I don't mean,' Rat said.

'What then?'

'Acos,' Rat said, 'I seen her one time say to one of them, "Goose," and in come a cold goose with sassingers. Then she said, "Rabbit pie," and in come a rabbit pie. And if you was to say, "Raw goose" and "raw rabbit," when down there with your two friends, it might be the saving of their pore lives.'

'I'll certainly do that,' Kay said.

'Ah,' Rat said. 'Yet I notice you never stop to think what you might say so as to rejoice a pore cellarman what toils in dust-bins for a living he don't get.'

'What can I say for you?' Kay asked.

'There was a thing come here once in the summer,' Rat said. 'He come done up so as he wouldn't burst, but he did burst; and he was to have come quick, but he didn't come quick, and so the sun got at him. And he was very baggy and people called him a Naggy. And he made folk go very white at dinner time, so you flung him away; but I didn't fling him away. No, I put him away and wished he was more. Now you just come into this little passage and hold that basket; then, if you will say Naggy, perhaps he'll come for you.'

'I know what you mean,' Kay said. 'The haggis . . .' He went into the passage, held the basket, and said, 'Haggis.'

Instantly there came a puddingy flump in the basket; a cold, bulging, blobby thing had fallen into it. 'Here you are, Rat,' he said, 'take it, will you?'

'Ah, that's what,' Rat said, taking it. 'Now you put on your shoes in here. You can get out at that jackdaw's place at the end.' As Kay sat down to put on the shoes, he heard Rat passing along the passage to the cellars singing a song:

> 'Of all the foods as good as tart,
> There's none like pretty Naggy;
> He warms the cockles of my heart,
> Though he is so cold and baggy.
>
> 'What though the wise eat mutton pies,
> Or pasties made of staggy,
> To all the wise I makes replies,
> Give me my pretty Naggy.
>
> 'O let my jaw lay down and gnaw
> Until my teeth are jaggy,
> Both cooked and raw the Scots whae ha
> My ain braw sonsie Naggy.'

Kay was not sure of the last lines, because, when Rat was singing them, he was whisking through the jackdaw's place under the eaves, holding his laden basket. He had slipped on the one league shoes, which were like scarlet goloshes of soft leather, then he had stamped one foot down, to make his shoe fit into it, and lo, away he had whisked, through the hole, over the garden, over the hill, over the wood, across Mile Meadow, which was said to be the best grass for milk in the seven counties, then along Yell Brooks, across Foxpits, then down, quite out of breath, at the third milestone. He had just time to say: 'That makes one league,' when he was off again. This time it was fun, because he was up among a company of rooks, who were changing their pasture. He had always longed to be among rooks.

'Hurraw,' they said, 'Hyaw's Kaw,' meaning, 'Hurray, here's Kay.' But in an instant, Kay was past them and coming down by Seven Springs to Condicote Old Mill, to the ruined lime-kiln where the entrance was. Luckily, no one was about.

He slipped off the red goloshes, lest they should take him further, then he put on his fox-eye spectacles, then he tied the basket round his neck, then he took out the lantern and examined the entrance. It seemed to him that no one had been there since he had left with Bat. He crept into the old cellar or stable from which Nibbins and Bitem had fallen. He peered down through the gap in the floor, and called: 'Nibs, Nibs, Nibs.'

'Is that you, Kay?'

'Yes, are you all right?'

'Well, we're feeling rather lost, as we couldn't face the look of the river when Otter showed it to us, and didn't quite know that you'd be able to help. But don't speak quite so loud, if you don't mind; we'll explain why presently.'

'I'll come down,' Kay said.

He was pulling out the rope-ladder to a proper length,

when he began to puzzle how to secure the end. 'I wish,' he said, 'I wish I had somebody here to tie the ends to the rocks so that they won't slip.' Instantly an invisible someone took the ladder from his hands, secured it to the rocks near him, went down it, secured the lower ends below, came back up it, said, 'Ladder-ends tied securely' (in a tinny, clicky voice, like a biscuit-tin lid being put on to the tin), and disappeared; that was one of the results of having a wish-basket.

Kay went down the ladder. Bitem and Nibbins were overjoyed to see him. Neither Bitem nor Nibbins was hungry, as Otter had given them a trout. He heard a noise as though a pick-axe were being plied against the wall of the cave from somewhere on the other side. He heard the click of the pick and the falling of stones after each blow.

'That is why I said don't speak quite so loud,' Nibbins said. 'They've been at it ever since daylight. They're digging into the wall from some other cave. If you come over here you will hear them.'

Kay went quietly to the wall of the cave. There the noise was so clear that it was possible to hear the voices of the workers when they stopped working. Whoever they were, they were not Edward and the Guards. Kay could make out that there were always two pick-axes working at the same time, for five minutes at a spell; then there came a pause, during which the broken stone was shovelled away; then the picking began again.

'They're a lot of people there,' Nibbins said, 'and they're making as little noise as possible; you'll notice that they don't sing; and they're getting within the last yard. Those picks will soon be through.'

'They will,' Otter said; 'they will be through in no

time, and that will mean another way into my place where I've been so snug. It may seem very selfish of me, but do you think, Kay, that you could block up the hole you made into my den, so that it won't be noticed?'

'I'll try,' Kay said. 'You go back into your den, and I will wish.'

He had no sooner wished, than invisible someones came silently, blocked up the approach to Otter's lair, tinnily reported, 'Entrance blocked securely,' and disappeared.

'That's your third wish,' Nibbins said. 'You'll get nothing more out of that basket this time until you've gone a league and crossed running water; that's how those things work.'

'Nibs,' Kay whispered, 'do you think that the diggers there are the Pouncer Seven?'

'They may be.'

'If they are, why don't they use the wish-basket?'

'You can only use a wish-basket for good things,' Nibbins said, 'so you may be sure that they don't use it much.'

'Where's Bitem gone?' Kay asked, looking round.

'He never says when he's going; he goes,' Nibbins said.

The picks at this moment struck some rotten piece of rock. One of the workers cried: 'Look out, she's coming.' On the instant there came a crashing fall as though all the roof had given way. There was a half-minute's pause, then the voice of Abner Brown sounded very distinctly through the rocks as he tapped with a hammer.

'That was a good clearance,' he said. 'Hark at the taps. Two or three more like the last will fetch us through. You can hear how hollow it is on the other side.'

The man called dear Brother Venom began to sing:

'Now Midnights All, my Fellow Six,
Just one more little spell of picks.
My Right Toes prickle on the mould,
Which shows that they are near to Gold.
My Left Toes twiddle in their shoe,
Which shows that there is silver, too.'

'Now, no singing,' Abner said. 'When we've copped the dibs we'll carol. Come on, Picks All.'

The voices and the pick-axes seemed so near that it was like having them in the next room.

'They'll get the treasure now,' Kay thought, 'if it's here. But is it here?'

He held up the lantern, over the casks and cases stowed at the lower end of the cave; he counted twenty-nine small wooden tubs, thirteen small puncheons of green glass, and eleven flat wooden boxes, some of which had rotted through, showing mildewed silk, rotted lace, and fungus where tobacco had been. 'This is not the treasure,' he said. 'These are things left by the Moonlighters.'

'Well, come along,' Nibbins whispered. 'Quick, before they break through upon us. Don't let us be caught by the Seven.'

'Wait a minute,' Kay said, 'I must just look round.'

'Oh, don't. Come along.'

'No. I want to see.'

'Well, I'm going,' Nibbins said.

Kay let him go, while he looked round the cave; there was no other treasure than the spirits. 'It isn't here,' he said. 'It will be a fine squish for the Seven when they break through.'

He noticed that at some time, long before, there had

been a heavy fall of rock at the landward side of the cave. Thinking that the fall might have buried the treasure, he walked to that side to look at it; something was there, lying on the ground.

It was not treasure, but the skeleton of a man, lying on his side in the rags of his clothes. He clutched a rusty knife in one hand, and the tin door of his broken lantern (which lay at a little distance from him) in the other. He had been scratching something on the tin at the time of his death. Kay picked up the piece of tin to read the writing, but at that instant, oh horror, there came another crash of rock followed by a cheer of 'Hurray, the pick's gone through.'

Kay did not wait another second; he pocketed the inscribed tin and hopped up the ladder after Nibbins. When they were at the point of coming out into the open air, Nibbins suddenly stopped him. '*She* is there,' he whispered. 'Just outside.'

Almost on the instant the voices of the pick-axe men, Abner and Venom, were heard outside calling:

'Mrs. Pouncer . . . Mrs. Pouncer. . . . Come on down. We've put a pick-head right through the rock into a cave as big as a wine-vault. We'll all be through into it in an hour or two, like into Tom Tiddler's Ground, picking up gold and silver.'

'How wonderful,' Mrs. Pouncer said. 'But what are those things you are carrying?'

'Yes, what *are* they?' Abner said. 'We found them in the outer cave. People had been digging there only this morning. Perhaps you can tell us whose they are.'

Mrs. Pouncer seemed to be examining the things.

'A handkerchief marked *Edward*,' she said, 'a collar marked *Brown Bear*, an old hat marked *Robin Pointnose*, a

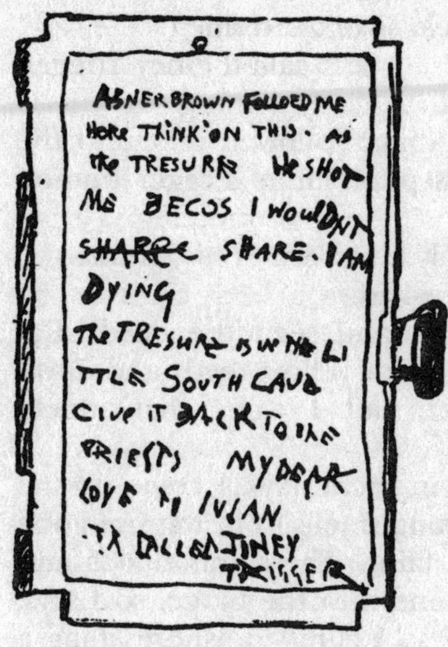

knight's cloak buckle, with the device of the Plough-stars, and a coloured waist-coat marked *Bruno Bree.* No . . . I really cannot say whose they are. But they must be the things of enemies, for, do you know, just as you began to bring them here I began to feel that pricking in my toes which tells me that enemies are near, about to thwart us.'

'Let us get back to the digging, then,' Brother Venom said.

'Yes; come; it's just upstream from here: and I pity whoever tries to thwart us now.'

As soon as they had gone, Kay slipped on the scarlet shoes, took up Nibbins, stepped out with his foot, and in another minute was in his bedroom. Nibbins ran away at once to purr to Ellen for the milk and sardine which she always gave to cats which had been missing. Kay looked at the piece of tin which he had taken from the dead man's hand. The oblong door of the lantern had been scratched with a knife-point thus, on the inner silvered side:

Abner Brown followed me here, thinking this was the treasure. He shot me because I wouldn't share. I am dying. The Treasure is in the little South Cave. Give it back to the priests. My dear love to Susan.

T.P. called Piney Trigger.

'There it is,' Kay said. 'Abner followed him into the cave and shot him. That is poor Piney Trigger himself that is lying there.'

'That's what,' Rat suddenly answered at his elbow.

'How do you know?' Kay asked.

'Acos I knowed the party, and seen the deed,' Rat answered. 'You think acos I got yellow teeth and a tail as I wot not what's what, but I wot's that which, howsomedever.

'I was marine cellarman in them days. I come up the river in a barge wot had strong smells in it, but not good to eat, only to sniff when faint. There was floods and bangings, and the water come into the barge, so I says, "I'd better get out of this," so I climbed ashore along a rope.

'Ah, and I need to hold on, too, doing it.

'There was a strong smell when I come ashore, so I followed it.

'I got down into a cave by the smell, and was just settling in, when in come a stout but pale party, with a lantern. He goes all about, looking at the casks and things and making notes and muttering. "So you're a cellarman, too," I says.

'Suddenly in come a white-haired party with another lantern. "Now, Ben Trigger," he says, "I've tracked you down," he says. "Are you going to share? I want half."

' "You can want," the other says. "You'll get nothing out of me, except another tooth out."

'Then BANG goes the white-haired man's pistol, and the other party falls. I was so scared of the bang, it did so clang, that I run out into the night.

'Bye and bye, the white-haired man comes out, all shakey and twittery, "I've killed him dead, and after all it isn't there . . . the treasure isn't there . . . and now I'm a doomed man. . . . Oh, what shall I do? Oh, why did I shoot? I didn't mean nothing, except just to scare him. . . ."

'And at that he goes too close to the bank, which was all rotten with the rain, and the bank had a bush on it, and bank, bush and he went swoosh into the river, which was all one foaming roar. It spun him right out into the white, and he go on screaming just like a pig, but not for long in a roar like that.

'I went back to the cave. The pale man had broken his lantern, so I ate his candle and come away. I don't like being cellarman where there are bangs; but if you ask what was what about what you know, I say that that's what.'

'Yes,' Kay said, 'that was what, I see it all. And by this time, I expect the Seven will have found the little south cave, and taken all the treasure.

'O, I wish that Edward and the others could have found it.

'I wonder who would stop the Seven from having it, because it isn't theirs. Who could stop them?'

The day passed as he puzzled over the question, who could stop them. The governess was not there for dinner, nor for tea; but just as Kay was going to bed two carriages drove up, with herself and seven others. They were all very dirty, hot and cross. 'They haven't found it after all,' Kay thought.

They all came into the house. Jane was ordered to build up the fire, as everybody was to have a hot bath.

After the baths, they were to have a high tea for eight, with sixteen poached eggs, and Ellen was to go to Farmer Chesses and bring two pounds of fresh butter and a quart of cream, because they had had such an exhausting day exploring the ancient history. 'And mind the tea is strong,' Abner said, 'for we shall all be up all night at this.'

'Yes, please see that the tea is very strong, Jane,' the governess said. 'And, Ellen, you might call at Mr. Clove's for a pound of his special tea; and Mr. Brown would like some of the Invalid's Brandy, that is in the cellar to mix with his tea, so please bring up a bottle, or rather, two bottles, for the others might like a little too. And as we are rather short of cakes, please go to the bakers and ask for any fresh crumpets, for there is nothing more delicious than hot crumpets thickly buttered and spread with sugar.'

As they were now beginning to come upstairs, Kay hopped into bed, where he very soon fell fast asleep.

He had slept for some little time, when he felt himself rudely shaken by the arm. He woke up to find the room full of light, as before. Nibbins was on his bed, shaking him.

'Wake up, Kay,' he said, 'wake up. We haven't got a moment to lose. I've only just been able to dodge her and get here.'

'What is it?' Kay said.

'No more witchcraft for me,' Nibbins said, 'after what I've gone through this evening. They caught me fast asleep in my chair after they'd had tea, and they took me up to their black room, as they call it. I knew when I saw the black room and all the Seven, as well as Abner, that they were going to do something awful . . . and I can tell you they did.'

'But what did they do?' Kay said.

'Do?' Nibbins said. 'What didn't they do? First they tried all the simple witchcraft. A fellow wouldn't object to that. There's nothing in that, it's rather fun. But when that didn't do any good, they said that they'd have to use stronger measures.'

'But I still don't understand,' Kay said, trying hard to wake up. 'What were they trying to do?'

'Why, to find the treasure, because they said that others were working against them, and they meant to find it first. They tried things that make my blood run cold, awful things; but they could get no clue. Then Mrs. Pouncer said, "Well, we'll find out who it is that's thwarting us," so they tried that. They asked it three times, and each time they got the answer, "Kay and his friends." Then Abner said, "O, indeed. Really. Right. We'll give Kay and his friends such a change as they little expect." They'll be here in a minute; any minute. Come along, Kay, quick.'

'Where to?' Kay said.

'Out of here, first. Quick. There are their steps in the corridor.'

Sure enough, there were their steps. Kay and Nibbins had barely time to slip through the little door in the wainscot, and bolt it behind them, before the Seven were in the bedroom.

Kay and Nibbins ran down the corridor into the garden. As they came out into the night, they ran into someone; they thought for an instant that it was Abner, but it was Bitem eating a rabbit. He knew at once that the hunt was up.

'Right,' he cried. 'Jump on my back, Kay. Hold me

round the neck; I can manage. . . .'

In a minute they were over the wall; the church clock then striking one.

'Down into the town, Bitem,' Nibbins said. 'They'll never think we went there.' They saw the lanterns of the Seven in the garden, all moving away from them. 'I was only just in time,' Nibbins whispered. 'We'd only a minute to spare.'

In a few minutes, they paused for breath in the street of the little town, which stretched to right and left in the silence of the moonlight. All the townspeople were abed; even Pimply Whatto. All the houses were shuttered, no lights shone in the windows; not even a cat moved along the broad green shaded with trees, where the stocks still stood beside the whipping post.

'We're not pursued,' Nibbins said. 'It's all right.'

'I don't know that it's all right,' Bitem said. 'This isn't exactly the kind of place that's all right for me. They've got scores against me that you little wot of, Nibbins, all of them. I'd a guinea-fowl out of that one. I'd three hens and a cock out of that one. At least you can't count the cock; he was the toughest I ever. Then, that one with the gate, he was turkeys, very innocent young things, very mealy. Then that one was ducks, just the three, if I remember; then that other one was a goose, and that one was a clutch of chickens. Then there was tame rabbits there, very juicy they was, only furry to the gullet, if you understand. There was only a guinea-pig there, nothing on him, but worth it just to try. Then in that one she thought that she'd shut me out, but she'd really shut me in. Nineteen they counted the next morning, but she didn't see me, because I got out while she swounded.'

'What we ought to do,' Nibbins said, 'is to cross

running water. That upsets magic.'

'Well, we have crossed running water,' Bitem said. 'There's an underground brook runs under here. Many's the time I've gone along it.'

'Are you sure of that, Bitem?' Nibbins said.

'Well, of course, I'm sure.'

Nibbins stopped still and began to shake.

'It's all very well,' he said, 'to be free from them for the moment, but we've got to go back. It's to-morrow morning that I'm thinking of.'

'Never you think about to-morrow morning,' Bitem said. 'You just be thankful that you're not caught to-day. If you'd been hunted like what I've been hunted, the hounds coming on you in the middle of your sweet sleep and you not expecting them nor hearing them, no, but just dreaming of your last juicy bit of gosling, all yellow fat . . . Ah, if you'd gone through that and heard the horn and the horses, and seen their sharp teeth, and run all day in front of thirty of them . . . Ah, if you'd done that and got away at the end, you wouldn't think about any to-morrow. No. "Let to-morrow fend for itself," you'd say, "but this is bliss." '

'What in the wide world is this?' Kay asked, interrupting.

Coming up the centre of the road that led from the river was a procession of small carts drawn by sturdy horses under escort. Kay looked at the carts and recognised them. There in front were the two which he had owned; they were very good ones which tipped up and had tailboards that came out. Then there was little Bill Gassle's cart and little Dick's cart from the Rectory and Charles's and Brian's carts from the Squire's. Then there were all the brand-new shining blue, yellow and scarlet carts from the village toy-shop; and a lot more carts, which he didn't recognise at all. But marching in front of the long procession of loaded carts was a figure, whom he thought never to see again. It was Edward in his fullest uniform, in his coat with the piping down the edges, his gun slung in a bandolier and his rapier at his side.

'Edward,' he cried.

'Ha, Kay,' Edward said in his usual extravagant manner 'I've got the treasure. We've jolly well got the treasure for you, Kay. We've been a long time about it, but, when I give my mind to a thing, I carry it through.'

'You mean you got it from the little south cave?' Kay asked.

'Yes, out of the little south cave: and it's going under the hearth-stone in your room before to-night's much older. And don't you have any fear, Kay. We're the guards, we are. We hear that the house has gone all to sixes and sevens since we left it, but that's going to be remedied now.'

Nibbins burst into tears of joy.

'Edward and the guards come back,' he cackled. 'Now there won't be any more witchcraft.'

'And are you going to the house, now?' Kay asked.

'Going straight there. Come on.'

'Look out, then,' Nibbins said, 'for they're all there, looking for us.'

'There's nothing I like better,' Edward said, 'than to have my enemy looking for me; then I don't have to look for him. Come on, boys.'

When they reached the garden, Nibbins said: 'Be careful, now. Halt the carts. They'll have sentries posted at the doors, you may be certain. Yes. Look. There, those little green lights near the holly; that's Blackmalkin;

those are his eyes. Greymalkin will be on the other side of the house, guarding the other doors.'

'Right,' Edward said. 'Bitem, let you and Tom creep round through the grass till you see Greymalkin; he'll probably be under the yew. Take a sack and scrobble him up in it, don't let him squeal. We'll settle what to do with him later.'

'He shan't squeal,' Bitem said. 'Nor yet won't he not gurgle.'

'We'll give you a full minute's start,' Edward said, 'to give you time to get round. Then Dogg here, and Peter Dogg, and you, Nibs, shall creep in with another sack on Blackmalkin there, scrobble *him* up and not let *him* squeal. We'll settle what to do with *him* later. Off you go, Bitem and Tom. We'll get in as soon as the guards are sacked.'

Kay saw Bitem and the rather melancholy-looking lad known as Tom steal away through the long grass. 'He's first rate for a night attack, Tom,' Edward said. 'He's so unexpected.'

After what seemed a long long time, the two Dogg cousins crept away with Nibbins. Presently Kay saw Blackmalkin's eyes glow up green. He had been pacing to and fro, and now had turned to stare in their direction. Edward nudged Kay's arm. 'Now watch,' he said.

Kay saw the green eyes become a little brighter as Blackmalkin took a few steps towards them. Then suddenly the two little lights went out. There was no squeal, nor any sound of a scuffle, only a little sigh as though somebody very thirsty had just had a cool pleasant drink. Edward nudged Kay again. 'They've bagged him,' he said. In a few minutes the two sets of scouts returned, bearing the two sentries, both neatly tied up in sacks. The Water Rat appeared at the secret door. 'You can go in,' he said. 'I've just been up part of the way. They are in a great tear and talking, all setting off for the river or somewhere.'

Kay and Edward crept up the secret stair into Kay's room. There they heard the voice of Abner Brown calling, 'Haven't you got them, Mrs. Pouncer?' and Pouncer's voice replying, 'It's too provoking. I must have put the lantern and rope somewhere, when I was tidying, and then, my one league shoes are gone.'

'Well, come on,' Abner said. 'We must do without them. After all, we've got some lights and a rope and the carriages are here.'

'I must just look a moment longer,' she said.

'Really you mustn't stay a minute longer,' Abner answered. 'We've got to get to the river and into the cave. It will be daylight before we lift anything at this rate.'

This seemed to convince Mrs. Pouncer, because she went downstairs muttering, 'It's too provoking,' and Kay heard her pass along the hall and out at the front door. Soon the noise of carriage wheels was heard on the gravel.

'That's it,' Edward said. 'They've learned where the treasure was by their magic, but they've learned it a little too late. Now come along, boys, let's get busy. All the stuff in these carts has to go underneath this hearthstone before daylight.'

There then followed a great bustle among the guards. One by one the carts were brought up and unloaded. The treasure was then carried up by hand and laid under the stone. All worked with a will. After two hours of hard work it was all stored safely away.

Kay stood with a light in the secret room looking at it

as it was carried down. First they brought in the gold and silver people which had so pleased the mermaids. Three of these were knights with swords, and one a queen-knight, leaning forward, with her hair blown back from her helmet. Then four were Bringers of Blessings, like King Cole of England, King Alfred of Wessex, Saint Nicholas of Bari, and Saint Augustine. Four other were lovely, calm women, Forgiveness, Mercy, Peace and Pity. 'According to the list,' Edward said, 'there should be one more of these people; but he is not there.'

'He is under the sea,' Kay said.

After the images, came the great gold and silver candlesticks that the goggle-eyes of so many fish had gawped at. Then came the censers and the church vessels. Then, when these had all been stored away, there came the marvellous caskets, each made like a church of gold or silver, with spires and pinnacles specked with jewels. The roofs of these churches opened like doors; inside were coloured glitterings from jewels, for each church was a box of precious stones, pearls, blue sapphires, yellow sapphires, opals like jewels with fire inside them, rubies like the heart of fire, emeralds like the depth of the green sea, diamonds like raindrops in the sun. Here and there on the treasures were relics of their travels, such as bits of the grass-mattings from Santa Barbara; chalk-marks and numbers put on them by Captain Harker or his mate Hollings, when they were brought on board the *Plunderer*; springs of coral, dried seaweed and a few spiky, pearly shells from their under-the-sea time; and much of the dried red mud of Old Man John's farm. On the last of the caskets was an old envelope with the following inscription in ink:

'Brought up the river, and safely landed by me at midnight, January 25th, 1850.—P. Trigger.'

'I don't know who helped him,' Edward said. 'Probably his Indians, whom he paid and sent home afterwards. He was a rough customer, Sir Piney, but he did do his best to make amends for it.'

It seemed to Kay and Edward that they heard a North Country voice say, 'Tha's reet, ma son.' Then, a moment later, they heard the same voice and a familiar female voice (now sweeter and fuller than it had been) singing in the garden:

'After long years alone,
Ironed to flesh and bone,
It is most sweet to pass
Like wind above the grass,
Free ever, and to find
The waiting mind.

'Then to set forth together,
To know the new strange weather,
And where the new road leads;
To put old burdens by,
And have the wind and sky,
Light as the wild-duck's feather
Or dandelion seeds.'

When the song had died away in the distance, Kay asked if he might speak to the guards. They all came in, in their dusty, rough, muddy working-clothes. They were very much sunburnt and wind-tanned; it was lovely to see them all looking so well, and to have them there again.

Kay spoke to each one and thanked them all.

'You must have had a dreadfully hard time,' he said.

'We had a lot of disappointments,' Edward said. 'We followed so many false clues. And I must say that yesterday, after all night in the mud with those two men whom Arthur lent, I must say that we came near to despair. It was little Maria who kept us at it. She made us all lovely beef-tea, and whipped up eggs in milk (and in cream for poor Brown Bear), and it was she and Susan who thought that there might be that cave to the south. I can tell you . . . when Otter gave us a hint, and it proved to be the fact, when we peered in and saw the treasure, it atoned for any troubles we may have had. I must say, that *was* a moment.

'But, however, we have found it; it is safely stored, and this stone is sealed. What I have to say now is . . .

'Up Guards and at them.

'It's time to set this house to rights.

'You, Lenda, take Jemima, Susan and Maria into this Pouncer's room, seal her cupboard, then lock everything up, so that she won't get in again.

'You, Peterkin, Snowball and James, and you, W. Brown, break open that magic room, fling everything that you find there out of the window and burn it in the bonfire.

'And the watchword, till further orders, is Keep Awake.'

While they were hurrying to obey, there was a scuttering in the passage, Otter came tumbling into the room.

'I say,' he said, 'there are such doings, down by the river. The eight of them came, with that man Roper Bilges and his brother, and the pimply man, and Brassy, who sets the traps. They have all been digging in the mud for hours. They're all filthy, blistered and as cross as two sticks. Then they got into the south cave and found the treasure gone; then they got into the middle cave and found a body. Now they're all fighting, quarrelling and blaming each other.'

'Serve them right,' Edward said. 'But tell me, Otter, as you came here, did you see any coastguard men?'

'I should think I did,' Otter said. 'Dozens of them, some on the roads, others in boats, all creeping in on them.'

'Right,' Edward said. 'My plans are working just as I could wish. John, just run down to the study, will you, and bring up yesterday's paper?'

Edward opened the paper and read:

> 'His Excellency, the Dictator of Santa Barbara, accompanied by the Archbishop of Santa Barbara and a numerous and distinguished suite, will arrive in London early tomorrow on a short visit to the Metropolis. They will be stopping at the Hotel Glorious.'

'There,' Edward cried. 'On the very day the treasure is found, the people arrive to take charge of it. I noticed that announcement yesterday, tired as I was; that shows you the kind of brain I have.'

'I showed it to him,' Maria whispered.

'I'll send them a letter,' Kay said. 'Come along to the drawing-room, where the embossed note-paper is kept.'

In the drawing-room, Kay wrote his letter:

'DEAR LORD EXCELLENCY AND ARCHBISHOP.

'I hop you are quite well.

'All the church treasure which was trusted to Capt. Harker, my great-grand-father, is now safely here. Please come with safe men to take it.

'I am quite well.

'KAY HARKER.'

'I'm afraid he'll never come for that,' Kay said. 'He'll think it's a rag.'

'Well, let's send it by someone who will make him come,'

Edward said. 'Not Ernest, he's such an ass. Bruno Bree is the man. Bruno, mount Peter Horse, gallop to London to the Hotel Glorious, and give this letter to the Dictator's hand. Tell him it's deadly serious and he must come at once.'

'I must put in a P.S.,' Kay said. 'The statue of St. George is under the sea.'

After Bruno had galloped off with the letter, Edward said, 'I must say, that your guardian has been an ass, Kay. However, someone else will be here this morning; then, perhaps, something can be arranged.

'Now I'll just post some guards, and you'd better get to bed for an hour or two.'

• • • • •

It was very late when Ellen called Kay that morning.

'O there have been doings,' she said. 'Your governess and a whole lot more of them have been taken trespassing down in a cave where they were smuggling. And what's worse is that there's a dead body where they've murdered someone. And, oh, the brandy they've found. Joe says it's enough to make the Army blind and the Navy mellow. And Sir Hassle has had to telegraph to your guardian.'

There were no lessons that morning, but a great deal of coming and going.

But long before lunch, at about eleven o'clock, there came a much greater surprise. While Kay was in the schoolroom wrestling with a portion of Mrs. Markham, Ellen came to say that he was wanted in the drawing-room. This was usually a message foreboding punishment. To-day Ellen brought it all smiling. 'Who is there, Ellen?' he asked. 'You are a tease not to tell a fellow.'

'You go down and you'll see,' she said.

He went down in a drag-leg sort of way, and opened the door. There, to his amazement, was the beautiful lady who had taken him to the weathercocks and to Miss Twiney Pricker. She came up to him and kissed him. 'You don't know who I am,' she said. 'But I know who you are. I am Caroline Louisa, who loved your Mother. I could not come before, but now I am going to live here and look after you. Will you like that?'

'Will I like that? I should rather think so. But what will she say?'

'She won't be here.'

'Oh.'

• • • • •

At half-past two that afternoon they were playing cricket in the garden, when His Excellency, the Dictator, with the Archbishop of Santa Barbara, and two very important-looking men, drove up to the door in the fly from the Cock and Pye. They were all as nice as they could be. Kay had the great pleasure of taking them to his room, rolling back the carpet and showing them the stone. The two men procured crowbars from the ironmonger's shop in the village. They hove the stone aside, there was the treasure neatly arranged as the guards had left it. Kay told them all the story of it.

They guarded it that night and then carried it away.

As for Abner Brown, Mrs. Pouncer and the others, they were all examined by the magistrates for being found unlawfully assembled, with arms in their possession, with intent to defraud the Queen's Majesty, by removing certain articles of contraband, to wit brandy, lace and tobacco from where they were to some other place, the said articles not having paid any duty. The magistrates were much puzzled by the case, because the people were not smugglers, and had not smuggled the goods, yet were plainly there with ropes, hooks and carriages to remove the same. The Seven were at last dismissed with a good scolding for taking part in a foolish frolic, but they were fined a large sum for trespassing in pursuit of game.

Abner Brown paid all the fines. Mrs. Pouncer left the district that afternoon.

Roper Bilges was discharged from his place for poaching. In revenge, he and his brother, Sir Hassle's footman, poisoned all the otter hounds. For this they were sent to Dr. Gubbins' Remedial Home for Scoundrels, where parts of them have been cut out, cleaned, and then put back; they are already much improved. Dr. Gubbins has great hopes of them.

Pimply Whatto and Brassy are now keeping a little pig farm.

Sir Hassle wears his grandfather's repeater, which goes

as well as ever it did. He takes Kay for a ride three times a week, out of the hunting season; he is going to give Kay a lovely little pony mare, called Christine, for his birthday, but of course this is a secret. Sir Hassle never draws for a fox down by the river.

The Squire will not buy any more otter hounds, otter hunting has therefore come to an end there. Water Rat and Otter have the river to themselves; they are very happy there, as the salmon have begun to come back.

Joe has taken the pledge, and is keeping it.

Bitem is very well. He has a fine summer lair in the hollow of Spring Hill. So far he has had one of my hens and three of my ducks this season. In the winter he goes down to the cave near the river where no hounds ever come. I hear him singing from time to time.

Blackmalkin and Greymalkin have turned over new leaves; but of course they will never be so nice as Nibbins, who is the nicest cat there is.

Old Blinky is still there, so is Bat.

Ellen and Jane say that they are never going to marry; but stop where they are to look after Kay until *he* marries.

Kay and Caroline Loüisa are as happy as the day is long. Last year they went to spend the winter as the guests of the Dictator of Santa Barbara, where they had a most happy time. While they were there, the Archbishop showed them the treasure, or some of it, in use, as it had been of old, the candlesticks on the Altar, the images against the screens in the quire, and the vessels in the side-chapels. Many of the precious stones from the caskets had been sold to build and endow a great College for the Study and Cure of Disease.

While at sea, both going and returning, Kay was quite sure that he saw the mermaids.

The guards are very happy, too. You may be sure that there is no more witchcraft in the house, nothing but peace and mirth all day and at night peace, the owls crying, the crickets chirping and all sort of fun going on among

THE MIDNIGHT FOLK.

THE END

The BOX of Delights

Contents

CHAPTER ONE

As Kay was coming home for the Christmas holidays, after his first term at school, the train stopped at Musborough Station. An old man, ringing a hand-bell, went along the platform, crying 'Musborough Junction . . . Change for Tatchester and Newminster.'

Kay knew that he had to change trains there, with a wait of forty minutes. He climbed down onto the platform in the bitter cold and stamped his feet to try to get warmth into them. The old man, ringing the hand-bell, cried, 'All for Condicote and Tatchester . . . All for Yockwardine and Newminster go to Number Five Platform by the subway.'

As the passengers set off towards the subway entrance,

Kay put his fingers into his pocket for his ticket: it was not there. 'Did I drop it in the carriage?' he wondered. He went back to the carriage. 'Stand back, master, please,' a porter said. 'We're going to shift the train.'

'Please, I think I've dropped my ticket in the carriage.'

'Oh . . . one minute, then,' the porter said, opening the door. 'Which seat were you sitting at, master?'

'Here,' Kay said. He looked under the seat and in what he called 'the crink' between the back and the seat: there was no ticket there.

'I don't seem to see it,' the porter said. 'Had you it when they punched tickets at Blunafon?'

'Yes.'

'Well, you'd better explain at the subway. We've got to shunt this train.'

The train presently moved away; Kay went to the bench where he had left his bag; he began to rummage through all his pockets. He felt that the ticket-collector who was watching him at the subway gate was beginning to think him a suspicious character.

An Irish terrier came up to Kay, sniffed at him and wagged the stump of his tail. 'Good boy,' Kay said. 'Nice old boy, then,' and rumpled his head for him, which made the dog bounce about with delight. Still, he could not find the ticket.

Two men, who had been standing near the subway entrance watching the people go out, moved up to the bench and sat down upon it. Kay had noticed them, for he had been told that detectives often stand near ticket-collectors, watching for escaping murderers. He had thought, 'Probably those are two men from the Yard, after somebody.' Now he thought, 'Supposing they arrest me, for not having a ticket?'

'Well,' one of the men said, 'he's diddled us. He's simply not on the train. Here's the description sent: "Travelling first class. In appearance like a French cavalry colonel, with waxed moustaches, very smart and upright, height five feet eight, age about forty to forty-five." He's hopped off the train where it slowed down somewhere; depend upon it.'

'We'd better telephone at once that he wasn't on the train.'

'Asses that we are,' the other cried suddenly. 'O silly chumps and fatheads . . . Of course . . . he got under a seat in a first-class carriage and he's been shunted out and away. Quick, quick . . . we may get him yet in the shunting yard . . .'

'Of course, that's it,' the other said. 'Lively, then.'

At once, the two men ran off, past the subway entrance and away along the platform in the direction in which the train had gone.

Now that the men were running, it seemed to Kay that some dogs, which he had not before noticed, were running with them. 'They are Alsatian dogs,' he thought, 'but they seem thicker in the shoulder than most Alsatians . . .

'Why, of course,' he exclaimed. 'They are Police Dogs, and they are going to be put on the scent. O, I do wish I knew what the criminal had done.'

As he watched, one of the men paused in his run to signal with his hand to a man on Number Five Platform, who signalled back with a real pair of handcuffs and then ran out of the station.

'I say,' Kay said to himself, 'I've never been so near to detectives before. O, I do wish I could find this ticket.'

The Irish terrier was at his feet again, begging to have

his head rumpled, which Kay did for him. Then he noticed that the owner of the dog was standing near him.

He was a little old man in a worn grey overcoat. He had travelled there in the end coach of Kay's train. Since leaving the train he had been at the platform end securing a big case in a cover of green baize. This he now carried in his hand.

'Ah, young Master,' the old man said, 'I see that my Barney Dog has made friends with you at first sight. That's the time that likings are made. And you are looking for your ticket, which, lo, is on the platform, dropped at your feet.'

'Why, so it is,' Kay said, picking it up. 'So it is. Thank you ever so much.'

'You must have slipped it out as you rumpaged,' the man said.

Kay noticed that the man had very bright eyes, alert as a bird's or squirrel's.

'We must be moving along, young Master,' he said, 'or they'll be wondering if we've got no tickets.'

'Could I give you a hand, please, to help you carry your case?' Kay asked. He noticed that it was an awkward load for a little old man.

'No, I thank you, Master,' the old man said. 'But if you would be so kind as to steady her when I swing her; then I could get her to my back, which is where she rides a-triumph. Only I do date from pagan times and age makes joints to creak. Or doesn't it?'

'I should think it does,' Kay said.

'Now, I'm going to swing,' the old man said, 'and keep it, you, young Master, from rolling me over, if you will be so gracious.' He swung his bundle up to his shoulder; and, indeed, if Kay had not been there to steady it, the load might have pulled him over; he had a frail little old withered body, 'like the ghost of ninepence,' as he said.

Kay walked with him through the subway to Number Five Platform, and there helped him to set down his bundle at a seat. After this, he went into the refreshment room and bought some biscuits for Barney, for which the old man was grateful. After this, as there was still half an hour to wait before the Condicote train came in, he tried to get to the shunting yard, to find out if the detectives had caught the criminal and what it was that the criminal had done.

He was not allowed inside the shunting yard. The young porter who headed him off at the gates told him that no one was allowed in. Kay asked if the detectives had found the criminal under one of the seats. 'What, just now?' the porter asked. 'Yes; they got him. He was under one of the seats dressing up as a Duchess. In another minute, he'd have finished, so that not even the Prime Minister would have told the difference.'

'What had he done?' Kay asked.

'Done?' the porter said. 'Er, he was a bad one. He had a row with his father-in-law, and he got a big sharp knife and cut the poor old man up, put him through the mincer and sold him to the dog's-meat man. The dog's-meat man wouldn't have noticed it, only one of the buttons stuck in a dog's throat and the lady who owned the dog complained, and then it all came out, and it's thought it isn't the first man he put through the mincer, it's a habit that's been growing on him for years.'

'What will be done to him?' Kay asked.

'He'll get the rope,' the porter said. 'Madame Tussaud's are offering any money already for the mincer he did the deed with.'

'I say,' Kay said, 'couldn't you let me peep in and just see him where he is, with the detectives?'

'Oh, they've gone, gone a long while,' the porter said. 'They'd a special car and went off at once to London with an armed guard.'

Kay was thrilled with the story, but as he walked back to the platform he wondered whether the porter had been telling the truth. He bought a newspaper but could find nothing at all about any such crime. While he was searching through the newspaper, the train came in. He got into a carriage and was soon on his way home.

When he had been taken to school in September he had gone by car. He was now returning home through a country quite new to him by a railway line over which he had never before travelled. The train passed out of the meadows into a hilly land beautiful with woodlands and glens. In spite of the bitter cold Kay was much interested in this new country. Some of the hills had old camps on them. On the headlands there were old castles; in the glens there were churches which looked like forts. He took from his bag a cycling map of the countryside. By this he picked out the hills, castles and churches as the train went past them. Soon all the land to the left of the railway was a range of low wooded hills of the most strange shapes. He read the name on the map—Chester Hills. 'What a wonderful place,' he said to himself. 'I do wish that I could come here to explore.'

While he was looking through the window at these hills he heard a scratching at the door. He saw that the Irish terrier, Barney, was standing on his hind legs in the corridor, looking at him through the glass. He went to him, opened the door and patted him, and after a minute the dog went scuttering off down the train. 'I suppose,' he said to himself, 'that the old man is in the train somewhere. I'd forgotten all about him in thinking about the murderer.' The train drew up at a station.

'Hope-under-Chesters,' he read. 'Then that little river is the Yock. And that is Chesters camp. It must be a Roman camp, from the name. And that is Hope Cross. There must have been a battle there, for it's marked with crossed swords. And the map shows a lake only a couple of miles away.'

He stared at the hills. It was a grim winter morning, threatening a gale. Something in the light, with its hard sinister clearness, gave mystery and dread to those hills. 'They look just the sort of hills,' Kay said to himself, 'where you might come upon a Dark Tower, and blow a horn at the gate for something to happen.'

The train was about to start; the whistle had blown and the station-master had waved his flag, when there came cries from the ticket-office of 'Hold on. Wait half a minute.' Two men rushed across the platform and scrambled into Kay's carriage just as the train moved off.

The men took the further corner seats; they panted a little, and looked at Kay. Both were in the black clothes of theological students. 'They didn't give us much time,' one of them said.

'The news has only just come through,' the other said. Both were youngish men (about twenty-three, Kay thought). Somehow, he didn't like the men, nor their voices. They made in some foreign tongue one or two remarks, which Kay judged to be about himself. After this, as the train went on, they spoke to him. One of them, who was a pale, eager-looking man, with foxy hair, said, 'Going home for the holidays, ha-ha, what?' and when Kay said, 'Yes, please, sir,' the other said, 'And very seasonable weather, too: we are to have snow, it seems. And no doubt you enjoy snowballing, and tobogganing and making snowmen?'

Kay said that he did: he began to like this other man, who had a round, rosy, chubby face, with fair hair; and yet there was something about him ... Kay couldn't quite put it into words ... he had a kind of a ... sort of a ... It was more in his eyes than in anything else.

'And are you going far, may I ask?' the chubby man asked.

'I'm going to Condicote,' Kay said.

'Ah, indeed ... Condicote Junction,' the chubby man said ... 'And I wonder if, in the Christmas holidays, you will ever do card-tricks?'

'If you please, sir, I do not know any.'

'But you are of a studious turn, I see, ha-ha, what? With your maps and food-for-the-mind,' the foxy-faced man said. 'I wonder if I might try to teach you a simple trick, since we are to be fellow-travellers.'

Kay said that it would be very kind, but that he was afraid that he would be stupid at it.

'I see that you will be very clever at it,' the foxy man said. 'Don't you think, Tristan, that he has the face of one certain to be clever at card-tricks; what?'

'The very face,' the other said.

'Just the facial angle and the Borromean Index,' the foxy one went on. 'Now let me see if I have my cards. I usually carry cards, because I am much alone, and find the games of Patience a great mental solace. Ah yes, I have my old companions.'

He produced a little packet of green-backed cards in a dull red leather case.

'Let nothing tempt you into playing cards with

strangers in a train or ship anywhere,' the chubby man said.

'I am inclined to agree with you, Lancelot,' the foxy man said, 'but there will be no harm in showing him one of the tricks by which sharpers deceive the unwary. Let me show you the commonest trick. It is often known as "spotting-the-lady." '

He dealt out three cards, one of which was the Queen of Clubs, the others two low hearts. 'See there,' he said. 'Mark them well. I twist them and shift them and lo, now, which is the Lady?'

'That one,' Kay said.

'So it is; so it is,' the man said. 'What it is to have young eyes, Gawaine, is it not?'

'It was not his young eyes, but your clumsy dealing,' the other said.

'Ha,' the foxy-faced man said, 'I lack practice, I see. I must give myself some incentive. I will back my skill. Now, then; prepare: if you beat me this time, you shall have sixpence, for, indeed, I must be put upon my mettle.

> 'Watch now the whirling cards,
> They shift, they lift, they dive.
> Twiddle. Twiddle. Twiddle.
> Pussycat and fiddlestrings.

'Can you tell the Lady, this time?'

'Yes,' Kay said. 'Here she is.'

'And here is your sixpence,' the man said. 'And yet I thought I was discreet. But you have an eye like a lynx. Now may I try once again? You are too young, you are too sharp; there is no getting round you. Now, no denial: if I beat you this time you shall give me half-a-crown for the Poor Box or next Sunday's collection.'

Kay was about to protest, for he had promised never to bet, nor to play cards for money; but the chubby-faced man said, 'Of course . . . that would be simply sportsman's honour.'

'Agreed, agreed, what,' the foxy-faced man said, as he twiddled the cards. 'Hark to Merlin: "Again the fatal sister spins her web. Mark well her hand, the hand of Destiny; so shoots the weft across the serried warp; and back the sword beats and the shear descends." Now, which is the Lady?'

'This one,' Kay said. 'I saw her from underneath as the cards went down.'

He was quite certain that he had seen the Queen, but when he lifted the card, it was not the Queen, it was the three of Hearts.

'Now how did that happen, what?' the foxy-faced man said. 'That will be just half-a-crown, please; for the collection in aid of the Decayed Cellarers, poor fellows. A debt of honour, you know.'

Kay felt very unhappy, but pulled out his purse and paid the half-crown. It may have been suspicion or error, yet it seemed to him that both men seemed very inquisitive, craning over, as it were, to see what money was in his purse.

'So you carry your money in a purse,' the chubby-faced man said. 'It is always a wise precaution; so much better than having it loose, when it will get pulled out with the handkerchief or what not.'

The foxy-faced man spread his cards. 'Now, Sir Lancelot,' he said, 'that is two to you and one to me. Won't you give me my chance to get equal?'

Kay thought that he was already past being equal and a good deal ahead. He was sorely perplexed as to what to say. At this moment, however, the train began to slacken for a station.

'Ha, we stop here, what?' the foxy-faced man said. 'Sir Dagonet, a word with you.' He tapped his left ear and went out into the corridor; the chubby-faced man followed him. The train was at a little junction, Yarton for Yockombe Regis; two or three people left the train and others got in.

'I won't play cards any more,' Kay decided. 'Nothing shall induce me . . .'

When the train started, the two men returned. Kay was again studying his map. He was afraid that the men would suggest more cards, but they had returned deep in thought. They talked to each other in low voices in a tongue which Kay thought must be Italian.

He glanced at them sideways from time to time. There was something in the way of their bending their heads together which seemed very sinister. Kay wondered that he had ever thought either of them nice. They were talking about somebody. They seemed to be looking out for somebody. Whenever the train stopped at one of the little stations: Gabbett's Cross, Lower Turrington, Stoke Dever and Radsoe, the men went out into the corridor, and seemed (as Kay decided) to watch all people leaving the train. They had friends (accomplices, Kay called them) in the train, for once (at Radsoe), as Kay was looking out for the landmarks of home, he saw the foxy-faced man, who had got out onto the platform, signalling to a man in a forward carriage.

'These men are up to no good,' Kay thought. 'They're after somebody. Very likely it's some farmer, coming home from the beast-market with a lot of money, whom they are going to rob. I do hope they won't talk to me again.'

He settled again to his map as they returned to the carriage. 'Still feeding the mind, what?' the foxy-faced man said.

'Yes, please,' Kay said.

'And can you tell me what country we are now coming to?'

'Yes,' Kay said. 'If you will look there, you will see Condicote Church ... Then, that wooded hill is King Arthur's Court: it's a Roman Camp ... Up there, is Broadbarrow, where there used to be a gibbet.'

'Indeed,' the man said. 'Well, well. Then this next station will be Condicote, I take it?'

'Yes,' Kay said.

'You hear that, Palamedes?' he said to his companion. 'Sir Lancelot says that Condicote is next stop, where the hawks get out to wait for the chicken ... if the chicken is still on the wing.'

'Not so loud, not so loud,' the chubby-faced man said, with a look of alarm. 'Good heaven, what was that?'

Some slight noise made them all look towards the corridor. It was only the Irish terrier of the old man, 'Barney Dog,' standing on his hind legs to look in to the compartment. With a scratching of claws upon the paint, the dog dropped from his post and slid away. Yet Kay felt somehow uneasy, for the dog had looked at him so strangely.

'A dog, I think,' the chubby man said, with a warning glance at his friend. 'One of the friends of man, as they are called. And do you keep dogs at Seekings, Mr. Harker?'

Kay jumped, for how did the man know his name and home? 'How did you know about me, sir?' he asked.

'Magic, no doubt,' the man said. 'But there is a proverb:

"More know Tom Fool
Than Tom Fool knows."

'Not that I want you to think that I think you a fool; by no means.'

'By no means, what?' the foxy-faced man said, as he put up his cards in their case. 'He is no fool, but a hawk with the eyes of a gimlet, our young friend from Seekings House. And this is Condicote Station?'

'It is,' Kay said, still marvelling that the men should know him. The train stopped.

There was always a press of people on Condicote platform at the coming-in of that train: there was on this day. Kay was bumped and thrust by people getting in and out. There in the press was Caroline Louisa come to meet him; then, among other familiar faces, the old 'bus man, Jim, came forward to help him with his bags. 'Why, Master Kay, how you have growed, to be sure. Learning seems to suit 'ee.'

He crossed the line with the crowd. At the exit gate he was bumped and thrust among the company. When he had won through the press and was safely in the car, he found that he had been robbed.

'I say,' he said, 'there must have been pickpockets in the crowd. They've got my purse and my dollar watch.'

'When had you them last?'

'A few minutes before we reached the station.'

'Did you feel any hand at your pockets?'

'No, of course not. I was pushed and shoved in the crowd, of course.'

'Did you notice any suspicious person near you?'

'No . . . Hullo. Here's my ticket . . .'

'But you gave it up just now.'

'So I did,' he said. 'Well. That's a queer thing. I couldn't find my ticket at Musborough: and an old man who was there said "there lo, it's on the platform"; and there it was, right at my feet. I must have picked up some other chap's ticket, perhaps it was the old man's own ticket. Why, there is the old man, that old fellow with the green baize case and the Irish terrier.'

'What is he?' Caroline Louisa asked. 'A Punch and Judy man?'

'I don't know,' Kay said. 'I'll ask him. And I'll ask if I had his ticket. And may I offer him a lift? He's rather a poor old chap to be lugging those loads about.'

'Ask him, if you like,' she said.

Kay asked him, had he given him his own ticket at Musborough.

'No, I thank you,' the old man said. 'I had my own ticket, thank you, and have now given it over.'

'Will you please tell me,' Kay said, 'if you are a Punch and Judy man?'

'I am, so to speak, a showman,' the old man said, 'and my Barney Dog is, as it were, my Toby Dog, when chance does call.'

'I was to ask you, would you like a lift down into the town, as it is rather a step, and it is so cold.'

'No, I thank you, my young Master,' the old man said. 'But if you would once more steady my show, why, then I should not stumble.'

Kay helped him a little, so that the case did not overbalance him as he swung it to his shoulders.

'And I thank you, my young Master,' he said. 'Time was when we had power, like the Sun, and could swing the Earth and the Moon, and now our old wheels are all running down and we are coming to a second childhood.

'Still, they say,' he went on, 'that it begins again, in the course of time. But the secrets of my show, they aren't to be had by these common ones, now, are they?'

Kay did not know what to say to this.

'Hearts, diamonds, spades, clubs, it goes,' the old man said. 'And then all the way back again.'

The old man paused an instant and looked about him. By this time, all those who had met or who had travelled by the train were gone from the station yard, while the porters and ticket man had gone back to shelter.

'And now, Master Harker, of Seekings,' the old man said, 'now that the Wolves are Running, as you will have seen, perhaps you would do something to stop their Bite? Or wouldn't you?'

'I don't know what you mean,' Kay said, 'but is there anything I can do for you?'

'Master Harker,' he said, 'there is something that no other soul can do for me but you alone. As you go down towards Seekings, if you would stop at Bob's shop, as it were to buy muffins now. . . . Near the door you will see a woman plaided from the cold, wearing a ring of a very strange shape, Master Harker, being like my ring here, of the longways cross of gold and garnets. And she has very bright eyes, Master Harker, as bright as mine, which is what few have. If you will step into Bob's shop to buy muffins now, saying nothing, not even to your good friend, and say to this Lady "The Wolves are Running," then she will know and Others will know; and none will get bit.'

'I'll do that, of course,' Kay said. 'But how did you know my name?'

'When Wolves Run it betides to know, Master Harker,' he said. 'And I do bless you.

'But Time and Tide and Buttered Eggs wait for no man,' he added. He swung away at once, bent under his pack, followed by his Dog Barney. He had that odd stagger or waddle in his knees that Kay had so often noticed in old countrymen.

'How on earth does he know my name?' Kay thought. 'And how does he know Bob's shop? I've certainly never seen him before today. . . .' He went back to the car.

'I'm sorry to have been so long,' he said. 'He's a queer old man. I should think he has been something very different once . . .'

'About your being robbed,' Caroline Louisa said. 'Who was with you in the train?'

'Two men, but I don't think they would have robbed me. They were two sort of curates. They got in at Hope-under-Chesters and got out here. The funny thing was that they knew my name and that I came from Seekings.'

'They could have read that from your luggage labels,' she said. 'If your curates got in at Hope-under-Chesters they may have been members of the Missionaries College there.'

'I say,' Kay said, 'are there any muffins?'

'No,' she said, 'teacakes, but no muffins.'

'Would you mind frightfully if we stopped at Bob's and got some muffins? Only you'll have to lend me some tin, for my purse is gone. I haven't a tosser to my kick.'

'Now, Kay, you mustn't use slang in the holidays.'

'That's nothing to some I know.'

At this moment, the car passed the old man. Kay waved to him and the old man waved back.

'By the way,' Kay said, 'are there Buttered Eggs for lunch?'

'Yes, specially for you. We must get on to them.'

'You know,' Kay said, 'there's something very queer about that old man. He knew that there would be Buttered Eggs. He said "Time, Tide and Buttered Eggs wait for no man." '

'I expect that a good many have said something of the sort.'

'No,' Kay said. 'He meant me, and that I ought to hurry up. There's something uncanny about him. I mean in a good sense.'

'Do you think that he could have picked your pockets?'

'No, I don't.'

'He was near you.'

'No, but I had my money and watch after I was near him and missed them before I saw him the second time. Look. Look . . . There are the two curate sort of men, both in the 'bus, there.'

'I can't look at them while I'm driving, I'm afraid. You're sure they didn't rob you?'

'Quite. Though I didn't like them much. I say, I wish you would let me drive.'

'Not for another five years, Kay.'

'I say; why ever not?'

'Because it's against the law, for one thing, and likely to be fatal, for another.'

'Fatal fiddlesticks. We've a man in the Fourth, at the

Coll, who drove the old Bodger's car once. What do the curates do at Chesters?'

'They read good books and learn how to be clergymen. They have to work in the farm and garden, I believe. Did they want you to join them?'

'They didn't ask me. I wish you'd tell me about them.'

'I don't know very much to tell. They're the other side of the county. I seem to have heard that most of them go off to missions after a time of training.'

'And get eaten by the cassowary?'

'Some of them, perhaps. But I'm not telling you the news. I've got rather a shock to give you. All the Jones children are with us for the holidays.'

'Oh, I say, golly, whatever for?'

'The parents have to go abroad, and I couldn't bear the children to have nowhere to go for Christmas. I do hope you won't mind frightfully.'

'I don't mind at all,' he said. 'I like the Joneses . . . some of them. No, I like them all, really. There's rather a gollop of them, though.'

'I'm putting Peter into your room,' she said. 'You'll have two little snug beds and can be like robbers in a cave.'

'We'll have some larks, I expect,' Kay said. 'I do hope Maria has brought some pistols. She generally has one or two.'

'I hope she has nothing of the kind. What do you mean by pistols? What sort of pistols?'

'Oh, the usual sort of pistols: revolvers: she got a lot of them from some robbers once. She's sure to have some still. She says she couldn't live without pistols now. She shoots old electric light bulbs dangling from a clothes-line.'

'She shall shoot none at Seekings, I trust.'

They sped on towards Seekings. 'I say,' he said, 'how far is Hope-under-Chesters from here?'

'Thirty or thirty-five miles.'

'Do you know it at all?'

'No, not more than one can know by passing.'

'I thought it looked a wonderful sort of place. I'd like to go exploring there.'

'It's deep, wild country,' she said, 'but it is just a little far away for winter exploring. Leave it till the summer.'

'When I grow up,' Kay said, 'I mean to explore all the wild bits left in England.'

'There aren't very many,' she said, 'but the Chesters are the wildest near here.'

'Do you think any of the people are pagans, there, still?'

'Not at heart, the Bishop says, but a good many in outward observance.'

'There's some snow,' he said. 'I do hope we shall have a real deep snow, so that we can make a snow-man.'

'The paper says that there will be snow, and the glass is falling.'

As they entered the little street, it was so dark with the promise of snow that the shops were being lighted. They were all decked out with holly, mistletoe, tinsel, crackers, toys, oranges, model Christmas trees with tapers and glass balls, apples, sweets, sucking pigs, sides of beef, turkeys, geese, Christmas cakes and big plum-puddings.

'I say, I do love Christmas,' Kay said. 'You'll have to give me a whole lot of tin presently, please, for I'll have to get four extra presents for the Joneses. And I wonder if I could get Jane to give me a plum-pudding that I could give to that old man? I wouldn't like him to have no plum-pudding on Christmas. And would you mind stopping at Bob's?'

'Jane will give you a plum-pudding,' she said, as she stopped the car in the busy market-place. There were open-air booths there selling all manner of matters for Christmas; chiefly woollen mufflers, nailed boots, cloth caps, hedger's gloves and the twenty-eight-pound cheeses, known as Tatchester Double Stones. The keepers of the stalls were flogging their arms against the cold; some of them were packing up before the snow began. Kay passed through these in some excitement. 'Of course, it's all rot,' he said. 'How can he know there will be a woman near the door there . . . And yet, there is one, sure enough. . . .'

Bob was the baker and confectioner of the little town. His shop was always sweet and pleasant with the smell of new bread. His window at this Christmas time was a sight to see. In it were two Christmas cakes, four storeys high, in pink and white sugar, both crowned with little dancers in tinsel who went round and round, each holding little electric light bulbs. All round these cakes were the most marvellous crackers that eye ever saw or child pulled. But Kay was not thinking of cake or crackers. He looked only at the figure of a woman who stood near the shop-window, with her back to the wall, staring at the man who was calling at a near-by booth:

'The very best warm caps and mufflers.
As worn by the great Explorer Shackleton.
The North Pole caps and mufflers.
As worn by Airmen.
North and South Pole caps and mufflers.'

She was plaided over the head and shoulders with a grey plaid shawl.

Now, as Kay drew near, the woman, who had been motionless, stirred. Her right hand came from underneath the plaid, drew the plaid closer about her, and held it there. Her hand was wearing what looked like a chamois-leather glove. On the middle finger outside the glove, and, there, very conspicuous, was a ring such as the old man had worn, a heavy gold ring arranged in a St. Andrew's Cross and set with garnets. At the same moment the woman shook the plaid back from her face, so that Kay saw a pair of eyes so bright that they seemed to burn in the head. She looked keenly at Kay. At the instant there was nobody very near. Kay looked at her. His heart beat as he said in a low voice, 'The Wolves are Running.' She looked hard at him, gave a very, very slight nod, and, as Kay went on into the shop to buy the muffins, she slipped away sideways, walking very swiftly with an erect bearing. An old woman coming out of the shop with a basket shoved Kay aside, so that he lost sight of her at that point. She had moved into the thickest of the crowd in the market-place.

'Well, it's very odd,' Kay thought to himself. 'I wonder what on earth he meant by "the Wolves are Running," and why it was so important that she should know?'

When he had bought his muffins, he stood on Bob's steps for a moment trying to get the packet into his pocket. He looked out with relish at the street, thinking how good it was to be home for the holidays. 'Well, I'm blest,' he said. 'There are some more of those Police Dogs . . . working a cold scent.'

Indeed, some Alsatian dogs were at the cross-roads, testing the air with their noses, swaying their heads with the motion of a weaving horse, as though trying to catch a difficult scent. There were three or four of them. They

CHAPTER TWO

When they reached Seekings, there were the Joneses; Jemima very smart, Maria very untidy, Susan like a little fairy and Peter, a good honest sort of chap.

At lunch, Kay said, 'What asses we were not to ask that Punch and Judy man to come here to give his show. Don't you think we might go down and find him and ask him to come? Do let's; we could have him in the study.'

'Yes, certainly, you can have him, if you can find him, and if he will come.'

'Then I vote we have tea at about half-past four,' Kay said, 'and have the Punch and Judy man at about half-past five, if we can get him, then.'

'I do wish,' Maria said, 'that we could hear of a gang of robbers in the neighbourhood, come down to burgle while people are at dinner, and hear all their plans, and be ready waiting for them and then have a battle with revolvers.'

'I hope we may get through Christmas without that,' Caroline Louisa said.

'Christmas ought to be brought up to date,' Maria said; 'it ought to have gangsters, and aeroplanes and a lot of automatic pistols.'

After lunch, Kay went out with Peter to look for the Punch and Judy man. It was a dark, lowering afternoon, with a whine in the wind, and little dry pellets of snow blowing horizontally. In the gutters, these had begun to fall into little white layers and heaps.

'I say, it is a foul day,' Peter said. 'I'll go back and get a coat. You go on; I'll catch you up. Which way will you go?'

'Down towards Dr. Gubbinses,' Kay said. 'But you'd better ask for the Punch and Judy man: and look for him, not for me.'

Kay went on alone into the street. He thought that he had never been out in a more evil-looking afternoon. The market-place had emptied, people had packed their booths, and wheeled away their barrows. As he went down towards Dr. Gubbinses, the carved beasts in the wood-work of the old houses seemed crouching against the weather. Darkness was already closing in. There was a kind of glare in the evil heaven. The wind moaned about the lanes. All the sky above the roofs was grim with menace, and the darkness of the afternoon gave a strangeness to the fire-light that glowed in many windows.

From the cross-roads behind him a rider came cloppetting up, the horse slipping a little, the rider bent into a long white overall to keep the snow from blowing down his neck. 'How d'you do, Master Kay?' the rider cried, checking his horse and looking down upon him.

Kay did not recognise the man, but he noticed that his eyes were very bright. The man suddenly put his right hand to his chin. The hand wore a pale wash-leather glove; outside the glove on the middle finger was a gold St. Andrew's Cross, set with garnets.

'They tell me, Master Harker,' the man said, 'that Wolves are Running. If you see Someone,' he added meaningly, 'say Someone's safe.'

'I will,' Kay said.

'And, look out for fun, Master Harker,' the man said, shaking up the horse and riding on. Kay watched him go. He went skittering a little sideways and champing on the bit. It seemed to Kay that the man's arms were hung with little silver chains which jangled. Later it seemed to him that it was not a horse and rider at all, but a great stag from the forest. Certainly the figure that passed round the bend out of sight was a stag.

' "If I see Someone," ' Kay repeated, ' "tell him that Someone's safe." I suppose he must mean the Punch and Judy man.'

At this moment Kay caught sight of the village policeman coming from the Beast-Market, and putting on his oil-skin cape.

'If you please,' Kay said, 'have you seen anything of a Punch and Judy man in the Beast-Market?'

'Why, it's Master Kay Harker,' the policeman said. 'Why, Master Kay, how you've grown. You are back for the holidays, I suppose. Now, a Punch and Judy man, now. Why, I saw one that might be called such with his show on his back. Would it be a one with a brown dog, Master Harker?'

'Yes,' Kay said, 'an Irish terrier.'

'Well, I did see such an one,' the policeman said. 'He

was down by Cherry Fields. He will be in one of the pubs, Master Kay, down by Lower Lock, sure to be. He wouldn't play in the snow and this bitter cold. It's going to be a bad fall, by the look of it.'

Kay thanked the policeman and walked on.

The Beast-Market was empty of people, save for one man who had just loaded a pile of hurdles into a cart, and was now turning for home with a horse thankful to be going from the cold.

'Please have you seen a Punch and Judy man?' Kay called. The man was singing:

> 'Though blind the seed, and dull the earth,
> Yet sweet shall be the flower.'

The horse's excitement, his song, and the noise of the great wheels on the paving kept him from hearing the question. He went on over the ridge and away.

At the top of the ridge, Kay saw the woodland about the camp known as 'King Arthur's Court' standing up black against the West. There was a stab of savage yellow and red over the wood. Every tree stood out distinct and seemed very near. He thought that he had never seen a landscape look so awful.

Kay went on to Lower Lock, which was a sort of double alley of very old houses near Tibbs's Wharf where the barges were lying up for Christmas. The two alleys were known as Lockside and Quayside. There was a brew-house at Lockside, and in between the two alleys was a little public-house known as the *Lock and Key*. A lot went on down at Tibbs's Wharf, around the *Lock and Key*. The bargemen used to come there, 'just like pirates from foreign parts,' so Ellen said, and would fight the landsmen for half-a-crown or a gallon of ale (or for the fun of it if times were hard). Then the poachers used to bring their game there, and plan their big drives with the men from the city shops. Then there was cock-fighting, and sometimes dog-fighting; and men would come in sometimes from the cities, to nobble a horse at the races, or to burgle a house, and so away. No matter at what time of the day or night you came near to Lower Lock you would always meet a dirty boy doing nothing in particular hanging about on the approaches. If the boy whistled 'God Save the King,' it was a sign that you were all right, but if he whistled 'Holy, holy, holy,' all those who felt uneasy used to get under cover.

There was said to be a great deal of cover, in between the two alleys, chimneys which would hide a couple of men, doors which opened from house to house, false floors, under which a man could hide or a body could be hidden, traps which took one into a cellar, or into a vault or into the big old drain of the monastery: there were hiding-places above and below everywhere, where wanted men could lie; and in the old brew-house who knew what went on?

However, Kay used to enjoy going down to Lower Lock, to look at the barges and at the small sea-going vessels, colliers, topsail schooners, brigantines, and barquentines which sometimes came there. He saw the usual dirty boy as he drew near. He recognised the lad as one called Poppyhead, which is the country name for ringworm. Poppyhead was sucking a straw, under the lee of the bridge, and beating his hands to try to warm them. On seeing Kay, he took the straw from his mouth and stared, but did not whistle. 'Please,' Kay said, 'do you know where the Punch and Judy show went?'

'What?'

'Do you know where the Punch and Judy show went?'
'Ah.'
'Where did it go?'
'He's gone.'
'Do you know where to?'
'He went along.'
'Up this way, was it?'
'Ah.'
'Was it this way?'
'He didn't say.'
'But did he go this way?'
'I don't know.'
'But did you see a man with a Punch and Judy show, passing along here?'
'Yes, I saw a man go.'
'Had he a Punch and Judy show with him?'
'I don't know.'
A couple of ragged little boys crept out from under the bridge: they stared, with their fingers in their mouths.
'What does he want, Poppy?' one of them asked.
'I don't know,' Poppy said.
'The man with the Punch and Judy show,' Kay said.
'He's not there,' a woman who was passing said. 'He's gone up to Cockfarthings in the Bear-Ward.' She was all wrapped against the snow in a grey plaid, and Kay did not know who she was, but he saw a pair of very bright eyes, and noticed a gold ring of odd shape on the bare hand that clutched the plaid close. She passed on over the bridge at once, without heeding Kay's word of thanks. Kay turned in the other direction for Cockfarthings. The three little boys called out to him to give them some ha'pennies, and as he did not, they flung stones after him and called him a Dinjer; but there were not many stones

lying handy, nor could they aim well, with the snow whirling into their eyes, like gritty dust.

A very long time before, when the Abbot had ruled there, someone had kept bears for the amusement of the pilgrims coming to the monastery: part of the village was still called the Bear-Ward, though perhaps no bears had been there for four centuries. Cockfarthings was the name of a man who kept a pub called the *Drop of Dew* there. There had been two brothers Cockfarthings, John and Henry, but John was now dead. Henry Cockfarthings made baskets when not serving in the bar. So Kay walked up to the *Drop of Dew* and again admired the sign, which showed a drop of dew as big as your head, all frosty with dust of glass. He went into the bar, expecting to see Henry Cockfarthings, but Henry was somewhere in the backyard doing something with a mallet, it seemed.

The only person in the bar was the little old bright-eyed man for whom he was looking. He sat in the settle by the fire looking at a book, which he closed and put into his pocket as Kay came in. Kay, who had very quick eyes, noticed that the book was full of coloured pictures. Kay never quite knew why, but as soon as he saw the old man sitting there in the lonely bar he said, 'If I saw Someone, I was to tell him that Someone is safe.'

'Ah,' the old man said, 'but I say that that's more than anyone knows when Wolves are Running, Master Harker.'

'Please,' Kay said, 'will you tell me what you mean by "Wolves"?'

'If you keep looking out for fun,' the old man said, 'you will see the Wolves as like as not. Or won't you?'

'I don't know,' Kay said.

'And now, Master Kay Harker,' the old man replied, 'you want me to go up to Seekings with my Punch and my Judy, and at half after five.'

'Did Peter tell you?' Kay asked. 'Did my friend, Peter Jones, find you?' The old man paid no attention to the question.

'I will be there, Master Harker,' the man said, 'with my Punch and my Judy and at half after five. And perhaps,' he added, 'maybe I'll bring more than my Punch and my Judy, for a travelling man collects as he goes, or doesn't he?'

'I should think he would,' Kay said, not knowing what else to say.

'Ah,' said the little old man. 'You would think he would. You're one that thinks right, then. And now, Master Harker, as I've heard tell that you're fond of birds, maybe you will tell me what bird you'd like best to see, of all the birds there are.'

'There is a bird,' Kay said, 'that I'd like frightfully to see, but I'm afraid it doesn't really exist.'

'Ah, but perhaps it does exist, Master Harker,' he replied. 'Come, look now at the desert sands, where the pebbles are diamonds: look now, the spice tree; smell the spice upon it.'

As he spoke he pointed at the fire. The kettle on its hob was steaming a little but not enough to dim the glow in the grate. As Kay looked, this seemed to open into a desert all glittering with jewels. Kay knew that it was an Arabian desert, for, somehow, Egypt with the Pyramids were behind him, and mirages were forming far, far in the distance. Then, lo, in the midst of the desert was the sole Arabian tree, oozing gum, its leaves dropping crystals of spice, its flowers heavy with scent, and its fruit shedding sweetness. Leaves, flowers, and fruit all grew upon it at the same time.

As Kay looked, a wind parted the boughs, and, within, on a nest of cinnamon sticks, was a Phoenix. 'It's a Phoenix!' Kay said. 'And now, I can say I have seen one. Oh, I wonder, will it begin to sing?' The Phoenix did begin to sing. She lifted her head, and the plumes changed from white to gold, and from gold to orange. As the song increased, so as to shake the very house, the plumes changed from orange to scarlet, and, lo, they were no longer plumes, but flames, which burned up the Phoenix, so that the song died away, and at last there was no Phoenix, nor any nest, only some ash blowing away in the wind and a few embers.

'Watch now,' the old man said. Kay watched. Something stirred among the embers. Something was being thrust from among the embers, so that it fell with a little click upon the jewels at the tree-foot. Kay saw another thing fall, and then saw that these things were white fragments of egg-shell, which the wind carried away.

Then out of the embers in the tree a little unfledged Phoenix rose. It hopped onto a branch, pecked a flower, then pecked a fruit and crowed.

'There,' the little old man said, 'that is the bird you were afraid didn't exist. But now, Master Harker, Master Cockfarthing is coming; so you shall see me at Seekings, with my Punch and my Judy and my little dog Toby at one half after five.'

'Oh, but please,' Kay said, 'I was to settle with you how much we were to pay for the performance.'

'As to that,' the man said, 'suppose you were to dig down at Seekings, and found the way into what was, what would you pay for going in?'

'I don't know,' Kay said.

'And suppose,' the man said, 'you were to dig through at Seekings, and found the way into what is, what would you pay for going in? One silver sixpence with a hole in it, isn't it?'

'I don't know,' Kay said.

'And I don't know,' the old man said, 'that what you give me for my great show will be a fair pay for all the wonders seen. But five new silver shillings won't break you; that and a biscuit for my Toby, and a dish of eggs and bacon afterwards for me.'

'Indeed, you shall have all that,' Kay said.

'In my box,' the old man said, 'that I carry about with me, I've other delights besides my show.' He tapped a little flat wooden box, covered with some black, shining waxed or tarred cloth against the rain. 'But perhaps you shall see that later, Master Harker, while I eat my eggs and my bacon, with my good grinder teeth.'

Kay thanked him very much, and went out from the *Drop of Dew* into the snow, which was now powdering the world and making all things dim. 'How on earth did he show me the Phoenix and know that I was thinking of it?' he wondered. 'And how did he know me, and all about me? I have never seen him before.'

Though he had not been long at the *Drop of Dew*, the storm had grown much worse while he had been there. It was so bad that he thought it wise to take the short cut to Seekings, through Haunted Lane as it was called, which was a way he did not like, for it was a very dark lane of old houses some of which were still marked with red crosses on their doors to show that within them, two centuries before, someone had lain sick of the plague.

He was very glad to get out of the lane into the open,

and so over the fence into the garden and into Seekings out of the snow. In the house he found Peter.

'I say, Kay,' Peter said, 'I've been all over the place and couldn't find your Punch and Judy man.'

'I've found him,' Kay said. 'He'll be here at five-thirty. And now let's get ready for Robber Tea.'

Robber Tea was one of Kay's delights. It was a game only played in winter evenings, in the dark old study that had shelves full of old books, and old guns on the walls above the shelves.

At the beginning of the game, the window curtains were drawn, so as to make a darkness. Then, the fire was built up with wood and coal, so as to make a hot toasting fire. Then, the table was pulled to one side of the room against the bookshelves, and some dark curtains were brought down and spread over the table and adjoining chairs, so as to make an inner cave. When the cave had been rigged, it was lit with some lanterns that had coloured glass slides. When all this was ready, a waterproof sheet was spread on the hearthrug with a supply of toasting forks, sausages, bread, butter, dripping and strawberry jam. Then, the robbers lay in the glow of the fire toasting bread and sausages, and afterwards eating them in the inner cave.

When they had feasted, the robbers decided to turn in for the night with Peter as a guard outside. The clock on the mantel struck for half-past five. There came a noise of pan-pipes outside the window.

'Here is the Punch and Judy man,' Kay said. 'I'll fetch him in.'

As he opened the door a whirl of snow sped in. There was the showman bent under the frame of his show, looking rather like a giant without any head or arms.

'Do come in out of the snow,' Kay said. The man came in and stamped the snow from him onto the mats, put down his show, and brushed the sleeves of his coat.

'Wild weather, Master Harker,' he said.

'It is wild,' Kay said. 'Would you like a cup of tea before you play?'

'No, I thank you, Master Harker, but it is as wild a night as any I've known, ever; and I've been a long time on the roads, Master Harker, first and last.'

'How long, sir?' Kay asked, for the man looked very old, although his eyes were so bright.

'I get a little out of my reckoning,' he answered. 'First there were pagan times; then there were in-between times; then there were Christian times; then there was another in-between time; then there was Oliver's time; and then there was pudding time: but there've been a lot since them and more coming: but the time I liked best was just before the in-between time, what you might call Henry's time.'

Kay didn't know what the old man was talking about, but by this time, he had brushed off the snow and was ready to begin his play: so, as soon as the room was ready, and everybody comfortable on the floor, he came in and played his Punch and Judy play.

'And now, Master Harker and friends,' he said, coming outside his stand, 'now that I've played my play, I'll play more than my Punch and my Judy, for a travelling man collects as he goes, or doesn't he?'

'He does,' little Maria said.

'Ah, he does, the bright Miss Maria says,' he repeated. 'He collects: and what he collects he shows.'

He propped his theatre against a bookcase, sat cross-legged in front of the door and produced a little white ball, which he tossed into the air. It broke into two balls while it was aloft, he tossed them repeatedly, till they broke into four balls, which shone as they flickered up and down. Presently, while three of the balls were in the air, he beat the fourth into the ground, where it became a little bright mouse which ran away into a hole: then he tossed another ball to the ceiling where it became a shining bird which flew away: then he caught the remaining two balls one in each hand: one turned into a red rose which he gave to Jemima, the other to a white rose which he gave to Susan.

'These are all little things,' he said, 'which a travelling man collects as he goes.'

After this, he turned to Maria, who was the smallest person there. 'And you, Miss Maria,' he said, 'I'm told you are fond of guns and that, so shall I see what will happen if I blow my bugle? But first I must tap the wainscot, to see if there's any gate there.'

He walked across to the western wall and tapped the wainscot. It was all dark old wood there, with no hole or cranny in it, yet now, after he had touched it, there was a tiny double gate of bronze, with gilded pinnacles, in the wood. As they all watched this, the old man blew a little bugle, and instantly from within the wainscot a little bugle answered. Then suddenly a little tiny voice called out an order from inside the wainscot, and instantly two little tiny men pushed the double gates open and stood aside. Then a lot of little drums and fifes and trumpets struck up a march, and out came a band of soldiers headed by a drum-major. There must have been at least a hundred of them. They had big drums as big as walnuts and little drums as little as filberts; and tiny white ivory fifes and lovely little brass trumpets. They were playing

Green Sleeves. They wore scarlet coats, with white facings, and neat little black trousers, but the beautiful thing was the way they marched. Then after them, there came a regiment of foot-soldiers, then a regiment of cavalry on little horses, and the horse of the Colonel, which was a white charger, shied at little Maria: then after these there came a regiment of artillery with guns and ammunition wagons: then after these there came wagons full of supplies of all sorts. The band halted in the middle of the room: but went on playing while the army marched about. Then presently, the army halted: the foot-soldiers piled their arms: the cavalry dismounted and tethered their horses; the artillery men parked their cannon and put their horses into lines; then they unpacked the wagons and put up tents, unrolled blankets, lighted camp-fires, cooked their suppers and went into the tents to sleep, except the sentries who marched about, and sometimes said 'Who goes there?' Presently the buglers came to the tent doors to blow the waking call. Everybody sprang at once to work: some struck the tents: others lit fires and cooked bacon and made coffee, or loaded up the wagons, or rubbed down and harnessed the horses, after giving them their feed. Then, when the men had breakfasted, they all fell in, the horsemen mounted, the artillery men climbed onto their guns, and away they all marched as the band played, three times round the room and then through the double bronze gates which closed behind them. After they had closed, the children heard the band fading away into the distance till it was silent. As they looked at the little gates, they began to fade, till in a minute no trace of them was there: the wainscot was old, dark wood, in a solid panel.

'That was lovely,' Maria said.

The old Punch and Judy man said, 'I seem to remember that little Miss Susan was once very fond of butterflies. I'll see if I can't call a few, in spite of the cold.'

He began to blow a low note upon his pan-pipes. Presently he said, 'The leaves are falling. All the cocoons are in the leaves.' It seemed to the children that the ceiling above them opened into a forest in a tropical night: they could see giant trees, with the stars in their boughs and fire-flies gleaming out and ceasing to gleam among the lower sprays. Heavy leaves began to waver down onto the floor, where they lay crackling, till it grew brighter, when lo, the sun was shining among the tree-tops, green and grey parrots and scarlet cardinal birds came pecking the fruits, and now, out of the fallen leaves, there came butterfly after butterfly, bursting out of cocoons and chrysalides of many strange forms into images of lively beauty, bright as jewels. They sunned themselves for a moment, then leaped into the air and flew about. 'Put a little sugar from the bowl into your hands,' the old man said to the children, 'then they will perch on your hands.' The children put sugar into their hands, moistening it from the milk-jug, and lo, the lovely gleaming blue and scarlet and golden creatures perched on their hands and glistened and quivered there, as they thrust long snouts into the sweetness. Little Susan had as many as nine on her hand at once, as well as a big shining blue one which perched on her hair. When all the butterflies had had some sugar, they flew up into the air, and danced in and out in a maze, as gnats will, but the maze danced by them was all in order and very beautiful. At last they all went spiring up into the bright tropic day, and flickered away among the trees, going round and round and round till they were out of sight, so far up. Then the tropic forest disappeared: it was the study ceiling again.

'And now,' the old man said, 'I'll show you yet another little play, which many an ancient queen has watched, in her palace by the banks of the Nile.' He produced two cubes of ivory, one red, one white; they looked like dice.

'Now,' he said, taking one in each hand and shaking them, 'look at these.'

He was shaking the dice in a strange way, so that suddenly the moving rhythm of the hands becames waves of the sea; the little red cube was a tiny little red shark, snapping after a little white skate; he swam round and round the room after it, always just missing it, and at last, when he had almost caught it, the skate turned into a skylark and went up singing to the ceiling. Instantly the shark turned into a hawk and went after her. They went round and round the room up and down: always the hawk nearly caught her, and once it seemed had caught her, but the lark turned into a little deer and ran among the children. The hawk turned into a wolf and chased her; yet just as he was about to pounce, the deer turned into a princess on a little white pony, and galloped away. The wolf turned into a red knight who called for a black horse and presently galloped away after her. The children could hear the hoofs dying away and away and away. A lot of little green fairies came dancing down onto the forest track by which the riders had gone. They pulled the sides of the forest inwards, so that at last there was the study wall again.

'Now,' the old man said, 'if you've been pleased with my shows, if I may have my silver shillings, my biscuit for my Toby, my egg and my bacon for myself, I will be taking my way.'

Kay paid him the silver shillings, and brought in biscuits and some good meaty bones for Toby, and then a supper of eggs and bacon, with hot buttered toast, and a jug of sweet chocolate.

The old man seemed suspicious about the French window. Before he sat to his supper at the table, he went to it, to make sure that the curtains were drawn completely across it.

While he ate, the children sat round the fire, talking of the wonderful show, and telling each other what they would like to see again. Suddenly the dog Barney pricked his ears and from just outside the French window two key bugles and an oboe struck up the tune of 'O come, all ye Faithful.' Some twenty singers outside in the snow broke into the hymn.

'Carol-singers,' Kay said, 'and very good ones. How silently they came up. I didn't hear a single step.'

Peter went to the window and twitched back the curtain a little. 'It's deep snow already,' he said peering out. 'They have got Japanese lanterns. Do look how beautiful they are!'

Outside was a party of twenty men and women wrapped against the snow, and bearing big Japanese lanterns hung upon sticks. Snow was whirling all about them. Their shoulders were covered white with snow. Their faces glowed in the lantern-light. The musicians had music stands with electric torches.

'That's not the Condicote Choir. We've not got a style like that. Who are they?' Kay said.

'That's the Cathedral Choir from Tatchester,' Caroline Louisa said. 'There are the Canons and the Precentor, and that's the Bishop himself.'

When the hymn had finished Kay and Caroline Louisa

went into the hall to the side door. The Bishop and his singers moved towards them as they opened.

'Good evening, Bishop,' Caroline Louisa said, 'come in into the warmth, while we brew some cocoa for you.'

The party came in stamping the snow onto the door-mats. They stood in the hall while Kay ran to fetch Jane, Ellen and Joe. Then they all sang 'Good Christian Men, Rejoice,' 'Christians Rejoice,' 'Deep was the Night,' 'O Night peaceful and blest' and 'Noël.' When they had sung, Kay and the others brought buns and hot cocoa for the singers. They sat about in the hall and ate and drank.

'And now,' the Bishop said, 'we have finished our tour here and must be thinking of getting back. I want you all to come tomorrow night to the Palace at Tatchester. We are having a children's party, with a Christmas Tree, at five o'clock, and I shall expect you all.'

The children said that they would be delighted and thanked him for the thought.

'Then, another thing,' he said: 'I want you all to come on Christmas Eve to the Midnight Service of the Thousandth Christmas Celebration in Tatchester Cathedral. There has been a midnight Celebration every Christmas Eve since the Foundation. We wish this Thousandth Festival to be really memorable.'

The children loved any festival which would keep them out of bed at midnight like grown-ups. They said that they would love to come.

He looked about the faces gathered in the hall: 'Ha,' he said, 'I think I have seen that face before. Aren't you my little friend, Miss Maria? Well, I am glad to see you again.'

Little Miss Maria showed some small confusion, for once, only a year before, she had started the Bishop's motor-car and driven it into a lamp-post. However, the Bishop seemed inclined to forgive and forget.

A moment later he caught sight of the Punch and Judy man, who was packing his puppets into a box.

'Ha,' he said, 'isn't this the famous Punch and Judy man, Cole Hawlings? We have met before, I think.'

'You've seen me a many times,' the old man answered. 'Yes, Your Grace.'

'And you're just the very man I was hoping to see; a Punch and Judy showman,' the Bishop said. 'At this party tomorrow we shall have a great many children. Would you consent to come to play for them?'

'Right gladly,' the old man said. 'I will bring my Punch and my Judy and my dog, Toby; for I have played a Christmas play on that Night ever since pagan times, so to speak.'

'Thank you,' the Bishop said. 'Will you be at the Palace at half-past four, then, tomorrow? Good. And now Good Night to all of you; a merry Christmas and a most happy New Year, and many, many thanks for your most warm welcome.'

As the members of the Choir swathed themselves up against the snow before venturing forth, most of the children scattered upstairs. Kay waited to open the door for the Choir and, while standing near the door, he heard, or thought that he heard, the noise of swift padding feet. The thought flashed into his mind, he did not know why, that these were the Alsatian dogs again. 'They move just like wolves,' he thought. The noise ceased and he thought that he must have been mistaken. Then he saw that the dog, Barney, had pricked his ears and was staring towards the door. Barney uttered a little yap.

'There was something passing,' Kay said to himself.

But now the Choir was ready to start. He opened the door and, as he opened it, he saw that three men were there at the French window which led into the study. Undoubtedly, they were trying to peer in through the window; as the door opened they wheeled round.

One of the first of the Choir to leave the house was the Precentor who lifted his Japanese lantern to see who the men were, and Kay saw that one of the men was the foxy-faced man who had done the card trick in the train.

He cried, 'Aha, Precentor, we were just too late for your concert, what?'

He and the other two caught step with the Precentor and passed along with him. Kay could not hear what the Precentor called them nor what they talked about, for the other members of the Choir were filing past, each saying something, such as: 'Burr-r-r, what a night!' 'I say, isn't it snowing!' 'Don't you stop at the door, Kay. You'll catch cold,' etc., etc.

Kay noticed that Cole Hawlings came to the door as the last of the Choir passed out; he leaned from it to watch the departing party. As he turned back into the house, Kay thought that his face was very white. He noticed that he walked somewhat unsteadily back into the study. 'He didn't like those three men,' he thought.

As Kay shut the door and slipped the chain onto it, he heard the bell of the back door violently rung. Someone beat on the knocker there. Jane and Ellen hurried to the kitchen to see who was knocking. Then the telephone bell in the porch began to ring. Caroline Louisa went to the telephone.

At this instant, little Maria, who was with the other children upstairs, leaned over the banisters and cried,

'Buck up, Kay! We are going to dress up and play Pirates.'

'All right. In a minute,' Kay said.

He went back into the study to look after the old man. He noticed that the curtains, which had been disarranged when Peter and the rest had stared at the carol-singers, were now carefully re-drawn over the French window. The Punch and Judy man stood in the corner near the door, looking very white and tense, as though the earth were about to open.

'So, Master Harker,' the old man said, 'we always used to say, "It's the snow that brings the wolves out." Many a bitter night did we stand the wolf-guard. Now here, once more, they're running. We must stand to our spears.'

'Everything's all right,' Kay said.

'Where did those three men go?' the old man asked in a whisper.

'I think they went with the Choir,' Kay said, 'but I couldn't see.'

The old man shook his head and pointed at the dog. Barney had stiffened in his tracks, with a bristling fell. He was showing his teeth and staring at the curtained window. There could be no doubt that somebody was outside.

The old man lifted a finger to the dog, perhaps to keep him from barking. He then shut his eyes and muttered something. It seemed to Kay that he was in great distress of mind. Then, as he opened his eyes, it seemed to Kay that he had found comfort, for he smiled, pointed, and whispered to Kay, 'Master Harker, what is the picture yonder?'

'It is a drawing of a Swiss mountain,' Kay said. 'It was

done by my grandfather. It is called the Dents du Midi, from the North.'

'And do I see a path on it?' the old man said. 'If you, with your young eyes, will look, perhaps you will kindly tell me if that is a path on it.'

As they stared at the picture, it seemed to glow and to open, and to become not a picture but the mountain itself. They heard the rush of the torrent. They saw how tumbled and smashed the scarred pine-trees were among the rolled boulders. On the lower slopes were wooden huts, pastures with cattle grazing; men and women working.

High up above there, in the upper mountain, were the blinding bright snows, and the teeth of the crags black and gleaming. 'Ah,' the old man said, 'and yonder down the path come the mules.'

Down the path, as he said, a string of mules was coming. They were led, as mules usually are, by a little pony mare with a bell about her neck. The mules came in single file down the path: most of them carried packs upon their backs of fallen logs, or cheeses made in the high mountain dairies or trusses of hay from the ricks; one of them towards the end of the line was a white mule, bearing a red saddle.

The first mules turned off at a corner. When it came to the turn of this white mule to turn, he baulked, tossed his head, swung out of the line, and trotted into the room, so that Kay had to move out of his way. There the mule stood in the study, twitching his ears, tail and skin against the gadflies, and putting down his head so that he might scratch it with his hind foot. 'Steady there,' the old man whispered to him. 'And to you, Master Kay, I thank you. I wish you a most happy Christmas.'

At that, he swung himself onto the mule, picked up his theatre with one hand, gathered the reins with the other, said, 'Come, Toby,' and at once rode off with Toby trotting under the mule, out of the room, up the mountain path, up, up, up, till the path was nothing more than a line in the faded painting, that was so dark upon the wall. Kay watched him till he was gone, and almost sobbed, 'O, I do hope you'll escape the wolves.'

A very, very faint little voice floated down to him from the mountain tops. 'You'll see me again'; then the mule-hoofs seemed to pass onto grass. They could be heard no more. 'He has gone for ever,' Kay thought, as he watched.

There came, as it were, a little gust of wind, blowing what looked like snowflakes from the mountain path. The snowflakes flew out into the room and fluttered about the ceiling, growing rapidly larger. They resolved themselves into shapes of coloured tissue paper, such as the caps and crowns sometimes found within crackers: there were also little paper balloons, in the shapes of cocks, horses, ships and aeroplanes: these floated and lifted and drifted down. Kay saw that there was one of a different shape and colour for each child there: and printed, too, with his or her name. Thus:

For little Maria,
from Cole Hawlings.
Shoot Not, Shock Not.

For Master Kay Harker,
from Cole Hawlings.
The Wolves are Running.

For good Miss Jemima,
from Cole Hawlings.
Happy Is that Happy Makes.

When the coloured papers had all floated to the floor, the lights seemed to grow dimmer. Caroline Louisa came into the study.

'Kay,' she said, 'I am so very sorry to upset your holiday. My brother is very ill again, in London, with his recurrent fever: and there is nobody to look after him at all. I'm afraid I must go up to him by the seven train tonight. Celia has been cabled for and should be on her way to him now: I ought to be there until she comes. I hate to leave you on the first night of the holidays, but I hope it won't be for more than just tonight, or perhaps tomorrow night as well.'

'I say, I'm most awfully sorry,' Kay said. 'I do hope you'll find your brother better. I say, can't I drive you to the station?'

'No, indeed, Kay, thanks,' she said. 'You will not drive any car for five years.'

'Well, can't I see you off?'

'No, no, thank you. I've told Joe to take me. He's putting on the chains now.'

'I will see you off though,' Kay said. 'It's an awful night. I hope your train won't be snowed up.'

'It's not so bad as that,' she said. 'Now I must run and be ready. I shall telephone to you at ten tomorrow morning.'

'You won't,' Kay said. 'All the wires will be down from the snow.'

While she ran to be ready, Kay slipped out of the front door to the garage, where he found Joe chaining the car-wheels to keep them from slipping in the snow.

'Even with the chains her'll slither in the drifts,' Joe said.

Indeed, when they started for the station a few minutes

later her did slither in the drifts. Kay went to the station to see Caroline Louisa away, and much enjoyed the car's skidding and the appearance of the engine of the express, glowing with fire and steaming, yet all hung with icicles from snow which had melted on the boiler and frozen as it dripped.

CHAPTER THREE

While Kay was out of the house and Caroline Louisa making ready to leave, the other children were in their rooms, dressing up as pirates, and giving themselves pirates' moustaches with burnt cork. Just as the front door slammed and the car lurched away to the station, they came down to the study for a dress-parade. There they found the paper toys which had floated down from the mountain. They much enjoyed seeing their names in print.

'Shoot not, shock not,' said little Maria. 'I like whoever it was's cheek. I shall shoot and I shall shock as long as my name's Maria. Now let's toss up for who shall be Captain. One of you's got to be a Merchantman and be taken and have to walk the plank.'

'No, let's be Christmas pirates,' Jemima said, 'and put all our treasure into poor people's stockings and let nobody know who did it: let the people all go to bed in despair wanting money, and then find it in their stockings in the morning and be made happy.'

'I say,' Peter said, 'of all the sickly sentiments.'

'It's a jolly good Christmas sentiment.'

'Well, I didn't dress up to be a pirate to have Christmas sentiment.'

'Hold on a minute,' Maria said. 'I believe there's someone just outside that window.'

'I expect it was only snow falling.'

'No, somebody coughed: it's carol-singers again. Well, I'll tell them to sing and then we'll get on with Pirates.'

'Let them ring the door-bell,' Jemima said, 'then somebody will attend to them.'

'Not a bit,' Maria said. 'They're probably a lot of foul little boys trying to peep in at the window. I'm going to open this window to them here.'

With that she flung back the curtain, unlocked the French window, and opened it into the night. There, directly outside in the snow, was the figure of a man. 'Good evening, my young friends,' he said in a gentle silky voice. 'I could not make anybody hear. This is the house called Seekings House, is it not?'

'Did you want Caroline Louisa?' Jemima asked.

'I am afraid you will think that what I want is very absurd,' he said. 'I was given to understand that a man called Hollings, or Hawlings, a Punch and Judy showman, is here.'

'There was a Punch and Judy showman,' Maria said, 'but he has gone.'

'Gone?' the man said. 'How long has he been gone?'

Although he had not been invited to come in out of the snow, he had come in, and had closed the French window behind him, and was shaking the snow from himself onto the mat.

Maria answered in good faith, believing that what she said was true, and little guessing what trouble her answer was to cause to others.

'He went away with the Tatchester Choir,' she said.

'D'you mean the party with the Japanese lanterns?' the man asked.

'Yes,' Maria said, 'they had a lot of Japanese lanterns.'

'That went off,' the man asked, 'in a motor-bus to Tatchester?'

'I don't know how they went off,' Maria said.

They saw that the man was dressed as a clergyman underneath his greatcoat.

'And so, I miss him once more,' he said. 'How very vexatious! I am interested, I should tell you, in the various forms of the Punch and Judy show, and this man is the son, and grandson of Punch and Judy men, who were on the roads many years ago. This man is known to have versions of the play which they played, and other versions still older, which are not played, and I do most earnestly want to meet him, and now he is off to this wild life of the roads in weather like this, where a touch of pneumonia, or a passing van, may wipe out his knowledge for ever.'

'You would get him at Tatchester,' Peter said. 'The Bishop asked him to give a performance there tomorrow.'

'Ah!' the man said. 'So that fixes him to Tatchester.' He looked at Peter curiously. 'May I ask,' he said, 'if you are the gentleman known as young Mister Harker?'

'No,' Peter said. 'I don't know where he is at the moment: probably upstairs somewhere, dressing up.'

The man looked at little Maria. 'And this little friend is your sister, I take it?'

'I may be little, but I am not a friend of yours,' Maria said, 'and you may take it, or leave it.'

'Indeed!' the man said. 'But I interrupt your Christmas gambols, and if the man is gone I must go too. Good night, my little Maria.' He slipped out, and closed the French window behind him.

'I say, Maria,' Peter said, 'you ought not to speak to people like that.'

'I'll speak to people as I like,' she said.

'But he was a clergyman.'

'I'll bet he wasn't. What would a clergyman be doing spying in at the window?'

'He wasn't spying in at the window.'

'Well, he was trying to, anyhow. As to his saying that he had been trying to make people hear, that's all bunk. If he had rung the bell, or knocked, we'd have heard him. He was creeping round, spying. What clergyman would come round hunting for a Punch and Judy man on a night like this? Any real clergyman would be going round carol-singing, or doing choir-practice, or visiting the sick or the poor. I vote we all go out and snow-ball that villain down his false neck.'

'Oh, chuck it, Maria,' Peter said. 'Now, come on and play Pirates. Where on earth is Kay?'

At that moment, Kay was driving home from the station. On his way through the market-square he asked Joe to stop the car. 'You go home alone, Joe,' he said. 'I must do some Christmas shopping. I shall be back in a minute by the short cut.'

He had drawn some money from Caroline Louisa. He bought a little scissors-case for Jemima, and a sheath-knife for Peter, at the ironmonger's. Then he went into Bob's shop, which was almost next door, and bought a bottle of acid drops for Maria and a box of chocolates for Susan. After stuffing these into his pockets, he turned for home up the Haunted Lane.

Near the most haunted part of the lane, there was a

short cut into Seekings garden across a derelict place known as Monk's Piece. There were still some stub ends of monkish building there, with the hollow of their fish-pond, now dry, and the vaults of some of their cellars, often full of water.

No one much liked the place after dark, but Kay liked it better than Haunted Lane, and in this night of snow it was a real short cut.

As he climbed the ruined wall into Monk's Piece, he saw an electric torch flash in the main ruin: several men were there. He had been told that the ghosts of monks always gathered there at Christmas time to sing carols, but ghosts of monks do not use electric torches. One of the men lit a cigarette with a pocket-lighter, another bent over a lighted match sucking at a pipe.

Kay would have slipped past without pausing, but:

'So he was among the Bishop's Choir and we never noticed, ha-ha, what?' a familiar voice said.

'Yes,' a silky voice answered, and the silky voice was familiar to Kay, too. 'And you never noticed. Do you notice anything, I sometimes wonder?'

Kay pressed close in to the ivy on the ruined wall.

'A clever dodge, though, what, to get in with the Choir,' the foxy-faced man said.

'No doubt it seems to you,' the silky voice replied. 'I should have thought it the obvious dodge that you might have expected. Now he has got right through our ring again. Those fools let him trick them at Musborough. Then by sheer luck we got his message that he would be here. Just as we learn his disguise and where he is, you let him go right through you, with the goods on him. O, if I'd only not been tricked to the *Drop of Dew* for him I'd have been here and I'd have had him.'

'You'd have thought him a carol-singer, just as we did,' a man growled.

'Would I?' the silky voice said. 'Would I, my gentle Joe, my far-seeing friend? But come on, now. The Wolves are Running. Get on to Tatchester. There seems no doubt that he's gone there, but he may slip off by the way. Overtake that motor-'bus, if you can. If not, find out where he's got to in Tatchester, and get the goods off him.'

'Won't you come, Chief?' the man called Joe asked. 'We're willing hands, maybe, but where are we without your great brain? Ha-ha, as our friend says, what?'

'You might well ask where you are without me,' the silky voice said. 'Are you going to start to Tatchester? Get to Tatchester, will you?'

All the silkiness fell from the voice at a breath: the men jumped as though they'd been kicked. 'All right, Chief,' the man called Joe said. 'We're going. I only asked, won't you?'

'I've got a report coming to me here,' the Chief said. 'Report to me at the inn in Number Three Code. My thundering sky, are you ever going to shift?'

Kay thought, from the voice, that he would strike them. The men hurried out of the ruin, going away from Kay, who was now pressed into the ivy on the wall. He heard the men clumping at a trot along the Seekings garden fence: presently he heard their car start off, taking the Tatchester road. Just before the car door slammed he heard a waif sentence from the foxy-faced man:

'Little Abner's in his little tantrums, ha-ha, what?' The others laughed.

'He'll tantrum you pretty soon,' the man growled from within the ruin.

'So it's Abner Brown and his gang again,' Kay muttered. 'I am up against Magic, then, as well as Crime. What report can he have coming to him here? I daren't move until he's gone from here. And if anybody comes here with a report he's almost bound to see me. O dear, O dear.'

Kay was standing pressed against the ivy outside. Under the vaulted roof inside the ruin Abner stamped his feet and flogged with his arms. Kay had not waited a minute after the starting of the car before he heard a sort of scuttering, scraping noise coming from somewhere below. There were also little splashes and snarls. He knew that under the ruins there were many queer underground ways. Someone was coming up by one of them into the ruin where Abner was.

'Is that you, Rat?' Abner asked.

'Ah, it's me,' a surly voice answered, 'and what's the good of being me? Up in the attic and down in the cellar, all weathers, all hours, for one who'd sell his mother, if he had one, for what she'd fetch as old bones. And what do I get by it? Bacon fat, you might say, or the green of that cheese the dog won't eat, or the haggie that made the hens swoon. But I don't, my Christian friend. I get rheumatics; that, and the dog sickt at me. That's what.'

'As a matter of fact, I've got some green-looking cheese for you,' Abner said. 'Look here.'

There was the scratch of a match; Abner lit a candle-end. Kay found that he could see through a hole in the wall right into the ruin. There, blinking at the light, was a disreputable Rat whom he had known in the past but had not seen for years. He was now much more disreputable than ever before. Kay had heard that everybody had dropped him, and that he had gone pirating. But there he was again; and a sickening object he looked.

'Ah,' Rat said, taking the cheese, which Kay could smell even in that cold weather. 'And you wouldn't give me this if you could sell it to a Tourists' Rest.'

'You're right,' Abner said. 'I wouldn't.'

'I understand you, Abner, and you understand me,' Rat said. He was eating the cheese with a sort of sideways wrench, while his little beady eyes stared at Abner.

'That man Joe, you'd better look out for, Abner,' Rat said. 'He's putting in for chief: likewise the "ha-ha, what?" man.'

'What d'you mean?' Abner asked.

'That's what,' Rat said. Here he dropped his cheese on the floor; he picked it up and ate it without wiping it. 'Ah, that's what,' he repeated.

'What's your report?' Abner said.

'Him what you wot of,' Rat said, 'is a getting rid of his Dog this evening.'

'That's nothing,' Abner said.

'A lady friend will take the Dog. There's many a Dog as I've loved more than that one now lies in a watery tomb with a stone round his neck. But some who claim to be friends never take a hint. That's what . . .

'Ah, and there's to be dark doings. You've scared 'em, Abner: and I beheld their scare.'

'Well, this is news at last,' Abner said. 'What did you see?'

'The *Drop of Dew*, upper room, the Lion and the Rose chamber as they call it.

'There's passages pretty near all under and round this city, to them who knows them. I've gone a dark stravage into pretty near every one first and last. They'd a meeting in the Lion and the Rose at the *Drop of Dew.* One what you wot of will be trying to get out of your ring at dawn tomorrow, by Arthur's Camp, across Bottler's Down, to Seven Barrows.'

'But Cole is at Tatchester,' Abner said.

'Well, one of what you wot of will be trying.'

'Will he have the goods on him?'

'Ah,' Rat said, 'that's what.'

'Well, will he? And which of them is it?'

'I been a cellarman, I have,' Rat said, 'and I've gone marine cellarman. And I've been a poor man, living in the dark, though others live in the light, with a haggy every day, and grudge a poor man so much as a old fishbone; yes, they do. You says to me: "Find out what they decide." Them was your words to me . . . "Find out" . . . you says . . . "what they decide." There I've been in those dark dwellings in danger of Dog, and found out what they decided. Now you says, "Will he?" and "Which of them is it?" You didn't tell me about that.'

'No, but you heard,' Abner said.

'I found out what they decided,' Rat said.

Abner seemed ready to box Rat's ears, for his stupidity; he seemed to gulp down his wrath and said very sweetly:

'So you don't know?'

'I know what they decided,' Rat said. 'And why? Because I found it out. And how? By going the dark ways, and being in danger of Dog. What your words was to me, that I done, although in danger of Dog.'

'And you did well,' Abner said. 'My brave Rat, you did superbly.'

'That's what,' Rat said.

There was a pause; Abner said nothing, Rat seemed to

expect something. At last he said, 'You said I was to have a bacon-rind, over and above the cheese.'

'So you shall have, my brave Rat,' Abner said. 'I'll bring you one tomorrow.'

'That's the bacon-rind to bring the plump on a man,' the Rat said, 'bacon-rind-tomorrow. That and marrow-bone-the-day-after proper makes your fur shine. Is there any little dark job you want done then, Master Abner, or shall I go now?'

'I want you to report at eleven tomorrow at the usual place, in case there should be anything.'

'Will I have the bacon-rind, then?'

'Yes.'

'That Kay Harker, what you wot of,' Rat said, 'if you was to saw his head off you'd do a good deed. He's to have a Dog give him at Christmas. That's what.'

'He won't bite you,' Abner said.

'Ah,' the Rat said, 'I hate him, and I hate Dogs.'

'Why?'

'Acos he's going to have a Dog give him.'

After this Rat smeared his paw across his nose and lurched off sideways to the candle-end. He blew out the light and took the candle-end: Kay judged that he bit the still soft tallow at the end. He moved off into the underground passage singing, with his mouth full of tallow, a song to his one tune, 'Sally in our Alley':

'Now nights are cold,
And on the wold
The wintry winds do whist-ol.
I ride my gray
On the high way,
To shoot 'em with my pist-ol.

'Now berries red
Hang overhead,
And pale berries of mist-ol.
It's my delight
To go by night
To shoot 'em with my pist-ol.'

Presently, the words died away underground. Abner took a few paces to and fro within the ruin. Kay could hear a few muttered words: 'Putting in for Captain, are they? We'll see. So Kay Harker is to have a Dog at Christmas. If that fool Rat would only choose the things that interest me, instead of what interests himself, he might be really useful. As for that intolerable child, Maria, at the house here, I wonder if she would be useful?' He seemed to reflect for a while. 'What did that fool of a Rat mean?' he muttered. 'Who is to get out of the ring by Arthur's Camp at dawn tomorrow? Could Cole double back from Tatchester and try it, or would it be one of the others? Going to Seven Barrows, too; what would they hope to do there? Well, the chances are that the Box will be on the man who tries to get out of the ring that way. Bottler's Down, eh? As nice a quiet place for a scrobbling as ever was made. We'll stop whoever it is. And, of course, it may be Cole, Box and all. I believe it will be. It probably will be . . .

'Rat, if it be, you shall have three rancid kippers and a haggis.

'Come now, I must telephone.'

So saying he flashed a torch on the broken stones of the floor, and walked briskly away, passing within two yards of Kay. When he had gone, Kay slipped from his hiding-place and returned to Seekings.

'Well,' he thought, 'they always say that "Listeners hear no good of themselves," but I never thought that old Rat in the old days would want to saw my head off. And who is going to give me a dog? I'll find out from Ellen.

'And what a world to come home to. Abner Brown and a gang, all dressed up as clergymen, and all after something that the Punch and Judy man has. I wonder what it can be. The Punch and Judy man is a wizard, if ever there was one, so it's probably some magic thing that he carries about with him. Why should Abner say that he has gone to Tatchester? I suppose he has heard that the Bishop asked him to come to Tatchester. Those spies at the window might have heard that. He might have been one of the spies himself for that matter.

'Then who are Cole Hawlings and the other two with the "Longways crosses" on their fingers?

'Well, when Caroline Louisa comes back tomorrow, I will tell her the whole story and ask her advice.

'Now what can I get for Caroline Louisa's Christmas present?'

By this time, he had reached Seekings. He shook the snow from him and went in.

'I say, Kay, wherever have you been?' Peter said: 'We've been waiting simply ages for you, and you aren't dressed, or anything, and we were just going to play Pirates, and there has been a clergyman sort of chap here asking for the Punch and Judy man.'

'What did you tell him?' Kay asked.

'Oh,' Maria said, 'I told him he had gone with the Tatchester Choir.'

'So that's how he thought that,' Kay thought to himself.

'What did he say?' Kay asked.

'I rather thought he was going on to Tatchester after him. But don't think for a moment that he was a clergyman. He was a burglar of the deepest dye. However, he didn't get much change out of us.'

'What did he want the Punch and Judy man for?' Kay asked.

'Oh, he had got some cock-and-bull story that he wanted some old versions of the Punch and Judy play. I'll bet that wasn't his real reason. I'll bet the Punch and Judy man is a member of a gang of burglars, and this clergyman is a member of a rival gang.'

'Oh, you've got gangs on the brain,' Peter said.

'If I have got gangs on the brain,' Maria said, 'whose brain is right as a general rule, may I ask? I've got a good deal more knowledge of life than you have, although you are so old and so wise, and go to a public school, and have to say "Sir" to the Masters. I'd "Sir" them, if it was me.'

'Well,' Kay said, 'he has gone on to Tatchester, you say?'

'Yes,' Peter said. 'I told him that the Bishop had engaged him to play tomorrow.'

'Come on then,' Kay said, 'let's play Pirates. I'll go up and dress.'

'Oh, no, you won't,' Maria said. 'We're not going to wait any longer. We've been waiting simply hours, as it is. You've had your chance of being a pirate and you haven't taken it, and now you'll be a merchantman, and you'll be captured and tortured, and then you'll have to walk the plank, and Peter and I are going to be the sharks that will eat you.'

After they had played Pirates, they had supper. After

supper, they sat round the fire and toasted chestnuts. Then, they told a chain ghost story, each telling a little piece and passing it on to the next one. Then presently, it was time for all the children to go up to bed. Kay and Peter were the last to go up. They got into their beds, and talked to each other across the room about what they would do in the holidays.

It was very snug in their room, for Ellen had built up the fire. Peter had just said that he thought he would be getting off to sleep, when Kay was thoroughly startled by the whining cry of the wind in the chimney. Often, on snowy nights, he had heard that cry of the wind in the chimney, but tonight there was something in the shriek that was very awful.

'I say, Peter,' he said, 'did you hear that? It was just like wolves howling.'

'Wolves are extinct,' Peter muttered, half asleep. Kay thought that he would turn off to sleep, and was just on the brink of sleep, when the wind again howled.

'It was wolves,' Kay said. 'It was what the old man said, "The Wolves are Running." '

Kay could not have been long asleep when he woke up feeling certain that there was something very important to be done at King Arthur's Camp. He rolled over, thinking, 'Well, it isn't likely that anything is to be done there at this time of night,' and was very soon asleep again. However, his dreams turned to King Arthur's Camp. He saw the place, half woke, then slept and saw it again. At this, he woke up wide awake, convinced that he must go there at once. He sat up in bed, struck a light and lit a candle. Peter woke up very grumpily. 'What on earth are you lighting a candle for?' he said.

'I'm going out to Arthur's Camp,' Kay said; 'will you come along?'

'Arthur's Camp?' Peter said; 'it's miles away. Whatever are you going there for?'

'I don't know,' Kay said, 'but I feel that I'm wanted there.'

'Wanted?' Peter said. 'You're talking in your sleep. What time is it?'

'Nearly midnight,' Kay said.

'Well, who on earth would want you there at midnight?' Peter growled. 'Do be sensible; you'll catch your death of cold. It's probably pouring snow still.'

'It isn't,' Kay said. 'Look.' He pulled back the curtains from the window so that Peter could see the bright moon shining on a world of deep snow. 'You see, it's stopped snowing; it's a lovely night now.'

'I know your lovely nights,' Peter said; 'freezing like billy-o, and about a foot of snow to slodge through.'

'It's jolly fine being out in the snow at night,' Kay said. 'You see foxes, white owls and tawny owls.'

'I never heard such rot,' Peter said. 'Do blow the light out and let a chap get to sleep.'

Kay said, 'I'll go alone.' He had wrapped himself up in thick things; now he took the candle and slipped downstairs. It was certainly icy cold in the hall. Some frosty snow had driven up underneath the doors and lay gleaming on the mats. He pulled back the bolts, took off the chain and opened. As he pulled the door back he became aware of something scraping the snow upon the drive. Somehow he had half expected it, and there it was: a shining white pony, with a proud Arab head and scarlet harness and headstall. 'Mount and ride, Kay,' the little horse said, 'for the Wolves are Running.'

Kay at once mounted; the horse sped over the garden with him, making no noise at all, but flicking up snow behind him as he sped. Kay could not be sure that these flicks of snow did not change into little white hounds.

All the town was fast asleep, there was only light in one window. Soon the houses dropped behind, and there was the open country, looking very wild and strange under the snow. 'Of course it's wild and strange,' he muttered; 'all the buildings are away: the two farms and the mill. Where have they gone? And those black pools . . . how did water come there?'

While he was wondering, the horse turned off on the track to Arthur's Camp. At this moment, Kay heard on the wind a note which he had heard once before that night. It was faint and far away, but it was the cry of wolves running.

At the Camp there was more strangeness. All the trees which had darkened the Camp the day before were gone; it was now a bare hill with a kind of glare coming from the top of it. By this glare, Kay saw that the earthen wall of the Camp was topped with a wooden stockade, which the horse leaped.

Kay slipped off the horse and kept a tight hold of the reins while he looked about him. Within the stockade a big fire was burning; it hissed and smoked as men put snowy branches onto it. By the light of the fire Kay saw that the Camp was busy with many short, broad, squat, shag-haired men and women, among whom some wizened savage children darted or cowered. Penned in one place were some half-starved cows, in another place some long-legged sheep. A dog or two skulked and yapped. There were some huts and ricks, and great piles of wood for firing. Whoever these people were, they had certainly been roused in the midnight by an attack of some sort.

In a moment Kay understood what the attack was. Somewhere down on the hill-slopes coming towards them that cry which had so scared him now burst out with a frenzy and nearness which made his blood run cold.

'The Wolves are Running,' he muttered. 'And now here they are.'

At this instant, the little white horse shied violently, plucked the reins from Kay and bolted. Kay saw the people running towards the stockade. The moon had come from her cloud and was shining brightly.

'Of course,' Kay said, 'this is only a dream. I shall wake up presently . . . But, no,' he added, 'no, it isn't a dream. They are wolves, and here they are at the pale.'

Just three feet from him, a big wolf leaped to the stockade and almost scrambled to the top. A man struck at it with a kind of adze, and missed it, Kay thought, but the fierce head fell back. As he fell back, there was a worrying, yapping snarl, as the rest of the pack came over the palisade in a body behind Kay. All rushed to meet them, flinging stones and lighted logs, shouting and striking. Kay rushed with them. Three wolves had got over, all the cattle and sheep were stampeding in the pens. There were the three wolves all hackled and bristled, snarling and slavering. Stones and burning embers fell all about them and hit them, they flinched and dripped and snarled but did not give way. Some men ran up and struck at them with spears and adzes; they gave way then and leaped easily back over the paling, to their fellows. In another instant, the pack was over the stockade in the darkest of the Camp. 'They're over again,' Kay cried. It was plain that they were over, for the cattle and sheep now cried out in terror and again stampeded, this time in such force that they broke their pens and scattered. The men shouted, and ran at the wolves. A woman thrust a great piece of gorse into the fire, lit it, and ran with it blazing. Kay seized another piece of gorse and did the same. A terrified little cow charging past him upset him. When he was again on his feet he saw that one of the sheep had been bitten, not too badly, and that the wolves were driven off. One wolf in scrambling back had had his backbone hacked through with an axe: another was being finished with spears. Three or four women had lighted gorse: for the moment the glare was too much for the wolves; they drew away; but they had not yet given up the attack. Kay could see them not far away, sometimes as green eyes glaring, sometimes as darknesses in the snow. They were waiting for the fires to die down, getting their breath, laying their plans, and licking their knocks and singes. Kay wondered how he was to get home to Seekings with the wolves in the fields. 'They always said there aren't any wolves,' he muttered, 'but there could easily be wolves in places like Chester Hills, and now, in this wild winter, out they come.'

The men now drove the stock to a space all lit and cornered by fire. Great flakes of fire floated away into the wind, as the dead leaves took flame: blots of snow fell hissing among the embers; the cattle flinched at both.

Kay had been reading a few days before that wolves are creatures of extraordinary cunning. Presently, he noticed that all the pack had shifted away from the palisade. The cattle inside the enclosure became quieter. The men and women put out the flares which they were burning. There was a general slackening of the tension. Then, suddenly, from the darkest point of the Camp, there came a howl and the noise of rushing bodies. The pack was over the stockade and into the Camp, and the cattle were stampeding, and the people shouting and lighting flares, and flinging weapons and burning embers again. Kay said to himself, 'This is the real attack. The others were only just feints to find out how the land lay.' Two enormous wolves, with red eyes and gleaming teeth, rushed directly at himself.

He felt himself plucked by the arm. There was the little old Punch and Judy man, but no longer dressed like a Punch and Judy man: he was wearing a white stuff that shone. 'You come here beside me, Master Kay,' he said. 'Don't you bother about those things: you only see them because I'm here. But it is like old times to me, Master Kay, to see this. I've had fine times in winter nights, when the wolves were after the stock. Many times we would stand to, like this, almost till daylight. And, then, the thing to do is to follow them, Master Kay, and never to let up till you've caught them; for the wolves lose heart, and they're not half what you'd think they'd be when you see them like this.

'But, I hoped that you would come, Master Kay, because other wolves are running. They're running after me, and they're running me very close. It's not me they want, it's my Box of Delights that you caught sight of at the inn. If I hand that to you, Master Kay, will you keep it for me, so that they don't get it?'

'Of course,' Kay said, 'I'll keep anything for you that you want kept, but, if you are in danger from anybody, go to the magistrates; they'll defend you.'

'Ah,' he said, 'the magistrates don't heed the kind of wolf that's after me. This, Master Kay, is the little Box, and there are three things I must tell you about it: you open it like this; if you push this to the right you can go small; if you press it to the left you can go swift. I've not had this long, Master Kay; it is Master Arnold's, not mine; and though I've sought for him and called him, I have not found nor been heard. He's gone a long way back, Master Arnold has.

'If I had time, Master Kay, I might best the wolves. But they run me close, with this New Magic, which I can't guard myself against. Going swift and going small will save you, you'll find; you're young. But they won't save me, Master Kay, not any more, for I'm old now, and only know the Old Magic. Now, will you keep this for me till I'm able to claim it, if I ever may be able, or till old Master Arnold can come back for it?'

'I will indeed,' Kay said.

'And, if they put me to an end, Master Kay, as perhaps they will, then you are to keep it till old Master Arnold comes; but above all things, keep it from coming to them. Will you do that?'

'If I possibly can, I will, of course. But who is this Master Arnold and how shall I know him?' Kay said.

'You'll know him if he comes,' the old man answered, 'for he'll come right out of the Old Time.

'Now, one other thing. If you and your friend, Master Peter, would come out this way towards dawn, you may see what comes to me. And now, good fortune, Master Kay, and I hope that I'll come back for this Box of Delights before so very long and give it to Master Arnold in person.' He handed Kay the little black, shiny box. Kay had seen one or two of the old men in the village with tobacco boxes that looked like it. 'Put it in your inner pocket,' the old man said.

He was about to put it into his pocket, when somebody thrust a big gorse bush into the fire. It flared up with a blaze and crackle. Instantly, the cattle and the tribesmen had disappeared. Kay seemed to be alone in a glare of light, surrounded by a ring of wolves all snarling at him and glaring with red eyes.

'Never heed them,' the little old man's voice said from far away. 'Press it to the left and go swift.'

He had the box in his breast pocket with his hand still upon it. He pressed the catch to the left, and in a flash, he was plucked up into the air away from the wolves and the hillside, and there he was, rather out of breath, in his bed at Seekings, with Peter sitting up in the bed opposite, saying, 'I say, Kay, what are you doing? Haven't you gone yet? What's the time?'

'Quarter-to-one,' Kay said.

'Uh,' said Peter with a growl, rolling over.

CHAPTER FOUR

Kay put the little box under his pillow, and was soon asleep again. He dreamed of wolves padding on the snow after the Punch and Judy man. At six o'clock he woke again, and heard the bells chiming for the hour. What with the moonlight and the snow-blink, there was light enough in the room for him to see the Box with its old, worn, shiny, shagreen cover, and magic knob upon it. 'He said I must go out towards the Camp at dawn with Peter,' he muttered. 'I must do that.' He waited for another twenty minutes, and then called to Peter: 'I say, Peter, wake up. Let's go out and explore.'

'Explore what?' Peter growled. 'What d'you expect to find—mushrooms, may I ask?'

'Oh, don't come if you'd rather not,' Kay said, 'but it's always rather fun being out in the fresh snow, and seeing all the animals' tracks.'

'But to get up before it's light on the first day of the holidays—I think it's the purple pim!' Peter said.

'Oh, get up, Peter,' Kay said. 'We can forage in the

larder. We can get heavenly breakfast foraging in the larder, then a real breakfast when we come in.'

'Oh, all right,' Peter said. So up they got.

They went down into the larder, and got themselves ham and bread, which they spread with blobs of butter. Then, each had a big mince-pie, and a long drink from a cream pan.

Before they set out together, Kay looked at the little black box in his inner pocket. 'I won't examine this till I come back,' he thought, 'when I can be sure of being alone. Now we must hurry, to see what comes to him . . . if it isn't all an absurd dream.'

They went out into the white world of the snow, and took the road to Arthur's Camp. Nobody was about yet: a few upper windows showed lights, a few chimneys smoked. The way looked very different from what it had been when he had ridden it at midnight. The buildings were back in their places and the lakes of water were gone. By the short cuts, it is only twenty minutes' walk to Arthur's Camp.

At the Camp, the wood (with its yew-trees) was again in its place. All bracken and brambles were prone under the snow; there was no close cover left. There were no wolf-tracks in the snow under the ramparts where the wolves had run: there were many rabbit-tracks. Now that it was beginning to be light, the boys found some fox-tracks and the tiny neat imprint of what they judged to be rats' feet.

Kay was soon at the very place where he had stood within the stockade, when the fires had burned and the beasts had stampeded. That was the place, with Oxhill dead in front and Broadbarrow, or Gibbet Hill, square to the right; the bearings proved it. Where the old man had spoken to him must have been a little to the left. Three great yew-trees grew there now close together, all very old. Kay moved towards them. In the space between them, which must have been the spot where the old man had given him the Box, someone had scuffled aside the snow, and had camped for the night, wrapped in a woven stuff which had printed its texture on the snow: it must have been a coarse woollen. The strange thing was, that no footprints led to the place, although footprints led away from it.

'Someone's been here for the night,' Peter said. 'Look out for creepy-crawlies.'

'No footprints to show where he came from,' Kay said.

'He must have come before the snow,' Peter said. 'Let's follow to see where he goes. What a night to have been out in.'

'Snow's said to be warm, if you get really into it,' Kay said. 'But I dare say that's one of the things they say.'

They followed the footprints, which were those of a man about the size of Cole Hawlings. 'But I don't think it can be Cole,' Kay thought, 'because there are no tracks of a Barney Dog: and he must have had Barney with him. But then, Rat said that the Lady was going to take the dog. Of course, she has him.'

The tracks led on over the Camp wall, across the ditch, and presently out of the wood onto the bleak upland known as Bottler's Down. There are some spinneys on the shoulders of Bottler, the tracks led past these, going due west. As the boys came over one of the shoulders past a spinney edge, they sighted their quarry two hundred yards ahead, a little old man, trudging the snow, bent under a green-baize-covered bale. He was near the spinney called Rider's Wood.

At that instant four men darted out of Rider's Wood and ran at the old man, who dropped his bundle. One of the men had something that flew up: Kay gasped, as he thought it was a club, but it seemed to be a sack or bag, which came down over the old man's head. A second man in the same instant lashed rope round the old man's arms and legs. In five seconds they had the old man trussed up and lifted. Three of them hurried with him to the other side of the spinney; the fourth man followed with the bundle. The boys were too startled to cry out or to do anything: they stood spell-bound.

There came the roar of an engine from beyond Rider's Wood. 'That's an aeroplane,' Kay said. They heard confused noises and the slamming-to of a door. The roaring of the engine became much louder and an aeroplane lurched into sight past the covert-end, going across the snow to take off into the wind. 'It will stick in the snow,' Kay said, 'and then they'll have to leave him.' However, it didn't stick in the snow. It lifted after a short run, and at once lifted higher and higher, with great lolloping leaps.

Now that it was in the air it was silent, of a grey colour and swifter in going and climbing than any he had seen. It had almost no wings and was in the clouds in no time (going north-west Kay judged).

'Well, they scrobbled the old man,' Peter said.

'Come along, Peter,' Kay said, 'we must go to see what tracks those people have left.'

'I say,' Peter said. 'I am glad I came out with you. I never thought I should see a gang scrobble an old man and carry him off in an aeroplane.'

'It's very lucky,' Kay said, 'that we've got the snow. All the tracks will be as clear as print. Don't let's run, and keep well to the side of the old man's tracks so as not to obscure them, and let's get it absolutely clear so that we can tell the Police: two men in white ran out, then two others, and there must have been another man in the aeroplane.'

'There were four who did the attack,' Peter said, 'and the first one, who had a bag, was the tallest of the four, and they'd all got something over their faces.'

They came to the scene of the kidnapping and then went into the copse to see where the gangsters had lain in wait.

They had been in the spinney some little time and had scuffled out their tracks: they had been resting in a yew clump among some tumbled stones clear of the snow. They had not smoked during their wait: there were no cigarette-ends, no matches, no tobacco ash. They had scuffled out their foot tracks from the aeroplane, but, of course, the tracks to the aeroplane were plain. All that they could see was that there were four men of different sizes, one a good deal bigger than the other three, and that all were wearing new rubber goloshes or rubber boots. The tracks of the aeroplane told the boys nothing: it had run on its wheels to a level strip near the spinney on a part of the down kept clear of snow by the wind.

'Well, that's that,' Kay said. 'They've got him, and they've got away with him, and I'm pretty sure it was our Punch and Judy man.'

'It looked jolly like him,' Peter said. 'Well, we'd better go back and tell the Police.'

They made a last examination where the aeroplane had rested, but there were no clues but a few spots of black oil. They took the short cuts home and called at the Police Station.

The big red-faced Inspector was an old friend of Kay's. He understood rabbits and was a clever amateur conjurer. Kay had always thought that there was a lot of sense in him. Kay told his story; Peter backed him up.

'Ah, indeed,' the Inspector said: 'that was those young officers from the aerodrome having a bit of a frolic.'

'It wasn't like a frolic,' Kay said; and Peter said, 'And they weren't in uniform, and it wasn't a government aeroplane.' 'And then,' Kay said, 'it was such a lonely place and such a time in the morning.'

'And what were you doing in that lonely place at that time in the morning, Master Kay?' the Inspector said. 'I hope you young gentlemen weren't trespassing in pursuit of game.'

'No, of course we weren't. We were out looking at the tracks of the animals in the snow.'

'Ha,' the Inspector said. 'Now, did this old man struggle at all or cry out?'

'He didn't have a chance to,' Kay said.

'Did he see you or did the other people see you?'

'No, they couldn't,' Kay said, 'from where they were.'

'And, did you shout or try to raise an alarm?' the Inspector asked.

'I'm afraid we didn't,' Kay said. 'We were just spell-bound, and it all happened in an instant. They ran out, scrobbed him up, put him into the aeroplane and away they went.'

'Well,' the Inspector said, 'it sounds like the aerodrome to me: those young fellows, Master Kay, serving their country and away from the civilising influence of their mothers, just full of spirits, the spit of what I was myself when I was a young man. It was a Christmas gambol and a bit of what you call "ragging." And you see, Master Harker, the Law isn't like ordinary things: sometimes the Law has to put its foot down, sometimes it has to shut its eyes. And the Law, Master Kay, makes much of what is called "motive": what's prank when meant as prank may become felony when meant as felony, and what you saw seems to me to be no more than prank.

'But all the same, I am obliged to you, Master Harker. We in the Law are always glad of evidence, first-hand evidence, from one who knows what's what. I'll keep my eyes and ears open, Master Kay, for anything out Bottler's Down way, but nothing's come in yet: no job for the Law has been done out Bottler's Down way. But we in the Law keep our eyes open as well as our ears. I'll ask what aeroplanes were out that way this morning.

'And you were a matter of two hundred yards from the scene of this fracas,' the Inspector said, 'and you didn't recognise any of the parties?'

'Well,' Kay said, 'we both think, and are almost sure, that the man was the Punch and Judy man who was at Seekings House last night from half-past five to half-past six. He was stopping yesterday at the *Drop of Dew* and his name was Cole Hollings or Cole Hawlings.'

At this moment the telephone bell rang. The Inspector lifted the receiver. 'Yes,' he said, 'Condicote seven thousand. What is it?' Someone talked to him for a minute or two. 'Now that,' the Inspector said, putting down the receiver, 'that's what we call in the Law a coincidence. That was our officer at Tatchester asking about your Punch and Judy man, Cole Hollings or Hawlings. The man is at Tatchester now and the Police are asking "Is he a fit kind of man to give a public performance at the Bishop's Palace this very night as ever is?" '

'And he's at Tatchester now?' Kay asked.

'Yes,' the Inspector said, 'at the Police Station, showing his licence. You heard me ask "Is he all right?": they said "Yes." You heard me ask "Does he make any complaints?": they said "No." So if he was the man you saw, Master Harker, he can't be much the worse, even if they did put him in the aeroplane. Now is he, Master Harker, a kind of man to perform before a Bishop and other holy men?'

'He's simply wonderful,' Kay said.

The Inspector took up the receiver and spoke again. 'I have every reason to suppose,' he said, 'from information received, that the man is a good performer and can be trusted not to disappoint nor yet to shock the company. By the way, is the man there?'

He listened and then said, 'Just bring him to the telephone. There's a young gentleman would like to know something. Hallo. Hallo. Is that Mr. Hawlings? Are you any the worse for being in the aeroplane?

'("No," he says, "none the worse, sir.")

'Mr. Hawlings, who was it put you in the aeroplanes?

'(He says some young friends, with more fun than sense.)

'And what brought you out Bottler's Down way in the snow, Mr. Hawlings?

'(He says it was the only flat bit where he could meet the aeroplane.)

'Now here's a young friend wants to ask how you are.'

The Inspector handed over the receiver to Kay.

'Is that you, Mr. Hollings?' Kay asked. 'I rang you up to ask how you are . . . if you're any the worse for the wolves or the aeroplane?'

The telephone was full of crackles and buzzes. A

female voice said, 'Pottington-Two-Five, please.' A distant man's voice said, 'Give up the strychnine and go on with the belladonna'; then from far away an old man's voice said, 'No, none the worse, I thank you: all the better.'

'You are really Mr. Hollings?' Kay asked, 'that found my ticket and was scrobbled into the aeroplane?'

'Really, truly he,' the voice answered. 'And you're the young gentleman?'

'Yes,' Kay said.

'Good-bye, my young Master,' the voice said. Kay hung up the receiver.

'So that's that,' the Inspector said. 'That's how Science helps the Law. You thought your friend was scrobbled. Now by Science and the Law you hear from his own lips that all is well.'

Somehow Kay wondered if all was well. The telephone was working badly and the voice was like the old man's voice, but still, somehow he felt uneasy.

'I'm very glad,' Kay said, 'that the man is safe. Please forgive us for taking up so much of your time.'

'A public man's time is the public's,' the Inspector said. 'It's my duty, as a public man, to listen to all and sundry at all times. Sometimes the Law has to shut its eyes, sometimes there isn't enough for the Law to go upon, sometimes the Law intervenes; but at all times, I say, let the Law in, Master Harker. Any tale that's first-hand evidence, you bring it to the Law, and, depend upon it, Master Kay, murder will out. However dark the deed, Master Kay, we bloodhounds of the Law, as they call us, will bring it into the limelight.'

Kay thanked him again, then they talked for a moment of brighter topics—rabbits, simple conjuring tricks, blue Persian cats, the Condicote Rugby Team, etc.—then they both shook hands with the Inspector and wished him a very happy Christmas and New Year, and then they went home to breakfast, for which they were a little late.

Just before they clambered over the garden fence of Seekings a puff of air came upon Kay's face, which made him look up at the sky. It had been bright clearing weather at dawn; now it was clouding over from the west on a muggy windless air. A weeping thaw had set in. As he entered the house there came the slip and splosh of snow dropping from the roofs. 'There's a thaw,' he said. 'We shan't get very far with that snow-man we were going to build.'

Before he went to breakfast, Kay tried to telephone Caroline Louisa, to ask how her brother was. Unfortunately, the line was out of order, owing to the snow. They said that the men were doing their best, but couldn't promise anything; they hoped to have the line ready during the day. The post had not come: that, however, was due to Christmas, not to the snow.

All through breakfast, the snow fell from roofs and trees, slither, slither, splosh. When they went into the field to set about their snow-man they found the snow rapidly becoming too slushy: they were soon working in slush.

'We'd better stop,' Jemima said. 'We shall be wet through. He'll never look up to much.'

'We'll give him a sort of a head,' Kay said. They did this. Maria topped it with an old top hat that had lost its crown, Susan put in some dark stones for the eyes, and Peter added a clay pipe. Then they flung some sploshy snow-balls at him.

Ellen called to them from the door: 'If you please,' she said, 'you're not to get wet through.'

'Oh, by the way, Ellen,' Kay shouted, 'have you had any telephone message?'

'No, the telephone isn't working,' Ellen said.

'Are they doing their best?' Peter called.

'Oh, Miss Susan,' Ellen said, 'you are naughty to go and get yourself wet through like this; and you, Miss Jemima. Miss Maria, your things will be ruined.'

'Jolly good job,' Maria said.

'No, Miss Maria,' Ellen said, 'it isn't a good job, and you know that it isn't; and you ought not to say such things. To be wet through in the cold is the way to take your Death. Come along now, like a good little girl. Come along in now; no nonsense. You must change all your things.' She shepherded the girls to the door, and then remembered the boys: 'And you, Master Kay, you are wet through too,' she said.

'Oh, come on, Peter,' Kay said. 'Let's get out of this. There's too much discipline here altogether.'

They slipped over the fence in spite of Ellen's calls. 'What shall we do now?' Peter said.

'Shall we go out again to Arthur's Camp?'

'But you've been there once this morning.'

'I know, but I don't think we've heard the last of that aeroplane . . . I can't help thinking we shall find out some more or hear some more, if we go out. And we might try tracking the foxes down. It's only a mile.'

'Well, all right,' Peter said.

Though the thaw was now streaming, they found their own tracks and those of the little old man. Besides these were the tracks of two other men.

'You see, two men have been along here since we were

here,' Kay said, 'and they are not country men, for they didn't wear nailed boots.'

'One of them was smoking a cigarette,' Peter said: 'see the ash. There's the cigarette-butt—Egyptian.'

'What on earth have they been doing here, sweeping the snow aside?' Kay said. 'I wonder why they've done that?'

'Oh,' Peter said, 'these bird enthusiasts are always doing things like that to let the birds get at the worms.'

'That's a bright idea,' Kay said. They went on, noticing that here and there the snow had been carefully swept aside. As they were now trackers on a trail, they went cautiously. When they came in sight of the spot where the old man had been set upon, they saw two men sweeping the snow with a sort of hard hand-brush.

'Keep under cover, Peter,' Kay said. 'There are your bird enthusiasts. The plot thickens. I see it all. They scrobbled that old man thinking that he'd got something which they wanted. They released the old man when they found he hadn't got it. Now they think that he's dropped it in the snow and they are looking for it. They won't find it in this slush, I'll bet. What d'you make of the two men?'

'They look like two curates to me,' Peter said.

'They're the two who were in the train with me yesterday, and I've a very shrewd suspicion that they picked my pockets.'

'You think that curates' clothes are a disguise?'

'Yes.'

'Golly!' Peter said. 'Well, let's watch.'

Presently, the two men wearied of their search and decided that it was no good searching longer. They went off down the hill. With some little trouble, the boys followed, unobserved (as they hoped). The two curates went downhill to the road, where a big, dark, shabby car was waiting for them: they got into the car and drove off. They went, as Kay noticed, in a north-westerly direction. Presently, as he chanced to look in that direction, he saw some bright, moving speck in the sky, which he judged to be an aeroplane.

'I wonder,' he thought to himself, 'if that motor-car could turn into an aeroplane.'

'I wonder what it was,' Peter said. 'I wonder what it was that the men were hoping to find,'

Kay knew very well what it was that they were hoping to find, but he did not feel that he had a right to say.

'Oh, these gangs,' he said airily, 'they always try to get each other's codes and passwords.'

'I shouldn't think they'd bother about those,' Peter said. 'They could always torture a prisoner till he told them all the passwords. I should think they were rival gangs of jewel thieves, after the same diamond necklace, and one of the gangs has got it and is trying to get it out of the country, and the other gang is trying to waylay it.'

'That's an idea,' Kay said. He was afraid that that might be the explanation. 'When I get in,' he thought, 'I will hide, and look at this Box. If it *is* a diamond necklace I'll take it straight to the Police Inspector.' They went home.

Now, at last, Kay felt that he was free to look at the Box of Delights. He went up to his bedroom. He was very anxious not to be spied upon, and, remembering how those three spies had been peering in at the window the night before, and how the repulsive Rat had crept about in the secret passages finding out all sorts of things, he was not sure that he could guard himself from being seen. His bedroom had two doors in it opening on to different landings. He locked both doors and hung caps over the keyholes: he looked under the beds. Then, as in the past, when he had wished to hide from his governess, he crept under the valance of his dressing-table: no one could possibly see him there.

The Box was of some very hard wood of a dense grain. It had been covered with shagreen, but the shagreen was black with age and sometimes worn away so as to show the wood beneath. Both wood and shagreen had been polished until they were as smooth as a polished metal. On the side of it there was a little counter-sunk groove, in the midst of which was a knob. 'I press this to open,' he repeated. 'If I push it to the right I can go small, whatever that may mean. If I push it to the left I can go swift, and that I've tried. I do want to see what's inside it. I wonder, is this wood that it's made of lignum-vitæ wood?'

'It's the wood the Phoenix builds in,' the Box said.

'Is it really?' Kay said. 'No wonder it smells like spice.'

Then he saw that the groove was inlaid with gold and that the golden knob within the groove had been carven into the image of a rose-bud, which was extraordinarily fragrant. 'I say,' Kay said to himself, 'this is a wonderful Box. Now I'll open it.'

He pressed the tiny, golden rose-bud and, at once, from within the box, there came a tiny crying of birds. As he listened he heard the stockdove brooding, the cuckoo tolling, blackbirds, thrushes, and nightingale singing. Then a far-away cock crowed thrice and the Box slowly opened. Inside he saw what he took to be a book, the leaves of which were all chased and worked with multitudinous figures, and the effect that it gave him was that of staring into an opening in a wood. It was lit from within; multitudinous, tiny things were shifting there. Then he saw that the things which were falling were the petals of may-blossom from giant hawthorn trees covered with flowers. The hawthorns stood on each side of the entrance to the forest, which was dark from the great trees yet dappled with light. Now, as he looked into it, he saw deer glide with alert ears, then a fox, motionless at his earth, a rabbit moving to new pasture and nibbling at a dandelion, and the snouts of the moles breaking the wet earth. All the forest was full of life: all the birds were singing, insects were humming, dragon-flies darting, butterflies wavering and settling. It was so clear that he could see the flies on the leaves brushing their heads and wings with their legs. 'It's all alive and it's full of summer. There are all the birds singing: there's a linnet; bullfinch; a robin; that's a little wren.' Others were singing too: different kinds of tits; the woodpecker was drilling; the chiffchaff repeating his name; the yellowhammer and garden-warbler were singing, and overhead, as the bird went swiftly past, came the sad, laughing cry of the curlew. While he gazed into the heart of summer and listened to the murmur and the singing, he heard another noise like the tinkling of little bells. As he wondered what these bells could be he decided that they were not bells, but a tinkling like the cry of many little long-tailed tits together. 'Where did I hear that noise before quite recently?' Kay said to himself. It was not the noise of long-tailed tits: it was the noise of little chains chinking. He remembered that strange rider who had passed him in the street the day before. That rider, who seemed to have little silver chains dangling from his wrists, had jingled so. 'Oh,' Kay said, as he looked, 'there's someone wonderful coming.'

At first he thought that the figure was one of those giant red deer, long since extinct: it bore enormous antlers. Then he saw that it was a great man, antlered at the brow, dressed in deerskin and moving with the silent, slow grace of a stag; and, although he was so like a stag, he was hung about with little silver chains and bells.

Kay knew at once that this was Herne the Hunter, of whom he had often heard. 'Ha, Kay,' Herne the Hunter said, 'are you coming into my wild wood?'

'Yes, if you please, sir,' Kay said. Herne stretched out his hand. Kay took it and at once he was glad that he had taken it, for there he was in the forest between the two hawthorn trees, with the petals of the may-blossom falling on him. All the may-blossoms that fell were talking to him, and he was aware of what all the creatures of the forest were saying to each other: what the birds were singing, and what it was that the flowers and trees were thinking. And he realised that the forest went on and on for ever, and all of it was full of life beyond anything that he had ever imagined: for in the trees, in each leaf, and on every twig, and in every inch of soil there were ants, grubs, worms; little, tiny, moving things, incredibly small yet all thrilling with life.

'Oh dear,' Kay said, 'I shall never know a hundredth part of all the things there are to know.'

'You will, if you stay with me,' Herne the Hunter said. 'Would you like to be a stag with me in the wild wood?'

Now, next to being a jockey, Kay had longed to be a young stag. Now he realised that he had become one. He was there in the green wood beside a giant stag, so screened with the boughs that they were a part of a dappled pattern of light and shade, and the news of the wood came to him in scents upon the wind.

Presently the giant stag gave a signal. They moved off out of the green wood into a rolling grass-land, where some fox cubs were playing with a vixen. They passed these and presently came down to a pool, where some moor-hens were cocking about in the water; a crested grebe kept a fierce eye upon them. They went out into the water. It was lovely, Kay thought, to feel the water cool upon the feet after running, and to be able to go paddling, although it had been winter only a minute before. 'And it's lovely, too,' he thought, 'to have hard feet and not get sharp bits of twig into one's soles.' They moved through the water towards some reeds. Looking through the stalks of the reeds Kay saw that there were a multitude of wild duck. 'Would you like to be a wild duck, Kay?' Herne asked.

Now, next to being a jockey and a stag, Kay had longed to be a wild duck, and, at once, with a great clatter of feathers, the wild duck rose more and more and more, going high up, and, oh joy! Herne and Kay were with them, flying on wings of their own and Kay could just see that his neck was glinting green. There was the pool, blue as a piece of sky below them, and the sky above brighter than he had ever seen it.

They flew higher and higher in great sweeps, and, presently, they saw the sea like the dark blue on a map. Then they made a sweeping circle and there was the pool once more, blue like the sky. 'Now for the plunge,' Herne cried, and instantly they were surging down swiftly and still more swiftly, and the pool was rushing up at them, and they all went skimming into it with a long, scuttering, rippling splash. And there they all were paddling together, happy to be in water again.

'How beautiful the water is,' Kay said. Indeed it was beautiful, clear hill-water, with little fish darting this way and that and the weeds waving, and sometimes he saw that the waving weeds were really fish. 'Would you like to be a fish, Kay?' Herne asked.

And, next to being a jockey, a stag and a wild duck, Kay had always longed to be a fish. And then, instantly, Kay was a fish. He and Herne were there in the coolness and dimness, wavering as the water wavered, and feeling a cold spring gurgling up just underneath them and tickling their tummies.

While Kay was enjoying the water Herne asked, 'Did you see the wolves in the wood?'

'No,' Kay said.

'Well, they were there,' Herne said; 'that was why I moved. Did you see the hawks in the air?'

'No,' Kay said.

'Well, they were there,' Herne said; 'and that was why I plunged. And d'you see the pike in the weeds?'

'No,' Kay said.

'He is there,' Herne said. 'Look.'

Looking ahead up the stream Kay saw a darkness of weeds wavering in the water, and presently a part of the darkness wavered into a shape with eyes that gleamed and hooky teeth that showed. Kay saw that the eyes were fixed upon himself and suddenly the dark shadow leaped swiftly forward with a swirl of water. But Kay and Herne were out of the water. They were trotting happily together over the grass towards the forest; Herne a giant figure with the antlers of the red stag and himself a little figure with little budding antlers. And so they went trotting together into the forest to a great ruined oak-tree, so old that all within was hollow, though the great shell still put forth twigs and leaves.

Somehow, the figure of Herne, which had been so staglike, became like the oak-tree and merged into the oak-tree till Kay could see nothing but the tree. What had been Herne's antlers were now a few old branches and what had seemed silver chains dangling from Herne's wrists were now the leaves rustling. Then the oak-tree faded and grew smaller till it was a dark point in a sunny glade. The glade shrank and there was Kay standing between the two hawthorn trees, which were shedding their blossoms upon him. Then these shrank till they were as tiny as the works of a watch and then Kay was himself again under the valance in his room at Seekings looking at the first page in the Book of Delights contained within the Box. 'My goodness,' Kay said, 'no wonder the old man treasured this Box and called it a Box of Delights. Now, I wonder,' he said, 'how long I have been in that fairyland with Herne the Hunter?' He looked at his watch and found that he had been away only two minutes. It was now ten minutes to eleven. 'My goodness,' Kay said, 'all that took only two minutes.'

CHAPTER FIVE

He was just wondering whether he should hide the Box in his secret locker, when he remembered that Abner had told the Rat to report to him at eleven at the usual place. 'I wonder,' Kay thought, 'if I could possibly be present when he reports.'

He took the Box of Delights in his hand and muttered, 'If I push this to the right I can go small, and if I push it to the left I can go swift.' He pushed the knob to the right and instantly found himself dwindling and dwindling, while the furniture in his room grew vaster and vaster, and there beside him, just beyond the edge of the carpet, was a little hole between two boards in the flooring. A mouse had once lived in the hole but had long since gone, and once Kay had dropped a sixpence there and had fished for it in vain with a bootlace smeared with cobbler's wax. He could see it shining there still now. Without any hesitation he slipped himself down the crack and picked up the sixpence, which was now bigger than his head and much too big to go into any of his pockets. The wonderful thing was that down there, where the mouse had lived, was a most charming corridor all as bright as day. It ran on and opened into a great space which had once been, as Kay knew, a secret hiding-place made by his great-grandfather. This was now laid out as a mouse's recreation ground. There was a little tennis-court, and a charming bowling-green and a little, tiny red pole hung about with ropes for the giant-stride. Then, in one corner, a part had been specially polished and a mouse was roller-skating here.

'Hullo, Kay,' the Mouse said.

'I say,' Kay said, 'you know these underground places. Could I get to the *Prince Rupert's Arms* underground?'

'Why yes,' the Mouse said, 'but, of course, it's a bit of what you might call a peradventure, getting to the *Rupert's Arms.* Parts of the way there are some very terrible fellows that lie in wait.'

'D'you mean cats and dogs?' Kay asked.

'Oh, no, no,' said the Mouse, 'but a party that has only come here lately. Of course,' he said, sinking his voice, 'I don't say anything against them. They're awfully nice fellows and good citizens and all that, but they've been away a lot. They've got foreign ways that take some getting into.'

'But, who are they?' Kay said.

'The chap who used to be cellarman here,' the Mouse said: 'I won't mention names. He went away. He said he went as marine cellarman, but, if you ask me, he was on the Spanish Main under the skull and crossbones. But, come along, Kay: I can fit you out with weapons.'

He led Kay along a little passage and unlocked a door labelled 'Armoury.'

Inside the armoury were some little light suits of chain mail. The Mouse pitched one over to Kay and took one for himself.

'You see, these will do for the body,' the Mouse said. 'That is, they will do up to a point. I expect you'd like a sword or something.'

He opened a cupboard in which there were some long shining rapiers made out of bodkins and darning needles. Someone had put them on to a whetstone and had given them edge and point.

'You see, these are very good,' the Mouse said, 'if you have time to use them; but the things that go for us are so sudden. And remember, when I put my finger to my lips that'll mean that we are at the danger point.'

'Tell me, before we start,' Kay said, 'what is the danger point?'

'Well,' the Mouse said, sinking his voice, 'when that one whom we named came home from the Spanish Main, he did not come alone; no; he brought Benito's crew with him, the Wolves of the Gulf they call themselves: and they're all there, drinking rum and plotting devilry. They've brought a reign of terror into what we call the Underworld. Oh, terrible things go on; every night.'

'Whereabouts are they usually?' Kay asked.

'The worst place is about two-thirds of the way there,' the Mouse said, 'in the old Powdering Cellar under William's Vintry. We shall have to go right past it.'

'Lead on, Macduff,' Kay said. 'If the worst comes to

worst, take my hand, for I think we shall be able to diddle them.' He thought that by pressing the knob on the Box he might be able 'to go swift' past any danger to which they came.

'Now the best way is this way,' the Mouse said.

Presently they reached the end of the Seekings cellar. Kay saw the barrels of cider and perry which they made in the orchard every year. The Mouse unlocked a little door out of the cellar into an underground passage. Someone had started digging under the door here. There was a mass of earth and rock and a pile of pickaxes.

'You see there,' the Mouse said: 'those pickaxes. Those Wolves of the Gulf that I told you of were up here last night. They were going to break into Seekings—you can see how they dug—but then that one you named came up and said: "I'll take you into Seekings by another way any time you like, but not yet," he said. "There are two cats in Seekings," he said, "which are just Doomsday in Fur. One of them is called Nibbins and the other is called Twiddles and they both ought to have their heads sawed off. And my advice is: don't break into Seekings till we've poisoned both of them. That's what." '

'And did they decide anything?' Kay asked.

The Mouse began to tremble violently and turned quite white.

'They did,' the Mouse said. 'They are going to poison the cats. I heard the whole plan.'

'Well, what is it?' Kay said. 'Forewarned is forarmed.'

'They said,' the Mouse said, 'they said, "First, we'll catch that Mouse when he comes along here and then we'll bathe him good and rich in the ratsbane they put down for us. Then we'll make him run across the room the two cats sleep in. Then the cats will pounce and eat him and then they'll die. That's what." And that's what they're going to do.'

'Well, we'll see about that,' Kay said.

'Oh, but Master Kay, Master Kay!' the Mouse said, 'don't tell them that I told you.'

'Come now,' Kay said, 'and don't be such a funk.'

The Mouse led by all sorts of strange ways towards the *Rupert's Arms,* along corridors, down steps, across forgotten cellars, behind a skirting-board, out onto somebody's backstairs, down into another person's cellar, then along an old wall and then downstairs and downstairs again to a very damp, chilly cellar, where the floor and walls gleamed with salt crystals and wept tears of moisture.

'This is the Powdering Cellar,' the Mouse said. 'It's here that we must look out.'

They stepped to one side from the Powdering Cellar and entered the thickness of the wall again. As they went on they found that it was becoming much warmer and, presently, it was hot.

'What makes it hot?' Kay whispered.

'This is near the furnace of William's Vintry,' the Mouse whispered, 'and it's near here that they've got their quarters.'

As they turned a corner, a reek of strong tobacco filled the air, there came a noise of a chair being pushed back, glasses were pounded, a drunken voice squealed with joy that Old Rum-Chops was going to sing . . . The Mouse put a warning paw on Kay's arm. 'They're at it . . . just inside there,' he whispered.

Indeed, just beyond them, the light fell into the corridor from an open door. From within the door there came cheers, mocking remarks of 'Good Old Rum-Chops,' 'Sick him Rum-Chops,' and the pounding of hands upon a table: then a coarse voice said:

'Pray silence now, gents, for the song.'

Kay and the Mouse paused, while within the room a most unpleasant voice broke into song. The singer may have been a little drunk, for he sometimes forgot his words and often forgot his tune, but whenever this happened the other members of the company cheered and pounded the table. These were the words of the song:

'We fly a banner all of black,
With scarlet Skull and Boneses,
And every merchantman we take
We send to Davey Jones's

'Chorus gents, please . . .'

And the company broke out into the chorus:

'And every merchantman we take
We send to Davey Jones's.
Sing diddle-diddle-dol.'

The singer went on with his song:

'To fetch the gold out of the hold
We make them shake their shankses.
Then over the side to take a dive
We make them walk the plankses.

'Chorus gents, please . . .'

And the company shouted with drunken cheers and laughter:

'Then over the side to take a dive
We make them walk the plankses.
Sing diddle-diddle-dol.'

They were going on with this disgusting ditty, but the company seemed so overcome by the beauty of the words and the sentiments that they all pushed back their chairs, rose to their feet, snapped their clay pipes and started to repeat the chorus.

'Quickly, while they sing,' the Mouse whispered.

As they slipped past the open door Kay glanced in. Oh, what a terrible scene was within! There, gathered round a table, lurching, shouting, swaying and clutching at each other to keep their balance, were the Wolves of the Gulf, all Benito's crew, whom the Rat would have described as marine cellarmen. On the table round which they lurched and carrolled were the remnants of a hambone without any dish, and a big bowl of rum punch. As Kay glanced, one of the ruffians fell forward with his head into the bowl. He splashed the rum over his head and another tried to set fire to him with a candle, but was too unsteady in his aim. All these men wore sea-boots, rough red caps and red aprons. No words can describe the villainy of their faces, all bronzed with tropical suns, purple with drink, scarlet with battle and bloated from evil living.

'Sing diddle-diddle-dol,'

they cried. Then they drew their pistols and fired them at the ceiling, so that the plaster came down with a clatter.

The Mouse plucked Kay on along the corridor. They turned a corner. There in front of them, at the passage end, Kay saw the familiar figure of Rat, with a younger marine cellarman. Kay and the Mouse slipped back so as not to be seen. They heard Rat saying:

'Now here we are at the door. Now, nephew,

remember what it was I told you. Don't you be afraid of the gent: speak out.'

'I ain't afraid of no gent,' the Rat's nephew answered.

'Well, that's what,' Rat said, and, stooping down, he knocked at a little door.

'What d'you knock for?' the nephew asked.

'To show respect to the great Abner Brown,' the Rat answered.

Kay heard Abner's silky voice say, 'Come in.' Rat and his nephew passed into the room and shut the door behind them.

'Are we in the *Rupert's Arms*?' Kay asked.

'Yes, this is the *Rupert's Arms*,' the Mouse said. 'If you will step up here there is a place where you can see right into the room.'

He led Kay up a fallen wooden moulding to a ledge behind the panelling of the old room. There was a crack in the panelling through which Kay could see. There was Abner in a green silk quilted dressing-gown, sitting at a table. Beside him was a rather stout, rosy-faced, but stupid-looking man whom Kay took to be the man Joe. Opposite Joe was the foxy-faced man. Opposite Abner was a lady, whose figure and bearing seemed familiar. She turned her head a moment to light a cigarette at a taper burning beside her and Kay saw that it was, indeed, as he had thought, one who had been his governess: Sylvia Daisy Pouncer, a witch.

'Come in, Rat,' Abner said. 'Who have you got with you?'

'I make so bold as to present my nephew, Master Abner,' Rat said. 'Make a reverence to the gentleman.'

'What's your nephew's name?' Abner asked.

'Oh, he answers to any name,' Rat said; 'Alf or Bert or

any name. He ain't earned a name better'n one of those.'

'Now,' Abner said, 'what will you take, Rat?'

'Well, since I've been marine cellarman,' Rat said, 'I can't stand the climate like what I used. I do like a drop of rum. Not because I like it, it's poison, but without it I can't stand the climate.'

'A drop of rum for Rat,' Abner said.

They gave Rat a tot of rum in a thimble. Rat wiped his lips with the back of his paw and said, 'Happy days, gents!' tossed it off and rubbed his chest. 'That's the stuff,' he said—'poison. I can feel it doing me good all the way down.'

'Now, Alf,' the Rat said, when he judged that he would not receive any more rum, 'stand there and tell the gentlemen what you seen last night.'

Alf Rat came forward and seemed much abashed at having to speak in company. Kay thought that he had seldom seen a more hardened young villain; he was pleased to see the brazen face now confused, the eyes downcast, sweat starting from the brow, and the cheeks flushing and turning white by turns.

'Speak up, Alf,' Abner said. 'What does he say, Rat?'

'He says so many of you makes it worse than being tried, Mr. Abner,' Rat said.

'Well, speak for him,' Abner said.

'Honoured company,' Rat said, 'my nephew, Alf, what is here, and doesn't often stand in such company, went faithful to orders to the *Drop of Dew*, by Henry Cockfarthings, at the hour of a quarter-to-five yesterday. He was told to keep an eye on One that you wot of, which was C.H., what keeps a Dog B. Danger of Dog my nephew Alf was in. But he don't flinch for that, no; he bides and looks. There is C.H. with Dog B. Presently in come Two that you wot of, a man with chains and a woman without chains. They talk of foreign talk. C.H. pulls out a Box thing, which they look at. He says, "The Wolves have come very close." "Yes," nephew Alf thinks, "they've come closer than you think." '

'Oh, I know all about this, you told me this last night,' Abner said testily. 'They agreed that the only way not guarded was out by Arthur's Camp, and that this C.H. could get away at dawn by Arthur's Camp; well, we waited for him at dawn at Arthur's Camp and got him. Tell me, Alf, when those three broke up, was the Box still in C.H.'s possession?'

'Ah, in his pocket,' Alf said.

'It was in his pocket?'

'That's where he put it.'

'He didn't slip it to either of the others?'

'No, they said, "You keep it." '

'He didn't hide it in the *Drop of Dew*?'

'No,' Alf said. 'He asked them if he should, but they said "No." '

'Now listen,' Abner said. 'After this, you followed this C.H. all the way to Seekings House, never letting him out of your sight?'

'Never once he let him out of his sight,' the Rat said.

'Let your nephew answer for himself,' Abner said. 'How close did you keep to him, Alf?'

'I kept him in my sight,' Alf said.

'In spite of the Dog?'

'Yes, sir.'

'Could you see if he hid the Box on his way, or before he left the *Drop of Dew*?'

'He had it in his pocket; he kept tapping his pocket to make sure it was there; all the way he tap his pocket.'

'It was snowing hard: did the snow get in your eyes?'

'No, sir.'

'You must have very odd eyes,' Abner growled.

'And you're sure,' the man Joe said, 'that on the way to Seekings he met nobody to whom he could have given the Box?'

'I take my oath on Hamlet he didn't,' Alf said. 'Not a soul did we pass, it being all snow, such as I never.'

At this point there was a pause. Kay saw Rat nudge his nephew, then nudge again. At a third nudge the nephew said,

'What d'you keep nudging me for?'

'Tell the gent what I told you to tell him,' Rat said. 'There was another thing, if you please, gent, that my nephew had to tell you.'

'What thing? What is it?' Abner asked.

'It was about that Kay Harker, Master Abner,' Rat said.

'What about him?' Abner said. 'Let your nephew speak for himself. What have you got to say about this Kay Harker?'

'Well, nothing much, sir,' the nephew said, 'except that he ought to have his head sawed off.'

'What for?' Abner asked.

'Acos he's going to have a dog give him for Christmas,' the nephew said.

'You infernal young lout!' Abner said. 'What d'you mean, Rat, by bringing your nephew here to repeat your folly to me? Get out, the two of you! Get back to your sewer and have a bath. You've got to bring someone, Nine; show these dolts out as you go. No, not by the way they came. I won't have them listening behind the skirting-board. Kick them both out of the back door.'

Joe and the foxy-faced man, who seemed to be 'Nine,' took the two rats out through the inn.

'Two infernal fools!' Abner said. 'They don't seem to have a very high opinion of your ancient pupil, my dear,' he said, turning to the lady.

'I don't wonder,' Sylvia Daisy Pouncer said placidly. 'He was a child for whom I had the utmost detestation and contempt: a thoroughly morbid, dreamy, idle muff with a low instinct for the turf, which will be his undoing later in life.'

'Well, now,' Abner said, 'the question resolves itself into this: what did that man do with the Box when those fellows let him get past them at Seekings House?'

'I felt, too late,' his wife replied, 'that we ought to have been there and not trusted it to those people. However, it is too late now to cry over the spilt milk.'

'It's not too late to make the spillers cry,' Abner said, angrily. 'Of all the blithering fools that I have ever had to deal with, Joe and those two are the most blithering. He got away right under their noses.'

'As for Cole,' Sylvia Pouncer Brown replied sweetly, 'if he hid the Box he must have done one of two things: either hidden it on one of the bookshelves in the study at Seekings—there are old books there hardly ever disturbed; or, possibly, in the old cupboard in the hall there, underneath the stairs. He did not go upstairs, that I know. I have been over to Seekings in the last twenty minutes and talked to two of the little girls. They told me everything. Cole gave a marvellous conjuring performance and did not leave the library until the Tatchester Choir interrupted the party; then, apparently, he went into the hall and from the hall went out with the

Choir. Therefore, if he hid the Box it must have been in the library or in the hall.'

'Not necessarily, my Brightness,' Abner said. 'While the party was singing carols in the hall he could have slipped upstairs and hidden the Box there.'

'I grant that he could have, my Astuteness,' Sylvia said, 'but the little girls said he didn't.'

'Whatever they said, my Inspiration, the point will have to be eliminated as a matter of routine,' Abner said. 'Besides, he may not have hidden it; he may have handed it to somebody. Who were there? These Jones children and this boy, Kay Harker, your ancient pupil. I think, my Ideal, and hope that you may agree, that he would not have trusted a treasure so great to any child whom he had not seen before that afternoon.'

'Well then, there remains the guardian,' Sylvia said: 'this Caroline Louisa.'

'Cole would have regarded her as the mistress of the house, certainly,' Abner said, 'and as a woman to be trusted. He must have been close to her in the hall. He could have handed it to her and whispered to her to keep it for him.'

'Your imagination is quite Shakespearean,' Sylvia Daisy said.

'Therefore,' Abner said, 'we shall have to take steps about Madam Caroline Louisa.'

'May a weak woman make a suggestion, my starlike Abner?' Sylvia said. 'Is it not more likely that he handed it to the Bishop, the Precentor, the Archdeacon or one of the Canons? You see, he was really in luck. There he was, unexpectedly in the midst of the most respectable company in the country, every one of which could be trusted to any amount.'

'It is only too likely, my Empress,' Abner said. 'Those three fools have let us in for a perplexing time. Supposing the Box is not hidden . . . and supposing he didn't give it to this Caroline Louisa, he'd have handed it, probably, to the Bishop. Whichever of the Cathedral staff had it would have called in all the others. He'd have called in the Dean, the Treasurer, the Seneschal and these other fellows in the Cathedral, and they'd have put the Box in the Cathedral treasure vaults. And you know what kind of vaults those are: Guy Fawkes and his powder wouldn't get through those, as we know from bitter experience. That's where the Box is now, depend upon it.'

'My dear,' his wife said, 'I think you look a little too much on the gloomy side of things. I do not doubt that in a normal season the Bishop, or whoever it was, would have acted as you suggest, but this isn't a normal season. At this time, so near to Christmas-time, the whole Cathedral staff is working overtime, and normal procedures are in abeyance. I think it very likely, my dear, that the Bishop, or whoever it was, when he got home to the Palace or the Deanery or the Canonry, put the Box into a drawer in his dressing-table among his collars and handkerchiefs and thought no more about it.'

Abner shook his head. 'My priceless Pearl,' he said, 'my blue and my yellow Sapphire, if I may call you so, I wish I could think it. But if Cole didn't hide it, he gave it to someone, that's sure; that's the first point to settle, and Our Routine will soon find out which . . .'

'Will you ask The Boy?' Sylvia asked, making a sign with her hand.

'I can't wait till I get home,' he answered. 'With luck we ought to know before then. Look here, Sylvia, I'm tempted to get rid of Charles, with his infernal "Ha-ha, what." '

'Oh no, my Emerald,' she said. 'He is one of our most precious workers. Get rid of Charles? Never. Whatever for?'

'He was in charge of Joe and the other,' Abner said, 'specially charged to nobble and scrobble Cole. He knew that Cole had a Punch and Judy show. He let Cole go right past him with the goods on him, with his Toby Dog in his pocket and the Punch and Judy show on his shoulder. Could a Prize Imbecile have been blinder or sillier, I ask you?'

'My Abner,' Sylvia said, 'you are unjust to our Charles. The terrier may have been in Cole's pocket: many terriers are very small. No doubt the show was also folded up very tight and not to be seen. Of course it was. How unjust of you to blame poor Charles. You must never, never think of getting rid of Charles. I repeat, my Emerald, never think of it. He did his duty well in a terrible night of storm and was deceived by a ruse. Get your Routine to work by all means, but then get home and ask The Boy.'

'The Routine is all at work,' he said. 'As to Charles, I shall follow my own judgment.'

'My Topaz and Diamond,' Sylvia said, 'your judgment is necessarily now mine. Can you not see that Charles is our only buffer against the stupidity and the craft of Joe? Can you not see that Charles is the only friend we have? But enough, my Idol, you do see; I see you see. Now as to this child, Maria Jones, whose ways you like. I admit, she sounds most promising. Remember that Cole may have given the Box to her.'

'I remember that,' Abner said, 'but even so, that

would be a point in her favour. I think you'll agree, that she would be an acquisition. She must be here with Nine, now, Nine and Charles. Shall I ring for them to bring her?'

'Do, my own Abbey,' Sylvia said.

Kay saw Abner stretch out his left hand and press a button in the middle of the table. An electric bell rang somewhere below in the house. Almost immediately the foxy-faced man and another curate, whom Kay had never before seen, entered with little Maria.

'Ah, Miss Maria,' Abner said, 'good morning. It was most kind of you to come over in answer to our message. Somebody was saying that you were very much interested in stained glass. We were making up a little party to go over to St. Griswold's this morning, lunching there, looking at the glass and being back at Seekings before tea. Would you care to come along? Oh, by the way, you haven't been introduced; this lady is Mrs. Brown.'

'Oh, thanks very much,' Maria said, nodding at Mrs. Brown, 'I'll be delighted. It's rather a mouldy lot of glass, isn't it, at St. Griswold's?'

'In the main church, yes,' the foxy-faced man said. 'Nothing a day earlier than fifteenth century; but in the Lady Chapel there is some of the very best that ever was done.'

'It's a pretty mouldy thing, English glass, if you ask me,' Maria said.

'Well, I think you will find that this isn't English glass,' the foxy-faced man said.

'Well, my dear,' Mrs. Brown said, 'before we start would you like to run back to Seekings and get some thick wraps?'

'No, I'll come as I am,' Maria said, 'thanks.'

'Would you like to leave word,' Mrs. Brown said, 'that you will be out until tea-time?'

'Oh no,' Maria said, 'thanks. They know that I can look after myself. They won't bother about me. I've generally got a pistol or two on me and I'm a dead shot with both hands.'

'How you must enjoy the quiet atmosphere of school,' Abner said.

'School!' Maria said. 'They know better than to try that game on me. I've been expelled from three and the headmistresses still swoon when they hear my name breathed. I'm Maria Jones, I am: somewhat talked of in school circles, if you take the trouble to enquire.'

'I count it a great honour,' Abner said, 'to entertain so distinguished an ornament of her sex. Then, we will start, shall we? We will have a look at the glass in the morning light. We will get to the *Bear's Paw* at Tatchester for lunch: the place still famous for duck patty. Then we will glance at the western window while it has the light behind it and bring you safely back to Seekings in good time for tea.'

They moved out from the room, Mrs. Brown with her hand on Maria's shoulder. Kay, crouched at the spy-hole, tried to cry out, 'Don't go with them, Maria: they're up to no good. They are the gang,' but being tiny as he was his voice made a little reedy squeak, like the buzzing of a fly.

'Back now,' he said to the Mouse, 'back now to Seekings as fast as ever we can go.'

At this instant round the corner of the corridor in which they were, came a party of the Wolves of the Gulf. They had been drinking more rum since Kay had passed them and there they were, pot-valiant, swinging lighted lanterns in their left hands and brandishing cutlasses in their right. Kay heard one of them say, 'There are their footsteps in the dust—two of them: a mouse and another —and we'll grind their bones to make our bread.'

'Yes,' another said, 'it's the cold-blooded cheek of it: coming past us when we were taking our ease round the bowl. We'll cut 'em into little collops. There they are!'

'Where?' said another. 'I'll eat their livers fried.'

'Up there,' the first one said, 'up there, where they can't escape.'

'Come on now,' they cried to Kay, 'come on. We'll mince you into collops and we'll eat your livers fried.'

Kay saw their gleaming teeth, their red eyes and their flashing cutlass edges. 'Give me your hand, Mouse,' he said. Quickly he caught the Mouse's hand and with his other hand twiddled the knob on the magic box that he might go swiftly, and, instantly, the two of them were plucked up into the air and whirled past the Wolves of the Gulf back to Seekings. He dropped his weapons in the Mouse's armoury, went back into his room and resumed his shape.

'Kay,' Susan was saying from the other side of the door, 'd'you know where Jemima is?'

'No,' he said. 'What d'you want Jemima for?'

'Well,' she said, 'I was out in the street buying Christmas presents and Maria went into a car with some total strangers at the *Rupert's Arms*, and she has gone off with them, and she knows she is absolutely forbidden to go into cars with total strangers.'

'What sort of a car was it?' Peter asked.

'Oh, it was a big, rather old, dark car. I didn't like the look of the strangers at all, though two of them were dressed like curates.'

'I expect it will be all right,' Kay said. He did not think that it would be all right: he was very much worried.

Kay did not know what to do; he wished that Caroline Louisa was there. As he went downstairs, Ellen met him.

'Oh, Master Kay,' she said, 'I didn't hear you come in. There has been a message from your guardian. She'll be here tonight by the eight-seven, she says, while you're all at Tatchester at the Punch and Judy show.'

'Oh, good; I am glad,' he said. 'Is her brother well, then?'

'Much better, she said, Master Kay.'

'Oh, splendid.'

He called the others into the study and told them how Maria had gone with Abner and the gangsters.

'She'll be all right,' Peter said. 'Maria can look after herself.'

'It is like Maria,' Jemima said, 'to go plunging off with any scoundrels who come along with a suggestion.'

'I say, it's rather sport,' Susan said. 'Supposing they say, "Miss Maria Jones, you will either join our gang or go down the oubliette for ever." '

'I pity any gangster who talks like that to Maria,' Peter said.

'Supposing she joins the gang,' Susan said. 'We might not see her again for years. Then, presently, when we are all old and frightfully hard up, suddenly a mysterious lady, covered with diamonds, will drive up in a Rolls, and say, "I'm your long-lost sister, Maria, come back. I'm the Queen of the Gang now and all your troubles are at an end." '

'She'll be Queen of the Gang, all right,' Kay said; but he felt uneasy, and wished that he knew what to do.

He went round to the *Rupert's Arms* to speak to the proprietress, Mrs. Calamine.

'Could you tell me, please, who the clergymen were who were here this morning?'

'Those, Master Kay?' she said. 'That was the Reverend Doctor Boddledale, with his wife and chaplain and private secretaries. He is the Head of the Missionary and Theological Training College at Chesters, in the Chester Hills.'

'I thought he was named Mr. Brown.'

'Oh, no, Master Kay, he's well known, and a very holy man, and his lady, Mrs. Boddledale; oh, she does wear lovely jewels. And she reminds me of someone whom I've seen somewhere: it's always on the tip of my tongue who.'

Kay knew who, but did not say.

By this time, a steady warm rain had set in from the west. Under it, the snow was falling apart into water: all spouts and gutters streamed and gurgled. The snow heaped at the sides of the roads had turned to a dirty grey. As it was very wet, the children stayed indoors after lunch. First, they played Work, then they played Murder. Kay thought, 'If Maria doesn't come back by dark I'll go to the Police about her. We shall have to start for Tatchester at half-past four. Somehow, I don't think the Inspector will be much help in the business.'

The darkness came before four o'clock that evening. Little Maria had not returned. Kay slipped round to the Inspector of Police and told his story with his suspicions.

'Have no fears, Master Kay,' the Inspector said. 'The Reverend Doctor Boddledale is a pillar of the Church and respectability. I've sung in the Glee Club with him time and time again. A very sweet tenor, Master Kay.

Now, depend upon it, Master Kay, you have come home, if I may say so, a little faint from the strain of learning. Your nerves want food. I often notice it in young fellows just back from school. Your young friend is in good hands, believe me, and as to her not being back in quite the time they said she'd be back, consider, Master Kay, the state of the roads, all swimming with sludge and filth, and the rain coming down on your windscreen so that you can't see a thing. She'll be back, you may be sure. Or, wait one moment, Master Kay, wasn't you to be tonight at the Punch and Judy show at Tatchester Palace?'

'Yes,' Kay said, 'I was. We were just going to start.'

'And wasn't Miss Maria to be there?' the Inspector asked. 'Well then, you say she's been to St. Griswold's to look at that old glass: why should she come back all the way to Seekings if she's got to be in Tatchester again at half-past five? She's a young lady who knows what's what. She'll have stopped in Tatchester, depend upon it, Master Kay; had tea there, and gone on direct to the Palace. You'll find her there when you get there.'

'I hadn't thought of that,' Kay said. 'Of course, that's very likely to have happened.'

'Ah,' the Inspector said, 'we in the Law, Master Kay, we've got a maxim, "It's the easy explanation that never occurs." You think all battle, murder and sudden death, and all the time it's only a tyre getting a puncture, or something equally simple. And we in the Law, Master Kay, have another proverb: "Never cross the water until you come to it." Time enough to think of making a bridge when you are at the water's brink, but until then, don't worry, Master Kay. And you get that good guardian of yours to see you take a strong posset every night. But you young folks in this generation, you don't know what a posset is. Well, a posset,' said the Inspector, 'is a jorum of hot milk; and in that hot milk, Master Kay, you put a hegg, and you put a spoonful of treacle, and you put a grating of nutmeg, and you stir 'em well up, and you get into bed and then you take 'em down hot. And a posset like that, taken overnight, it will make a new man of you, Master Kay, while now you're all worn down with learning.'

Kay thanked him and hurried back to Seekings, where all the children were clamouring for him to hurry up or they would be late for the Punch and Judy.

'It's all right,' Kay said. 'We shall be in lots of time. It's not much of a run to Tatchester. On a Roman road most of the way.'

They got into the car, and, in spite of the slush upon the roads, they were soon at Tatchester Palace, where the Bishop and his sister gave them a royal tea.

CHAPTER SIX

'Please,' Kay said to the Bishop, 'can I talk to the Punch and Judy man?'

'I am afraid not,' the Bishop said. 'He asked specially that the children should not talk to him either before or after the performance. He is giving two performances. He is an old man, and is suffering rather from his throat and doesn't want to talk in addition to having the strain of the two performances.'

'But, it is Cole Hawlings, isn't it?' Kay asked: 'the old man who was at Seekings last night?'

'Oh, yes,' the Bishop said, 'it's Cole Hawlings.'

'Well, could you tell him from me,' Kay said, 'that I am so very glad that it's all, all right?'

'Certainly, I will tell him that,' the Bishop said. In spite of the Bishop's words, Kay hoped very much to talk to Cole Hawlings.

Presently, they were all taken to the room in which the performance was to be given. Kay thought, 'Now I'll be able to speak to him,' but in this he was disappointed. The room was a long room, once the guest room of the pilgrims; at the end of it there was a stage covered with a curtain. Kay realised that the performance would take place on the other side of the curtain and that there would probably be no chance whatever for him to speak to old Cole. The Bishop made a little speech and welcomed them all. Then the curtain was partly drawn aside. On the stage was the theatre for Punch and Judy. It seemed to be exactly the theatre that Cole had used and the Toby dog was an Irish terrier, but at the end of the play when Kay called, 'Barney, Barney,' the dog did not answer to his name. Kay wondered several times during the performance whether the performer's voice was quite that of Cole. He couldn't be sure. After all, the shrill of one Punch is very like another.

'And now,' the Bishop said, 'Mr. Hawlings will give you a much older version of the Punch and Judy play, which his grandfather used to play upon the roads.' It was a very interesting performance and the children hugely enjoyed it, but not so much as they had enjoyed those magical tricks which he had played at Seekings.

Presently, the curtain fell and that was the end of Kay's hopes of speaking to the old man, for the Bishop at once said, 'And now, everybody, I want you to move into the next room, there behind you, to dance round our Christmas Tree and receive the gifts allotted to you.'

The door opened behind the company. Beyond the room in which they had seen the show was another room, also a part of the hostel. Pilgrims had come to that place in hundreds in the Middle Ages, for the Cathedral had then held the Shrine of the great Saint Cosric, Saxon King and Martyr, who had worked such famous miracles in the cure of Leprosy, and Broken Hearts.

In the midst of this room was the biggest and most glorious Christmas Tree that had ever been seen in Tatchester. It stood in a monstrous half-barrel full of what looked like real snow stuck about with holly and mistletoe. Its bigger boughs were decked with the glittering coloured glass globes which Kay so much admired. The lesser boughs were lit with countless coloured electric lights like tropical fruits: ever so much better, Kay thought, than those coloured candles which drip wax everywhere and so often set fire to the tree and to the presents. At the top of this great green fir-tree was a globe of red light set about with fiery white rays for the Christmas Star.

The boughs were laden with the most exquisite gifts. For the little ones there were whistles, drums, tops of different kinds, whips, trumpets, swords, popguns, pistols that fired caps and others which fired corks. There were also many dolls and teddy-bears. For the older boys there were railways with signals and switches and passenger trains and goods trains, some of which went by steam and others by clockwork. There were goods yards with real goods: little boxes, bales and sacks, real cranes by which these could be hoisted, and pumps by which the engines could get water. There were aeroplanes which you could wind up so that they would fly about the room. There were others which you made to fly by pulling a trigger. There were farmyards with cocks and hens which really pecked and cows which waggled their heads. There were Zoos with all sorts of animals, and Aquariums with all sorts of fish (in real water which could not splash out). Then there were all sorts of mechanical toys, of men boxing, or wrestling, or sawing wood, or beating on anvils. When you wound up these they would box or wrestle or saw or hammer for three or four minutes. Then there were squirts of all kinds and boxes of soldiers with cavalry and cannons, boxes of bricks and of 'Meccano,' and all sorts of adventure books and fairy books. Then for the girls there were needle-boxes with silver thimbles and cases of needles. There were acting sets with costumes of different colours, so that they could dress up to act charades. For each girl there were necklaces, bangles and brooches, and each brooch had the girl's name done in brilliants. There were also boxes of chocolates and candied fruits and great glass bottles of barley-sugar, raspberry drops, peppermint drops and acid drops. Then for both girls and boys there were toy boats, some with sails, some with clockwork engines, some with steam engines that would make real steam with methylated spirit furnaces. Hanging from the boughs here and there were white and scarlet stockings all bulging with chocolate creams done up in silver paper.

All round this marvellous tree were wonderful crackers, eighteen inches long. The Bishop made all the children stand in a double rank round the tree, each with one end of a cracker in each hand. The musicians struck up a tune and they danced in the double rank three times round the Christmas Tree. Then the Bishop gave the word: they pulled the crackers, which went off with a bang together, like cannons. And then, inside the crackers there were the most lovely decorations—real little tiny coats of coloured paper that you could put on, with the most splendid hats and necklets like real gold. Then the Bishop's sister and her friends gave each child two presents. Then they all played 'Hunt the Slipper' and other merry games and, then, suddenly, Kay remembered that he had not thought about little Maria since he left the Police Inspector and that she wasn't there.

'Good heavens!' he thought, 'Maria isn't here. What shall I do?' He went up to the Bishop's sister and asked her if little Maria had been there.

'No,' she said. 'No. And the Bishop said just now to me, "I'm sorry not to see little Maria here. She may think that I bear malice for the smashing up of my car that time, but, indeed, that isn't so. I should have loved to have had her here." '

'D'you mind if I telephone?' Kay said. He went down and telephoned to Ellen.

'No,' Ellen said, 'Miss Maria hasn't come back.'

'By the way,' Kay called, 'we shall be a little late in getting away from here. Will you ask the *Rupert's Arms* to send a car to meet the eight-seven?'

Ellen said that she would do that. Then, presently, the evening came to an end and all the happy children got ready to go away.

Just as they were crowding into the hall, going off in instalments as the cars came for them, the butler came to the Bishop with a look of great gravity on his face. Kay was standing close beside the Bishop at the moment. The Bishop said, 'What is it, Rogers?' and the butler said, 'I am sorry to tell Your Grace, but during the performances the burglars have been in every room of the Palace. They have turned the place just topsy-turvy, Your Grace.'

'Indeed,' the Bishop said. 'Warn the Police, Rogers. I will be with you in a moment as soon as my young friends have gone.'

'If you please, Your Grace,' Kay said, 'd'you think I might say good-bye to the Punch and Judy man?'

'I am afraid he has gone,' the Bishop said. 'Somebody in an old car came for him as soon as the performance was over.'

'D'you know where he went to?' Kay said.

'I seem to know. I really can't quite recollect. He did say, but I have forgotten,' the Bishop said. 'I shall think of it when I go to bed tonight. Somewhere not very far from here.'

Kay thanked the Bishop for their glorious treat. Presently, they were in the car driving home in the slush.

'The Palace has been burgled,' Peter said, 'while we were at the Punch and Judy. A gang got in. They got every single thing that there was worth taking.'

'How d'you know?' Kay said.

'I was up there talking to Rogers,' Peter said. 'The Palace is full of guests—seven old dowagers at least—and they have all brought their family jewels, and they're gone. A cool forty thousand wouldn't pay the insurance.'

'The footman said we shall have the Police on us tomorrow,' Kay said, 'and we shall have our finger-prints taken to see if we were accomplices.'

'I say,' Susan said, 'd'you think we shall?'

'Sure to,' Peter said, 'it will be a matter of Police routine.'

Kay thought that the burglary was a matter of Abner Brown's Routine.

'Well, I do hope,' he said, 'I really do hope that little Maria hasn't been in it with the gang. It would be just like her to do a thing like that.'

'Oh, I do wish it was tomorrow morning,' Jemima said, 'and we could see the papers about it. If the motor-cars have gone from the garage, then we may suspect that Maria has had a hand in it.'

'Maria won't have had a hand in it,' Susan said, 'except to collar all the swag and bring it back to its owners.'

When they reached home there was no news of little Maria, but in some strange way the news of the burglary had reached Ellen. She greeted the children with, 'I do hope the burglars didn't frighten you.'

'No, they didn't,' Kay said. 'But has Miss Maria turned up?'

'No, not yet, Master Kay,' Ellen said.

'Is my guardian back?' he asked.

'No, Master Kay,' Ellen said. 'The *Rupert's Arms* man met the eight-seven, but she didn't come by that train, and there's no other train from London tonight.'

'Has any message come from her?'

'No,' Ellen said. 'I telephoned through to the number you gave. She'd started to catch that train.'

'Well,' Kay said, 'I suppose the trains are all upset, partly with Christmas and partly with the snow. She may have gone a certain distance and then had to come on by car.'

'It may have been something like that,' Ellen said.

'You see, sometimes,' Kay said, 'they have to run the trains from London in two parts at this time of year. She may have come by the second part.'

'Something like that, I dare say,' Ellen said.

They telephoned to the station, and the station telephoned to Paddington, and Paddington replied that the train hadn't started in two parts. Then they telephoned to the address where she had been staying. They replied that Caroline Louisa had started and hadn't since returned.

'Well, I don't know,' Kay said. 'D'you think I had better speak to the Inspector of Police?'

Then he remembered the Inspector's maxim 'That the simple explanation was always the last one thought of' and thought, 'Well, the Inspector would only laugh and tell me to take a posset.'

'Ellen,' he said, 'can you make possets?'

'Yes, Master Kay,' she said, 'I can.'

'Well, I wish you'd make me a big one,' he said, 'because I'm feeling very miserable.'

He went up to bed. He found Peter already in bed, reading a murder story. Kay got into bed. Presently Ellen brought him a posset in a mug. He drank it down, thinking that the Inspector certainly knew a good thing. After he had drunk it the comfort seemed to tingle through him, which put an end to his miseries. He half heard Peter chuckling and saying, 'I say, Kay, do listen to what the detective said.' He knew that Peter went on to read what the detective said, but he paid no heed. He was fast asleep. When he woke the fire was almost out, but the moonlight shone in through the open curtains, and outside on the hard asphalt of the walks round the house came the clank of weapons and the stamp of feet marching in time. A trumpet blew and a stern voice cried, 'The Wolves Guard setting out for Duke's Heath! Guard against the wolves! Just starting for Duke's Heath! You coming there?'

Kay looked out of the window and there he saw in the moonlight a pack of armed men with bronze scalearmour, helmets and short spears.

'Are you coming, Kay?' the captain said. Duke's Heath was a couple of miles away, but it seemed to Kay much too good a chance to miss.

'Yes, of course I'm coming,' he said.

He took his precious Box, which had been under his pillow, and in a minute he was out of the house.

'Very strange lot of men,' he thought. 'Even in the

moonlight they seem to be sunburnt and tanned.' They had shields on their left arms, short swords by their sides and each man had two short spears.

'Well, you'll want a coat of armour, Kay,' the captain said, and put a lovely little coat of mail over his shoulders. It was lined with wash-leather and very warm, so that Kay was very glad that he had not stopped to put anything on over his pyjama coat. Then they gave him two lovely little spears and a little short sword, and away they went.

Kay thought that the officer, beside whom he was marching, was very good-looking and agreeable. He was young, pale, with quick eyes and black hair; some of his dash was in his men: they marched like one man, with snap and swagger.

'Will you tell me who you are, please?' Kay asked.

'We?' the young officer said. 'We're the smartest squad in the finest cohort in the star wing of the crack Legion of the whole Imperial Roman Army, search it where you will; you'll not find anything anywhere to touch or come near the Blue and White Stripers of the Tatchester Toms.'

'I suppose not,' Kay said. 'And are you going to camp at Duke's Moor?'

'No, no,' the man said. 'We're the Wolf-guard passing that way with the mails. We go on to the frontier.'

'Are the wolves very bad?' Kay asked.

'So, so,' the man said. 'It's best to keep your eyes skinned. Duke's Moor is none too good a place. There are some of the old lot there, who used to hold Chester Hills.'

'There's a Roman Camp at Chester Hills,' Kay said.

'There had need to be,' the officer said.

'Were you ever fighting there, please?' Kay asked.

'You'd call it so,' he said. 'A bad place and bad people. Men disappeared—sentry after sentry; and were never seen again. You see, it's a limestone country, all honeycombed with caves, and these Wolves as we called them were all underground. It cost us a lot of men to get them out of it.'

They marched so swiftly that very soon they were out of the town in the open fields with Duke's Moor already black to their right front.

'You're looking for a friend,' the officer said. 'Well, here's the bridge over the brook. There's a dingle to the right where you could shelter in case the rain should come on again. If I were you, I'd wait here for your friend. Don't cross the brook. Some of the Wolves may be out on the other side, and they're none too good.'

'You mean men wolves?' Kay said.

'See now,' the officer said, 'that flat bit near the brook. When we were operating here, we were camped on that bit of slope behind us, and had double sentries out, visited every half-hour. Well, on that flat bit, one of our posts saw a calf come out in the moonlight to feed; just one of these wild white calves that you see. Well, nothing odd in that; the calf fed, and scratched and stamped like any other calf; but the posts noticed that it was always drawing nearer. At last, one of the men in the post didn't like the look of it, so he flung a stone and called "Get out of that," and at once the calf tossed off its skin and charged the post, hurt one man and got away with two spears. The calf was two of these young Wolves under a cow-skin. That was only three years ago, just here. They're none too good, the Wolves.

'Now if you stay here, your friend will soon be with you; and we'll go on.'

The squad's music, a strange kind of horn and drum, broke out into a march; the squad stepped out to it with a stamp and jingle. Soon even the noise of the march was gone. Kay was alone near the swollen brook and the dripping trees of the dingle. 'Duke's Brook,' he thought. 'I wonder who Duke or the Duke was.' He had been told that the real name was Duck's Brook. Kay wished that the soldier had not told him that tale about the wild white calf. The night was now black as a pocket; and there in the blackness, oh horror, was a white calf moving towards him just as the Roman had described.

Was it a calf? He remembered, that Cook had said, that there was a White Lady who 'walked' out Duke's Brook way. This thing that was coming was a White Lady . . . but supposing it was a White Wolf, standing on its hind legs and ready to pounce. It looked like a wolf: its teeth were gleaming. Then the moon shone out again; he saw that it was a White Lady who held her hand in a peculiar way, so that he could see a large ring, with a glittering 'longways cross' on it. She was the Lady who had been outside Bob's shop, waiting for the message.

'Come, Kay,' she said, 'you must not stay here; the Wolves are running: listen.'

The midnight was still enough, save for the babble of the brook, and the occasional running patter of drops from the ash-trees. Now above these noises, from out to the north by the straw yards, came the cry of Wolves in pack, 'all mad,' Kay thought, 'like the bark of foxes, but much more awful.'

'Come with me,' she said, giving him her hand.

As he took it, he felt himself lifted from the grass, so

that he glided beside her up the stream to the pool from which the stream rose. Near this, to the right, was an oak of great age, which Kay had always called King Charles's Oak and the country-people called the She Oak. It was hollow with age, but the mighty shell was alive still.

'There are the Wolves,' she said. 'Look.'

There in the moonlight, racing over the grass to them, were the Wolves in pack, with their ruffs up and their eyes glaring. The oak-tree opened behind Kay, the woman stepped within it drawing Kay with her. Instantly they were within the quiet of the tree in a room panelled with living oakwood and hung with tapestries of oak-leaves in which the birds were alive.

Kay marvelled, for the birds came out of the tapestries and perched upon his hands. 'They want some strawberries,' the woman said. 'Won't you give them some?'

'Please, I haven't any,' Kay said.

'Ah, here they are,' the woman said. 'Now you can give them some.'

Out of a little door in one of the walls a red squirrel came cocking, with very bright eyes. He carried in his fore-paws a cabbage-leaf heaped with strawberries. He hopped down to the table and offered the leaf to Kay, who took the berries and gave them to the birds. It was charming to have the little birds' claws upon the fingers and to see the little bills peck the berries.

'Squirrel would like some nuts,' the woman said. 'Bring some nuts, Mole.'

Three black moles came swiftly out of the floor, each bearing dock-leaves, one with beech-nuts, one with walnuts, one with filberts. As the squirrel cracked and ate these he sat on Kay's shoulder (and tried to drop the shells down his neck).

'Now Kay would like some supper,' the woman said. 'For indeed, Kay, things are not going too well, when the Wolves have the best of us underground, and are still Running.'

Indeed, they were Running; they were sweeping past the tree with every kind of shriek and madness.

But Kay in the happy oak never bothered about the Wolves, for the woman was now grown young before his eyes: she was all bright, shining and beautiful, and humming a most beautiful tune which brought more and more birds out of the tapestries, so that perhaps there was no kind of bird known to Kay not fluttering near him. Whenever he thought, 'I don't see a gold-crest,' or 'There's no golden-crested wren,' or 'I don't see a lesser spotted woodpecker,' lo, that bird would be hopping onto his finger. 'These birds are lovely,' he said. 'However do you make them so tame?'

'Oh, I have a way with them,' she said. 'But tell me, now, which season do you like best, Kay?'

'I like them all,' he said. 'I suppose I like April best, on the whole.'

'Look, then,' she said.

All one side of the room changed to a rolling red ploughland stretching down to a blackthorn hedge where a brook was running. The blackthorn was in blossom; there were marsh-marigolds in the mud near the brook and a few primroses in the dead grass of the bank. Nearer to Kay, at his feet, a couple of lambs were nibbling. A patch of daffodils grew in the grass. It was April beyond all doubt.

A blackbird flew suddenly with a chackering cry onto

the blackthorn near him. Before the spray had ceased to shake, a missel-thrush settled beside him: the spray swayed and settled; then the blackbird sang:

'Out of the many-coloured earth,
That eats the lights and drinks the rain,
Come Beauty, Wisdom, Mercy, Mirth,
That conquer Reason, Greed and Pain.

'My laughter ripples in the corn,
In the green leaf it claps its wings,
In summer's rose it blows a horn,
In brook and flying cloud it sings.

'Come missel-thrush with merry will
Ring out your jolly notes agen,
And April will come up the hill
A million bright green little men.'

As soon as the blackbird had sung, the missel-thrush lifted up a magical voice and sang in answer:

'The withered thorn-trees on the hill
Mope on the rabbit-barren dry,
I flute their thin blood to a thrill
Of quicking bud as I go by;

'The dormouse drowsy to the soul
In warmth of mossop where he lies,
Uncurls his beech-nut-battened roll,
And is all dart and is all eyes;

'And out along the hedge the curled
Green little buds that lambkins bite
Spring, and the blackbird calls the world,
And all the cherry-trees are white.'

'Spink, spink,' said a chaffinch. 'That's a very good song to *me*-oh.'

'Sing the song again,' said Jenny Wren, so the missel-thrush sang.

As she sang, the squirrel, the moles, the most beautiful little mice and seven little foxes brought Kay strawberries, raspberries, red and white currants, ripe mulberries, plump blackberries, red and yellow cherries, black cherries, walnuts, beech-nuts, hazel-nuts, filberts, little round radishes, little pointed wild strawberries, sloes all cracking with ripeness, a mushroom for a relish, a chip cut from a turnip, an apricot from the south wall and a peach almost bursting its skin. Then there came blue grapes, black grapes, yellow grapes, almonds, raisins, all so ripe and so sweet and so good; and the animals were so charming, offering them on dock-leaves held in their front paws, and all the time the beautiful woman hummed. At last she said, 'They have taken Cole, they have taken Maria, and they will take others; but don't lose courage, Kay, even if the Wolves are Running. You will beat the Wolves, won't you, Kay?'

Kay said he would, and at once there he was back in his bed at Seekings, in daylight, with Peter saying, 'It's about time you woke. You've been snoring like a stuck pig. Have you had a nightmare?'

When he came down to breakfast there was no letter from his guardian, but there was a newspaper and the children pounced upon this for news of the burglary at the Palace.

'REGRETTABLE INCIDENT AT TATCHESTER
PALACE
ALLEGED BURGLARY

'We are informed that a serious and very successful burglary was carried out at Tatchester Palace last evening. According to the Bishop's laudable custom before Christmas the Palace was the scene last night of a large children's party with a Christmas Tree and other festivities. While these were in progress the burglars, who, it is thought, were assisted by someone secreted within the Palace, went through the guest-rooms and escaped with considerable booty, including the jewel-cases of five ladies who were guests of His Grace's sister. The Police preserve a professional reticence over the affair, but it is understood that they regard the work as that of smart London men and are at present engaged upon exhaustive enquiries. It is understood that dramatic developments may be expected shortly.'

'But that's what they always say,' Peter said. They talked among themselves about how lovely it would have been if they could have caught the burglars at work, and held them up with pistols till the Police came.

Kay was very much worried about Maria being still absent, but Maria's brother and sisters said that she would be all right. 'She always falls on her feet,' they said. 'Don't you worry about Maria.' But Kay did worry. As soon as breakfast was over he went across to see the Inspector of Police.

'And so, you haven't seen Miss Maria,' the Inspector said. 'Ha, that doesn't look so well, but you leave the matter in my hands, Master Kay, and I'll make what enquiries are called for. And your guardian, I hear, hasn't come back.'

'No,' Kay said, 'that's another point. She ought to have been back: she started out yesterday to catch a certain train and she didn't come by the train. We have had no word from her since.'

'So I understand,' the Inspector said.

'How did you know?' Kay said.

'Well, in the Law, Master Kay,' the Inspector said, 'it's our duty to hear all things: "Information Received" we call it. But I will put through the necessary enquiries, Master Kay. You leave the matter to the bloodhounds of the Law, and, depend upon it, information will be received.'

Kay was cheered by his confident manner and by his repeating. 'The simple explanation is always the last thing thought of.'

When he reached Seekings Ellen said, 'Oh, Master Kay, your guardian's brother has rung up. There was so much fog and such a crowd at the station yesterday that she didn't start, but went back to her brother, and one or two other little things have sprung up since, so she won't be back today, but she may be back tomorrow. And she sends her love and tells you not to worry, and she hopes you are having a good holiday.'

'Well, that's a jolly good thing,' Kay said, and being much cheered by the news, he went upstairs to get his catapult and some bullets. He kept these in a little secret hiding-place underneath his bed. After he had put them in his pocket he looked out of the window towards King

Arthur's Camp, and there in the fields below the Camp he saw the gleam of water. He ran down at once to the others. 'I say,' he said, 'it's splendid. The floods are out. We'll go for a mud-lark. We'll get out all our ships and sail them on the floods.'

Both Peter and he had received ships from the Bishop's Christmas Tree. Kay had a ship called the *Hero* which went by methylated spirit, Peter had a ship which he called the pirate ship, the *Royal Fortune*, which went by clockwork, and Kay, in addition to these, had an old cutter which he called *Captain Kidd's Fancy*. 'We'll launch these and christen them properly,' they said.

'It's perfectly lovely,' Kay said, 'that the floods are out. We'll pretend that these ships are real ships, and we'll provision them with almonds, raisins and chocolates and we'll all take long sticks so as to poke them off if they get stuck anywhere. And we'll take sandwiches, cakes and hard-boiled eggs and we won't come back till tea-time.'

'I've got some lovely little things that would do for the ships,' said Susan. 'In the stocking which they gave me from the tree there were those little tiny wooden barrels filled with Hundreds and Thousands. They were just the sort of barrels to go in the ships.'

She fetched the little barrels and they divided them up among the three ships, and they put raisins and currants and bits of biscuits in each barrel.

'I vote,' Jemima said, 'that the other barrels shall be filled with ham, which we will pretend is salt pork.'

'They don't take salt pork any more,' Peter said. 'They take pemmican, which is beef chopped up with fat and raisins and chocolate and beer and almonds and ginger and stuff. It must be a sickening mess, but it's very nourishing. It's supposed to be what the ancient Britons had. They could take a piece as big as a currant and live on it for a week.'

As there weren't enough barrels to provision the ships, Kay got some match-boxes and egg-collector's pill-boxes, which they filled with food. Jemima produced some drapers' patterns of woollen goods. 'The ships ought to have these,' she said. 'They'd be exactly the size of thick blankets for the little sailors.'

'I tell you what we might do,' Susan said. 'When we get to the water we might take a little plank and make a landing-stage of it, and take some of those little flags that we've got, and we'll pretend that these ships are Christopher Columbus's ships going out to discover. We'll tie the ships to the landing-stage and then Jemima shall be the Queen of Spain and Kay had better be the King of Spain, and we will all be monks and nuns and people and sing to Columbus, and then we'll push him out into the Atlantic.'

'That would be a good idea,' Kay said. 'And then, presently, we could be Sir Francis Drake, and some of us could be Indians and some of us could be Spaniards. And then one of us will be going to be burnt by the Inquisition, and, just at the end, we'll rush in and kill all the Spaniards, and take all their treasure and sail away to Plymouth. And we could fire red-hot shot, to tell the truth, if we didn't get the cannon too wet. You see, we can't fire gun-powder, but we could get the caps from toy pistols and load the guns with those, and then, if you put a match to the touch-hole they sometimes go off with quite a bang.'

'You'd better have some anchors,' Jemima said. 'All ships have anchors, otherwise they wouldn't be able to stop.'

'You've got to be jolly careful with anchors, with ships so little as these,' Kay said. 'Very often, if you try anchoring little ships like these, the anchor will pull them right underneath the water.'

They made ready the ships. Peter found a plank and rigged up some flags upon it for the landing-stage. Ellen brought sandwiches, cake, boiled eggs, fruit and ginger-beer. Kay had a bottle of methylated spirit for the engine. Then they went out to the wood-shed to Joe, who gave each one of them a long wand or stick for poking off the ships if they got stuck. Then away they went in bright, sunny, clearing weather, with the noise of running water everywhere. When they came to the meadows there were pools in all the hollows and many of the mole-hills were bubbling up water like running springs. When they came to a suitable place on the mill stream they fixed the landing-stage and the children poked about among the banks with their sticks, while Kay and Peter got the methylated spirit furnace to make steam in the boiler.

Kay had the Box of Delights in his inner pocket and sometimes poked his hand inside to be sure that it was there.

Presently all was ready. The King and Queen of Spain, with the monks and nuns and people, sent off Christopher Columbus on his voyage, and away the ships went down-stream with the children following, shouting and cheering and poking them clear of the banks with their sticks.

When they had gone about half a mile down the stream, Susan, who was looking up at the sky, said, 'There's an aeroplane: no, two.' The others didn't see the aeroplane at first but then saw them like two bright specks against a dark cloud. 'It's odd we didn't hear them,' Susan said. They hadn't heard them.

They went on with their ships, paddling in the water, getting very wet and enjoying themselves so much that they forgot about all other things, till Kay suddenly saw a shadow running across the field in front of him, and, looking up, saw two aeroplanes circling silently overhead. 'I say,' he said, 'look at the aeroplanes, absolutely silent.'

He didn't say so, but the thought flashed through his mind that the aeroplanes were there after them, but the other thought also flashed that no aeroplane would dare to land on ground so rotten with springs as that low-lying field. 'They'd stick in the mud if they tried that,' he thought.

'They're going to land,' Susan said. 'They're coming down by the copse there.'

'I'll bet they're after us,' Kay said to himself. 'Bring the ships in to the banks.'

They saw the two aeroplanes come down on to the big dry open field near the copse on the other side of the stream. There were some old willow-trees where Kay was standing. He climbed up one of them. 'There are four men getting out of the aeroplanes,' he said. 'They've got pistols and ropes and they're coming this way. I think it would be wise to get out of the way.'

'Do you think they're after us?' Susan said.

'I shouldn't wonder,' Kay said.

'But it's all tommy-rot,' Jemima said. 'Who'd be coming after us with pistols and ropes? They're probably mole-catchers coming to set traps over these fields now that the moles are working in the soft earth.'

'That's a champion remark,' Peter said. 'When did you

ever hear of mole-catchers coming in aeroplanes with pistols?'

'They're the men who kidnapped the Punch and Judy man,' Kay said. 'That's the man who was in the front of that attack: the tall one with the white splash of paint on his leggings. I'll bet they're after us.'

'What shall we do?' said Susan. 'Shall we run to the mill or the farm?'

'They'd beat us to either of those,' Kay said.

'Could we get down into the gully there?' Susan said.

'The gully's full of water in this flood,' Kay said.

'Well, what can we do?' Susan asked.

'Well, I've got here,' Kay said, 'a sort of magic dodge. If we all hold hands while I touch a button on it, we shall all shrink into little tiny creatures, and then we'll pop on board our ships and go down the stream.'

They held hands, and he twiddled the little button, and instantly, each one of them felt lighter and brighter than ever before. The earth seemed to shoot up and to become enormous, and there they were, clambering on board their gigantic ships. They cast loose the strings which tied them to the bank and away they sailed down-stream, round a bend and on. 'All very well,' Kay thought, 'as long as we can keep in mid-stream, but in a flood like this if we jam against some wreckage or fallen tree we shall be sucked right under.'

Just as the ships went round the bend, Kay saw the four men coming in sight close to the bank. It was plain that each man had two long pistols stuck in his belt and they were coiling lassoes ready for a throw. The ships went gaily down the mill stream into the mill-race. At the mill-race came a roaring and terrible torrent, down which the ships plunged so swiftly that they were through it before they had time to be afraid. In an instant they were in quiet water out of all the currents, gently rubbing the ships' sides against the roots of an elmtree, which grew in the high bank. Kay and Peter hooked the anchors onto some of the roots of the tree. They secured all three ships alongside each other.

CHAPTER SEVEN

'And now,' Kay said, 'I vote we have our pemmican and decide what we'll do next.'

At this moment a little voice sounded from up above. 'Hullo, you people,' it said. 'Come indoors. There's going to be a shower. You can have your feast in here. I'll let down a cage to hoist you up.' Then they saw a little field-mouse leaning over a platform which projected from the trunk of the elm. He had a little crane on the platform. Evidently he hoisted all his stores from the water by means of it. Presently the little cage came dangling down from the crane and the Field-mouse said, 'Not more than two of you at one time.'

Peter and Jemima got in and the little mouse went to a winch and set the works going, and, instantly, the cage was up at the platform. Then the cage was sent down for Kay and Susan.

'Well, here we are,' the Field-mouse said. 'Come in.' He led the way from the platform into a corridor to a room with little windows which looked out upon the river. The floor was covered with dry leaves and moss, and the wall had lockers all along it, labelled: 'Beech-nuts,' 'Corn,' 'Pig-nuts,' 'Best Berries,' 'Second-best Berries,' 'Berries,' 'Assorted Seeds,' 'Hazel-nuts,' 'Honey,' 'Dried Minnow,' etc., etc.

'Well, now let's lunch,' he said. They all got out their provisions: pemmican, ham and the rest. The Field-mouse told them where to look for other things. He produced some blackberry wine and some beech-nut loaves, which Susan toasted at the fire. While they were feasting in this happy way they heard a great clumping noise outside. 'That's men,' the Field-mouse said. 'They might be elephants the noise they make.' Almost at once the men began to talk.

'Well,' one man said, 'they seem to have got away from us. They must have come down-stream under cover of the banks somehow. We'd have seen them if they'd gone up-stream, because there aren't any banks.'

'Well,' another said, 'if they've gone into the stream the flood must have got them,' and another said, 'Well, if the floods have got them, we've got to fish them out.'

'Well,' the first one said, 'there's nothing like little children for leading one a dance: little devils! I thought we were making a mistake bringing both the 'planes down and losing sight of them. You see, those little creatures have popped away into almost nothing.'

'How would it be to look under the bridge there?' one of them said. 'They'd time to get to the bridge.'

'Yes, the bridge is a good idea,' they said, and then the voices and footsteps moved away.

When they had gone the Field-mouse said, 'Perhaps you'd like to see some of the wonders of this tree.'

'We should love to see the tree,' the children said. The Field-mouse threw up a shutter in the wall. In the hollow behind the shutter was a little cage like that in which he had hoisted them from the ships. 'You see,' he said, 'I have to have a good many places like this. Chaps like me sometimes have to leave the room in a hurry; if I hear someone coming whom I don't want, you understand; I name no names, but there are several round here; uncertain sort of chaps, and you never can tell in a place like this which door they will come in at. But now that I've got the lifts fixed, if I hear anyone suspicious I nip into one of these places. Just step in here, will you? And I press a button and up we go.'

The cage shot upwards. When it stopped, the Mouse opened the door. 'See, it's rather a bare loft here,' he said. 'If you will just come to the window here you'll be able to see down.' They looked out of the little window. They were amazed to find that they were right at the very top of the great elm-tree. Close to them was an old rook's nest: it looked like a mass of black timbers, big as a church. Just beyond it, on a twig, was a rook swaying in the sun: his back, which was towards them, glistened purple. 'Dangerous chaps, those,' the Field-mouse said. 'I keep out of their way as a rule. Now just come this way. Now here,' he said, 'is one of the slides. If you just let yourself go you can't hurt yourself. You just slither down on to moss.'

They slithered down and found themselves in another bare corridor, in which there was a strange droning noise, which the children took to be the wind in the boughs. There was a strong smell of honey in the air. The Mouse opened a little shutter and told them to look within to the hollow of a tree. They saw that within the tree there were a multitude of bees which had almost filled the hollow with their honeycombs. Although it was winter they were moving there, making the place drone like a thrashing-machine. The place smelt as though all the summer was still there with lime-blossom and bean-blossom. 'This is a fine place on a cold winter night,' the Field-mouse said, 'curled up in a blanket and letting the bees drone you to sleep. And in any place you can get a draught of honey. Lots of the tree is all blocked with very old honey which the bees will never get to now. And, of course, here and there in this part of the tree there are woodpeckers, the green and the spotted. They're very nice people, of course. The rooks are very nice people too: very wise. But all those chaps have got rather a snappy way. They don't mean anything, of course, but if you get one good snap with those great beaks I ask you, where are you? Oh, and then, of course,' he said, 'there are the jackdaws. Very odd chaps, the jackdaws. If you will look in the corner here you'll see the kinds of things they bring.'

In a corner near an opening, where a knot in the wood had fallen, was a heap of stuff which sparkled. The children went to it and pulled the things over. There was a lady's little, old gold watch, two rings set with brilliants, a pin with a fox's head top, a bit of quartz which gleamed, two scraps of Roman glass, irridescent from being in the earth for eighteen hundred years, the red cut-glass stopper of a bottle, a broken glass marble with a coloured spiral in it, a bit of brass chain and a crystal seal set in gold. 'They just bring these things in and leave them,' the Mouse said. 'Queer chaps.'

'But come on down now. Oh, before we go just come up this stair. You will see a sight.' They crept up a little stair and looked into what seemed like a cavern. Within the cavern, just below them, a big white owl was perched, fast asleep, gurgling and growling. Peter dropped a bit of bark on to him. He half opened an eye and gurgled back to sleep again. 'He's the oldest thing around here,' the Field-mouse said. 'He's ever so old: he remembers when this tree was a sprig and when the Very Good People were here. He makes my blood run cold, he's so old. But come on down. His place is a bit bony and birdy and he's a graveyard of my relations, if the truth were known. I never come here except in winter,' the Field-mouse said, as he went down the little stair. 'This is really the birds' quarter. In the season there'll be a matter of seventy or eighty young jackdaws in this tree first and last, and about half that of young rooks. And they knock the place about and nothing's safe from them.'

He opened another little door, a trap-door in the floor. The children could see a long shoot leading downwards. 'It's perfectly safe,' the Mouse said, 'if you just let yourself go. Nothing but weed and moss to fall on to: you can't hurt yourself.' And with that he let himself drop and the children followed. 'Now this,' the Field-mouse said, as they got on to their feet in a strange room, 'this is a part of the tree that's really worth seeing.'

The room in which they were had been a music-room. There was a stage still set with music-stands and torn music propped up: against the wall were old 'cellos and pretty little fiddles: a drum with the end knocked in: and parts of brass trombones. It had not been used for many years: it was dusty and cobwebby. 'Now this, you see, is a part that was made by the Very Good People, who don't come here any more.'

'D'you mean Fairies?' Susan asked.

'No, very, Very Good People,' the Field-mouse said: 'very clever, very beautiful and very wise. But they went away. It's a long time ago,' the Field-mouse added. 'I don't know the rights of it. It isn't wise to talk about those People, but, of course, everybody knows they were very, very good.'

He led the way out of the music-room to a beautiful staircase hung with tapestries and lit still with glowing lights. The staircase was carpeted with scarlet. The banisters were beautifully carved with flowers growing on stems. The tapestries showed countless little people carrying coloured baubles to a queen of extraordinary beauty who sat upon a mushroom.

'Now, this place,' the Mouse said, when they reached the foot of the stairs, 'this place I don't quite like going into, but it's so beautiful I can't keep from it.' He opened a big door, so that they pressed into a great room which seemed to fill the whole hollow of the tree. The walls were hung with banners and with portraits of extraordinary brilliant people, whose eyes seemed to move in their painted heads. This room was lit like the staircase with a soft, glowing light: it was carpeted with scarlet: at the end of the room was a dais with a throne, and in front of the throne a table on which lay an ivory horn. Underneath the horn, written in letters of flame which flickered to and fro, were the words:

'He that dares blow must blow me thrice.
Or feed th' outrageous cockatrice.'

'Oh, I would love to blow,' Kay said, 'just to see what would happen. What is a cockatrice?'

'Oh, don't,' Susan said. 'Anything might happen. A cockatrice is a fearful thing, like a cock and a cobra mixed.'

'Oh, I wouldn't touch the thing, sir,' the Field-mouse said. 'Oh no, you mustn't think of doing that. Nobody's done that: even the Owl wouldn't dare to do a thing like that: why, the Fox wouldn't.'

'Do blow it, Kay,' Peter said. 'Just for a lark.'

'Oh, don't, don't!' the Mouse said. 'You don't know what they are. Of course, they're awfully Good People; very beautiful and very good and very, very clever and wise, but that's why I wouldn't like to hurt their feelings.'

'Oh, if they're beautiful and good and clever and wise,' Kay said, 'their feelings wouldn't be hurt.'

'Oh, but you don't know,' the Field-mouse said. 'Remember I'm not saying anything against them.'

They could see that the Mouse was in a twitter with terror, but Kay picked up the horn, put it to his lips and blew. He had had a little practice in the blowing of horns. He had an old hunting-horn that had belonged to his father and sometimes the Police Inspector had let him try an old coach-horn, so that he could blow without fear of splitting his lips. He blew once and a strange noise as sweet as the winter singing of the storm-cock came from the ivory. With a little tinkle and clack all the frames fell from the portraits on the walls. The little Mouse shrieked with terror and got underneath the table.

Kay blew a second time. This time the note was louder and stronger: it was like the first calling of the cuckoo when he comes in April. The children heard a sort of gasp of breath from the portraits on the walls and all the figures of the portraits turned their heads and looked at Kay.

'Oh, Kay, they're looking at you,' Susan said.

'Never mind,' Kay said. The Mouse had by this time got his head underneath the carpet.

Kay blew a third blast, and at this all the lights in the room burned out a thousand-fold more brightly, and the blast of the horn became like the song of all the birds in June singing together, with a noise of the little silver bells that had hung on the sleeves of Herne the Hunter. And at this all the beautiful people in the portraits stepped down into the room. The air became fragrant as though all the flowers and spices of the world had come suddenly together there. The glorious creatures formed in two lines. The portraits over the door were those of a King and a Queen. As the children turned, they saw this King and Queen advancing through the company towards the throne. They took their seats upon the throne and all the company burst out into singing. The children stared in amazement, for they had never seen people so beautiful as these: all were exquisitely lovely and so delicate and so swift. Some were winged, but all could move with the speed of thought, and they were clad in the colours of the dewdrops in the sun. And as they sang, countless other marvellous people of the sort thronged in through the doors and at once they fell to dancing to music so beautiful, so moving, that to listen to it was almost too great a joy. Some beautiful little men moved up to Jemima and Susan and asked them to dance; beautiful princesses caught Kay and Peter by the hand and swept them into the dance; and as they danced they all seemed to understand what it is that makes the planets dance about the sun and the great stars keep their place in the constellations as they move for ever in the heavens. Kay, as he danced, could not help the thought that the Field-mouse might be a little out of it, but as he came round a second time he saw that someone had placed the Field-mouse in a corner near the band, where he was eating what looked like wedding-cake with Hundreds and Thousands on it. When the dance ended seven exquisite little fiery horses came into the room and galloped round and round; and all those who cared could run after the horses, leap on their backs and dance upon them as they galloped, and leap from horse to horse. Kay couldn't resist these beautiful galloping horses. He leapt into the ring with them and found that he could spring upon their backs and leap from horse to horse. Then, presently, the horses trotted out of the room and were gone. Then out of the ceiling little coloured flowers began to fall, and these the Fairies caught as they fell and put to their lips. Kay did as they did: a little white violet fell into his hand and when he put it to his lips it was as though all the honey and every sweetmeat that he had ever tasted were pressed into his mouth at once. A joy thrilled through him such as he had never before known. Then the King of the Fairies said, 'Friends, the long enchantment has been brought to an end. What can we do to Kay, who has ended it for us?'

As the Fairies didn't answer, the Queen of the Fairies said, 'We will grant him the power to come again into Fairyland on one day in every year.'

At this moment Kay heard again that heavy tread which had so disturbed him at lunch. 'Kay's enemies,' the King of the Fairies said. At once the lights went out: the Fairies vanished. Groping in the dark the children found each other. The Field-mouse, with chattering teeth, was saying to them. 'Well, it ended all right, but I was never so scared, not even that time with the sparrow-hawk.'

He groped his way to the trap-door, which he opened, and they slid back into his dining-room, where they heard the voice of a man saying, 'Well, it's no good waiting any longer. Wherever they've gone they've got right away from us. Now, it's my belief that they've been in the mill the whole time.'

'How could they have been in the mill?' another man said. 'In all this mud their footprints would have shown. Inside the mill in all that flour their footprints would have shown, too. They've beaten us, but how they beat us I'm blessed if I can think.'

'I can't think,' another said.

'Abner won't be too pleased,' another said, 'when he hears the result of today. I told you one of the aeroplanes had better keep up in the air to observe.'

'Oh, you told us a lot, didn't you?' another voice said.

'Blessed if I haven't got pins and needles all over me, crouching there by that bridge,' one of the men said, as they moved off.

'And I have,' another said.

'It isn't pins and needles,' Susan said; 'the Fairies are pricking them. Look there.'

Indeed, down at the tree-foot the children saw

countless little Fairies jabbing and tweaking the men. They looked like little fireflies darting to and from the great dark figures.

'Blest if we haven't all got rheumatics waiting like this,' a man growled. 'Come on. We'll get home before we're paralysed.'

After this, the men hurried away.

'I say,' Kay said, 'it's quite dark. Whatever time is it? I say, Mouse, I'm awfully sorry that we've stayed so long.' By his watch, it was half-past six.

When they had said good-bye, the Field-mouse opened the front door at the foot of the elm. The children joined hands, Kay pressed the button of his Box and they resumed their shapes and fished out the boats from the hollow of the elm-tree roots. 'Come along,' Kay said. 'We'd better hurry.'

As they came into the garden of Seekings they saw that the house was lit up at every window: the doors were wide open. 'Good heavens!' Kay said, 'look at this.' While they had been away the study and hall had been turned topsy-turvy: the carpets taken up and rolled back; every drawer and cupboard ransacked; every book moved on the shelves. The house had been thoroughly searched. Susan and Jemima cried out that their rooms had been turned topsy-turvy, by someone who had smoked strong shag tobacco. While they were marvelling, Ellen and Jane came back. They said that they had been called away to look to Ellen's mother who was said to be very ill, but when they reached her mother they found her never better.

'Well, while you've been away a gang's ransacked the house,' Kay said. 'Do look at what they've done. They don't seem to have taken much.'

'Oh, Master Kay,' Ellen said, 'whatever shall we do? Whatever will your guardian think?'

'This is more of Abner's Routine,' Kay thought. 'I must go and find the Inspector,' he said.

The Inspector was soon there with his notebook. 'Ah,' he said, looking at the study, 'they've been in.'

While the Inspector began to examine the house for clues and finger-prints, Kay went to his room. That, too, reeked of strong plug tobacco. 'I know who has been in here,' he said. 'Those Wolves of the Gulf have been in; that's the plug tobacco they were smoking in the cellar there.'

Hanging on the bed-post of Peter's bed was a dirty red bonnet or Cap of Liberty such as the pirates had worn at their carouse. It was very old and greasy. Inside it was stitched a piece of card with the legend:

R CHOPPS KAP
HANS ORF
This MEENS U.

The Inspector went rapidly through the house and examined door-handles for finger-prints through a strong lens. 'Yes,' he repeated, after the examination, 'they've been in. Smart London men, Master Kay: old hands. They've all worn gloves. I'll just ask what the maids say about it.'

Ellen and Cook said that at about half-past three a car had come from the *Rupert's Arms* with the word that a telephone message had come from Ellen's mother at Naunton Crucis to come at once as she was dangerously ill. So she and Cook had gone and had found, on arrival, that the mother was well. 'Well, that may be a clue,' the Inspector said. 'We may be able to trace where the telephone message came from, but it's none too rosy.'

'And Maria hasn't come back,' Kay said.

'Ah, that reminds me,' the Inspector said. 'I've got a message for you about that. Your young friend, Miss Jones, was at St. Griswold's looking at the glass with some clerical gentlemen and Father Boddledale. Then they had lunch at the *Bear's Paw*, and after that Father Boddledale says he and his young men said good-bye and came away, and Miss Jones was to come by a later 'bus. What happened to her since we don't yet know, but she was seen at the *Bear's Paw* long after Father Boddledale had gone. But you leave the matter in the hands of the Law, Master Kay. The Law is said sometimes to be slow, but it never sleeps. While you are snug in your bed, Master Kay, the Law is up and about taking thought for you, and your Miss Maria won't be long missing, you take my word for it.'

Presently the Police had made all their examinations and had questioned everybody remotely connected with Seekings. They went away. Kay longed for his guardian to be back: even to have a word from her would have been much in this time of trouble, but there was no word from her. But as Ellen said, 'The posts are all upset for Christmas.'

After supper that night, as the four children were sitting round the study fire, the hall door opened and somebody came in. 'I wonder is that my guardian,' Kay said. He went into the hall and there was little Maria. 'I say, Maria, I am glad to see you,' he said. 'Where on earth have you been?'

'I don't know where I've been,' Maria said. 'I've been

scrobbled just like a greenhorn. I knew what it would be, not taking a pistol. Well, I pity them if I ever get near them again. They won't scrobble Maria Jones a second time.'

'But what on earth happened to you?' Peter said. 'You aren't usually the one to get scrobbled. Who scrobbled you?'

'I don't know,' she said. 'I went with those clergymen people and looked at the stained glass: then we had lunch. It was the only good part of the proceedings: I'm very partial to duck patty. Then, presently, they went out: said they'd got to go. Well, it was beastly wet, as you know, so I thought I'd take a taxi to the 'bus: telephoned for a taxi from the *Bear's Paw*: taxi came: I got into it: "Drive me to Market Square, please," I said. Presently I saw it was going a different way, so I said, "Market Square!" The driver said, "The road's up, miss: got to go this way," and at that he put on speed and a sort of cast-iron curtain came down over all the windows. There I was, shut up in a black box, going about fifty miles an hour, right out of Tatchester. I beat on the shutters, but they were cast-iron and I might have spared my strength; and the car went faster and faster and at last, from the queer lurch it gave, I knew that it was up in the air.'

'Oh, that's rot,' Peter said. 'How can a car go up in the air? And a Tatchester taxi! Poor old crocks tied together with boot-lace!'

'This wasn't a taxi,' Maria said. 'I don't know what it was: it was some marvellous invention, but it was an aeroplane or a car that became an aeroplane. And there we were, lurching through the air, going lickity-spit in absolute darkness—I hadn't a ghost of a notion in which direction we were heading: we were making hardly any noise, too.'

'It couldn't have been an aeroplane, then,' Peter said. 'You must have an enormously powerful engine to go fast, with an enormous number of cylinders and an enormous number of explosions every second, so, of course, you have noise.'

'I tell you,' Maria said, 'this was an aeroplane, and it was silent, and it was going lickity-spit.'

'I say,' Kay said, 'you are in luck, Maria. And what happened then?'

'Well, it would have been about a quarter-to-three when I got into the taxi,' she said. 'Presently I felt that the aeroplane was dipping down. Then it touched the ground and went bumping over grass for a while, then I heard it scraunch on gravel. Then I heard a sort of door clang to behind it, and I said to myself, "Now we're in the garage." Then there came a sort of sickening feeling, as though we were dropping down a well. The shutter went up on one side and the sort of door of the thing opened, and I saw a light.

'Well, the light was along a little passage. It seemed to me that the car or taxi or aeroplane or whatever it was was in a small stone cellar. The door was open and, as I said, I could see into this little passage with the light at the end. I didn't see anybody, but I got out of the aeroplane and I walked towards the light. I came into a small room with no window, but a sort of a little ventilator high up. The walls were rock: I touched them; and they had been whitewashed. It was lit from the ceiling about twelve feet up. I was no sooner in the room than a great iron door shot up behind me and there I was, shut in. Then rather high up on the wall an iron shutter slid to one side and there was an iron grille with what I took to be a lady's face; and a very silky female voice said, "Miss Maria Jones, please forgive any inconvenience we may have caused you in bringing you here and, above all, don't be afraid." "I'm not used to being afraid," I said; but all the same I was afraid. "We only brought you here," the female said, "because we hope that you may be interested. We are rather in need of a dashing young associate at the moment and we wondered whether we might persuade you to become that." "Oh," I said, "what are you: a gang of crooks?" "Oh no," she said, "a business community." "Oh," I said, "what business does your community do?" "Social service," she said. "Setting straight injustices with the least possible inconvenience to all concerned." "And how do you do it?" I asked. "Oh, sometimes in one way, sometimes in another," she said. "You would soon learn if you would join us." "Why d'you want me?" I asked. "Well, you are young," she said, "and full of dash. It's an interesting world for our younger agents: lots of motor-cars, lots of aeroplanes. Life is one long, gay social whirl." "And what is the work?" I asked. "Ah," she said, "we shall discuss that if you expressed a willingness to become one of us." "If your job were honest," I said, "you'd say what it is. It can't be nice, or it wouldn't have you in it." "If children are pert here," she said, "we make them into dog-biscuit. Many a good watch-dog is barking now on insolent little chits like you." So I said, "If ladies are pert to me I make them into cat's-meat. Many a good caterwaul have I fed on meat like you, cold."

'We should have become quite eloquent, but a black-bearded man's face appeared at the bars and he said, "Now, ladies, ladies, ladies! The first word in business of any kind is unity. Do let us have unity. Without that we can never get anywhere. Now, Miss Jones, if we cannot have unity from you, let us have some information. When Mr. Cole Hawlings gave his performance of Punch and Judy at Seekings, did he hand you a small black box?" "No," I said, "he didn't." "Did he leave it with one of the others of your party there, or hide it in Seekings House?" "How on earth do I know?" I said. "That's the point," he answered. "Do you know?" "Well, I don't know," I said.

'This time, by the light from the bars, I looked at my watch and found that it was four o'clock. "You need not look at your watch," the woman said. "You will have lots and lots of time. If I were you, sir," she added, "I would put this young person into the scrounger. D'you know what a scrounger is, my dear?" "Yes," I said. "I don't think you do," she replied. "It's a place that we put people into. It has a thing in it that goes round and round and round, which is the scrounger; and then, presently, of course, the thing scrounged becomes dog-biscuit." At that the shutter went across the bars and the light went out. I was in absolute darkness and utter silence: I might have been fifty feet underneath the ground. I don't know how long I was in that absolute blackness. I stood perfectly still for some little time because I was afraid that there might be a trapdoor which would let me down into some dungeon.'

'I say,' Peter said, 'you're making all this up.'

'Am I?' she said. 'Let something of the sort happen to you and you'll see whether you can make it up.'

'Presently, I couldn't bear standing still. I thought that I might perhaps come to some door in the wall that would lead somewhere, so I groped to the wall and felt my way all round the room. I reckoned that it was fourteen feet by twelve feet: cold stone walls, cold stone floors; but not damp and the air neither chilly nor foggy; it was well ventilated. I had gone all round the room feeling the wall and there wasn't so much as a knob or a crack. I had gone round once and was starting round in the opposite direction to make absolutely certain, when suddenly, down came something thick and warm and woolly right over my head and shoulders and I was pinioned. I couldn't see, but I felt that the light went on and that horrible woman's voice said, "All right, you needn't kick and you needn't try to bite and you can't scratch. I only just want to know if you have got this box upon you."

'Well, I was searched, and then I was carried along the little passage by which I had come and I was put into the taxi which had brought me. They removed my woollen, and, though I hit out pretty hard when they took it away, the woman was a lot too quick for me and I only rapped my knuckles on the taxi door, which was sheet-iron. They turned on a little light in the taxi roof and I saw that they had put me a pot of tea and some cold ham and some bread inside the taxi, so I thought, "Well, nothing like keeping one's pecker up," and so I made a hearty meal.'

'Was there any knife with the food?' Kay asked.

'No such luck,' she said. 'I had to eat it with my fingers. I'd have soon hacked my way out if they had left me a knife.'

'Weren't you afraid of the food being drugged?' Jemima asked.

'No, that never occurred to me,' Maria said. 'I'd been

through a good deal of mental strain and had to restore my nervous force.

'Well then, after I had made a meal I looked about and there on the floor of the taxi was a little bit of pink tissue-paper. I picked this up and it was a bit of one of those coloured papers which floated down after the Punch and Judy man had gone. You remember you, Susan, had one with a bit of your name torn from it. Well, this is the very bit. You see: ". . . san Jones": it was the one designed for you.'

'I've got the torn cap here,' Susan said. 'You see, it does fit. How very, very strange.'

'Yes,' Maria said. 'That Punch and Judy man was one of the gang.'

'He was nothing of the sort,' Kay said. 'He was scrobbled by the gang the morning after his performance, and he was scrobbled in the sort of aeroplane that carried you. But what happened next?'

'Well, I waited and waited for what seemed like hours: I didn't hear any sound of men, only from time to time I thought I heard, very, very far away, the noise of water falling; quite a lot of water: a sort of waterfall. Then the light went out and I was in the dark. I suppose, what with fatigue and fear and one thing and another, I fell asleep, and the next thing I knew the taxi was moving. I heard some roller doors clang open, and we scraunched on the gravel, and then we ran upon grass, and then we gave that sort of lurching leap that an aeroplane does and we were away in the air, going higher and higher and making no noise. And then, presently, we were on the ground, running along the road. We stopped. The bottom of the aeroplane quietly opened and dropped me through it and, before I could get on to my feet, it had moved away. And there I was in the churchyard, with the Condicote church clock striking nine and chiming, and the taxi or aeroplane or whatever it was was away. It just lifted up past the church and was gone.'

'Did you see which way it went?' Kay asked.

'It just went behind the church and then I couldn't see it any further. I haven't the vaguest notion where I've been. I should think we were flying for an hour and a quarter both times and I don't doubt that we were going at a frightful speed. We might have got to Scotland for all that I know. We might easily have gone three hundred miles.'

'I say,' Peter said, 'you do have all the luck.'

'Well, I'm awfully glad you've got out of it. Would you like to go round to tell your story to the Police Inspector?'

'I'm not going to tell any more story,' Maria said. 'What I want is underdone chops and plenty of them. I'm going to build up my nervous system before anything else, and then I'm going to bed.'

'Well, come along down to the larder,' Kay said. 'And, Jemima, you might put on a kettle and we'll boil her up some cocoa.'

'I'm not going to drink any poison like cocoa, thank you,' Maria said. 'When one's had a nervous strain such as I have, one wants a posset with three fresh eggs in it and a spoonful of sherry.' They went into the larder and found a nourishing meal after Maria's own heart. Then Jemima and Susan took her up to bed and gave her a posset.

Kay and Peter went up to their rooms. 'Well, I'm blessed,' Peter said, 'we are having a holiday. I wonder what was in the black Box that the gang wanted. I shouldn't wonder if it wouldn't be the Duchess's diamonds that were stolen.'

'I hope they won't kidnap any more of us,' Kay said; and with that he slipped the black Box under his pyjama coat next to his skin, rolled over and fell asleep.

He hadn't been long asleep before he woke in a state of perplexity and excitement. He kept thinking of what Maria had told him. He said to himself, 'She might have been fifty feet underneath the ground, in cold stone walls and cold stone floors: well, she must have been underground. And where was it I was reading about, or heard about, caves underneath the ground? It was that Roman chap last night, talking about Chester Hills: he said, "It's a limestone country, all honeycombed with caves; and those wolves, as we call them, were all underground." I wonder whether this gang is at Chester Hills? There would be nothing like a lot of underground caves for the secret quarters of a gang. Get down there with their aeroplanes which can become taxis by pressing a button and the Police might hunt for years and never find them. And then, what if this Theological Missionary College should really be a gang in disguise? It's just what I should do if I were a gangster: pretend to be a clergyman. And I'm sure that Abner Brown is that man they call Father Boddledale—the Reverend Father Boddledale D.D. He's a magician and a gangster of the deepest dye, and now that he's married to the Pouncer he's probably five times as bad as he ever was before. And I do wish my guardian were here and then I could ask her advice.'

He fell asleep again, but could dream of nothing but caves, dark and damp, with the noise of dripping water and long stalactites hanging from the roofs. When he would wake up from being, as he thought, a prisoner in one cave he would fall asleep and dream of another, black as a pocket, with water falling into some almost bottomless pit. Now he remembered something that somebody had said to him of the people at Chester Hills in the old days stealing and killing sheep and dropping them down pot-holes into the underground waters, which would carry the carcasses of the sheep for some miles and bring them out at other pot-holes where people waited for them. He seemed to remember that in the story somebody had said that once, when the people were waiting for the sheep to appear, the body of the thief appeared. 'That was at Chester Hills,' he thought. Then he slept again and seemed to hear the voice of Caroline Louisa calling to him in great distress from a great distance and, in his dream, it seemed that he answered her and asked, 'Where are you?' and heard her cry, 'Here,' and ran towards the voice and found nothing but stone walls, against which he beat and thrust, but could find no door nor any window. But through the thickness of the stone came the voice, 'I'm shut up here in the darkness, Kay. I don't know where it is, but it's somewhere where I can hear the noise of water falling.' Then he woke up, but found nothing but the dark night with a little glimmer of moonlight coming through the curtain and the fire in the grate almost out. 'I'm almost sure that they've got her in Chester Hills, somehow,' he muttered. 'Though why,' he wondered, 'and how? Of course, if they'd got her into one of those taxis they could have flown her to Chester Hills in less than an hour, even from London.' He fell asleep again, but passed an uneasy night. When he woke again it was time to get up, so he dressed and was down by eight o'clock.

By some fortune or freak the post was in, in spite of the Christmas rush, but, as Ellen said, it was probably the post of two days before. There was no letter from Caroline Louisa.

CHAPTER EIGHT

While he was looking through the letters Ellen brought in the paper. 'Oh, Master Kay,' she said, 'have you heard the news? The Bishop of Tatchester has disappeared.'

'What?' Kay said.

'The papers are full of it,' Ellen said. 'The reverend gentleman went out of the Palace last night for a brisk walk before going to bed according to his custom and he hasn't come back, Master Kay.' Kay opened the paper:

'STARTLING DISAPPEARANCE OF THE BISHOP OF TATCHESTER

'Considerable alarm was caused,' he read, 'in ecclesiastical circles last night when it was known that His Grace, the Bishop of Tatchester, had failed to return to the Palace and was not heard of at the time of our going to press. The very reverend gentleman had passed the evening at the Palace in making ready for the Christmas season and in dispatching his Christmas cards to the clergy of his Diocese, a duty that His Grace leaves to no hands but his own. On conclusion of this pleasant duty His Grace signified to his sister, Dame Eleanor Chasuble, that he would go for a brisk walk through the Precincts before retiring to rest. According to her nightly custom, Dame Chasuble prepared tea for His Grace on his return. As he had not returned at the accustomed time she proceeded to the Precincts, but could not see him. At first she thought it likely that His Grace had joined some body of carol-singers and might be singing carols in the neighbourhood, but at midnight as he had not returned she became alarmed and telephoned to the Dean, who enquired at once at the Hospital if His Grace had been the victim of some accident, but, receiving a negative response, they communicated with the Police and, although an active search was at once instituted, we regret to announce that no news has been received of His Grace's whereabouts. It will be remembered that the Palace was the scene of a serious burglary the night before last and it is thought that the Bishop's disappearance may be connected with that earlier outrage. Dame Chasuble is confident that the Bishop has no enemy who would lay violent hands upon him and flouts the opinion that he may have become subject to some sudden loss of memory. The Police are inclined to the view that the reverend-gentleman may have received some shock, as from a passing motor-car, which may have caused a temporary aberration. Anyone who may have seen anyone answering to the description of His Grace or any occurrence which may seem to throw light on his disappearance is earnestly asked to communicate with New Scotland Yard, or with the Tatchester Constabulary: Tatchester 7000.

'Naturally His Grace's disappearance has cast a gloom upon what would otherwise be a festal city. We would remind our readers that on Christmas Eve at midnight His Grace hoped to celebrate the thousandth anniversary of the dedication of the Cathedral, for which great occasion the usual Christmas decorations and expectations have been increased thousand-fold. We are sure that we voice the feelings of thousands of our readers when we extend to Dame Chasuble our heartiest sympathy in her anxiety, and our liveliest hopes that His Grace may soon be restored to the bosom of his household and his Diocese.

'Few figures in the church of today are more eminent for piety and the Christian virtues than His Grace, the Very Reverend Michael Chasuble, D.D. Our readers will remember that Dr. Chasuble in his young days was a famous oarsman, long-distance runner, cricketer and heavyweight pugilist. In the scholastic field he carried away not only the prize for Greek verse, the Newdigate, the Latin Oration and the Ponsford Laurel Crown for Hebrew, but took first-class honours in Natural Science and in what are known as "Greats." Few people of his time at the University have attained such universal distinction in the provinces of sport and learning.'

'I say,' Kay said to himself, when he had read this, 'now they've got the Bishop. I won't mind betting it's the same gang, and they're after this Box of Delights and they think that the Bishop's got it.'

While he was meditating this in the dining-room, Peter came down. It was about ten minutes past eight, and, being a dark winter morning, was still hardly full daylight. 'You look pretty gloomy, Kay,' Peter said.

'I am pretty gloomy,' Kay said. 'They've scrobbled the Bishop. I'll bet it's the people who scrobbled Maria.'

'And who d'you think they are?' Peter said.

'Well, I'm worried, Peter,' Kay said. 'I know you think it's absurd, but I think they're the Missionary College people out at Chester Hills. Would you come with me, Peter,' he said, 'to Chester Hills, to see what kind of place it is?'

'Well, I don't mind,' Peter said. 'Shall we go after breakfast?'

'I was thinking we might get there and back before breakfast,' Kay said, leading the way to the door. 'Breakfast won't be till nine.' He paused just outside the door. It was a gloomy morning.

'How on earth could we get about forty miles and back?' Peter said.

Kay caught hold of Peter's arm, and, with his other hand, twitched the button on the magic box and, instantly, both of them were plucked through the air in a north-westerly direction so swiftly that they saw the fields and the brooks in a kind of blur beneath them. Then, suddenly, they were whirled downwards and there they were, on a hillside, standing on what was the rampart of an old camp. Both the boys were a little out of breath.

'Now, this is Chester Hills,' Kay said. 'Look there: that's Hope-under-Chesters, the railway station where the curates got into the train who I believe picked my pocket. And you can see that this was once a Roman Camp. This is the Chester.'

'Well, where d'you want to go now?' Peter said.

'I think down there, into that valley,' Kay said.

Looking down on the valley the boys saw nothing but a

great sea of woodland which began a little way below the camp and filled all the valley; but there were folds in the valley and what there was in the folds they could not see.

'I say, it's a lovely country,' Kay said.

'It looks all right,' Peter said. 'I vote we go and explore in the woods.'

Kay looked first at the Roman Camp. The line of the rampart was still firm and sharply cut; the gates were just as they were when the Romans had marched out of them for the last time.

'Jolly good chaps, the Romans,' Kay said.

'Oh, I don't know,' said Peter. 'They were rather a mouldy lot. They were lucky chaps not to have to learn Latin grammar, but to know it naturally.'

'I don't know, I admire them enormously,' Kay said. 'You see, we are a thousand miles from Rome and they hadn't any trains and they hadn't any steam and they walked here, carrying all that they wanted on their backs; and when they came to the sea they made ships and sailed here. And when they were here they made the only roads that we had, that were any good, for the next eighteen hundred years, and the only baths that people took until about fifty years ago. You see there, you can see from the lie of the land that a road ran out of this gateway down the hill. I'll bet if you had a spade to clear away the turf you'd come upon a pavement underneath.'

He led the way down the hill and presently, the lines of the Roman track became more difficult to follow. When they came to the edge of the wood the track was barred with a locked and chained gate. There was a notice nailed to a tree:

'TRESPASSERS WILL BE PROSECUTED.'

and on another tree there was a bigger notice:

'DANGER!'
'MAN-TRAPS AND SPRING-GUNS.'

The track inside the wood was hardly more than a narrow woodland path. The wood looked curiously forbidding and evil. It contained a great deal of yew and other dark evergreens. The undergrowth was curiously grown and in the darkness and wetness, with its profuse mass of close, sinister growth, it put a chill onto both boys' hearts.

'It doesn't look a very cheery place,' Peter said. 'I don't think we ought to risk those notices.'

'Oh, rats!' Kay said. 'I don't believe in any of those notices. For years I was scared of a notice that said "Bloodhounds" and there wasn't a bloodhound within the county. Come along in. But we'd better not talk much and we won't make more noise than we must.'

He clambered over the gate and Peter followed. They went down the woodland track. It was a still, sinister wood, very thick covert, even for the depths of winter. As they went along it seemed to Kay that somewhere on his left hand there was the noise of water falling, much as he had heard it in his dreams. The little track led down the hill: it wasn't straight, but bent and twisted; Peter went with a beating heart: Kay went forward boldly.

'I say, Kay,' Peter said, 'I wish you wouldn't hurry on like this. You ought to go cautiously.'

'It's absolutely safe,' Kay said. 'Do look; nobody has been on this woodland track for weeks.'

'But a keeper might come at any minute,' Peter said.

'There aren't keepers,' Kay said. 'You can see that this place isn't preserved. If it were preserved we should have seen pheasants long ago or, if not pheasants, we'd have seen keepers' vermin boards, or dead stoats and weasels and poor, beautiful owls.'

Presently they passed from the woodland into a rather denser part, that was more like a neglected shrubbery with azaleas and overgrown rhododendrons. In this part of the wood a very great deal of box had once been planted. This had straggled and grown to a great height and made the wood even darker than it would otherwise have been. There the track ended in a double line of box-trees. No doubt the trees had once been trimmed into a box walk; now they were all straggled and overgrown and untidy. Between the lines of box-trees, however, a path, that seemed to be in considerable use, led to right and left, and through gaps in the dense shrubbery the boys saw the gleam of water just below them.

'That will be the lake,' Kay said; 'it's marked on the map. Let's go on down and look at the water.'

They left the path and thrust through the shrubbery where it seemed thinnest and presently were just inside a rhododendron bush on the very lip of the water, which stretched to right and left in a long and very beautiful lake of deep water. It was not much more than a hundred yards across, but it gave to Kay the illusion of great depth and of being very evil, it was so dark, being fringed on both sides by beautiful trees nearly all dark.

'I say,' Kay said, 'what a place!'

'It gives me the fantods,' Peter answered. 'I don't like this place.'

'Well, we've come here now,' Kay said; 'do let's examine it before we go.'

A little to the right of where they were they saw among the trees the roof and part of a building, and what was either a boat- or a bathing-house. Away to the left, about five hundred yards from where they were the lake came to an end in some tumbled rocks and boulders. Beyond this the ground rose with shrubberies and ornamental trees and, beyond the trees, there were buildings seemingly of great extent: yellowish, Kay thought, as though built of Cotswold stone, which must have been imported there. From somewhere in the mass of these buildings, which were mainly screened by the trees, a little bell chimed gracefully for the half-hour.

'Now, I'm going along here to have a look at the house,' Kay said. 'You coming?'

'No, I don't think I will, thanks,' Peter said. 'You go and look at the house if you like. I'll just go along and look at the boat-house and to see if one could come here in the summer for a swim.'

'Well, do look out for yourself,' Kay said. 'That little clock has just chimed for half-past eight. When it chimes for nine, you be inside the track we came by. You can easily take cover and wait for me.'

'All right,' Peter said, 'but I do wish you wouldn't go into this place. You'll get dropped on most frightfully hot if they catch you.'

Kay went off along the path between the box-trees, and he hadn't gone very far before he heard footsteps and voices coming towards him. He nimbly took cover between the path and the water and listened as the voices and steps drew nearer.

Presently Kay could distinguish the voices of those who were approaching. He heard the unmistakable high voice of the foxy-faced man saying, 'So you'll get them all in the soup, ha-ha, what?'

Then something followed which Kay couldn't quite catch; but the next voice which spoke was undoubtedly that of Abner.

'As to that matter, sir,' Abner was saying in his silky, soft voice, 'that's a question that must wait till we have had our bathe and our breakfast. Perhaps they will be in a better mood and more disposed to be reasonable after their good night's rest.'

The men passed where Kay was hidden without seeing him. The foxy-faced man said, 'It will be mighty cold. One plunge and then out will be enough for me.'

'It will be exhilarating,' Abner said. 'By the way, I think I shall recommend Eleven for service abroad. But my head will be clearer after my bathe.'

Kay heard the men enter the bathing-box a little distance from him. He heard feet running upon spring-boards and two splashes, followed by sputterings. The foxy-faced man was saying, 'It's like iced water, what?' Kay heard them crawling up the steps from the water and Abner saying,

'Enough for honour: we will leave the rest to the British.'

He heard them rubbing themselves down and muttering with clacking teeth that 'their blood would never run warm again.' Soon they had their robes round them and were running back along the path by which they had come.

Kay went out from his hiding-place and crept along in the direction in which they had gone. Presently he came to the end of the lake among the tumbled rocks and boulders. At first he could see no outlet to the waters but then heard, above the sighing of the pine-trees, a sort of wash of water. Somewhere underneath his feet some water at any rate from the lake was falling into a passage underground. The path by which the bathers had come led above the tumble of rock. He followed it through a dense shrubbery and presently came into a thicket of laurel bordering on a drive. Through the laurel he could see the spacious mansion, built in Cotswold stone somewhere early in the reign of George the Third on a foundation much older.

He was looking directly across at great double front doors within a portico. They were lofty doors paned with glass to give light to the hall within and, as the morning sun was now shining onto the glass, he could see something gleaming inside the hall: it looked like a suit of armour. The hall had the look of having been built on after the main structure had been finished. While he watched, there came from within the house the sweet banging of a gong. Almost immediately half a dozen men wearing black cloaks came out of the outhouses to the right of the house and passed through the front doors. 'That's the gang,' Kay said to himself, 'or some of them—this college of young clergy—and the gong was for their breakfast, and I can creep in and see them while they're at breakfast.'

Just as the last of the men in the black cloaks passed under the portico, there came a loud hissing noise, something between a whistle and an escape of steam, from somewhere up in the air. The laurel was rather in the way of Kay's getting a good view, but he saw the men in black look up towards the noise and looked up himself. To his amazement he saw a silvery aeroplane poising just like a kestrel above the house: it had come noiselessly and there it was, hovering in a way that Kay hadn't thought to be possible for any aeroplane; and the whistle or hiss of steam was plainly a signal, for a moment later the aeroplane sank slowly down vertically, as though into the very body of the house.

'I say,' Kay thought, 'whoever would have thought that an aeroplane could do that.' He thought to himself at once, 'Well, I suppose that's the kind of aeroplane that scrobbled little Maria, and, of course, if they've got a thing like that they could do all sorts of things that nobody would suspect. Now, I wonder,' he said, 'if poor old Cole Hawlings and the Bishop, and perhaps Caroline Louisa, are shut up in dungeons only a few yards away.' Almost at once, as he listened, he heard a lot of men's voices singing together a familiar hymn. 'Well, I don't know,' he thought, 'that sounds like a Missionary College; but what would they want with Abner Brown and what would they be doing with an aeroplane like that, if they were only missionaries?'

However, it was now time to start back towards Peter. As he crossed above the tumbled rocks he looked again, hoping to see some opening among them. This time he saw what he ought to have noticed before, a sluice with its winch, beside which was a rusty iron grating, so covered with drift of different sorts that it could not easily be distinguished. The water seeped and trickled through this grating and fell, as he judged, some little distance. 'I would like to go down there on a rope,' Kay thought, 'with torches, and explore.'

At this moment the bell above the Missionary College struck nine and chimed the hour. Kay hurried to the agreed place where Peter was to be, but Peter was not there. Kay looked in the thickest cover nearest to the agreed place, but there was no sign of Peter. He certainly had not entered the cover there. Kay waited some minutes, thinking, 'Well, Peter always was an ass. He never had much sense of time and will always go wandering on and blundering into something.' He waited a few more minutes, but Peter had not come. Then Kay thought, 'Well, perhaps, if he has gone on by himself, he will have left a patteran.'

He had often played gypsies with Peter and had read in one of George Borrow's books that gypsies put what they called a patteran, some sign or mark of leaves or twisted grass on the ground, to show the direction they have taken; the agreed sign between Peter and himself was a handful of leaves squeezed and dropped on the ground. He looked on the paths for such a mark, but could find none. 'Oh, where has he gone?' he thought. Then he wondered, 'Well, what should I have done if I had been in Peter's place. He had gone on probably past the little bathing-box and would have kept on the further side of the bathing-box while the men were bathing; but what on earth would he have done then?' He followed along the path by which he thought Peter might have gone on his exploration. Presently a little brook ran across the path; in the mud by the brook's bank was the mark of Peter's shoes. 'He did come as far as this,' Kay thought, 'and he hasn't come back this way. Well, of course, he wouldn't come back this way.' It was the maxim of these young scouts never to come back the way by which they went in a strange or dangerous country.

Presently the ground began to be very soft: a good many springs broke out there and the channels by which they had fallen into the lake had been allowed to become choked. Peter's tracks were plain indeed. On the farther side of the soft patch the track turned a corner and there, to Kay's horror, were other tracks. Two or three men had been there and there were little fresh, unmistakable signs of rapid trampling and scuffling. 'There's no doubt about it,' Kay thought, 'they've scrobbled Peter. Somebody's been here and they've got Peter. Just like that silly ass to go right into the lion's den. But if they scrobbled Peter what did they do with him? Where did they take him? They didn't take him to the house at any rate: they took him away from the house.'

He reckoned up the chances and decided that it would be safe to follow after these people, whoever they were. They had got Peter and were removing him. The chances were that they would not be expecting anybody else and that it would be safe to follow in that direction. He had not gone far before he heard the noise of oars on the lake. Going down towards the water and peering through the branches he saw that a boat was pulling towards the mansion on the other side of the lake. In the stern-sheets of the boat was something that looked like a roll of blanket. 'That's Peter, scrobbled,' Kay thought. Two sinister-looking men in black cloaks were at the oars; two sinister-looking men were sitting in the stern-sheets beside the bundle; one of them was steering and the other was trailing for pike. 'They've got Peter all right,' Kay thought. Then he wondered, 'Should I go to the village of Hope-under-Chesters and rouse the Police there?' Then he thought, 'No. The Policeman is probably one of the gang and I should be arrested for trespassing. I'll get back home and speak to the Inspector and, perhaps, by that time there will be a word from Caroline Louisa.'

He took up his Box of Delights and pressed the knob.

A sort of whirlwind plucked him up above the tree-tops and snatched him south-eastwards to the box-tree walk at Seekings, where he was set gently upon his feet.

He found the other children at breakfast. 'You're very late, Kay,' Maria said. 'Have you seen the latest?'

'No,' he said, 'what is it?'

'Something like a mystery,' Maria said. 'Here.' She unfolded the paper for him. In the middle page were large black headings:

'MYSTERIOUS DISAPPEARANCE
THE MERRY DEAN DISAPPEARS
DEAN OF TATCHESTER MISSING SINCE
TEA-TIME

'Ecclesiastical and other circles have been convulsed at Tatchester by the strange disappearance of the well-known Dean from the Precincts. It appears that the Dean went out shortly after dark last night, in response to what was said to have been an urgent summons, and has not yet been heard of. He was first missed at six p.m. when he should have attended a meeting connected with Cathedral business, but it was not until he failed to return to the Deanery for dinner that the family became concerned. At the time of going to press no news has been received of the reverend gentleman.

'It is feared at the Deanery that he has been the victim of a motor-car accident, but we are entitled to our own conviction that the disappearance of the reverend gentleman, coming so soon after the recent burglary at the Palace and the disappearance of His Grace, the Bishop, are crimes perpetrated by some local gang. Until a late hour the Cathedral Clergy were indefatigable in their search for their friend, who is perhaps the most popular figure in the Establishment. Something like a reign of terror exists at this moment throughout Tatchester. The Police preserve a becoming reticence in the matter and, though they scout the notion that the reverend gentleman has been the victim of a practical joke, they abstain from committing themselves to any definite theory.

'It is hardly necessary to remind our readers that the Dean of Tatchester is the well-known author of "Possible Oriental Influences in Ancient Philosophies" as well as the famous handbook "Cheerfulness: The Christian's Duty."

'We are sure that we voice the feelings of the rest of the world when we wish that Christmas at the Deanery may be gladdened by his speedy return to the bosom of his family.'

'Now, what d'you think of that?' Maria said. 'That's the gang that scrobbled me.'

'I believe they've scrobbled Peter,' Kay said, 'and as soon as I've had some breakfast I'll go round to the Police Station.'

'I love to see the sleuths at work,' Maria said, 'so I'll come too.'

They went round and the Inspector welcomed them. 'Come in, Miss Maria and Master Kay,' he said. 'What is it now? More clues for the Law to follow?' Kay told his story and all his suspicions.

'Ha,' the Inspector said. 'And footprints in the mud, you say, and the roll of blanket in the boat. But you know, Master Kay, you ought not to have gone trespassing at Chester Hills. I was there as a young man and it's a dangerous place. They have a lot of those holes that they call "dings," like old mines. Lots of folk break their necks going into them and I hope your Master Peter hasn't gone and done the like. But you are quite wrong, Master Kay, in saying that the Principal of the Training College is a Mr. Brown: it's Father Boddledale, as I told you. I will telephone him now.'

He telephoned: 'Is that you, your reverence?' he asked. 'I'm the Inspector of Police speaking. I want to ask if you have seen anything of a lad aged ten, by the name of Peter, who was out at your place this morning. . . . You haven't seen him? . . . Hasn't been seen at all? . . . Thank you. And have you with you a gentleman by the name of Abner Brown? . . . No? . . . You don't know the name. You train simply young men for parish and missionary work, isn't that so, your reverence? . . . Well, you will forgive my disturbing you at your good work, but Duty is the policeman's watchword, as you will understand, sir. I'm much obliged, I'm sure, sir . . . Thank you, sir, and I wish the same to you.

'You see, Master Kay,' he said, hanging up the telephone, 'they know nothing of Master Peter there; but it's my belief about boys, Master Kay, that "leave them alone and they'll come home." '

Kay thanked him and they returned home. 'Pompous old ass,' Maria said.

'He's a jolly good chap, really,' Kay said. 'He mayn't be quite a Sherlock Holmes, but he's most awfully good about rabbits.'

As they went into the little street more newsboys came rushing from the station shouting, 'Special edition of the *Tatchester Times*!' They were shouting, 'Another disappearance—Special!' . . . 'Canons of Tatchester disappear—Special!' . . . 'Murder gang suspected—Special!' . . . 'Bloodhounds on the trail—Special!' . . . 'What clergyman is safe?—Special!' . . . 'Another dreadful religious mystery—Special!'

'There you are,' Maria said.

Kay bought a paper, for which the boy charged him sixpence. He read the little sheet which was still wet from the press:

> 'We feel that this morning's events are so extraordinary that we are warranted in making them the subject of a special edition of our paper.
>
> 'The night before last our deservedly popular Prelate was torn from us; last night the World's Dean, as we may call him, similarly disappeared; early this morning, while they were walking back from the early morning service, Canon Honeytongue and Canon Balmblossom, his friend, were met, we learn, by a messenger who told them that the Dean had met with a motor accident, was suffering from a slight concussion and was asking eagerly to see them. The reverend gentleman then hurried to the waiting car and, on asking the driver how long they would be, were told "Less than an hour." They called to their friends, others of the Cathedral Clergy who were accompanying them through the Close, that they would be back to breakfast. After this the car—a Rolls-Royce according to some, a large Daimler according to others—drove rapidly away. At that early hour few people were about and no one seems to have taken the number of the car. The anxiety of the people of Tatchester may be judged when the breakfast-hour passed without any

message whatsoever from the missing Canons. Becoming seriously alarmed, Mrs. Honeytongue telephoned to the Police, who at once instituted a widespread enquiry, so far, we regret to say, without result. Though some people are inclined to believe that our Cathedral Clergy have been the victims of a practical joke, these events are so strange and follow so closely upon the burglary of the Palace that serious people may be excused for having the gravest misgivings.

'We ask all the inhabitants of the Diocese to come forward at once in aiding the Police by reporting the movements of all cars likely to have been concerned in the removal of the reverend gentlemen. The car is reported to have been a large black, dark blue, dark brown, or even dark green or grey saloon, with a clean-shaven driver in a dark suit. Anyone who may have seen such a car in any of the country roads in the hours between five and seven-thirty this morning are asked to telephone at once to the Chief of the Tatchester Constabulary: telephone number, Tatchester 7000.

'In the meantime we would convey to all the members of the Cathedral Establishment our heart-felt sympathy with their anxiety. We would also reprehend in the strongest terms all those who venture to criticise the work of our splendid Police Force. We are sure, what indeed we have never doubted, that they have the matter well in hand, and though it is against the public interest that they should divulge at this juncture the point to which their investigations have proceeded, it is an open secret that they are in the possession of certain clues which may lead to startling denouements in the near future.'

'Now what d'you think of that?' Maria said.

'Wait a moment,' Kay said. 'There's some "Stop Press" news here at the side:

'STOP PRESS NEWS

'The rumour current that the missing Prelate was seen near Chester Hills last night turns out to be without foundation. The gentleman mistaken for the Bishop was the Reverend Father Boddledale, of the Ecclesiastical Training College, who has long been known as the Bishop's double. Father Boddledale went yesterday afternoon with the Clergy's Christmas offerings to the children in the village school of Hope-under-Chesters and, wearing clerical dress, was again mistaken for the Prelate. No reliable information has reached the Authorities about any of the missing dignitaries.'

'Well, what d'you think of that?' Maria repeated.

'Well, I know what I think of it,' Kay said. 'They've got the Bishop, the Dean, the Punch and Judy man, the two Canons and Peter in that den of theirs at Chester Hills.'

'Well, if I were you, I'd telephone to the Yard,' Maria said. 'It's no good going to your champion rabbit man, or whatever he is: go to the sleuths whose job it is to sleuth. Let's telephone the Yard.'

They telephoned to the Yard, who referred them to the Chief of the Tatchester Constabulary: telephone number, Tatchester 7000. When they did this they were told that the matter would meet with every attention and that, though no news had come about any of the missing gentlemen, they expected developments before the evening.

At lunch-time Kay was called to the telephone. Caroline Louisa's sister wanted to speak about her brother who was now better. Kay explained that Caroline Louisa had not returned from London and had left no word: had neither written nor telegraphed.

'Well,' the sister said, 'she set off from here two days ago. Whatever can have happened?'

Kay had a very shrewd suspicion of what had happened. He said, 'Perhaps she's been kidnapped like the Cathedral staff.'

The sister said, 'That doesn't sound very likely to me, but I will telephone to the hospitals to find out whether anybody has been brought in as the result of an accident.'

She said that she would telephone later if she heard anything. She did telephone later to report that she could learn nothing of her sister whatsoever. Kay went back to lunch feeling very miserable. After lunch it came on to rain. There was no news of Peter. It wasn't possible to go playing in the garden. He went upstairs to his room; locked the doors; put caps over the keys as before; climbed under the valance of the dressing-table and looked again into the Box of Delights.

This time he looked into an entirely different scene. There was a little hill with a beech clump upon it and a vixen playing with her cubs on some tumbled chalk outside a burrow. A badger was padding about; from the glow upon the wood it seemed to Kay to be about sunset on a fine May evening. The cubs rolled over and over, playing with themselves or with a bit of rabbit-skin, and presently Kay was aware that some of the glow upon the trees was due to the presence of multitudes of butterflies of the most brilliant colours—painted ladies, red admirals, peacocks, purple emperors, chalk blues, commas, tortoise-shells, purple and green hairstreaks: and besides these there were others—Camberwell beauties and swallow-tails—and all these began moving suddenly towards him; he noticed that they were drawing an airy chariot made out of rose-leaves from some sweet-briar rose. It was liker a basket than a chariot and, although it looked very fragile, it was held together with silk; Kay said to himself, 'Silk is really the strongest of all stuffs;' he stepped into the chariot. At once the butterflies lifted him up high over the tree-tops, going much more swiftly than he would have thought possible and, although their flight wavered now up, now down, it was extraordinarily delightful.

'Of course,' he said, 'we are going to Chester Hills;' and very soon they were indeed flying over the very wood from which Peter had disappeared, but inside the wood and all round the great house, as Kay drew near it, there were wolves running and snarling with their hackles up and with their teeth gleaming: he had never thought it possible that there could be so many. He saw them leaping and snapping, trying to reach the butterflies, who kept well out of harm's way. They floated up to the great house and then round it, though the wolves came out of the chimneys and through trap-doors onto the roofs and yapped and snarled and showed their teeth.

Then, at one little window, as Kay floated past, he saw Caroline Louisa stretching out her hands to him, calling, 'Help me, Kay!' Then, instantly, two great she-wolves dragged her from the window and pulled down an iron shutter.

The butterflies changed their direction and floated

away and away from Chester Hills, and at last brought Kay to a bare mountain which he had never before seen. In the mountain-side there was a little door with a knocker. Kay knocked at the knocker and a little old man opened the door and said,

'Will you please to walk in, Master Kay? And what would you like to see: the treasures or the work?'

'I should like to see both, please,' Kay said.

The little old man opened a door and there was a little furnace with a bellows and an anvil, with little men hard at work making extraordinary things out of metals and precious stones. In cases on the wall were the most marvellous weapons and knives, coats of armour, crowns and jewels. And there were also strange things shaped like hands and, when the little man pressed a button, these hands took hold of hammers or tongs, plucked molten metal from the furnace and beat it into whatever shape the little man ordered. Kay was so delighted with these things that he stared and stared and, at last, one of the pairs of hands plucked a piece of gold, beat it rapidly into the shape of a little rose-bud and thrust it into Kay's buttonhole. Then the little old man said that it would be time for him to be going and led him to the stone door on the hill-side, and there was a sort of boat harnessed to wild duck.

When he got into the boat the wild duck flew with it high into the air over the dark woods, then down and down and down, till at last, the boat was just over Seekings House and Kay had only to drop down the chimney, as it seemed, into his room. And there he was in his room, snapping-to the Box and putting it back into his pocket.

Just as he snapped it to in his pocket there came a clattering at the door.

'Kay! Kay!' Maria cried.

'What is it?' Kay said.

'What isn't it?' she said. 'Come on down at once.' In the study, she showed him a paper. 'Look at this,' she said. 'There's a special edition of the paper. They've got the whole of the Cathedral staff.'

'No,' Kay said, 'they can't have!'

'They have, though,' Maria said. 'Look here.'

The special edition was a single sheet still damp from the press; the big black headings easily smudged.

'UNPARALLELED ATROCITY!
MORE HORRORS AT TATCHESTER
HAVE THE BOLSHEVIKS BEGUN?
A FEARED TERRIBLE PLOT
REIGN OF TERROR IN CATHEDRAL CITY.'

And there was a note:

'We had thought that the mystery attached to the disappearance of the eminent Clergy of the Tatchester Establishment would by this time have been cleared up with the return of the Bishop, the Dean and Canons to their functions. We regret to say that our confidence was gravely misplaced. Tonight we have to report the complete disappearance of the Precentor, the Vesturer, the Bursar, the Canons Minor, the Archdeacon, Vergers, Organist, and, it is feared, other members of the Cathedral staff.

'These gentlemen, according to their custom on the afternoon before Christmas Eve, were proceeding in a motor-bus to the Tatchester Alms Houses laden with suitable offerings for the old Men and Women Pensioners. They set off, according to custom, at half-past three and, it is thought, were beguiled into entering a motor-bus other than that sent for them. From that moment no word has been received from any of them.

'Anyone able to throw the slightest light upon this very dark mystery are adjured to communicate at once with the local Police (Telephone, Tatchester 7000), and to spare no pains in bringing the offenders to justice.'

'But what time is this?' Kay said.

'It's nine o'clock,' Maria said. 'We've been wondering where on earth you've been.'

'Oh,' Kay said, 'I suppose I fell asleep.'

'What a very pretty shiny buttonhole you've got,' Maria said. 'What is it?'

'Oh, that's a little rose,' Kay said, looking down; and indeed, there in his buttonhole was the little golden rose that had been made for him in the mountain.

'I suppose you got it from a cracker,' Maria said. 'But just think of their bagging the whole Cathedral staff at one swoop! They must have had the brains of buns. You see, they've had warning: the Bishop went, the Dean went and then the Canons went. And then, the whole of them go and plunge into a motor-bus and are whirled off, very likely into eternity.'

'Well, I hope they've not been whirled into eternity,' Kay said. 'They were awfully nice to us, some of those clergy: we had a lovely party there the other night. What on earth will they do for the Christmas services? We'll get the news on the wireless. We'd better wait up till then.'

They waited up until the news on the wireless. They

heard that the Archbishops were determined that, in case of need, the services should be held in the Cathedral in spite of the absence of the regular staff and that certain clergy had been asked to proceed to Tatchester to officiate there if the need arose. The announcer said that the matter was viewed with the greatest seriousness and that the public was asked to co-operate with the Police by giving instant, accurate information of a red, white, blue, grey, brown or black motor-bus—the colours had been variously given by various observers—proceeding at a frightening pace in the direction of Tatchester some twenty minutes before the alleged outrage. He asked that those who had any information to give should telephone at once to the Chief of the Tatchester Constabulary: telephone number, Tatchester 7000.

'Well, I should think,' Maria said, 'that even the sleuths at Scotland Yard will begin to think that they are up against a gang by this time. I should think the gangsters are dropping them biting post-cards: "Don't you know my methods, Watson?" etc. However, I should think we'd better get to bed. We've not heard the end of this yet: some more of them will be gone, you'll see.'

'They've got the whole boiling,' Kay said. 'I don't see how many more they could get.'

'The choir-boys aren't there,' Maria said.

'I think you'll find they've got the choir-boys,' Kay said.

'Well, I know who they'll get,' Maria said, 'and those are all the clergy who have gone to Tatchester to take office in case. Blithering asses they were, to let the gang know that.'

'I say!' Kay said. 'There'll be a fine old twitter in Tatchester.'

'Well,' Maria said, 'if they survive they'll have something to talk of as long as they live. Next to being martyred I should think being scrobbled would be the greatest joy a clergyman could have. I should prefer it to being martyred myself, but tastes differ.'

With that she went to put some holly in Jemima's bed and then retired to rest.

CHAPTER NINE

Kay went back to his room, sorely perplexed. It was time for bed, but the sight of Peter's bed without Peter reminded him that the Wolves were Running: he could not think of sleeping. 'Oh, if I could only find out where Cole Hawlings is,' he thought, 'then I could give him back his Box, and put an end to all this kidnapping.'

He stayed, looking at the fire, without any thought of undressing. At last, in his misery, he opened the Box, thinking, 'Perhaps I may see Herne the Hunter. He might be able to give me some advice.'

When he opened the Box, it seemed to him that he opened it at a stone gateway, through which he passed to the waters of a lake, where a boatman sat in a little green boat. 'Going across?' the boatman asked. 'Step in.'

So Kay stepped into the boat, the boatman thrust her off and rowed her over the lake, which was so clear that Kay could see the golden and scarlet fishes on the pebbles at the bottom. Kay landed at the other side of the lake, and walked up an avenue of fruit trees all glowing with the ripe fruit, apples, pears, plums, apricots, peaches, those five, all golden, scarlet, blue and orange-coloured. At the end of the avenue was a Castle surrounded by a lawn of the greenest grass with the whitest daisies. Some gazelles were nibbling the grass; they ran up to Kay to be petted. There were many little goldfinches flying about. Kay walked towards the steps of the Castle. All sorts of birds were there, herons, white ibises and scarlet flamingoes on the steps, and many finches flying. Out of the Castle, to meet him, came the Lady who had feasted him in the oak-tree. She still wore the ring with the 'long-ways cross.' She seemed to be about twenty now, and more beautiful, Kay thought, than even Caroline Louisa.

'Ah, Kay,' she said, 'I know why you come to me today. You will hear more tomorrow, if you go to Chester Hills. Now that you are here, what of all the things in the world would you like to eat?'

Kay thought and thought, at last he said, 'I think, mangoes, please.' Instantly out of the wall three plates appeared laden with mangoes. The plates had neat little legs which walked. They walked up to the table and bowed down before him, so that he could eat the mangoes; afterwards a sponge walked up and mopped off the stickiness.

'And now, Kay,' the Lady said, 'what, of all things, would you like to see?'

'Well, of all things, I think,' he said, 'a tournament.'

Instantly, one wall of the room rolled away, so that he

could look into the courtyard of the Castle, which was now divided into two by a gaily painted barrier. The sides of the yard were lined with tiers of seats, full of people and gay with banners.

At each end of the lists two Knights, one in scarlet, one in white armour, were taking position on horses excited by the music and the crowd. Suddenly, the trumpeters in the royal box blew all together, the Knights dropped their lances to the rests, drove in their spurs, and hurtled at each other on different sides of the barrier. Under the royal box, they struck each other's shields with their spears; they themselves reeled in their saddles, but were not unseated: the spears broke at the guards and leaped a dozen feet into the air: the Knights finished their courses, then wheeled round and waited for fresh spears.

'Would you like to do that, Kay?' the Lady asked.

'Oh, I would,' he said.

Instantly a squire led forth a war-horse with blue and white trappings for him. Out of the wall, the pieces of a suit of armour walked towards him and buckled themselves about him, first the footgear, leggings and cuisses, then the body-armour and arm-pieces, lastly the helmet with its plume. A squire came forward to give him a leg-up into the saddle; another squire brought him a lance.

'It is not always wise to take part with the Past, Kay,' the Lady said. 'Arnold of Todi did so, as you may hear tomorrow, and where, in the Past, is he now? He is lost, Kay.'

But Kay could not think of Arnold of Todi; he was on a great horse, feeling his mouth, and staring through the slit of his helm at his enemy at the other end. His enemy was a red Knight, just gathering his shield, which now turned to Kay, so that he saw upon it a black wolf rampant. A squire handed him a white shield with blue chevrons on it, but before he could take it, the trumpets blew. At once he drove forward at the Wolf Knight. The horses whinnied with delight, the joy of the charge surged up in him, he saw the red helm crouched above the Wolf; then, crash, they met.

'I've got him,' Kay shouted, as he felt his spear drive home on to the Red Knight's chest, and the Knight go backward over the crupper.

He *had* got him, but something odd had happened to himself. 'My girths are gone,' he cried. He felt the saddle turn under his horse's belly while himself was flung headlong, endlong, anylong, down, down, down, back to his chair by the fireplace in his room at Seekings.

'Well, tomorrow,' he said, 'as soon as ever it is light, I'll go out to Chester Hills to hear more.'

Next morning, as soon as ever it was light, he dressed. Taking the Box, he turned the knob first so that he might become tiny; next, so that he might go swiftly; instantly, he was whirled up through the chimney, out through the cowl and away, just as it was growing to be light. He felt so minute that he trembled lest a sparrow should peck him in mistake for a caterpillar. In a moment or two he was whirled down to the door-step of the great house at Chester Hills, still clutching the Box. He was shrunken to the size of one of his leaden soldiers. The front door was open. He was on the top step; he walked towards the hall.

Unfortunately, at that instant, a boy and girl were coming towards the house carrying between them a basket of packages. The sun shone at that instant on the door-step. The girl dropped her end of the basket and made a dart up the steps.

'Quick, Bert!' she cried. 'There's a fairy. Quick, catch him! We'll catch him and sell him.'

As she darted up the steps Kay slipped into the house and dodged to cover under the hangings of a window-seat. The two children followed and peered about at the door, whispering together. Plainly they were afraid to come further.

'What was it you saw?' the boy asked.

'A fairy dressed like a little boy.'

'Oh, go on!'

'But I did and he can't have gone far.'

'What d'you mean by a fairy?' the boy asked.

'A fairy, like a little boy—a little, tiny boy no bigger than my little finger.'

'Go on,' the boy said. 'There aren't such things as fairies: it's all rot about fairies.'

'But I tell you, I saw one,' the girl said.

'Well, we'll cop it if we are caught in here,' the boy said.

'Here,' the girl said, taking a walking-stick from the walking-stick-stand just inside the door, 'I'm going to give a prod underneath the seat there.'

The stick which she took was a sort of alpenstock with a long steel spike at the end of it. She thrust it under the hangings of the window-seat and raked with it there. Kay saw it coming at him like the head of a battering-ram mounted on a tree-trunk. It missed him by about an inch.

'It was in there he went, I'll bet a dollar,' the girl said.

The steel spike came prodding round again. Kay, crouching against the panels, gave himself up for lost.

There came the pad of straw-soled slippers on the

stone corridor and the squeaky voice of an old man said, 'What are you two doing there?'

The battering-ram fell with a crash. Kay heard the children rush away, pick up the basket and fly off. The old man came slowly limping to the door. Kay could see his feet in straw-soled slippers, with old trouser ends dangling down over them and the end of a dark green apron; also the head of a broom which the old man was trailing after him.

'I shall report them,' the old man muttered. 'They're not allowed in. They know that just as well as I do. I shall report them. It's not the first time. I'll report them as sure as my name's in the Bible. It was that girl and boy who cried "Hoi!" at me, and I shall report them and they'll get stick pie, as sure as my name's in the Bible. I'll teach them to cry "Hoi!" at me!'

He kept muttering how he would report them and how his name was in the Bible as he began to sweep out the hall. The broom began its work under the window-seat. In one instant the broom was rushing at Kay with a row of bristling hairs like a small plantation. They were soft hairs but they did not seem soft to Kay. They swept him off his feet into a collection of dust, pins, wool, matches which looked like stakes of wood, and cigarette ends which to Kay seemed like great logs all covered with charred grass. Kay was rolled over and over into the open hall, with his eyes tight shut for fear of being blinded and clutching the Box of Delights lest he should lose it. Another thrust of the broom buried him deep in grits, bits of gravel, mud and dead leaves which had been knocked off on the hall floor from boots coming in. He saw the old man's foot poised above him and thought, 'Now I shall be trodden on and squashed flat.' The old man pitched the door-mat out of doors, picked up his broom, gave three vigorous thrusts with it and rolled Kay with the last of them right out on to the porch.

Kay picked himself up and contrived to press the knob on the Box, saying, 'I want to go fast to the chief room in this place.'

Instantly he was plucked through the hall, along a corridor into a room where he was set down on a shelf of books, six feet from the floor. Near to him on the shelf was a sand-glass and behind him a row of the works of the English Poets, edited by somebody called Gilfillan. The walls were hung with hunting pictures and one specially he noticed which represented a small waterfall sweeping away a fox and three hounds; just beside the waterfall a hunter in a red coat was climbing to his feet from a fallen horse; with the legend: 'The Chester Hills Day: February, 1841.'

He heard the bell of the house chime for half-past eight. Then a pleasant, silky voice came towards him from along the passage singing a popular song.

'That's Abner Brown,' Kay muttered; 'and he wouldn't sing unless he were doing something pretty bad.'

Kay slipped in between two of the English Poets as Abner entered the room.

'What news? What news?' Abner muttered.

He pressed the button of a bell and sat at his desk. Presently someone entered.

'Did you please to ring, oh Father?' the newcomer asked.

'Yes, Nineteen,' Abner said, 'I did ring. Send Seven here, will you, please?'

Kay saw Abner take up various typewritten slips.

'The latest wireless,' he said. 'Ho, he won't, won't he? Oh, so the Police have a clue, have they? Clever chaps, the Police; clever fellows. Ha! She offers seventy thousand for the sapphires. Ah no, Madam: this is not a bargain-sale. Eighty-five thousand is our price.'

Presently a robust voice was heard approaching from the back of the house. It was singing a song which was certainly not the song for a young clergyman:

'A rum-rum-tiddly-um,
Who'll have a drink with me?'

The door was shoved open and a man came striding in. He was the big man whom Kay had seen at the *Rupert's Arms*: the man called Joe. He was laughing and singing in a breath.

'You want me, Chief?' he said.

'You might close the door, perhaps,' Abner said: 'Gently.'

The man, from where he stood, made a long leg and kicked the door to; then he drew near to Abner's desk and stood there, waiting.

'You sent for me, Chief?' he said at last.

'Yes,' Abner said. 'I hear you've permitted yourself some little criticisms of my orders about these clergymen.'

Kay, who could see Joe's face, saw at once that Joe was asking himself, 'Who on earth could have told him that?'

'Odd how the news gets about here, isn't it?' Abner said.

'You're right,' Joe said.

'So you *have* been criticising my orders. Why?'

'Well,' Joe said, 'if I knew why the orders were given I might see sense in them, but to kidnap a lot of clergymen, who can't afford any ransom worth your while, seems to me a lot of foolishness. You've roused the Press, you've roused the Yard and you've roused the Nation . . . here's the morning papers . . . all to get a Box, you say, that belongs to the Punch and Judy man.'

'Correct,' Abner said. 'That was in the possession of the Punch and Judy man would be better, perhaps.'

'Well, then, that's why we criticise,' Joe said. 'You know that this old man, Cole Hawlings, had the Box when he went to Seekings House. You know that he hadn't got it next morning. Well, you've got Him, haven't you? What we can't understand is why you don't make him tell you where he put it.'

'How would you make him?' Abner asked.

'He's an old man: a bit of talking-to would make him tell. No need to hurt him; threaten him with a red-hot poker, or keep him awake with Itchy Powder. If he'd scratched all these last two nights he'd have told you by this time.'

'Then you don't realise who Cole Hawlings is?'

'We don't. To us, he's a prisoner with information which you want. I say threaten him (or hurt him, if he's stubborn), till he gives you the information. If that's not cold sense, what is?'

'Cold sense,' Abner said; 'the English strong point, like "fair play" and "justice" and these others.'

'Well, they're things you get the benefit of,' Joe said, 'little as you may like them. What about it?'

'Ah,' Abner said, 'what indeed?'

Some of his words had been spoken with such savage sarcasm that Kay had trembled in his shoes; now all the savagery went out of his voice; he spoke again, with the utmost gentleness.

'Joe,' he said, 'can I trust you with a secret?'

'Why, Chief,' Joe said, 'you know you can trust me with anything, except perhaps a cold drink on a hot summer day.'

'I think I can, Joe,' Abner said. 'As a general rule, if a man can't keep a secret he needn't expect anybody else to keep it for him. Still, in this case, I will tell you why even I dare not threaten or hurt Cole Hawlings. It will go no further, of course,' Abner said.

'It will be secret as the grave with me,' Joe said.

'Yes,' Abner said. 'As secret as the grave; I think it will be; as secret as a very secret grave.

'Did you ever hear of Ramon Lully, Joe?' Abner asked.

'You mean the chap who did the box trick at the Coliseum?' Joe asked.

'No, Joe, not the Coliseum man,' Abner said. 'The man I mean was a philosopher of the Middle Ages. They show his tomb at Palma. Remember the name, for I shall allude to it later.'

'Right,' Joe said. 'I can remember. But if you are going opening tombs don't ask me. It's a job I don't hold with, though, of course, I know some people have done very well out of it.'

'Well,' Abner continued, 'did you ever hear of Arnold of Todi?'

'No, I can't say I ever did,' Joe said. 'What was he, or is he?'

'Well, he too was a philosopher of the Middle Ages,' Abner said, 'and not very, very much is known of him. But the son of one of his disciples left some papers which say that he and Lully, were rivals. Lully was all for finding an Elixir of Life that would make him last through the Future: Arnold was always trying to find some power of entering the Past.'

'Golly!' Joe said, 'they were a couple of queer cough-drops, if you ask me.'

'I'm not asking you,' Abner said: 'I am telling you. This unknown man whom I mentioned says in his papers that Arnold, by some extraordinary magic power, created a Box, by means of which he could enter the Past at will.'

'In fact, he did the box trick,' Joe said; 'like that chap at the Coliseum.'

'Now,' Abner said, 'some think that Arnold entered the Past by means of this Box and could not get out of it, but is wandering there for ever. Anyhow, he disappeared; but the Box, the man says, remained. He thinks that Dante had it, and that two of the great painters of Italy had it, and then a lesser painter, Zaganelli. I have reason to believe that Shakespeare had it and that he gave it to a poet called Wilkins, who was afraid to use it; and Wilkins gave it to a lady—one of the Stiboroughs—who was afraid of it. She kept it in Stiborough Castle, about twenty miles from here. In the Civil War Stiborough was besieged and she buried the Box in the Castle vaults. When the Parliament took the Castle they blew up most of it, so that the vaults were filled with the ruins.

'This woman, Aurelia Stiborough, when she was old repented of her folly. She wrote down the bearings of the hiding-place.

'The actual bearings were in cipher, but above the cipher she wrote some verses in English, which suggested that the cipher was worth deciphering.

'You won't have heard of the Historical Commissions,

which went about examining papers in old houses all over the country and printing brief summaries of all that they found. In their wanderings they came upon the Stiborough papers and printed the cipher for the sake of the verses at the beginning: that was in 1882: and there were the bearings for anybody with the wit to see what they meant. But perhaps, my dear Joe, I worry you with this. I should be desolated to inflict boredom on an old friend.'

'Go ahead,' Joe said. 'Now we've begun I may as well know it all.'

'Well, we came here,' Abner said. 'I have always been interested in magic, as you know. For many years I have been aware of all the stories about Arnold of Todi, but, like most students of magic, I believed that the Box must have fallen into the hands of Inquisitors or Puritans and been burned.

'I have always been interested in ciphers of different kinds and, quite by accident, came upon this Stiborough cipher while I was stopping with the Bishop at the time of the Missionary Conference. As I said, the poem at the beginning of the cipher showed that it referred to something very important. You are not interested in ciphers, Joe?'

'Well, I did a little ciphering at school,' Joe said. 'That's been enough for me so far.'

'So I gather,' Abner said. 'Well, a cipher will always yield its secret if you go on long enough and this one gave way to me, although it was a very ingenious thing. That Aurelia Stiborough was not the fool I thought her by any means.

'You're not an imaginative man, Joe, but you can imagine my excitement at finding that this amazing treasure of one of the amazing men of all time was buried in the earth less than twenty miles from here—a thing that Shakespeare and Dante and the great painters had used? That I had only got to go and dig it up and have it for my own—a thing that Ramon Lully had sought to buy from Arnold and been refused? Think, Joe, if you can think; there were those two great men, each supreme in his own way of thought. Lully travelled through Spain and across France and over the Alps and down through Italy to Todi to offer his secret for Arnold's, and Arnold refused.'

'So then, I suppose, you got busy,' Joe said.

'Busy!' Abner said. 'You little know, Joe, what I went through. I learned what the cipher contained at two in the morning here. Before three I was on the site of Stiborough Castle; pitch dark night, gale blowing, rain coming down in torrents, the ivy blowing loose from the walls, bits of boughs flying everywhere, the Castle in such a mess of old broken stones and earth and bramble that I almost broke my neck half a dozen times. And then, gradually the autumn dawn appeared and I could get proper bearings: a hill with a nick cut in it, a church spire and the entrance gate of Stiborough; and then, Joe, I made my measurements. I was wet through: was cold to the marrow. I didn't mind wet: I didn't mind cold. And there, by the first rays of light, I saw that I was too late: someone had read the cipher a little before me. There were the brambles cut away and the shaft sunk in exactly the right place and, at the bottom of the pit, the marks showed that I was too late.'

'Gee!' Joe said, with feeling, 'it isn't often you're too late.'

'I was too late. Here,' Abner said. Kay saw Abner pull

open one of the drawers of the desk. He took out some wrappings and covers of leather, much perished, of rotten wood, of a harder wood that was not rotten, and what looked like wool and silk. 'These were the outer wraps,' he said. 'Inside was this jewel-case—plain silver: time of James the First—marked "A.S." for Aurelia Stiborough; but the inside box was gone. I had been beaten, as you would put it in your poetical way, on the post by a short head. He had got the things at sunset on the night before, just before the rain began.

'Well, there it was: the Box was gone but it hadn't been gone long, and the next question was to get it from the man who had it. Who had it? Who'd been digging at Stiborough and making enquiries there? It is not difficult to find out in a countryside as lonely as that. The only man who had been near the ruins was a little old man who played a Punch and Judy show.'

'Cole Hawlings,' Joe said.

'As he calls himself now,' Abner said. 'He was the man who had been taking measurements at Stiborough and borrowing a bill-hook to cut away some of the brambles and undergrowth.'

'Well, you've got Cole Hawlings all right,' Joe said. 'You've no cause to complain. I suppose it wasn't hard to run him down: an old man with a Punch and Judy show?'

'I have other ways of finding things that I want,' Abner said, 'than by questioning all those who happen to be in the tap-room of the *Blue Dragon.* I used certain magical ways. But, of course, you don't believe in magic, Joe.'

'Well, sometimes, Chief,' Joe said, 'sometimes you talk in a way that makes me think you've got bats in your belfry.'

'Ah, so you don't believe in magic,' Abner said. 'That's a pity. Just look at me, Joe.'

Joe looked at Abner, who moved his left hand strangely. Instantly, the door opened and through it came queen after queen, crowned, smiling and wearing scarlet. They looked into Joe's face and said, 'Don't you believe in magic, Joe?' then smiled and passed out at the door. After them there came little scarlet horses that whinnied and tossed their manes. They, too, looked into Joe's face and whinnied, 'Don't you believe in magic, Joe?'

Then, immediately it seemed to Kay that the room had disappeared into a waste of thistles and dried grass blowing in the wind. Over this expanse came an old donkey with a matted, thick fell, one ear lopped down and the other cocked. He trotted up and turned to look at Joe. He looked extraordinarily perverse and very clever. Then he brayed, 'Don't you believe in magic, Joe?' Then he cocked the ear that was lopped and lopped the ear that was cocked and brayed again, 'No, Joe doesn't believe in magic:' and there was the room just as it had been before.

'For goodness' sake,' said Joe, 'how did you do that? I suppose you've got a magic lantern somewhere.'

'You might call it that,' Abner said. 'But by some such body of friends as those you have just seen I was able to find out who Cole Hawlings really is.

'When you see your friends again, Joe, you will be able to tell them who he is and why I have never hurt him. Cole Hawlings is Ramon Lully.'

Kay, who was watching Joe's face, saw Joe gasp, and then assume a look of pity, contempt and tolerance for a man plainly gone mad.

'But you said he was dead, Chief,' Joe said at last.

'I said, "They show his tomb at Palma." He discovered the Elixir of Life and flew away from his disciples in the likeness of a golden cock, and here he is now as Cole Hawlings.'

There was a pause at this, Joe looked at Abner, and at the floor, then back to Abner: he was plainly trying to find something tactful to say: at last he found it:

'That thing you say he discovered, the liquor of Life and that, would be a kind of cough-mixture?'

'If you can imagine a cough-mixture that will make a man eternal, able to survive pestilence or any other way of death . . .'

'It would be a good mixture to get on the market, I can see,' Joe said. 'Abner's Cure-All, at one and six the half-pint bottle. These patent medicines just rake in the money. But it wouldn't cure crashing in an aeroplane nor being run over by a lorry, you don't pretend?'

'Why not?' Abner asked. 'Why shouldn't that which makes tissue unkillable make bone unbreakable?'

'I see,' Joe said, scratching his head, 'it's like one of those rubber solutions they used to pump into tyres; they made the tyres solid, so then you couldn't puncture. Well, if you could get a stuff like that on the market you'd beat all the pill-merchants, and all the salts fellows. And should we all be in it with you?'

'My dear Joe,' Abner said, 'if there is one thing I pride myself on it is my loyalty to my colleagues. For whom do I toil here? For whom do I think and worry and scheme, but for the Brotherhood? We have lived through all these years of danger and adventure together. What could be a greater joy to me than to share all our little takings and enter into partnership for the marketing of the Elixir, for an Elixir, for an eternity of happy quiet?'

'Chief,' Joe said, 'if you don't mind, I'll sit down. Some of what you've told me is a bit of a knock-out.

'Well, that's that then,' he said at last.

'That is that,' Abner answered.

'About these clergymen,' Joe said; 'what still we don't see, is why you keep scrobbling the clergymen. See here now in *The Daily Thriller*.

> 'The latest outrage at Tatchester, culminating in the disappearance of the Bishop's Chaplain, the Reverend Edward Charity, D.D., and his friend, the Chief Theologian, Doctor Isaiah Dogma, points to the existence of an organised conspiracy, possibly, as been suggested, to prevent the holding of the Millennial Christmas Service advertised for the early hours of Christmas morning. If this be so, and no other explanation of the outrage, so far suggested, seems to meet the case, we would warn the scoundrels responsible that the Establishment will contrive to defeat their machinations.
>
> 'THE SERVICE WILL BE HELD'

'You see that, Chief, and the heading "Church Defies Bandits." They mean business.'

'So do I, Joe,' Abner said.

'Is it your game to stop that service?' Joe asked.

'I'll stop that service if they don't deliver the Box or tell me where it is.'

Kay saw looks of anger, bewilderment, contempt and mutiny cross Joe's face in quick succession; he noticed, too, that none of these looks was missed by Abner, who was watching Joe intently. Joe rose from his chair and walked the room for a moment.

'Chief,' Joe said, 'I don't like what you're doing. While you were just a fair and square burglar, like the rest of us, I respected you; but this dabbling in magic and scrobbling up the clergy will come to no good. You'll find it so, when it's too late. The Press respects burglars like us who only burgle the very rich; but you're going now against children, women and the clergy, and you've turned the Press dead against you. Of course, I've got no intellect; don't go by what I say . . .'

'I congratulate you on your knowledge of yourself,' Abner said sweetly. 'You're not employed for your intellect, but for your nerve. Are you losing your nerve?'

'No,' Joe said sulkily.

'Good,' Abner said.

'I take it, Chief,' Joe said, 'that you're not keen on going dead against your own interests in this?'

'No,' Abner said, 'why?'

'Of course,' Joe said, 'the profits are too small for you to bother about. A thousand quid is nothing to you, but to us poor chaps, who do the work, they're a thousand quid.'

'Come to the point; what is it?' Abner asked.

'Well, Chief,' Joe said, 'now would be the time to stop this clergy business. The Archbishop is offering a reward of a thousand pounds for the return of the Bishop or Dean, with reduced sums for the rest; it's twenty-five quid even for a choir-boy. It would be quite a profitable little haul if you chose to take it. Tomorrow, or even today, you'll have the Yard poking about.'

'The Yard! The Yard could be in this room, and those

clergy could shout, "O Come, all ye Faithful!" at the tops of their voices, yet not be heard. Come to breakfast.'

'All right,' Joe said. 'But there is another thing. There is a boy at Seekings; Kay Harker. He was here with that boy Peter whom we scrobbled; and I don't see why Cole Hawlings shouldn't have given the Box to him, if it comes to that.'

'You don't see a good many things,' Abner said.

'I dare say I'm as blind as a bat,' Joe said, 'and as for intellect I never claimed any, but blind and balmy as I am I never talked such tosh as you've talked since I came into this room; nor I never sold my soul to the devil. What with that and going to the films you've got bats in your belfry. I thought so before and now I know it. You'll come to a bad end, let me tell you, and it won't be long hence. . . .'

Kay saw Abner's pale face turn a little whiter; he was plainly very angry and about to answer savagely. At that moment, the door opened. In came Sylvia Daisy Pouncer Brown, who had no doubt been listening at the keyhole. On seeing her, Joe muttered what sounded like 'Crikey, now here's his Missus.' Sylvia D. P. Brown looked at Joe and drew her own conclusions.

'Abner, my dear,' she said, 'you've talked and talked. Do come to breakfast before it's all cold. Remember, you've got to speak a Christmas talk at Tatchester Alm Houses at half-past ten.'

'Certainly, my dear,' he said. 'We've said all that we had to say.'

Kay could not be sure, but thought that Joe muttered, 'Oh, *have* we? You'll see.'

'I was forgetting the Alms Houses,' Abner said. 'Those

poor deserving old men and women, we mustn't forget them, must we? Well, Joe, that will delay our business till half-past two, in my room. Do you get that?'

'Half-past two, in your room; very well, Chief,' Joe said.

Abner walked past him to the door, 'Come along to breakfast, Joe,' he said. 'We're both starved.'

They walked out of the room together. After a moment Kay pressed his Box, resumed his shape and slipped into the corridor after them.

To his right, the corridor led to the hall and main staircase. To his left, it led to a closed door where breakfast was now in progress: cups, knives and forks were clicking; there were strong smells of bacon and of coffee; Abner's voice said, 'May I beg you to pass the butter?'

Almost in front of Kay, a second corridor led towards the kitchen or pantry; there, coming from the kitchen, was the old man who had swept in the hall, carrying a dish on which his eyes were fixed. He was muttering aloud to himself:

'Chop small with best green bacon. Add a pinch of powdered cheese. Add chopped mushroom or, as some prefer, chopped sardine. Served hot with melted butter.'

He tapped at the door and entered.

Abner said, 'You anticipate my every wish, David. You bring us more when hope was failing.'

As David closed the breakfast-room door, Kay slipped towards the kitchen and pantry. To his right was the pantry with a chafing-dish from which a savoury smell came; to the left was a big kitchen where a man's voice called:

'Jim, haven't you done the scullery floor yet? They'll be inspecting in a minute.'

'Danger here,' Kay thought. He turned swiftly back on tiptoe and ran up the main staircase. At the top of the stairs was a long, broad corridor with doors and passages opening to right and left. All the doors were shut and labelled 'Dean,' 'Sub-Dean,' 'Prior,' 'Sub-Prior,' 'Bursar.' Kay opened the Bursar's door very cautiously and peeped in.

A preoccupied voice said, 'No, no; you must wait just a minute longer. I haven't finished the accounts.'

He slipped back into the passage and shut the door.

'Nearly caught there,' he said. 'I'm much more likely to be caught than to discover anything.'

Then, as he walked along, a door opened down below and there came a clatter of voices and a rush of feet coming up the back stairs. It came upon him in a flash that these were the younger members of the brotherhood who had finished breakfast and were running upstairs to tidy their rooms for inspection. They were shouting together like schoolboys, evidently chasing each other and, as they were coming very fast, he hadn't an instant to lose.

'I'll come back at half-past two,' he thought, 'and hear what those two are up to.'

He turned the knob of the Box, so that he might go swiftly. At once, he was sped away from those shouting collegiates, yet not before he was seen. He heard one young man cry out, 'I say, look . . . a swallow,' and a second answered, 'Rats. Swallows come in April.' But now, he was borne away upon unseen wings back to his late breakfast at Seekings, with the three girls, each sure that Peter would be all right, and all thrilled at the disappearance of Mr. Charity and Dr. Dogma.

'Now,' Maria said, 'they have scrobbled every single clergyman attached to the Cathedral. The *Thriller* has got a name for them now: the Red-Hot Atheists: Red-Hot Atheists at it again. Wholesale Murder Feared. Shrieks heard from Shuttered House. Bloodstains in the Snow.'

'The gang has put the clergy's backs up now,' Susan said. 'I'm simply thrilled to think that Maria and Peter have been scrobbled as though they were clergymen. But the whole English Church is resolved now, to hold that service tonight. You see what the Archbishops say, "That they are happy to state that five clergy from the diocese have proceeded to Tatchester to supply the Christmas services if by any unhappy occurrence the rightful Ministers be unable to officiate." '

'They ought not to have mentioned that,' Maria said. 'Now the gang will scrobble those, too, you'll see.'

'I expect they will,' Kay said, 'but all the same, they had to let people know that the services will be held.'

'What makes my blood boil,' Maria said, 'is the cheek of the gang, thinking they can prevent the services.'

Kay did not answer this, he was thinking how very powerful the gang was, and how miserable the beautiful Caroline Louisa must be shut up in the rock with two women like she-wolves as guards.

After breakfast, he went round to the Inspector.

'If you please,' Kay said, 'would you like to win the Archbishop's reward of a thousand pounds? If you would go to the Tatchester Barracks and fall out the Tatshire Blues and raid the Chester Hills College, you'd find the clergy there, I'm sure you would.'

'Why, how you run on about the College, Master Kay,' the Inspector said. 'This is what in Medical Circles is spoken of as a Hobsession. No, no, believe me, the College is all full of young Reverends. However would young men like that go scrobbling the very men who'll ordain them?'

'By an aeroplane that can turn into a motor-car and then back into an aeroplane. And it can hover just like a sparrow-hawk and settle down in through the roof.'

'Ah no, Master Kay, no aeroplane can do that; none.'

'But I saw the aeroplane settle through the roof . . . I did.'

At this moment, a car dashed up to the door. The Chief Constable of Tatshire was there. 'Are you there, Drew?' he called. 'Come along, will you, we need every man we can get: we're to give Police protection to the clergy detailed for duty in the Cathedral. Bring a truncheon, you may need it.'

The Inspector unhooked a truncheon and hurried away in the car.

'He simply will not believe me,' Kay said. 'And in a few hours it will be too late.'

He went back in deep distress to his room at Seekings.

CHAPTER TEN

'Perhaps,' he thought, 'if I look into the Box, I may meet with Herne the Hunter again, and oh, if I do, I'll ask about Arnold of Todi, for he's the cause of all this trouble: it's his Box, and if he had it again then perhaps all this hunt for it and scrobbling folk would stop. So, here goes.'

This time, as he opened the Box, it seemed to him that he was looking between two columns, on which the snow lay thick. Here and there on the stone the snow had partly melted and had again frozen, so that little icicles dangled from the ledges. Kay passed between these columns into a wintry wood, full of snow, where even the rabbits had turned white. In front of him was what seemed like the bole of a ruined tree, but it was Herne the Hunter, clad in some pelt, powdered with snow.

'I know what you want, Kay,' he said. 'You want to know about Arnold of Todi. He went back into the Past, looking at it, and was caught in it somewhere and is lost, never able to get back.

'And the Past, Kay,' he added, 'is a big book with many,

many pages; if you go looking for Arnold in the Past, who knows if you will ever find him?'

'I have this Box. Won't this Box help me to find him?'

'No,' Herne said. 'Arnold left that Box behind him, because he made another way of getting back, which he liked better. The Box is good for Europe, but Arnold wanted the East.'

'Could you take me to Arnold, please?'

'No,' Herne said. 'We do not know where he is. He is somewhere in the Past; that is all we know.'

'Well, what part of the Past d'you think he went back to?' Kay said.

'Well, as to that,' Herne answered; 'there's one part that everybody goes to and that's the Trojan War.'

'Could I get down to the Trojan War to ask about him?' Kay asked.

'You could,' Herne said. 'There are generally people there, and one of them may have noticed Arnold, or heard where he went; he didn't stay there probably, people don't: and if he *had* stayed there he wouldn't be lost, would he, and we know that he is lost.'

'How do you know?'

'The word got about,' Herne said.

'How could I get to the Trojan War to ask?' Kay asked.

'I could get you there,' Herne said, 'but you must leave the Box behind you, and I strongly advise you to do no such thing. You may never get back, if you once get there. I can't be sure that I can get you back.'

'I expect I could get back,' Kay said.

'I'm not so sure of it. You're bent on going?'

'Yes, please,' Kay said.

'Well, in a way, it won't be you that goes, it will only

be a shadow of you: the rest will be asleep. The you that goes will cast no shadow. People won't like that, you'll find.'

'I shan't mind,' Kay said.

'*They* may,' Herne said, 'and they're a pretty rough crowd in parts of the Past.'

'I'll chance it,' Kay said.

'It's a dangerous thing to get mixed up in the Past,' Herne said, 'but if you must, you must.'

He beckoned to Kay, and Kay felt that he became two Kays, one asleep at Seekings, the other beside Herne.

He noticed then that the sea had come almost up to where they stood. There, running into the sand at his feet, was a strange black ship, looking rather like a dolphin. She had one mast and one big sail and a lot of men sitting on benches with the oars. The captain of this ship was a fierce-looking man with long yellow hair. He had a curious breastplate of some blue metal on which a wolf had been inlaid in gold.

'If you are for Troy, step on board,' this captain said.

Kay stepped on board, and, instantly, the rowers began to row and the sail filled and the ship leaped like a dolphin. The men sang as they rowed. They went past island after island, all bright in the sun, and, presently, they were beached on the sandy shingle between two rivers. All the beach was lined with ships of different sorts, all rather like the ship in which he had travelled. There were lanes between the lines of ships and in these lanes there, were huts, where men were cleaning their armour, cooking, or washing their wounds.

Beyond the gate of this and crossing the beach Kay saw on a little hill beyond them the wall of some castle from which a dense smoke was rising. As he went towards this, he saw more soldiers, wearing those blue breastplates with the inlaid wolves. These were driving down parties of unhappy men, women and children, laden with packages of booty.

'Goodness,' Kay said. 'This is really Troy. There are the walls and that's the Tower over the Skaian Gate, and I have come just too late: the city has been sacked.'

He came presently to the river, but he saw at once that, as a road led from it on the other side, it could be easily forded. There it was very shallow and did not do much more than cover his ankles. There were plenty of little fish in the clear water.

Beyond the river there were marks of frequent fighting: the graves of men marked by broken spears with helmets on them, fragments of broken weapons or chariots and some dead horses. The ground rose from this point, and out of the Skaian Gate, coming towards him, were the last of the Trojans being beaten forward by the butt-ends of the spears of their conquerors.

'Oh dear,' Kay said. 'There are all the poor Trojans driven into captivity and the beautiful walls all racked and ruined.'

After the party had gone past with the wailing captives and cursing guards, Kay went into the Skaian Gate and looked about him at the desolation. The doors of all the houses were open; the things which had not been worth carrying away lay smashed or torn in the ways. There was nobody left in the city except a stray cat or two, mewing in misery. The pigeons which had once nested in the temples were flying about in the smoke. As Kay went up towards the temples a gust of wind caught the fire; it burst out with a savage crackle and fierce flame.

He noticed then that an old, old crone was sitting at

the corner of the ways. She looked as though she had been too old to be taken away.

'You are looking for Arnold of Todi?' she said. 'He was here, but he has gone.'

'Where did he go?' Kay asked.

'He went with the Wolves,' she said.

'Has he gone long?' Kay asked.

'A matter of five hundred years ago,' she said.

It did not seem very hopeful to Kay, but he went back down the hill and across the ford to the beach, but the beach now was deserted. The ditch had fallen in, the stockade was gone and all the space where the ships had lain now seemed ruined by floods from the two rivers.

But there, drawing near to the shore, was a boat manned by long-haired, dirty men, most of whom wore ear-rings. The boat had a name painted on her bows in clumsy red letters. Presently, as she drew near, Kay read this as *Seawolf.* As the boat touched the shore the man who was steering hailed him and said:

'Are you sick of the Mediterranean? We are.'

Kay said he did not know very much about it, but the man said, 'You will, if you stay. Come on board.'

Now that he could see their faces, Kay was not very eager to come on board. He remembered to have seen, in an old print, by Hogarth, of the 'Idle Apprentice,' a representation of a boat-load of evil-looking men. It seemed to him that the men in this boat might have been the brothers of those whom Hogarth drew. There was a pale and toothless look about them that was very awful. They looked at him slantwise, and spat sideways in a very crooked manner. Perhaps he would not have gone aboard their cutter, had he not seen that a party of spearmen, wearing breastplates stamped with the images of wolves, were slinking down the beach as though to seize him. They were coming down the sands behind and on both sides of him; they were closing in on him. Though they all made a pretence of looking for shells, or watching the sky, it was quite plain that he was their mark. He did not like the looks of the cutter's crew, but these Wolf-men terrified him, so he climbed aboard the cutter, which at once shoved off into the sea. The Wolf-men at once turned back: plainly, they *had* been after him.

Kay saw that the cutter was heading for a ship in the channel. As he sat in the stern-sheets, looking at the crew, he found their eyes fixed on him. He had seen a cat looking at a little bird with that sort of look; he had heard that snakes will look at mice with that sort of look. He began to notice their dress: they wore short buckled shoes, no stockings, rude red canvas petticoats or kilts, and canvas jackets. In their belts were stuck pistols, knives and hangers. The boat was old, dirty, and had once been painted red.

He looked a little anxiously towards the ship. He had heard that Mediterranean cruises are delightful, and that the ships in which they are made are spotlessly clean, brightly lit and very comfortable. There was nothing of all this about *this* ship. For one thing, she flew no colours; for another, she was not in any sort of order. There was a sort of green grass at her water-line; the paint had long since gone from her sides. It seemed, too, that she had been in action not long before, for splinters had been torn off her planking, leaving white wounds, sometimes jagged and irregular, sometimes round like the shot which had caused them. She was rolling slightly to the swell; some of her gear gave out a melancholy creak as she rolled. One of the rowers in the boat spat some tobacco juice over his shoulder and said, 'She creaks, just like Old Bill after he was hanged in chains.'

Kay noticed that the fore-topsail was loose. He knew enough of the sea to know that this meant that the ship was about to sail. He was shocked to notice that she was not flying the Blue Peter. He had always heard that a ship about to sail invariably flies the Blue Peter. The boat ran alongside the ship and the stroke oar said, 'Up with you, young Master'; so Kay clambered up the ladder to the deck. He was shocked to find that the deck was dirty, scarred like the sides, and cluttered with gear. The ropes were not coiled up; the hammocks were not in the nettings. There were heaps of old clothes and hats on the deck. Two or three of the crew lay asleep in the scuppers. The ship had guns upon both sides of her deck: on her bulwarks were little swivel-guns which could be turned in any direction. On the quarter-deck, just above the ship's wheel, was a scroll-work which had once been gilded. Within the scroll was a painting of the ship as she had been on her setting forth. 'She must then have been a beauty,' Kay thought, for the picture showed her gay with paint and hung with colours. Her name had been painted underneath her, in white letters: *The Bristol Merchant.* Somebody had run a streak of red paint across this name and had painted over it a new name: *The Royal Fortune.* 'I see what this is,' Kay thought. 'She is a merchant ship which has been captured by pirates.'

He had not time to think of his discovery. A pale man, who seemed to be the captain, blew a whistle; all the crew gathered to him on the quarter-deck.

'Brothers,' the captain said, 'I have called you all together . . . Steward, a bowl of rum . . .' A bowl of rum was brought forward. It was a tub of rum, not a bowl. The captain said, 'Brothers, fill your pannikins. We are going again on the Grand Account.'

The crew gave three loud cheers, dipped their pannikins in the rum, lifted their pannikins, called out each one of them a different sentiment, such as: 'Here's how,' 'Drink hearty,' 'Success to *The Royal Fortune*'; then they all drank success to their cruise, drank a second, then a third success, and fired a salvo of guns.

Instantly the ship began to sail. Malta dropped astern in half a minute; they cleared Gibraltar a moment later. The ship slipped swiftly towards the west.

Very soon the ship was in the tropics, not far from land: there in the water were scarlet seaweeds, rainbow-coloured fishes, bits of wreck with coral stuck on them and branches with strange leaves and fruits. Kay kept away from the evil-looking men, who smoked short clay pipes, and sipped rum, as they sat on deck dicing for the old clothes.

Soon Kay saw an island rising ahead. It must once have been a volcano, for it rose up in a cone, from which the slopes lapsed to the sea, under dense wood. At one side, the island was sheer cliff against which the surf was bursting: elsewhere little valleys ran down to beautiful white beaches. Kay could see the sparkle of brooks tumbling down the hill.

He was so intently watching the island that he was surprised to find one of the crew intently watching himself. This man had a bloated mouth with only two front teeth in it. Suddenly this man seized him by the collar.

'I have got you,' he said. 'Here he is, boys; here's another of them.'

The captain, hearing this commotion, turned and said, 'What is it, there?'

'It's another of them, please, Captain,' the man said. 'I have been watching him for some time and he has got no shadow.'

'Bring him up in the sun,' the captain said.

They brought Kay up into the sun; they stood round him with their pistols drawn; they turned him about, so that he caught the light.

'It's true,' they said. 'He's got no shadow, no more than that other one we had.'

'Well, we'll soon settle him,' one of the men said, drawing his cutlass and running his thumb along the edge. 'One good whack with this,' he said, 'it'll let the shadow out that he's got tucked away inside of him.'

'Hold on there, brother,' another pirate said. 'That's Death: it's well-known sure Death to cut a man with no shadow. Never take an edge to such. Tie ropes to him, that is the way, and pull him underneath the ship from side to side till he is torn in three; then let the sharks have him, shadow and all.'

'That's a soft way to be rid of him,' another said. 'It's plain that you're New to the Coast, talking like that. That is just the way to start disease among the fish. The sharks would swallow the shadow and die, the fish would eat the sharks and die; then men would eat the fish and die. It's just sheer murder, all the way along. Hang the sculpin up by the heels till the shadow falls out of him, *I* say.'

Then another man said that it was well known that the thing to do with a person of that sort was to shoot him with a blessed bullet. This sentiment met with general applause that that was undoubtedly the way, but when they came to apply it to Kay they found that they had not a blessed bullet. In fact they found that the only blessed thing on board was a church candlestick, which had been in use so long on board for lighting pipes and warming rum that it was probably no longer blessed. The general vote was that it was probably, by this time, not blessed, and that in any case it would be a pity to spoil the candlestick for a two-penny sculpin with no shadow.

'Wait now,' the captain said. 'Once before we had one of this sort with no shadow, but we found a way of dealing with him. We marooned him on the Tiburones. There are the Tiburones. I say that we should maroon this man there too.'

This met with immense applause. 'Yes,' they cried to Kay. 'The Tiburones. You will stay there and live with the other fellow till you get your shadows back. That's the place for them—the Tiburones.'

Kay heard one of the men say in an Irish voice, 'That's a queer sort of a name to give a place. What did they give it a name like that for?'

'Well,' one of the men said, 'Tiburones is its name, and Tiburones is its nature. It's the Spanish word for sharks.'

Having decided Kay's fate, they filled the bowl with more rum. Some of the crew dragged Kay to what they called the Bilboes, which were two iron rails fixed to the deck. They chained his wrists to one rail and his ankles to the other, so that he sat with great discomfort, with his hands behind him and the back of his neck being scorched by the sun. After this, all hands drank their rum, fired their pistols and flung sea-boots at Kay's head. In a few minutes, the ship glided into the quiet of the anchorage: instead of the roaring surf Kay heard a queer, dry, snapping noise.

'You hear that, sculpin?' one of the men said. 'Those

are the Tiburones, champing their teeth for you. Each has got three rows of teeth; one to grip, one to tear, and the third to chump up tiny.'

By this time some of them had lowered a boat. They thrust Kay into it and rowed him towards the shore. The water in the bay was of the most vivid, pure green, so curiously clear that far, far below he could see shark after shark, all spotted, spangled and striped. From time to time an enormous shark would heave silently alongside, just out of reach of the ends of the oars. It would turn over on its back a little and show its awful mouth with the three rows of teeth.

'Now, out you get, you shadowless sculpin,' the captain said, as the boat ran into the sand. They pitched Kay out head first on to the beach. 'If you look among the woods,' they cried, 'you may find your brother.' With that the boat turned for the ship. Kay was left alone on the desolate beach.

He thought, 'Perhaps I would have been wise not to come exploring into the Past.'

The sun was exceedingly hot and he was without a hat. The beach was composed of millions of tiny white shells, some of them flushed with pink. They scrunched under his feet as he walked towards the shelter of the forest. As he reached the line of the trees he turned to look at the ship, which was now heading for sea again. A bright flash darted from her stern port and Kay instantly jumped to one side, thinking, 'They have fired at me.' He saw a column of water leap up from the bay, then another and then another, as the shot skimmed towards him. Just as the bang of the report reached him, the shot buried itself in the beach close to where he had been standing. A shower of little shells came pattering on the leaves near him, and all the birds of the island (it seemed) screamed and mewed and rose up out of the tree-tops.

'Well, here I am, marooned,' Kay said to himself; keeping well under cover lest they should send another cannon ball. 'Now I am like poor Ben Gunn in *Treasure Island*: unless I am able to run down the goats, if there are any, I am not likely to get much dinner. I am frightfully hungry.

'I wonder,' he said, 'what I could do for food. There are lots of berries and things on the trees, but they may be poisonous.'

He remembered to have read that berries which the birds ate freely could usually be safely eaten by men. He saw that birds were pecking various red and yellow fruits, but these fruits were high in the trees, and the trees were bare of lower branches; there was no climbing to them. There were coconuts on some coco palms, but no monkeys to hurl them to him, as he had read that monkeys did. He saw no goats, and he had no pin about him with which to make a fish-hook. Now that the ship had gone he thought that perhaps he would be able to creep down to the rocks to find shell-fish. There were some shell-fish stuck to the rocks, but so tightly stuck that he could not get them away. He repeated to himself an old poem:

> 'Said gorging Jack to guzzling Jimmy,
> "I am extremely hunger-ee." '

He remembered to have read of a sailor who used his white toes as bait, dangling them in the sea to attract the fish and then spearing them as they came to nibble. He found a stick and with great trouble rubbed it to a point on the rough shells of the shell-fish on the rocks. Then, finding a rocky pool on the beach, he drew off his stocking, slipped his foot into the water and gently waggled it about. Suddenly, what seemed like the bottom of the pool rose up in a mass towards him. He snatched his foot from the water, dropped his stick and fled, but had time to see two terrible jaws snap within a inch of his foot as he withdrew it. The worst of it was that in his hurry he knocked his shoe into the pool. Turning round he saw this floating like a little boat for a moment; then the great jaws rose and snapped it up.

'Now I've only got one shoe,' Kay thought; 'and shipwrecked seamen have to eat their shoes. Well, I suppose I had better do that . . . eat the other shoe . . .'

He took it off and tried to bite some of it, but it was extraordinarily tough and the taste of blacking was not very pleasant.

'Oh come,' he thought; 'animals can live on grass and leaves and things. Why shouldn't I?'

He picked some leaves, but they were so very bitter that they shrivelled his mouth up. Then he picked some grass, but this was very salty. Then he picked some other grass, which was so rough and sharp that it made his lips and tongue bleed.

He seemed to remember that some shipwrecked man or tribe of savages of whom he had read had made elegant fish-hooks of sea-shells. Among the tiny shells on the beach there were many bigger ones, but he could not find the knack of cracking them into hooks.

'Well,' he thought at last, 'perhaps this island is inhabited. There may be people somewhere or other in it who will help me.'

He set off to walk through the jungle. He held his one

shoe in his left hand as that was his only supply of food. He found the going extraordinarily rough with so many fallen trees and branches, but he had not gone long before a most appetising smell came to his nose.

'Oh,' he said, 'there are people. That's something being cooked.' There was no doubt about it: something very nice was being cooked not very far away. Then Kay thought, 'Supposing, when I came through the jungle I find that it is a whole lot of cannibals cooking Man Friday or his brother. I wish I knew what cooked man smelt like.'

Somehow the smell in his nostrils seemed too pleasant to be the smell of toasted man. He went on with increasing hope that he would soon come to someone who would feed him. He heard on ahead the pleasant splash of falling water. At this point, somewhere beyond him in the jungle, an old man's wavering voice began to sing a song. As from the first it seemed a very queer song, Kay sat down on a fallen tree to listen to it. This was the song:

'When I was three, or two, or one,
I used to go to bed on Sun,
And wake on Mon.
And when I went to bed on Tues,
I woke on Wed, as true as trues,
I could not choose.
When Thurs, on Fri; when Fri, on Sat;
When Sat, on Sun; it all fell pat;
And that was that.

'Now that I'm four, or five, or six,
It is another bag of tricks;
It is a mix.

'For, when Tomorrow's bed-time, say,
I never, never wake Today,
But Yesterday,
Yesterday, or the Day Before.
Or Two Months Since, or Three, or More,
In Years, Long O'er.

'Sometimes, of course, I find this pleasant,
I never greatly loved the Present,
Except when eating roasted pheasant,
Or reading Greek:
But still sometimes I stand aghast,
Stuck in the Week before the Last,
With all the Present turned to Past,
And Now, last week.

'And what is worse, I sometimes fear
It isn't Now at all that's here . . .
No, but Next Year;
Next Year, or worse, some year beyond
In future time unkenned, unconned,
As far away as Trebizond,
From Todi Weir.

'And this I ask, and fain would know:
Will Now be in a day or so?
Is this-time-next-year Now or no?
Or did Now happen long ago,
Long, long ago?

'And was Tomorrow Yesterday?
Or has it been and gone Today?
Will no one say?
I wish someone would say.'

The voice trailed off from the tune here, and the song ended. The singer muttered to himself two or three times, 'Yes, indeed, truly, I wish someone *would* say. The fact of the matter is, they don't know.'

Something in the voice made Kay feel sure that the singer would not harm him; he rose from his log and pushed through the scrub towards him. After a few yards, the jungle was less thick. He came through the jungle to a clearing, where he saw the mouth of a cave, a bubbling spring falling down some rocks near the cave-mouth into a rocky pool, and an old man sitting beside a fire, toasting two bananas stuck upon skewers, which he held, one in each hand.

Kay limped towards this old man, who looked at him and said, 'Italiano?' Kay shook his head.

The man said, 'Français?'

Kay, who was on surer ground here, said, 'Non—English.'

The old man looked at him in astonishment and interest. 'Come then,' he said kindly; 'sit, eat, drink;' he took the toasted bananas from the skewers, put them on a broad leaf and offered them to Kay with a big shell full of water. Kay, who was really very, very hungry, ate the bananas with thankfulness. He looked at the man who had welcomed him. He was extraordinarily old, ragged-haired and tatter-bearded. He was dressed like a scarecrow in a most strange patchwork of palm leaves, pieces of old sail and what may once have been leather. Presently the man spoke in strange English:

'You excuse me,' the man said. 'Make pardon. What year in Anno Domini is this?'

'Nineteen-thirty-five,' Kay said.

'What you say? Nineteen—nineteen hundred?'

'Yes,' Kay said, opening his hand three times and then showing four fingers. 'Nineteen-thirty-five.'

'In the Future, or in the Present?'

'In the Present,' Kay said.

'Oh,' said the old man. 'What a thing is Time. I have got lost in Time.'

'Tell me, please, sir,' Kay said, with interest, 'are you Mr. Arnold of Todi?'

'I was once, young Englishman,' he said, 'but that was when I belonged to the year of Our Lord, which I went out of, by my own act. I would have none of it: I went back into the Past, and should therefore have a name from the Past, such as Alexander.'

'Why did you go back into the Past?' Kay asked.

'Why?' Arnold said. 'Because of the dullness of the Time into which I was born.

'But tell me; you, you say, are English. You will please excuse and pardon. The English I have never seen. It is true that we Italians conquered the land. We have a legend that the English are like rabbits, in that their front teeth stick out, but that they are unlike rabbits, in that they have tails. You are a strange people.'

'We haven't tails,' Kay said.

'The fact is well known,' Arnold said.

'But about Time: I am rather behind hand in Present Time. Perhaps I am not in Modern Time at all, but in Future Time. It isn't Past Time. You asked me why I went back into the Past. So many things happened in the Past. In my young days, life in my country was tedious to a man of thought. I made a way to get back into the Past . . . a certain Box . . . You may not credit it, but a man came all the way from Spain to offer me the Elixir of Life in exchange for it. He gave me a sip of the Elixir and I let him see my Box, but I would not make the exchange; for I could get back into the Past by my Box, that is into the Past of Europe. Young Englishman, I do not consider that the Past of Europe is worth consideration.'

'I don't know,' Kay said. 'A good many things have happened in Europe . . . The Roman Empire, the Spanish Empire, Napoleon the Great, the Battle of Waterloo . . . and the Great War.'

'The Great War!' Arnold said. 'It was to see that that I gave away my first Box and spent years finding a way into the Past of Asia. Tell me, in the Time that you know do they speak much of Alexander the Great?'

'He is mentioned sometimes,' Kay said.

'Imagine it,' Arnold said. 'Mentioned sometimes. Is not that typical of European things and people? Rulers and ruled alike—childish, trivial, wanting in will.'

'You can't call Julius Cæsar that,' Kay said.

'He only imitated Alexander,' Arnold said. 'Besides he was bald. I was delighted that he met the end he did. My race, the Italian, has ever been renowned for intelligence. They never showed it more clearly than in ending that public pest. What is your Christian name, young man?'

'Kay,' Kay answered.

'You ought to change it to Alexander,' Arnold replied. 'Young men should have prosperous names, names to live up to. Kay isn't a name, it's a letter of the alphabet. It is the Greek Kappa. We Italians dispensed with it.'

'Did you ever meet Alexander?' Kay asked.

'Young man,' Arnold said. 'I was weary of life in Todi, so I made my Box and wandered into the Past of Europe. Oh, it was so dull . . . dreary kings, dreary murders, silly wars; so I got out of it as soon as I could. I went into the

Past of Asia. And d'you know, a lot of that is very dull . . . silly wars, you know, rather dreary kings, not very much thought; and then suddenly, in one of those cities in Asia Minor, I first saw Alexander. You never met Alexander?'

'No, indeed,' Kay said, 'I never did.'

'You ought to set to work,' Arnold said, 'to make yourself a Box like mine that would take you where you would meet with Alexander. As to the Present (not that this is the Present, it seems like the Future), I do not know where he is, but he exists for ever in the Past. He was the finest young man that ever trod this planet: beautiful, like young Apollo. The sculptors and the painters, when they wanted to carve or to paint a god, all turned to him. He was all beauty and strength and wisdom. He had only to ride down the street on that horse of his, that spoke with a man's voice, and every man would come out with his weapons to follow him to the world's end. Everybody saw that he was the king. In the camps, the men would hurl the spear, or shoot with the bow, or throw the quoit, or wrestle or run: he could beat the best of them at all these things. And then, too, think of his Army, the Earth Shaking, and his Fleet, the Sea Taming, and his Horses, the Thunder Bearing, and his Trumpets, the Spirit Lifting. Think of his god-like scheme of making the world one kingdom under one worth-while king instead of all these little dreary kings. But, of course, you know of this as well as I do. You have seen Alexander . . .'

'No, indeed,' Kay said, 'I have not.'

'Well, it is hard to believe that anybody has not seen Alexander,' Arnold said, 'for who knows what Beauty is that has not? His hair is beautiful, young man, he has marvellous eyes, and he has a way of leaping on to his horse's back or into his chariot. I saw him last driving in a chariot with white horses. He was dressed in leopard-skins and had a crown of laurels on his brows, and people flung themselves down, crying that he was a god . . .' He paused for a moment, thinking of Alexander.

'I am behind in my Time, if you understand me, young man. I was in the Anno Domini, and then I went back into the Past and the Anno Domini has moved on and I have only partly moved on, or perhaps I have moved on too far, if you understand.'

'I think I do partly understand,' Kay said. 'It was Ramon Lully who came to you from Spain with the Elixir.'

'I never paid much attention to the man's name,' Arnold said. 'He was a thinker of my time. I do not believe in the thinkers of my time. Now the thinker of Alexander's time—Alexander's teacher, Aristotle—he was a real thinker.'

'Do you know, I have got your Box of Delights at present,' Kay said. 'It belongs really to the man who came to you with the Elixir.'

'It is a trivial toy,' Arnold said. 'I ought to have let that Spaniard take it and had his Elixir in exchange, and drunken deep of it; then I could have gone on and on with Alexander over the Chorasmian Wastes and other Wastes.

'But permit me to offer you these raisins. I dried them myself in the sun. Alexander used raisins in his campaigns. Other soldiers wanted meat, bread, wines, sweetmeats; Alexander only a few raisins and a little water.

'What was the race that you said that you belonged to, young man?'

'The English,' Kay said.

'Some very small unimportant race,' Arnold answered. 'I had a list of all the nations of the world that marched with Alexander; there were no English among them. We were in a great plain covered with tents. One morning he hung out his golden banner, and all those countless nations blew their trumpets and hung out their standards and away we went. It took a week for the army to pass out of the plain, and we went on over mountains and across rivers, and the cities we visited we sacked; but usually the cities opened their gates to us and came out with gold and silver and precious stones.

'But allow me to offer you this pomegranate.'

Kay ate the pomegranate and a second one which the old man offered. The old man stood up and said:

'Now, there was one special thing about Alexander that I have not yet told you; when I have told you this you will understand why it was that his soldiers thought that he was a god.

'We were marching, if you understand, across a burning waste. Whether it was the Chorasmian Waste, or the Acheronian Waste, I cannot now be sure. It may perhaps have been the Gedrosian Waste. Know only that it was a burning pitiless desert of glare and death and dead men's bones. There were asps in the sand. The glare of that sand made men's blood so thin that an asp-bite killed in three minutes. Men died of asps, thirst, glare and giddiness. The sand stretched, the sky arched, glare below, glare above, and the moon at night in terrible cold with jackals howling. I made a poem of the sky:

"It arched, it arched,
We marched, we marched,
And parched and parched."

'Some men's tongues shrivelled dry and dropped out with the parching. No water there, no drink: only pebbles and buttons to freshen our mouths with.

'Now, some of the soldiers found in a rock at dawn a little scoop of cold water. They thought, "Now we will win promotion for ourselves by taking this to Alexander," so they brought it to him. It was not more than is in this shell here, but in that place, under that sun, it was Life itself, young Master. Did Alexander drink it and give those men promotion? He was as thirsty as any soldier there. "No," he said, "I will not touch what I cannot share with my men," and he poured it out in the sand to his Fortune. I tell you once more, that there has been nobody in this world like Alexander.

'Allow me, now, to recommend to you this egg of the Island Pheasant which I have baked for you. For salt, here is salt of the sea, and for bread this meal of pounded almond. Eat, eat, for the young can enjoy what they eat.'

Kay ate gladly; for he was indeed hungry.

'You mentioned, young man,' Arnold said suddenly, 'a certain person who had made a figure in the world.'

'Julius Cæsar?' Kay said.

'Do not name that person to me. No, another whose name I didn't catch. You called him great.'

'Napoleon?'

'That was the name,' the old man said. 'Who was he?'

'He was a soldier who conquered nearly all Europe,' Kay said.

'Conquered Europe! That miserable collection of barbarians conquered. Could it ever be anything but conquered?' Arnold said. 'And you dare to place these petty pugilists of yours beside the god-like figure of

Alexander. You talk with parochial insolence. Were you not so ignorant, it would be my duty to strike you dead . . . that you debase thus a god-like and glorious figure, whose achievements cannot be weighed because there is no balance with which to weigh them, nor other with whom to compare him.

'Presently, young man, I shall perfect yet another Box, much greater than any that I have made yet. I entered the Past of Europe by one Box; I entered the Past of Asia by another; but with this third box I will go after Alexander, where he rides on some planet, in some starry place in heaven. I will harness the comets for him, and we will come down, young man, and we will sweep away all these paltry kings and you English with tails.'

'We haven't got tails,' Kay said.

'You know nothing even of your own race,' Arnold said angrily, 'and you dare to presume to speak about Alexander.'

Kay was, by this time, terrified of Arnold of Todi, this extraordinary figure of fun, whose matted beard was stuck with twigs and leaves, whose coat was of sail, palm-leaf and old leather, who seemed to be seven hundred years old and to have gone with Alexander the Great into India. He was now standing with flaming eyes, glaring down at Kay.

'Mad as a hatter,' Kay thought. 'Now he will probably tear me piecemeal.'

At this instant he heard himself called: 'Kay! Kay!' There behind him in a little bay of the sea, so bright and beautiful, were two figures whom he saw to be Herne the Hunter and the woman of the oak-tree. On their left hands were these curious rings with the longways crosses upon them.

'Come, Kay,' they said. 'We can take you home. You must not be lost in the Past in this way.'

'Could you take Arnold of Todi too?' he said. 'He has been most awfully kind to me.'

'Yes,' they said, 'let him come.'

Kay did not quite see how they were to come, but, when they reached the beach, the two called and out of the sea there came tumbling the most beautiful dolphins, drawing a chariot made of one big sea-shell, of the colour of mother-of-pearl.

By the side of these were three bigger dolphins, one, with no saddle, for Herne the Hunter, two, with high-backed saddles of white and scarlet coral, and stirrups and reins of amber beads, for Kay and Arnold.

'You will mount these, Kay,' the lady said, as she stepped into her chariot and gathered the long reins of seaweed; 'then follow me.'

'Stick on tight,' Herne said. 'They're odd mounts at first.'

The woman had already set off in her chariot. Kay, Herne and Arnold mounted: the dolphins at once leaped from the water, plunged in, and again leaped out, on the long rush towards home. Soon, they were speeding level with the chariot, going swifter and swifter, racing fish against fish, while the woman called to the team and sang to them:

'Fin on, leap, skim the foam,
Swim the green toppling comb
Of blue seas rolling home
Under the west wind
From Yucatan to Ind.

'Shear the sea-flowers to stubbles,
Crush the blue floor to bubbles,
Gallop, forget your troubles,
Skimming in gladness
The salt sea's madness.

'Come, flying-fish, come, whales,
Come, mermaids with bright scales,
Come, gulls that ride on gales,
And albatrosses
That no gale tosses,

'Speed with us as we thrust
The blue ways none can trust,
The green ways without dust,
The salt ways foaming;
Attend our homing.'

Instantly, as they sped, the mermaids shot to the surface beside them; many white, grey and gleaming birds swooped out of heaven to them; the whales surged out from below, snorting out glittering fountains. With little whickering flickers the flying-fish leaped beside them like tiny silver arrows. The first moment or two, on setting forth, had been terrifying, but now, in all this glitter and leap and speed, with the lady singing, the dolphins ever going faster, the mermaids splashing water at him, and himself splashing water back at the mermaids, Kay loved it more than anything that had ever happened to him. It was exquisite to feel the dolphins quivering to the leap, and to surge upwards into the bright light with flying-fish sparkling on each side; then to surge down into the water, scattering the spray like bright fire, full of rainbows, then to leap on and on, wave after wave, mile after mile. In the thrill and delight of this leaping journey Kay fell asleep. He was presently aware of Arnold getting off his dolphin at Tibbs Wharf near the *Lock and Key*. He half opened his eyes, thought he heard the church bells chime, and then woke up drowsily in his seat at Seekings, under the valance of the dressing-table, where the Box lay on the floor. He went down to lunch. It was lunch-time and the others were there.

'Well, Kay,' Jemima said, after a while, 'you have seemed to us half-asleep ever since lunch began. Aren't you going to say something?'

'Say something?' Kay said. 'Where is Arnold?'

'Arnold?' they said. 'Who's Arnold?'

'It's very odd,' Kay said, and he went to the window in order that he might pull himself together. It was very strange, but there at the top of the garden was a strange figure of fun, dressed seemingly in old leather, bits of sail and palm-leaf, staring with admiration at the church tower.

Kay hurried out to speak to him, but he was no longer there.

CHAPTER ELEVEN

When he returned to the house, Maria had a little special edition of the Tatchester paper.

'YET ANOTHER CLERICAL OUTRAGE'

'Kay,' she said, 'you're losing all the fun. They've tried to scrobble another clergyman who was walking into Tatchester from Tineton.'

'Did they get him?' Kay asked.

'No, they didn't get him,' Maria said. 'Here is the account. I'll read it.

'CHURCH BANDITS FOILED

'It now seems undoubted that the recent outrages at Tatchester are the work of an organised gang, sworn probably by some subversive maniac to prevent the millennial celebrations. We are happy to state that on this occasion the scoundrels were defeated. The Reverend Josiah Stalwart, Rector of Tineton, had undertaken, in answer to the Archbishop's plea, to be prepared in case of need to help with the services in the Cathedral tonight. While proceeding to Tatchester along the Roman Road he was passed by a dark motor-car in which were two men. The car stopped, the two men got out and coming towards him asked if he would like a lift. He noticed that one of the men had a white splash upon his leggings and held his right hand behind his back. Not quite liking their looks, and being naturally on his guard in view of recent events in Tatchester, he declined the lift and at once the taller man attempted to fling over his head what seemed like a felt bag, while the accomplice tried to deal him a short arm punch in the ribs. The Reverend Stalwart avoided the felt bag and smote his shorter assailant on the head with the holly cudgel which had been lately presented to him by his admiring col-leagues of the Tineton Hockey Team, which he has so often lead to victory. Being an exceedingly athletic gentleman as well as a very good heavyweight boxer, Mr. Stalwart proceeded to deal with the bagman. The ruffians, realising too late the kind of man with whom they had to deal, exchanged rapid passwords, which the Reverend Stalwart thinks may be of assistance to the Police. The shorter man said, 'Kool slop.' The taller man said, 'Mizzle.' They succeeded in tripping the reverend gentleman by a throw unknown to him, darted into the car, the engine of which had been kept running, and were at once out of sight, going at great speed.

'Mr. Stalwart proceeded at once to Tatchester Police Station and a full description of both bandits is being broadcast at half-hourly intervals from all stations. Mr. Stalwart is convinced that both criminals will bear marks of their meeting with him for some weeks.

'We would point out that the mystic words uttered by the reprobates are common thieves' slang: 'Kool slop' is what is called back slang: the words Look, Police turned backwards. It is a familiar warning in the underworld. The other word, 'Mizzle,' of doubtful derivation, means escape, fly or hurry away.

'It is hardly credible that armed bandits should thus beset a public highway in broad daylight to kidnap members of a holy calling. We are delighted that, in this case, a little resolution and British pluck have defeated their purpose. Needless to say, the precautions of the Police have been trebled on every road leading to Tatchester. In future no clergyman will proceed to Tatchester to take Christmas duty save under Police protection.

'We understand that the Tineton Hockey Club has sent a long telegram of congratulation to their victorious captain.

'You see,' Maria said, 'they've been diddled this time. The Reverend Josiah must be a bit of a boy to take on two.'

'I say, they will be furious,' Kay said.

'I don't know,' Maria said. 'You see here, the Stop Press News. They've got the two Rectors and Curates from the Parish Churches in Tatchester: the Reverend Arthur Pure, the Reverend William Godley, Thomas Holyport and Charles Lectern: all disappeared, no one knows how. "Consternation and anguish in Rectory and Curacy alike." '

It was now very nearly half-past two. Kay went back to his room thinking: 'They've had a good deal of success, but this set-back, coming at this time, will make Abner furious; and he may proceed to extremes. I must find out what he intends to do.'

He locked himself into his room and climbed underneath the valance of the dressing-table. He turned the knob of the Box, so that he might go swiftly and little to Abner's room at Chester Hills.

He was set down in the upper corridor of the Theological College, near a door that stood ajar under the little label 'Chief.' Kay listened near this door. Nobody seemed to be within. He peeped in: no one was there. He slipped inside and then, as he wished to examine the room, he resumed his proper shape and closed the door. The door clicked to with a snap. When it was fastened he realised, too late, that it was a spring lock. He was shut in.

'That may be awkward,' he thought. 'But here I am in Abner's own room; I must look about to see what I can see.'

By the clock on a little table near the wall, he saw that it was two-twenty-seven. 'I'm early for the meeting,' he thought. 'I've got a minute or two, before they come.'

Plainly this part of the house was of the sixteenth century, or more than a hundred years older than the rest of the building. It was a small, irregular room, with a low ceiling and little Elizabethan windows, still glazed with old, thick, greenish glass in little panes like the bottoms of bottles. The walls were covered with tapestries, much worn and faded. The mantel was great, solid, black oak reaching to the ceiling, all carved with grotesque figures. There was a small alcove at the room's end; it contained a hard, little camp-bed that had not yet been made.

'Abner may be fond of food,' Kay thought, 'but he's pretty tough if he sleeps in a bed like this.'

There were books in the bookshelves: *Sermons on Several Occasions*, Tillotson's *Sermons*, Dr. Beatty's *Sermons*, Dr. South's *Sermons*, the Reverend Hart's *Sermons*, the Reverend George Crabbe's *Sermons*, *Sermons for the Year*, etc., etc.; but on all the books the dust was thick. Kay went to the window to see what could be seen from it. The window was shut and the glass was so thick that he could not see through it. To his surprise, when he opened it, the window, which had looked like four loopholes divided by stone mullions, opened all in one piece. He found that it opened on a charming little leads between two pitches of steep roof. There were ladders up these pitches and, apparently, ladders leading down on the other sides of them. 'Here is a way of escape,' Kay thought, 'in case of need.' He could judge from the shadows that this window opened to the south-east.

After this, Kay spent a minute poking the knobs in the carved mantelpiece, hoping that one of them might work a spring and reveal a secret stair. Then, suddenly, he heard voices just outside the door.

Abner was saying, 'But I left this door ajar!'

A key pressed into the lock. Kay just had time to press the knob of his Box so that he might go small when the door opened and Abner and Joe came in. Kay squeezed into a recess by the fireplace behind the tapestry.

'Funny thing about that door,' Abner said. 'I left it ajar purposely. Someone's been in here and left the window open.'

He shut the window. He went into the alcove, took a hasty glance round under the bed and behind the tapestries: 'I'll enquire about that door and window,' he said. 'I wonder who's been in. Do you know who's been in?'

'No, Chief,' Joe said. 'Of course I don't.'

'Well, why don't you? You've been in charge here while my wife and I have been in Tatchester. Have you been in?'

'No,' Joe said. 'Of course I haven't.'

'No "of course" about it,' Abner snapped. 'But as I've told you all many times, there's a little trap in store for the man who comes prying in here and you're most of you too scared to try it. I shall know tonight who's been in. Look out for squalls if I find it's you.'

'It wasn't me.'

'Now then, listen to me. Who sent those two fools to tackle Josiah Stalwart?'

'I did,' Joe growled.

'Didn't I give strict orders that no scrobbling party was to consist of less than four; three to scrobble, one to keep the car ready?'

'That was before we were short-handed.'

'Did I or did I not give those orders?'

'I suppose you did.'

'Don't you know that I did?'

'Now, Chief,' Joe said, 'chuck it. I'd have sent four after Stalwart if I'd had four to send. I hadn't four. You never told us Stalwart was a champ. We didn't know. You told me I was to get him scrobbled and I did what we could. If you had seen Eleven and Twelve before Seventeen dressed their wounds you might feel a little sorry for them.'

'Sorry? I'd have made them a little sorry. What did Stalwart do to them, two against one, too?'

'He cracked Twelve's crown across, a fair treat. He give Eleven an eye like a stained-glass window. They're marked for a month, the pair.'

'And a jolly good job,' Abner said. 'I wish Stalwart had

given them each a cauliflower ear. I wish he'd knocked their silly noses west and banged their ribs blue, and yours, too.'

'Now, now, Chief,' Joe said. 'That's not fair. They've only done their duty and were badly hurt doing it.'

'They were hurt disobeying plain orders.'

'Chief,' Joe said, 'we'll set that aside, if you don't mind. I've other things to say to you now.

'You see, Chief, while you've been in Tatchester, I've been thinking of things, and I've made up my mind.'

'Oh,' Abner said. 'Repeat that, will you?'

'I've made up my mind,' Joe said.

'So you made up your mind, did you?' Abner asked.

'Yes, Chief, I did.'

'I didn't know you had a mind, but I am glad to hear it. And so you've made it up?'

'Yes, Chief, I have.'

'What did you decide?' Abner asked.

'Tomorrow's Christmas Day.'

'So I hear. What about it?'

'Christmas Day's rather a special day. We don't like keeping all those poor captives away from their homes on Christmas Day.'

'*We* don't like. Who are *we*?'

'All the lot of us. It's not Christmas dealing. We've spread a lot of misery taking these poor people, just now; fathers from children, husbands from wives, and the poor little Choir-boys who'd been looking forward to hanging up their stockings. It's more than we can bear.'

'Well?' Abner asked.

'We want you to return all the captives tonight, by air, with a ten-pound note apiece, the ones we got at the bank-robbery. Then the whole thing would pass off as a rag . . .

and it would tell in our favour, if we ever come to be tried.'

'So,' Abner said, '*we* don't like, and *we* want this and that; and a made-up mind all piping hot with mutiny. Were you thinking of getting rid of little Abner, Joe, and then putting in for the command yourself? You, with a made-up mind, would run this brotherhood to some tune.'

'I was thinking nothing of the sort, Chief,' Joe said. 'But you're making a mistake and so we warn you.'

'Ah,' Abner said, 'a mistake. Well, forewarned is forarmed. Thank you, Joe. And now, we'll go down to see the captives.'

'There was another thing we've got to speak about,' Joe said stubbornly.

'*Got* to speak about,' Abner said. 'Then speak it . . . proceed.'

'I've been telling them about your magic and that,' Joe said. 'What we don't see is why you don't use magic to find this Box that you set such store by.'

'You're a cricketer, aren't you, Joe?' Abner said, 'a fast bowler, with a terrifying in-swerve?'

'I suppose I can plug 'em in a bit,' Joe said, with modest pride.

'Sometimes I suppose even you come up against a bat who hits you all round the compass?'

'That might happen to anyone,' Joe said.

'It's the same with magic,' Abner said. 'You don't believe in magic, I think, but perhaps this may convince you. Watch, now . . .'

He lifted his hand in a strange way and uttered some foreign words in a loud, clear voice. Instantly, the figure of a boy, with a bony, unintelligent and unpleasant face, appeared through Abner's desk.

'What d'ye want me for now?' he growled.

'No pertness,' Abner said. 'Tell the gentleman what Cole Hawlings did with his Box.'

'He gave it to somebody to keep for him,' the Boy said. 'I told you that before.'

'Learn civility,' Abner said. 'To whom did he give it?'

'I don't know. He put spells round it. I couldn't see the person. Let me go.'

'If you're not careful and civil I'll peg you into the waterfall,' Abner said. 'Am I nearer to getting the Box than I was?'

'Yes. You're very near to it,' the Boy said.

'Shall I get it?'

'You'll have it under your hand today. Now I want to go—I've told you everything.'

'Don't try to dictate to me,' Abner said. 'The gentleman would like to ask you something. Ask him anything you want to know, Joe.'

Joe did not much relish speaking to the Boy, but at last asked:

'What is in this Box?'

'The way into the Past. I will not be questioned by you.'

'Yes, you will,' Abner said. 'Anything else, Joe?'

'Yes,' Joe said, 'there is. If Cole Hawlings had hold of this Box, why couldn't he go into the Past by it and escape from Abner here?'

'The Master there put spells on it. Shut your mouth now and let me go,' the Boy said angrily.

'You shall suffer for this,' Abner said. 'Is there anything more you wish to ask, Joe?'

'Yes,' Joe said. 'What will win the National?'

'Kubbadar, by seven lengths. Now I'm going.'

'Wait, my young insolent friend,' Abner said. 'You will have a little lesson before you go. Come here.'

As the Boy approached, Abner tapped him on the top of his head with a time-table. The head at once telescoped into the chest, and the legs telescoped into his body.

'Off, now,' Abner said. 'You'll stay plugged under the waterfall for seven weeks for insolence. Perhaps that may teach you . . .'

The Boy vanished into the desk, howling loudly from the middle of his chest.

'A general tendency to mutiny, it seems,' Abner said. 'I must take steps, I see. Now come on down to the Zoo.'

Kay was peering from his little cranny to see exactly what was done. Abner touched something, Kay could not see what, in the corner over his head; then he went to the hearth-rug and stamped upon it with some force. There came a clicking, clacking noise. Kay saw the fireplace slide open like a door, revealing a lift lit with an electric light.

'Come on, then,' Abner said.

The two men stepped into the lift. Kay, who was only two feet from the door of it, darted into it after them as the fireplace closed-to upon them. Abner pressed a red button in the lift wall and the lift slowly began to move down. Kay counted and tried to guess how far down it went. It went slowly. It passed two different possible landings. When at last it stopped it did so with a jolt as though it were at the bottom of its shaft. The Chief opened the door; as he and Joe stepped out, Kay followed.

He was in a wide, high cavern or gallery in the rock. It

stretched out to right and to left. It was not less than fourteen feet high by ten broad. It had every sign of being a natural cavern worn by water and smoothed underfoot by man. In the main, it was now a dry cavern. The walls glistened with wet here and there; in some places they shone as from some quartz-crystal in the rock. There was a little pause and silence when they left the lift. Kay heard water dropping, drop by drop, like the tick of a very slow clock. Far, far away, too, water was running over a fall.

The two men turned to the right; Kay followed. At every ten yards or so Abner would stop, turn out the light and turn on another to light the way ahead. When they had gone perhaps forty yards from the lift, Kay saw what seemed like a range of ships' cabins stretching along the side of the gallery. Abner went to the door of the first of these, pulled aside a shutter, turned on a light to light the cell within and spoke through the opening:

'And how is the dear Bishop?' he said. 'Christmas sermon getting on well? Well, well, well! And will you tell me where the package is?'

'I tell you, ruffian,' the Bishop answered, 'that I know nothing of any package. These pleasantries had better cease.'

'Tell me where the package is,' Abner said, 'and they shall cease, and starvation shall cease. You shall have a savoury omelet and coffee and rolls and honey. What, you won't? Water from the well, then, and darkness to meditate upon it.'

He switched out the light, fastened the shutter and moved to another door.

'Dean,' he said, 'still cheerful? Splendid! Can you tell me of the package yet? What, you don't know anything about it? That won't do for me, my Dean: think again. Keep cheerful.'

He switched out the light and moved to another door.

'Ha,' he said, 'the Precentor, I think.' Here he began a song:

> 'Tell me, shepherd, have you seen
> My package pass this way?'

'A strait-jacket's on its way to you,' the Precentor said, 'and then you'll sing another tune. What d'you mean by a "package" and shutting us up here?'

'Oh, a proud stomach, still?' Abner said. 'A little cold water is very cold Christmas fare, you'll find, and not one of you proud prelates will taste more until you tell me where the package is.'

He went from cell to cell asking the inmates where the Box was. Some said, 'We don't know what you mean.' Others said, 'You are mad. The Police will soon run you down, to be sure.'

'Don't you be too sure,' Abner said. 'And here, I think, are the Canons Minor. How that brings back my Latin—major, minor, minimus! And are my Minor Canons going to tell me of the package?'

'A judge and jury will give you your package, and a heavy package it will be and you will carry it for a long time,' said young Canon Doctrine, who had once been the famous three-quarter.

By this time Abner had reached the end of the cells. He raised his voice so that he could be heard all along the gallery.

'So you are all stubborn,' he said. 'You'll find that I'm stubborn, and the rock is stubborn and not all the Police in Europe could find you where you are now. One of you knows where this package is. Tell me and you shall be at home within the day. If not, I can last and the rock will last, but I don't think you will.'

He then turned to Joe, who was at his side.

'By the way, Joe,' he said, still in his loud voice, 'this cell at the end here—we put the Earl into it, you remember, because he wouldn't pay the ransom. Seven years ago, I think it was: you remember?'

'I remember well,' Joe said. 'A dark, handsome man, the Earl: very well-dressed.'

'That's the man,' Abner said, unlocking the cell door. 'Just step in, will you, and see if his bones are still there? The ransom didn't come, if you recollect, but I expect the rats did, or am I wrong?'

Kay saw Joe step into the lighted cell and pretend to rummage in the corners.

'Do you see any bones still?' Abner asked.

'Just the skull and a rib or two,' Joe answered. 'Oh, and his marriage ring.'

'Quite so,' Abner said, locking him into the cell and switching out the light. 'And now, my dear Joe, with the made-up mind, meditate with these holy men on the errors of your ways. Another time you may not be so brave as to tell me that I am making a mistake.'

Joe, who was a very strong man, leapt at the door and beat upon it. 'Let me out, you hound,' he cried. 'Let me out, or I'll wring your neck.'

'You mean, "*and* I'll wring your neck," ' Abner said. 'I'll keep you there for the present, thank you, because I think you really might. Sleep well, dear Joe. The floor of that cell is a little uneven, but you won't notice it much after the first week.'

Joe continued to beat upon the door and to shout threats and curses. Abner moved away whistling a few bars of Schubert's Unfinished Symphony. Kay, who was horror-struck, moved away after him. Then suddenly, from a cell not yet visited, Peter's voice piped up.

'If you please,' Peter said, 'I think I know where the package that you want is.'

'Ha,' Abner said, 'so! And where is the package?'

'I can't explain it,' Peter said, 'but I could take you there.'

'Oh, could you?' Abner said. 'And give us the slip on the way, no doubt. We are not quite so green. Where is it?'

'Please I can't explain,' Peter said.

'I say that you can explain. Where is it? In Seekings House? In the garden? In the town? At the Inn? Where is it?'

'I think it's peeping out of a rabbit-burrow somewhere on King Arthur's Camp, please,' Peter said.

'Whereabouts on the Camp?' Abner said.

'I could take you to it,' Peter said, 'but I can't explain just where.'

'Oh yes, you can,' Abner said. 'You could mark the very place on a six-inch-to-the-mile map. When did you see it?'

'If you please, I thought I saw a package just before they scrobbled the Punch and Judy man up on the Bottler's Down.'

'Ha,' Abner said. 'Well, you thought wrong, then; think again. . . . And think of mushrooms for breakfast. Have you thought of them?'

'Yes, please sir,' Peter said.

'Well, that's all the breakfast you'll get,' Abner said.

'That may teach you not to try to deceive me another time. Now snivel!'

He moved away up the gallery so rapidly that Kay could hardly keep pace. As he came near Joe's cell Joe cried:

'Let me out, Abner, let me out, I say!' Finding that his cries had no effect and that Abner was going past paying no attention, he changed his tone: 'I say, old man,' he said, 'a joke's a joke, but don't leave an old pal here in the dark: not old Joe, Abner.'

'Yes, old Joe,' Abner replied. He had gone past Joe's cell when something seemed to strike him. 'By the way, Joe,' he said, 'you don't believe in magic, do you?'

Instantly, out of the air, there came little faces, grinning and wicked. They had pointed ears and pointed teeth. These faces flitted swiftly through the bars of Joe's cell; they buzzed round Joe's head, and spoke, sometimes in squeaky, sometimes in shrill and sometimes in very musical voices: 'You don't believe in magic, do you, Joe?' Joe beat at them as though they were wasps, but they were too quick to be hit.

Abner watched the effect of these imps with their words upon Joe's terror-stricken face. 'No, he doesn't believe in magic, Joe doesn't,' he said. 'However, take your time. You will, presently, Joe,' he said; and at that he switched out the light and marched on, turning swiftly up a gallery which Kay had not noticed. Kay followed, running, where Abner's footsteps led. Presently a light went up. Abner had opened the door into a lighted room; Kay slipped into the room behind Abner before the door closed.

It was a bare room carpeted with a thick red carpet. Certain strange magical symbols were painted on the walls in red. In the middle of the room on a pedestal was a bronze head which Kay had seen before. Kay noticed that the bronze head's eyelids were closed and the head drooped as though asleep when he entered the room, but, as Abner lifted his right hand, the eyelids opened, the head raised itself, the lips moved and a voice from within it said, 'Command me, Master.'

'Tell me of our plans,' Abner said.

The voice spoke from the head: 'Your agents have now captured every clergyman attached to the Cathedral, as well as most of the Cathedral servants and staff.'

'Is anything going wrong?'

'Yes,' the bronze head replied. 'You should have begun (as I told you) much later in the day. You have given them time to act against you.'

'Don't criticise me, Slave,' Abner said; and the head at once cowered down upon the pedestal and began to whimper.

'Stop that,' Abner said. 'Tell me, now, what are they trying to do against me?'

'All sorts of things,' the head said. 'Mainly telephoning, and telegraphing, trying to get substitutes.'

'With what success?' Abner said.

'Not much yet,' the head said. 'It is Christmas. All the clergy are busy in their own parishes. But substitutes will be found. There is a body of Friends of the Cathedral; I told you of them: the Tatchester Trusties: they are the ones. They will rake up clergy from all sorts of places, you will see.'

'Will I?' Abner said. 'Will they? We'll try that.'

He raised his right hand in a peculiar manner. Instantly, a red-winged figure rose up out of the floor and bowed before him.

'Cut all the Tatchester telephone-wires and telegraph-wires,' he said. 'Wait. Bring in those Tatchester Trusties.'

'I go, sir,' the winged figure said and disappeared through the ceiling.

'That won't see you very far,' the brazen head said. 'Some of the substitute clergy have already started.'

Abner raised his right hand again. Instantly, another red figure rose from the floor:

'Command me, Master,' it said.

'Dislocate all railway traffic for twenty miles round Tatchester. Jam the points.'

'I go, sir,' the figure answered and disappeared through the ceiling.

'That won't be much use,' the bronze head said. 'They will come by road.'

Abner raised his hand again. A third red figure rose from the floor and asked for orders.

'Make every road impassable for twenty miles round Tatchester,' he said. 'But stay, that won't be enough. We must make the air impassable too. Stay here one moment.'

He lifted his left hand in a strange way and, instantly, an old, old crone was thrust through the floor by little red hands, towards him. She looked so old that she might have been a thousand years or more: nose and chin almost met; her face was the colour of old wood. She seemed terrified of Abner.

'What d'you want with me, Master?' she said.

'I want a storm out of the north and the east,' Abner said, 'with snow.'

'I can't give it. I can't give it,' the old woman said. 'You ask too much. I can only sell a storm for a great sum—a bag of amethysts.'

'Give me a storm from the north and the east,' Abner

said, 'or I will torment you in a way that you'll remember.'

'No, give me at least half a bag of amethysts,' the old woman said, 'for I need them for a cordial that I am making.'

'I will give you a quarter bag,' Abner said. 'Now let me have the storm.'

He produced from his pocket a little canvas bag which did contain amethysts: Kay saw the stones as he emptied them out. A very meagre quarter of the bag was handed to the old woman, who produced in turn from her pocket a little leather bag tied with three strings at the mouth.

'Don't open more than two of those strings,' the old woman said, warningly, 'or you may be sorry.'

'Don't tell me how I am to proceed,' Abner said. 'Away with her!' At once the little red hands plucked the old woman away.

'Servant, here!' Abner cried to the red figure. 'Away with this to Tatchester. Open two strings from the mouth of this bag and fill the roads and the air with snow, so that neither cars nor aeroplanes shall come near Tatchester: let any clergyman who tries to get there be buried six feet in snow and not be found until the spring.'

'He cannot do that,' the brazen head said. 'He cannot take life.'

'Do not interrupt me, you,' Abner said. 'As for you, Servant, take that bag to Tatchester. Open all the strings and flood that countryside with the deepest snow since Wolves Ran. Make the drifts eight feet deep round each Cathedral door. Away with you.'

'I go, sir,' the figure said and vanished through the ceiling.

Abner turned to the brazen head.

'You have interrupted me, you have criticised me,' he said. 'All this establishment seems given over to mutiny. I will have you learn respect. You shall be upside down for a while.'

'I implore you, Master, not,' the head said, whimpering.

'I say, yes,' Abner said. He plucked the head from its pedestal and jammed it violently down upon it upside down. It whimpered and wailed in that position.

'Shut up,' Abner said. 'Listen to me, and tell me truth: Am I to have that Box today?' he asked.

'You will have it under your hand,' the head said.

'To do what I like with?'

'To toss and to tumble. It will be your plaything.'

'Then I can open the sluices when I choose?' he asked.

'Whenever you choose.'

'Ha,' Abner said. 'Who will bring me the Box?'

'It will come under your hand,' the head said.

Kay was by this time trembling lest the head should say where the Box was at the moment. It was at this instant that the poor upside-down eyes caught sight of the tiny figure of Kay near the door. The eyes showed astonishment, then Kay felt that they showed excitement. 'He'll betray me now,' Kay thought, 'so as to be turned right-side-up again.' Then he saw that the head was rebelling against Abner for being turned upside-down, one of the eyes winked at Kay to reassure him.

'What are you rolling your eyes for?' Abner asked.

'You'd roll *your* eyes if you were upside-down,' the head said.

'Who will bring me the Box?' Abner repeated.

'The spells won't let me say.'

'How soon will it be here?'

'It's on its way to you now.'

'Is it near?'

'It is very near.'

'Right,' Abner said. 'Now mend your manners there.'

'Oh dear,' Kay thought. 'He is to have the Box after all, and what will happen to me when he gets it? And what will happen to all the captives? And what did he mean by "opening the sluices"? Did he mean that he is going to let water into the caves?'

He had no time to consider these questions, for Abner strode swiftly out of the room; Kay had to follow him at once to avoid being shut in. Abner moved so swiftly to the left, that Kay lost touch with him. Following on, as fast as he could, he heard something which made his heart leap:

'So Miss Caroline Louisa,' Abner was saying, in some dark den in the rock. 'You would not tell me about the Box, though you must know all about it. Now you may like to know that it is on its way to me; nothing can stop its coming to me.

'Once before you stood in my way and were the cause of great trouble to me and mine. I promised then that I would be even with you. I am going to be even with you, never fear, quite soon; as even as water can make me, for water, when released, finds its own level, they say. This time I shall pay off all our old scores. Good-bye.'

Caroline Louisa did not answer, but Kay heard her cough and knew that she was there. Abner came striding back past Kay; there came a sudden noise of a door rolling in a groove; the cave became suddenly bright with light.

Kay saw that a door in the rock had slid back; beyond

it, a curious motor-car, thickly sprinkled with snow, was being opened by masked men, who dragged from it two figures whose arms and legs were lashed and whose heads were in felt bags.

'Ha,' Abner said, 'the Tatchester Trusties, I presume. Working, no doubt, double time, like good friends of the Cathedral, to find clergy for the services. Excellent work, but it must now be interrupted for the time. First, action, then, contemplation. Remove them to the cells . . . but stay one moment . . . it is snowing, I perceive.'

'Snowing,' one of the masked men said. 'You've said it. I never knew anything like it. It came on all of a sudden, so blind I thought we'd never get through.'

'Nice seasonable Christmas weather,' Abner said. 'A white Christmas, eh? Well, well; remove them.'

After the two men had been dragged away into the darkness of the corridor, Abner went to a recess where there was something which looked like a typewriter let into the rock; he touched some of the keys of this, then spoke into the mouthpiece:

'Is this the *Tatchester Evening News*?' he asked. 'The News and Associated Papers? . . . Father Boddledale speaking. I wish to give a message to your evening edition—perhaps you could make it a special edition—that there need be no alarm whatever about the services in the Cathedral at Tatchester. Got that? Even if none of the missing clergy be restored in time, it will be possible for my organisation to supply all the services with qualified clergy. . . . You can print a special edition to that effect at once, can you? . . . Actually have the copies in the streets in half an hour, can you? . . . Splendid! . . . Let there be no anxiety whatever. And you will acquaint the London evening papers, will you, that all is arranged? . . .

Father Boddledale of the Ecclesiastical Training Centre will see that services are supplied, although there can be little doubt that the practical jokers, for such they must be, will relent in time. . . . Thank you so much. And will you allow me to wish you the very happiest of New Years and of Christmastides? Are you running any particular Christmas charity for the Old or the Sick or the Poor? . . . Oh! will you allow me to put my name down for twenty-five pounds? . . . Father Boddledale. . . . Yes: B-o-d-d-l-e- . . . Thank you. . . . A most happy Christmas. . . . Thank you. And add that Father Boddledale wishes the good people of Tatchester a most happy Christmas and New Year. . . . Thank you.'

He closed the recess and moved away; Kay saw a happy smile upon his features.

In deep thought, Abner moved along the rocky gallery. Kay followed with some difficulty, for this gallery was badly lit. Kay heard a continual murmur of water falling. Presently, he judged that this noise was not from falling water, but from violent sobbing and lamenting. When they came near to the noise, Abner turned on a light. Kay could see an iron cage, at the bars of which were pressed some white faces, whose haggard, dark eyes made black patches on the flesh.

'Ha,' Abner said, 'my vocal and orchestral friends from Tatchester! The Choir, I think? And is our cocoa as you like it? And do you admire our brand of bun? Now listen to me, boys. There is something very disgusting to me in the undisguised grief of boys who do not carry handker-chiefs and use the backs of their hands. Stop snivelling, you little beasts. Do I see Dr. Blowpipe, the famous Organist? Now then, tell me, you, Dr. Blowpipe, and you, Organist's Assistant, and you, members of the Tatchester

Choir, which of you has the Box of Delights and where is it?'

Dr. Blowpipe and some of the elder members of the Choir asked him what on earth he meant.

'You know quite well what I mean,' Abner said. 'Where is it: Cole Hawlings' Box of Delights?'

All repeated that they knew nothing whatever about any box; they protested against their imprisonment and asked to be set free at once.

'Very well,' Abner said. 'You have had your chance, then; your bloods will be on your own heads. You are doomed. Tonight there will be no more Choir-boy, no more tenor nor baritone nor bass, no more Dr. Blowpipe. Somebody else will play the "Requiem in D Minor" and very soon; because little Abner will turn on the tap and let the water in.' He paused and then added: 'Midnight will soon strike on the Cathedral clock, and there will be no service in the Cathedral—no! for the Cathedral staff will be rolling:

> 'Where Alph, the sacred river, swishes,
> With Organist and boys and Bishes,
> Down to a sunless sea.

'The Box is coming to me, let me tell you. I shall turn on the taps, let me tell you, and you'd better turn off your taps, let me tell you, for you will have water enough when that happens.'

He walked away, followed by threats from Dr. Blowpipe and cries from the baritones and basses:

'You let us out of here, my joker. This has gone far enough!'

There were piteous wails from the Choir-boys:

'Oh please, sir, do let me go home. Oh sir, have mercy!'

The voices and crying died as Abner sped swiftly into the recesses of the cavern. Kay followed as quickly as he could. Abner, who knew the way, walked by the aid of a torch, which he flashed on from time to time. Kay, on his little tiny feet, had to hurry as best he could after the occasional flashes. Sometimes he fell into some pit in the floor and bumped himself; sometimes he ran into a projecting stone and bruised himself. He felt to the full the misery of being tiny. From time to time, he thought, 'If there should be a cat anywhere down in these cellars, I shall be pounced on and done for.'

Presently, Abner turned on a permanent light. Kay could see that they were in a broad gallery, in the side of which, backed against the rock, was a cage of strong iron bars, raised a little from the floor. In the midst of the cage, heavily chained, was old Cole Hawlings.

Abner walked up to within a few feet of the bars.

'Master Cole,' he said, 'or Master Lully: great Master, the time has come for us to speak together. You are so beset by my power that you can never escape from here without my leave. I come to tell you that the Box is now on its way to me: nothing can stop its coming.

'Once, long ago, you walked from Spain to Italy to buy the Box, with your Elixir of Life. I will sell you the Box for the Elixir. Will you deal?'

'No,' Cole said, 'because you are a greedy scoundrel, unfit to have long life.'

'I will repeat the offer once more,' Abner said, 'but only once. After that, you will see.'

As he turned away up the gallery, seizing a shoe-lace, Kay swung himself into the fold of Abner's turned-up trouser, so that he might not be left behind. He was so light, that Abner did not feel him scrambling there, but walked swiftly on. Kay found his perch pleasanter than the walking had been, but still a giddy way of travelling.

Hanging within the fold of cloth he was tossed and banged by the rapid going till Abner stopped, unlocked a strong-room, entered it and shut it to behind him. It was a stronger room than any that Kay had thought possible. No sound of any sort came within it. The walls might have been more than a foot thick of solid iron. It was brightly lit. It was about nine feet high and twelve feet across. On one side, there was a small sofa with cushions. On another side there was a table on which stood an open iron deed-box; a chair was near the table. On the walls opposite were shelves holding iron deed-boxes, labelled with capital letters—R. E. P. S. D., etc., etc., Abner went to the table and burrowed in the open box.

'Yes,' he said, 'we have done not badly with our little ventures; not badly at all. When the Box of Delights comes, I can sail with these to my quiet island. Ramon Lully will see wisdom: he will grant me the Elixir too before I go. But I must have a look at these once more.'

He felt at the door to be sure that it was closed:

'Strange,' he muttered, 'once before when I had my hand on a great treasure that little boy, Kay Harker, upset my schemes. Why should he come into my mind now? He'd better not come into my presence;' at this he produced from his hip pocket a pistol, which he put upon the table beside him. Kay slipped from the trouser-end to the floor, where he could watch.

Abner opened one of the bags in the deed-box:

'Ah, the Duke's rubies!' he said. 'The setting is rather

coarse—those Victorians were heavy in the hand—but they are a rare crimson: worth thirty thousand, if they are worth a penny. And these—those emeralds: twenty thousand. And these are the pearls. We have done well in pearls and they are very light—very light to carry. Fashionable things—pearls. Liver disease in the oyster, I understand, but ladies don't know that. Ah! this was the Countess's that there was such a fuss about. And this was Mrs. Julius K. What's-her-name's, who offered the big reward. And this was the dancer's: a very foolish young woman, if I am any judge. Ninety-four thousand the three. That shows you what love will do. Then these big ones: anything up to fifty thousand, these. And these are my sapphires—blue and yellow: my favourite stone.' Kay saw him turn out a little bag of sapphires onto the table. 'Ah, I could never part with these,' he muttered. 'There is something about this blue and this yellow. Why anybody should prefer other stones I cannot think. But now for the real box—the rich box.'

Kay watched him open a silver jewel-box which contained what looked like rolls of brown paper. He unrolled some of these. Kay could see the glitter of pendants, necklaces, coronets and stars of glittering diamonds. Abner chuckled as he played with them.

'All the clever jewel thieves in this world,' he muttered, 'have worked for little Abner getting these; and then those stones from the mines that the kind black men kept for little Abner. What a lot of burglars have had anxious nights so that little Abner might have his quiet island! Dear! Dear! And where are the burglars now? Boxed up in iron bars and granite, most of them. Well, they meet their friends there and they have time for thought. There must be a matter of three hundred thousand in this little box alone. I shall retire. It's enough, even for me.

'Strange,' he said, 'strange! That little mildew of a boy is in my thoughts the whole time. The trouble with me is that I have been doing too much in these last anxious days; I have had no proper rest. It's as wearing as a war, this kind of thing. I think I will take a nap; that will do me good.'

Kay saw him slip off his shoes, take off his coat, lie down upon the sofa, settle the coat over his toes, shake the pillows a little and fall instantly asleep. There Kay was, shut up in the strong-room for what seemed like hours, while Abner slept.

'What shall I do?' Kay thought. 'Shall I go home and tell the Lord-Lieutenant or the Colonel of the Tatshire Regiment that there isn't a moment to lose? No, no, of course, I know what I'll do. I'll go to Caroline Louisa and ask her advice.'

He had only to twirl the knob and speak his wish to be whirled to the corridor where she was prisoned: but here he found himself beset by magic; he called, but she did not hear; he groped, but could not find the prison; heavy felt blankets came in his way, tripped him up and baffled him. Besides these, horrid little aeroplanes with snouts like wolves came snapping at him. He was soon glad to wish himself back in Abner's strong-room, where he found Abner just waking from his nap; he was growling as he woke, that 'he would soon teach them.'

Kay realised suddenly that, tiny as he was, his suit of grey was very conspicuous against the red carpet. 'If I am not careful,' he said to himself, 'I shall be seen.' Abner rolled over towards him and opened his eyes, then rubbed them. Kay pressed back towards the wall and lay down along the edge of the carpet. Abner sat up, slipped on his shoes, put on his coat, rose and stretched himself.

'Ha,' he said, 'a very snug little snooze. Now let me see; let me see . . . Of course, the first thing is this boodle. I have packed most of it. There is nothing like going over things a second time. I may have left out something.' He looked at his watch: 'I *have* had a sleep,' he said. 'Come on now.'

He took the deed-box from the table and laid it on the floor close to Kay. Then he knelt down and unpacked its contents. Some of the bags of jewels almost fell upon Kay, who trembled in every limb lest he should be seen.

'Oh, what shall I do?' Kay thought. 'He is bound to see me. Shall I twiddle the knob and go home? It is no good going to the Inspector, he simply will not believe the things I tell him, and I must stay here to learn more of this place, if I am to rescue the others.'

He lay still, hoping that Abner would not see. Abner was intent upon the jewels:

'Rubies,' he said, 'Emeralds, Pearls, Diamonds, my own Sapphires . . . there, I knew I had forgotten something: the Cat's-Eyes. I do not value those silly stones myself, but those Eastern Kings think the world of them and pay just what one asks. Well,' he said, 'we have done quite well in Cat's-Eyes . . . here we are.' He took some packages from a shelf, removed some of the packages already packed and began to restow the box. 'No,' he said, when he had finished, 'even now it won't do. I must get some amethysts in.'

He pitched out some of the packages, poured loose amethysts into the box, shook the box to make them settle down and then snatched the packages lying on the floor and crammed them in on the top. In his hurry he picked up Kay with one of the packages, not noticing him, pitched him with the package into the box, jammed him down tight, so that Kay's bones were nearly smashed, and then squeezed him fast with a couple of packages. Then he shut the lid, sat on it to make it close, locked it, passed a chain round the outside of it, apparently secured the chain with a padlock, then lifted it with a jerk and banged it down on the table with a jolt, so that Kay was shaken, squeezed, banged, bruised and battered, as though the coals had been delivered on top of him. By kicking and struggling Kay managed to reach the top of the heap, so that he could breath what little air there was.

'This is enough for me,' he muttered. 'I will go home.' Struggling hard he contrived to move his arms and felt in his pocket for the Box, but alas, it was no longer there: it must have been jolted out as he struggled among the jewel bags. The precious Box was gone. There he was, no bigger than a mouse, perhaps forty miles from home, in a strong-room in a prison in the rock, padlocked and chained within a locked iron box, which was perhaps soon to be carried to some distant island. He heard Abner putting things on the table beside him. He heard a cork drawn; then he heard Abner apparently cracking walnuts. There came the glug-glug of something poured from a bottle. He heard Abner's teeth crunching nuts and his lips smacking over his drink.

'A very pretty little port,' Abner was saying. 'A little lacking in body, but a pleasant afternoon drink.'

Kay heard the glug-glug repeated more than once; then Abner picked up the deed-box from the table and shook it.

'Ah,' he said, 'not many people shake half a million

pounds of jewels at one go. Now, soon I shall be aboard the submarine, speeding through the billows. This day next week, instead of a foot of snow, there will be the tropical island; instead of my Pouncer, there will be peace; and instead of this Brotherhood, I shall have that Box of the Past, to enter at will. Oh, happy Abner!

'And think of all the benefits that I have conferred; the stimulus that I have given to the jewel trade. Half the noble families of England, you might say of Europe, have had to buy new jewels because of me. Think of the impetus that this has given to the mining industry. Many black and brown creatures in remote parts of the world are munching the banana of content in full employment when, but for little Abner, they might be sitting in the sun doing nothing—starving. Now, very likely, they can even go to the cinema. Then, too, the benefit that I conferred upon the Church. All the clergy of the diocese who have perhaps had embittered years thinking that they would never get promotion—what is the clerical name, by the way? Not promotion, not translation—preferment. Now, at one swoop, the curate becomes a rector, the rector a canon, the canon an archdeacon, the archdeacon a dean and the dean a bishop. Think, too, what I do to the tourist industry. Thousands will come to Tatchester to see the scene of the recent outrages: hotels will prosper: tea-rooms will enlarge their premises. The master masons of Tatchester will obtain an enormous sum of money by public subscription in order that they may put up a memorial to the martyred clergy—Tatchester represented as something between Britannia and, shall we say, Miss Garbo, will be seen weeping in a recumbent position, or perhaps clinging to the foot of a big stone cross. In my retirement in the peaceful island I think I will send them some designs—the tears of Tatchester for the missing Bish. When the memorial is unveiled of course, there, too, Tatchester will benefit through me: a general holiday: the Lord Lieutenant of the Country; Yeomanry parading; a platform in the Cathedral precincts: and the Tatchester Light Infantry Brass Band.

'And this romantic pile here will be all water underneath and charred ashes above. I will open the sluices now. I have emptied six gallons of petrol in the older parts of the house downstairs, where the wood is driest. A wax vesta on my return from Tatchester will suffice for that. With what splendour shall I pass from here: a gurgling flood deep down in the caves and a roaring bonfire above.'

Having finished his speech, Abner said, 'Now, come along.'

His rest and refreshment had put him into a merrier mood. Kay heard him open the strong-room door, which he slammed-to behind him. He set out walking fast, swinging the deed-box to and fro and singing light-heartedly. Each swing drove hard knobs in the bags onto some part of poor Kay, who rolled this way and that, out of breath, banged, bruised, almost suffocated, and forced to lie face downwards with arms outspread, to keep from being shaken under the bags.

CHAPTER TWELVE

Presently Kay realised that Abner had reached a lift. He heard the little grille thrust back, then closed. He felt the lift started. Presently, it stopped at the top of the shaft. Abner came out into what Kay judged to be Abner's bedroom.

'Hurray, hurray,' Abner carolled. 'No more of the worry of thinking for all these fools.'

He put the box upon his table. 'There are one or two things I still must do,' he muttered. 'I say, how it is snowing. I wonder what fool left my window open. There is a foot of snow on my pillow. No doubt about this being a storm. No clergy will get to Tatchester through this.'

Kay heard him slam the window to and judged, from the muffled sound of the slam, that the snow kept it from shutting. Abner had to clear it before he could snap-to the hasp.

'Now, wait one moment,' Abner muttered to himself. 'It might be just as well if I heard what my merry mariners are up to. They aren't exactly the kind of lad to trust further than there's need. I'll tune in the wireless to their mess deck.'

Kay heard Abner turn a switch. Instantly, from just beside him, as it seemed, there came a confused growling murmur of knives and forks, and conversation. Then somebody pounded a bottle on a table, and a voice said, 'And now, gents, please silence for a intellectual treat. Our gallant Captain, known to his enemies as Death-Chops, but to us as Rum-Chops, is kindly going to oblige with a song of his own make about one we all wot of. Gents, all, pray silence for our great commander's melodious joy.'

There were loud cheers. Kay heard a chair pushed back. Rum-Chops cleared his throat and at once burst into his melodious joy, as follows:

'Our Abner is a captain bold,
    the nimblest ever seen-O
He thinks to fly with all his gold
    aboard our submarine-O,
To leave his gang to wreck or hang,
    or languish in a jail-O,
While he in his isle does sit and smile,
    and lives on cakes and ale-O.
Says Abner Brown, "I will do you down,
    and none shall find my trail-O." '

Loud cheers followed this ditty.

'That is very clever of Rum-Chops,' Abner muttered. 'I had not given him credit for so much wit. So he has guessed that I am leaving for good. Wait, now; there is to be some more. I love the simple mirth of these rough diamonds. Hush, now.'

As the coarse laughter, cheers, banging of pots, table-pounding, guffaws, and stamping of feet died away, Rum-Chops called, 'Hold on, gents, all; there's some more about Abner.'

'Good old Rum-Chops,' they shouted. 'Hark to Rum-Chops about Abner. He does old Abner to the life.'

Rum-Chops prepared to sing a second stanza. 'I'm going on about old Abner,' he called. 'Wot d'jer think of this, boys?' Then he sang:

' "For O," he says, "I'll love my time,
all secret in the sea O,
Where blushing peach and yellow lime
are dangling from the tree-O,
Where the bread-fruit-bun toasts in the sun
and comes to lunch on trays-O,
In a hammock cool by a shady pool
I will read my book and laze-O,
While the gang will be still in Pentonville
in cells for all their days-O.

'Chorus this, gents, please,' Rum-Chops called.

All the terrible sea-wolves, bursting with laughter, shouted the last line three times:

'While the gang will be still in Pentonville
in cells for all their days-O.'

After they had sung it, they mocked, and roared with laughter. There were cries: 'That's exactly Abner; that's Abner all through: him to the island, the gang to Pentonville. My, don't old Rum-Chops hit him off?

Good old Rum-Chops. At it again, Rum-Chops. Rum-Chops, once more. Encore de Rum-Chops. Encore, Rum-Chops; Rum-Chops, a second helping with more sauce. Hurray.'

'Well, gents, since you are so pressing,' Rum-Chops said, 'I'll try your patience yet once more. There's nothing like good company for making a man do his best; that's sure. Now will you all load your pistols and charge your glasses; we'll give the last chorus Fiery Honours. Are you all ready now . . .?'

There came the glug-glug of rum pouring from bottles, and the click of many pistol-catches being snapped and resnapped. 'All ready, governor,' several voices said.

'I wonder what is to follow,' Abner muttered. He was not long left in doubt. Rum-Chops pounded the table with a bottle and began a third stanza:

'This may be nice for Abner Brown,
but not so nice for us-O,
And so we plan to let him drown
without unpleasant fuss-O.
When the submarine is seething green
and the water's far from shoal-O,
We'll weight his heels for all his squeals
and drop him through a hole-O . . .
Then Bim Bam Bon for Abner gone
And Hot Rum Punch in a bowl-O.
His golden showers will then be ours,
sing hey what joy to the soul-O.'

All through the stanza, there had been sounds of ill-suppressed joy, but when Rum-Chops reached his fourth line there were shrieks of ecstasy; at the fifth line all present rose to their feet, and towards the end of the sixth Bang went all the pistols, Crash went all the glasses, there were yells and cheers, and the last two lines were repeated and repeated . . . A young pirate called out, 'I know another line we could sing:

'Though Abner Pi has scored the try,
yet Rum-Chops kicks the goal-O.'

This was repeated a good many times. At last, as the noise abated, the voice of Rat, much excited and rather confused, was heard saying, 'I know another line what we could sing.'

'What line is that?' someone asked.

Rat gurgled with laughter. 'I'll die laughing at it,' he said.

'Come, out with it, Rat,' some voices said. 'Stand up and sing it . . . up, on your hind legs, now.'

Kay could hear Rat's chair pushed back: the clamour ceased for the new line; there was silence. Rat gulped with laughter.

'Come, spit it out, man,' someone said.

Rat gurgled with laughter: 'You'll die laughing at it,' he said. 'This is what it is: I don't know that I can, for laughing:

'Ho, something . . . diddle and diddle and
something . . . and something diddle
and Olo.

'That's what.'

He gurgled with laughter: there was a long silence. Then Rum-Chops said:

'I don't think I quite followed. Would you repeat it?'

The wretched creature repeated it, but seemed to feel that something had gone wrong. There was a long, awful silence. Then Kay heard one of the pirates say:

'Where's that nephew of his? Here, Alf Rat, help your uncle up to bed.'

Abner turned off the wireless set with a click.

'So,' he said, 'mutiny even here. I rather feared it. No matter. They shall pay the penalty and I will go to my island by aeroplane. Number Three Plane is at all times ready for the voyage. And these clumsy brutes think to pit their wits against me . . . So be it. They shall pay dearly, that I promise them. Very good . . .

'And now,' he added, 'now for the great moment. Now for my Pouncer. Much as I have suffered from these fools, I have suffered more from my sweet Pouncer, but to make sure of my sweet Pouncer will be but the work of half an hour.'

So saying he left the room, singing a little ditty with a chorus:

'Hey trolly-lolly-lo.'

The clock ticked slowly. It struck for a half-hour, then for ten o'clock, then for half-past ten, but Abner did not return. Presently, Kay heard the door open. He thought for a moment that it would be Abner returning, but two people came in.

'You see, my Pouncer, what,' a familiar voice said, 'I told you he was going to put a double-cross on us. There is the boodle, all packed up.'

'False-hearted, treacherous Abner,' the Pouncer said.

'Ha-ha, what,' the foxy-faced man replied. 'My masterkey will soon resolve the matter.' Kay heard him unlock the padlock on the chain and unlock the deed-box. 'Ha-ha, you see, what,' the foxy-faced man said, thrusting back the lid. 'Cat's-Eyes, Diamonds, Pearls, Emeralds, Rubies—everything; even the special blue and yellow Sapphires.'

'Never shall he look upon them again,' the Pouncer said. 'Quick, into our suit-case.'

The pair had a suit-case. 'They are going to fly together,' Kay thought.

In their hurry and excitement they did not notice Kay, but they thrust bag after bag of jewels into the suit-case.

'Wait, you have left something,' the Pouncer said.

'Ah, it is only a bit of rag,' the foxy-faced man answered. It was not a bit of rag: it was poor, trembling Kay at the bottom of the box. The foxy-faced man picked him up between thumb and forefinger and pitched him into the grate, where luckily he fell into the ashes, not into the fire. 'It was only a bit of old chamois,' the foxy-faced man said. 'A bit of jeweller's rag. Now we had better be off.'

'Wait,' the Pouncer said. 'Fill the box up with coal.'

'My Sylvia, what an inspiration,' the foxy-faced man said. 'Never was your equal born.'

Nimbly he placed some big lumps of coal from the scuttle inside the deed-box; he then carefully muffled their jolting with a towel and a table-cloth.

'My dear Charles, you think of everything,' the Pouncer said.

'Who would not, inspired by Sylvia,' he answered, taking up the keys. 'Now, swift . . . there it is, locked . . . there is the chain . . . and there, finally, the padlock. Beautiful, and no traces left.'

'And now, away, my Charles,' the Pouncer said.

'Wait yet, my Sylvia,' the foxy-faced man answered. 'He has put old Joe in one of the dungeons. We must set old Joe free first. Did you ever see his Zoo?'

'I never did,' the Pouncer said.

'You shall now,' the foxy-faced man said. 'We'll have time before the Police are here.'

Kay saw them work the mechanism of the lift and disappear within it. As soon as they were gone, he crawled out of the grate, which was unpleasantly hot. He was half stunned by his fall into the grate, and half choked by the ashes. He was too miserable at the loss of the Box to mind these things. All that he could think was, 'Now I shall be tiny, like this, unable to help those people, who will all be drowned; and for my own part I shall be burned when he sets fire to the house.'

He was crouching in a corner of the room when he heard the lift drawing near. Sylvia, Charles and Joe came out. Sylvia was wearing nine diamond necklaces. Kay saw that the suit-case had gone. Joe carried a small bag; Charles had a big dressing-case. 'They have been re-packing for their journey,' Kay thought.

'There's the box that he'd packed the boodle in,' Charles said, pointing to the deed-box.

'I'll boodle him, the beauty,' Joe said. 'What can I do against him, I wonder.'

'Oh come along, Joe,' Charles said.

'I'll put my boot through his window first,' Joe said.

He kicked through each pane: snow came driving in in a cloud.

Sylvia Pouncer peered into the fireplace. 'Didn't you throw away a bit of chamois, Charles?' she asked. 'I'd like it now, if you could find it, to give my diamonds a rub with.'

Charles peered into the grate beside her. 'It was just a bit of dirty chamois,' he said. 'Like a little rag, what? I'm afraid it went into the fire and got burned. It doesn't seem to be there now. Perhaps we'd better come along now. Come along, Joe.'

'No, wait just one minute,' the Pouncer said, 'for perhaps it didn't go into the grate, but beside the fire-place here. I thought I saw it, to tell the truth.'

She poked about quite close to Kay, but luckily didn't see him.

'If it's chamois leather that you want,' Joe said, 'you'll find a piece in the kit-box in the aeroplane; if that would do.'

'Yes, that would do,' Charles said. 'We had really better go.'

They stole out of the room and were gone.

'I shall never find the Box again now,' Kay said to himself. 'If it's in the deed-box, Abner will find it, as the Boy said he would. If it isn't in the deed-box, it is probably in one of those bags which they are carrying; they've been sharing the spoils evidently. There is just a chance that it has been spilled out onto the floor here . . . Oh, I do hope it has.'

He looked, with a beating heart, but could not see it. While he was looking, the door of the room opened: Abner came in.

'Confound this window,' he said. 'The snow's drifted in all over the place again and broken the window, too.

'Where on earth has the Pouncer got to? Well, I must get going, and leave that deed undone.'

He picked up the deed-box. As he did so, Kay clutched Abner's shoe-lace and swung himself once more into the turned-up trouser end. Abner did not notice him doing this. He took the lift down to the gallery and walked swiftly to Cole's cage. Near the cage, all muttering, snarling and snapping, was a pack of little aeroplanes and motor-cars, each headed like a wolf, plainly ordered by Abner to be guards and annoyances to Cole. Abner stopped, put down the box, sat upon it and spoke:

'Now, Ramon, or Cole, my merry old soul,' he said. 'I have only one thing to say to you: I want your Elixir. How about it?'

'No,' Cole said, 'nothing that you can offer shall buy the Elixir from me. You are unfit to possess it.'

'You realise the alternative,' Abner said. 'If I am not to have the Elixir, be sure that you will not profit from it. You see this iron wheel in the rock-face? It works sluices by which I can flood these cellars at will. I think the Elixir would hardly preserve you from twenty feet of water, chained as you are.'

'Whether it will preserve me or not,' Cole answered, 'will be known later. But my secret shall not preserve you from anything through any weakness of mine.'

'So?' Abner said, 'you remember of course that I am offering to bargain . . . Your Box for your Elixir . . . It is a fair exchange.'

'You have nothing with which to bargain,' Cole answered. 'You say that you have my Box, or will have it. You are wrong: you will not have it. But I most absolutely refuse to bargain with you in any way whatsoever. I defy you.'

'Very good then,' Abner said. 'In any case, there is no need to continue the conversation.' He walked over to the wheel in the rock and cast loose its safety-catch . . . 'You still refuse?' he asked.

'I do,' Cole said. 'I most absolutely refuse to bargain with you in any way.'

'Very good then,' Abner said. 'The water shall come in.' He took the wheel and was about to swing it round, when a thought seemed to strike him; he turned again to Cole. 'Wait one moment,' Abner said. 'I confess I do set a little store by your Elixir of Life. You are not ignorant of Magic. If you see my Helper, you will hear from him that your Box of Delights will be mine before midnight. That may convince you.'

He lifted his hand in the familiar way. There came a noise of dripping, mixed with a limping, hobbling, shuffling step, difficult to describe. In the corridor appeared that boy whom Abner had smitten with the time-table. The creature's head was still deep within his chest, his legs were still telescoped into his body; but his sulkiness and pertness were gone. He was dripping wet. Dead leaves and bits of sodden twig were stuck about him. He came limping, hobbling, shuffling up to Abner, where he stood and dripped and whimpered.

'So,' Abner said, 'the waterfall has taken some of the insolence from you, it would seem. Now, tell this gentleman the truth. The Box that I search for, shall I not have it by midnight?'

'No,' the boy whimpered.

'You told me that I should have it,' Abner said.

'I didn't,' the boy said. 'I said you'd have it under your hand and you've had it under your hand. You've had it under your hand for something like an hour this afternoon and you didn't know. Now, it isn't under your hand and it won't be under your hand again, and you don't know where it is and you'll never know where it is.'

'Tell me instantly where it is,' Abner said.

'I won't tell you another thing more,' the boy said. 'You can peg me under the waterfall, or melt me in the fire, or bury me, or blow me through the winds, yet I'll never tell you another thing, except that you had the Box and didn't know it and now won't have it again, ever. So that's what I call Squish to you.'

Abner smote the boy on the top of his neck and Kay saw him telescope up under the blow: this time his legs went right through his body, and out at the shoulders.

'Get you back to your waterfall,' Abner said; 'and you will stay there for seven years.'

At this moment, Kay saw Cole Hawlings in the cage lifting his right hand in spite of his irons. As he did so, the boy slowly began to untelescope: the legs went down; the body rose up from the legs; the neck and head rose up from his chest, till there he was, a boy again, looking, Kay thought, rather less bony and unpleasant than he had looked in Abner's study.

'Well, I shan't,' the boy said to Abner. 'I shan't be pegged under the waterfall, for I've been set free, see, from you and yours. You had the Box under your hand and didn't know it and now you'll never get it again. A jolly good Squish to you—Squish, Abner!' At this he suddenly became fainter and disappeared upwards.

'You see,' Cole Hawlings said, 'you have deceived yourself. The Box will not be yours, nor shall my secret be yours, whatever happens to myself.'

'Very well,' Abner said. 'I have other Helpers beyond any power of yours. I am not to have your Elixir, it seems, and I am not to have your Box. Very well; but I shall have something, and that's revenge on you. D'you know what this river and lake are famous for?'

'I know what they are infamous for,' Cole answered—'a very ugly scoundrel.'

'They are famous for crayfish,' Abner answered, 'little fresh-water lobsters, excellent with mayonnaise. Before midnight some of them will have begun upon you: for I am going to drown you, Cole Hawlings, like a rat in a trap.'

He seized the wheel and spun it round. Kay heard a distant clattering noise, a thud, and then a great, fierce but still distant roaring rush of water.

'You hear,' Abner said. 'The sluice is working beautifully. I love the noise of running water. As one of the poets says:

> "Beauty born of murmuring sound,
> Does pass into my face."

'You feel that draught of air rush past? That's air driven out by the water. There's a great head of water in the lake: thirty feet of dammed-back flood water is coming after you. It won't take very long to reach you. And now I shall set off with my little earnings to a place of rest and beauty.'

'You will not set off,' Cole answered. 'All the exits to this place are now guarded by Police.'

'No Police can guard the exit by which I shall go,' Abner answered. 'Good-bye. My last act before I leave will be to drop a wreath down the sluice for you and your clerical friends. Sleep well, Cole.'

He kissed his hand to his victim and turned to walk away. As he turned, Kay slipped from the folded trouser-edge; he had had enough of Abner.

Abner whistled to his guard of little wolves that were

yapping and snarling. They came to heel with their little headlights glaring like radiant eyes. One of the little motor-cars snapped at Kay and almost got him. They passed rapidly along, following Abner like a pack of dogs at the heel of their master.

From far away Kay heard something give way at the intake of the water. The rush of the flood water increased suddenly threefold.

'Mr. Hawlings,' Kay said. 'Mr. Hawlings.'

'Ah, is that you, Master Harker?' Cole said, leaning towards the bars of his cage. 'If I were you, I wouldn't keep that size, Master Harker.'

'Mr. Hawlings,' Kay said, 'I have lost your Box: I had it: it was shaken out of my pocket somewhere, and now I can't get back to my proper size.'

'That's a pity,' Cole said. 'You are not much bigger than my thumb.'

'Yes, and the water's roaring in,' Kay said; 'and he's got you all chained up here in these caves. How can I help?'

'I told you, Master Harker,' Cole said, 'that the Wolves were coming very close and now they are here.'

'Could you suggest something, Mr. Cole, please,' Kay said, 'that I could do to help?'

'It is not so easy, is it?' Cole said: 'hard rock floor, hard rock ceiling, and thick iron bars in the walls. From the sound of the water, too,' Cole said, 'the lower cellars are pretty nearly full up already. There's a lot of water coming in. And it is nearly here, mark me; the air hasn't been coming past in such a draught for some minutes. Do you remember the time, Master Harker,' Cole said, 'when the Wolves came very close at Seekings, yet I got away?'

'I do, indeed,' Kay said. 'Could you do something of that sort now?'

'Why, I am not so sure, Master Kay,' Cole said. 'Have you such a thing as a pencil and a bit of paper?'

'No, I have not,' Kay said.

'That's a pity,' Cole answered; 'but if you'd come up into my cell here through the bars . . . That's the style: well climbed indeed, sir. Now you see in the corner there my coat that they took from me: I can't reach it: I am chained. If you can rummage in the pockets you should find a bit of paper and a pencil.'

Kay went to the corner of the cell. There was Cole's coat tossed in the corner. To such a tiny being as himself it looked like the mainsail of a line-of-battle ship. Sticking from one of the pockets was a piece of timber, which looked like a bridge pile sharpened for driving or a newly-cut larch sapling. Near it was a pocket-book some four times bigger than himself.

'I can't use these,' Kay said. 'I can't lift the pencil nor open the pocket-book.'

'Get down into the pocket, Master Harker,' Cole said, 'for inside, if you grope, you may find a bit of lead that was broken off, and a crumpled sheet or two.'

Kay crept into the pocket. It was rather like going into a coal-mine. There were some crumbs, so dry that they were now rough and sharp, like lumps of rock; further down, beside a penknife bigger than himself, and a spectacle-case that might have been a coffin for him, he found a piece of lead, in weight and shape like a poker; near it was a piece of folded paper. He dragged these out into the light.

'I have got them,' he said.

'Good, Master Harker,' Cole said. 'And now, perhaps,

it may just be that the wind will set a little in the favour of a travelling man. Now are you a good hand at drawing, Master Harker?'

'No, I am not very good,' Kay said, 'except at horses going from right to left.'

'Well, I am not very good at drawing,' Cole said, 'with two hundredweight of chain on each wrist, but can you unfold that paper, Master Harker, and draw on it two men with hammers and cold-chisels, smiting off these irons?'

'I'm afraid I'm not very good at drawing men,' Kay said. 'I can draw horses going from right to left, and trains going a bit the other way.'

'Well, suppose you draw horses, Master Harker,' Cole said, 'coming to bite these chains in two.'

Kay opened the folded sheet of paper, which was Mr. Hawlings' bill at the *Drop of Dew* by Henry Cock-farthings.

He had never before realised how troublesome a sheet of paper can be when it is rather bigger than a blanket, naturally of a stiff quality, and already crumpled from some days in a pocket. As he drew it out, opened it and bent back the crumpled corners, he became suddenly aware that the Wolves were Running with a little whirring snarl. Little motor-cars with wolf heads rushed at him from different points of the cave, and snapped at him.

'Don't heed those, Master Kay,' Cole Hawlings said.

It was not so easy not to heed them, for they came at him with such malice that the snapping of their bonnets was very terrifying. Any bonnet of them all was big and strong enough to snap him down into the engines, where he would have been champed up in no time.

For about half a minute he wrestled with the paper, trying to get it flat. The little motor-cars snapped at him all the time. Snap, snap. One of them would run behind him and snap at his ankles, while another darted at him to bite his toes. Then he realised that though they snapped very near, they never really bit him; he himself was in some way safe, they could only annoy and hinder. Presently, he straightened out one corner of the paper; instantly, one of these snapping motor-cars rushed over it and crushed it back.

'Hit them with the pencil, Master Kay,' Cole Hawlings said. This was very much like saying, 'Hit them with the lamp-post,' or 'Whack them with the telegraph pole.'

'I don't think I can lift the pencil,' Kay said; 'it's too heavy.'

'Well try now,' Cole said.

Kay tried, and to his great delight found that he could lift this great fir-tree of a pencil. For a moment he felt like one of those heroes at the Scottish Games tossing the fir-tree for a haggis. As the motor-car came at him once more, trying to force the paper from under him, he smote the bonnet a lusty blow. The car at once upset and rolled over and over and over with a puncture in all four wheels. A little whimper of pain came from its klaxon, and the other little wolf motor-cars drew to one side and clashed their bonnets at Kay, snap, snap.

'Now draw, Master Harker,' Cole Hawlings said, 'two horses coming to bite the chains in two.'

'D'you mean coming head-on?' Kay said. 'I don't think I have ever drawn horses coming head-on. I always make them look so like cows.'

'Well, try it, Master,' Cole said.

Kay went at it with the piece of lead like a poker on the

crumpled paper big as a blanket which kept rolling up and hitting him. Somehow it seemed to him that what he drew was (for once) rather like a horse. Then, suddenly, at him out of the air with a whirring yap, came little aeroplanes with heads like wolves. They snapped their propellers at him and tried to knock the lead from his hand. This was very much worse than being attacked by hornets, and, while he was dodging their attacks, the wolf motor-cars began again.

'Bat them with the pencil, Master Harker,' Cole said.

Kay put down the lead and seized the pencil, but the creatures were as cunning as wolves; they skipped away. When he put down the pencil they were at him again: the motors snapping at his heels, the aeroplanes all round him. Kay lifted the lead with which he was drawing and smote with it on the propeller of one of the aeroplanes. The propeller snapped, the aeroplane crashed into two others, they spun round and round in flames and set fire to one of the motor-cars, which exploded.

'That's the way, Master Harker,' Cole said. 'Now the other horse.' The Wolves stood aside while Kay finished the second horse. 'There you are, Master Kay,' Cole Hawlings said. 'You come over to my side now a moment, and stand that paper up on its end so that we may take a good look at it.'

Kay propped the paper on its end and stood beside the old man, who was indeed laden down with chains: there were great shackles on his ankles and knees; which were chained to ring-bolts in the stone; a great weight of chains secured his wrists to his ankles. 'Watch the paper, Master Harker,' Cole said, 'don't heed the chains.'

Kay looked at the horses in his drawing. Sometimes, in

earlier days, when he had drawn horses, he had felt that his effort had some merit. These today were the first end-on horses drawn by him; somehow they did really look liker horses than cows. They hadn't got the Newfoundland dog look that some of his horses had. He thought, 'I'd like to keep those drawings. They are the best I've done.'

In fact, the drawings did stand out from the paper rather strangely. The light was concentrated on them; as he looked at them the horses seemed to be coming towards him out of the light, and, no, it was not seeming, they were moving; he saw the hoof casts flying and heard the rhythmical beat of hoofs. The horses were coming out of the picture, galloping fast, and becoming brighter and brighter. Then he saw that the light was partly fire from their eyes and manes, partly sparks from their hoofs. 'They are real horses,' he cried. 'Look.'

It was as though he had been watching the finish of a race with two horses neck and neck coming straight at him at the winning-post. They were two terrible white horses with flaming mouths. He saw them strike great jags of rock from the floor and cast them, flaming, from their hoofs. Then, in an instant, there they were, one on each side of Cole Hawlings, champing the chains as though they were grass, crushing the shackles, biting through the manacles and plucking the iron bars as though they were shoots from a plant.

'Steady there, boys,' Cole said to the horses, as he rose and stretched himself. He put on his coat, pocketed the paper, pencil and lead, and placed Kay on one of the horses. 'Now, Master Harker, I will put you up on this one,' he said. 'Hang on to the mane. I will take the other; we will see if we can get out of this. I will lead the way, Master,' he said. 'Hang on to the mane, for you are rather small for a horse this size.'

He turned the horse along the rocky corridor. No light burned in that part, but the horses gave such light that it was like daylight wherever they went. They had not gone far down the corridor when Cole said, 'No, we are a little too late to go this way. The water's coming in.'

There before them, the water was coming in. Little wave followed little wave, each marking the rocky walls at a higher level. It came in, muttering and snarling, from somewhere far away to the left. Angry little eddies spun away with dead leaves and bits of twig; the corridor was windy with the air displaced by the water; everywhere in that expanse of caverns there was the booming, roaring, drumming of water echoes. The horses shied at the water. When their hoofs touched the stream, they hissed and smoked, as white-hot metal will when wetted.

'Back a little, Master Harker,' the old man said. 'These horses are fiery. They can't abide water, which puts out fire, as you know. We must get back up the passage a piece, and we have not too much time by the look of things. The water's coming in very fast.' He swung himself down from the horse and helped Kay down. 'Steady there, boys, and give us light,' Cole said. 'We must proceed once more as before,' he said, 'with this paper and pencil. Draw me a long roomy boat with a man in her, sculling her.'

'I'm not very good at boats, and I've never drawn a man sculling,' Kay said.

'Draw now,' Cole Hawlings said; 'and put a man in the boat's bows and draw him with a bunch of keys in his hand.'

'I shan't make much of a hand at that,' Kay said.

However, it was not so difficult as the horses had been. Old Cole was there to hold the paper and to keep away the Wolves. They were there, muttering, at some little distance. He could see their wicked little red lights and hear them snarling. The thing that he was afraid of was the water, that was rising rapidly. He could see that the horses were alarmed.

'Well, here's the boat,' Kay said. 'And then, here's the man sculling. Now, this is the man standing in the bows with a bunch of keys.'

'Won't you give him a nose?' Cole said. 'Men do generally have them and they are fine things to follow on a dark night when you can't see your way.'

'I'm afraid the nose is rather like a stick,' Kay said.

The old man took the drawing to the water, set it afloat, and watched it drifting away. Somewhere far away to the left there came the noise of another rock or barrier collapsing under the pressure of the stream. Instantly, the swirling of the water intensified and took to itself an angrier note. Bigger waves rushed out of the darkness at them and licked up more of the floor.

'The sluice-mouth has given way,' Kay said.

'That is so,' Cole Hawlings answered. 'But the boat is coming too, you see.'

Indeed, down the stream in the darkness of the corridor, a boat was coming. She had a light in her bows; somebody far aft in her was heaving at a scull which ground in the rowlocks. Kay could see and hear the water slapping and chopping against her advance; the paint of her bows glistened from the water. A man stood above the lantern. He had something gleaming in his hand: it looked like a bunch of keys. As he drew nearer,

Kay saw that this man was a very queer-looking fellow with a nose like a piece of bent stick.

The boat drove up into the corridor beside them. The man with the nose like a piece of stick steadied her with a boat-hook. The sculler was a bushy-bearded man with his face hidden under a boat cloak. He bent down in the stern of the boat and thrust over a plank. Cole lifted Kay into a safe place in the stern-sheets and then turned to fetch on board the horses, who stamped, snorted and backed, not liking the water. Kay, who was always thrilled by the presence of horses, clambered up on to the gunwale to see them come on board. He half expected to see the boat upset, but Cole and the boatman so trimmed the boat that the first horse clambered on board without trouble. The second horse was more nervy and made the boat rock. Cole brought it on board and soothed it down in the stern-sheets. His eyes stared and his crest rose at the rising water.

'There, there,' old Cole said. 'And now, perhaps, we'd better shove off to see if we can save some other prisoners. We haven't too much time, the way the water's coming in.'

Kay looked along the corridor in the direction from which the water was pouring. It was now so brightly lit that he recognised stalactites which he had passed earlier in the day with Abner. There, near one of the stalactites which he had specially noticed, something was shining on the floor just above the edge of the stream. It caught the light and sparkled. Kay looked at it with attention. 'It must be some of Abner's diamonds,' he thought. Then he thought that the thing was shining not from reflected light, but from light of its own. He wondered for a moment whether this were an underground snail or slug that had a power of phosphorescence: he seemed to have read that there were such things. Then the lipping water touched it and seemed to lick it away an inch or two; then, as the next gush of water came, it sidled from its place onto the current, drifted a couple of feet towards them, stuck an instant, and then came dallying along on the edge of the stream.

'Oh,' Kay said, 'look, look! It is your Box! However did it get there? The foxy-faced man must have dropped it.'

'That is what it is,' old Cole said. 'And what quick eyes, Master Harker.'

The old man went swiftly along the boat's length and vaulted over the gunwale into the stream, which was now over his ankles. He had been quick, but the little aeroplanes now darted down at the shining prize. One of them swooped at it and missed, tried to rise from the water but failed and went directly under the current with a great noise of sizzling. A second darted out; all the wolf motor-cars dashed to the brink of the stream. Cole knocked the aeroplanes aside, caught the glittering treasure as it sailed by; then, scooping the water with his free hand, he splashed it into the champing bonnet of the nearest motor-car wolf, which at once stopped working and sputtered.

Cole vaulted into the boat. 'Shove off,' he said. He reached to Kay and at a touch restored his shape. 'That's rather better, Master Kay,' he said.

'Indeed it is,' Kay said. 'And look, there are some oars floating; they must have come from the lake.'

He leaned over the side of the boat and salved one oar: Cole salved a second.

'Now, here we are,' Cole said. 'You stand on that side,

Master Kay, and shove her off the rocks. I will do the same on this side.'

The current drove the boat into the alleys of blackness. The gallery in which they were floating was now almost full: they had to stoop to avoid the roof; often they snapped off the stalactites as they passed. The boat drove into another gallery. There, clinging to a stalac-tite, submerged up to the waist, was a drenched and sodden Rat, crying, 'Pity a poor drowning man; an old naval pensioner what give his youth for the Empire.'

The man with the boat-hook said, 'I'll fetch that chap a clip as we pass.'

'No, no,' Kay said. 'He will help us to find the prisons.'

Cole Hawlings leaned over and pulled the Rat on board by his mangy collar. He was very cold with wet and terror; he shivered with chattering teeth.

'That's what comes,' he said, 'of having cisterns what burst. Time was when a cellar was a cellar, but now, in these upside-down-side days, folk keep their water with their wine, it seems.'

'You know these cellars,' Kay said; 'where are the prisons with the clergymen in them?'

'Would they be what you call "religious parties"?' the Rat asked. 'They're along here, quite close. I was having as nice a little bit of a religious biscuit as ever I ate, out of one of their pockets, when this water came in and I had to leave it. That's Life, that is: a poor man works for five years and gets nothing, then, when he gets a bit of biscuit, the cistern bursts. And such is Life. That's what.'

'They were along here?' Kay asked, pointing into the cave.

'They were along there,' the Rat said, 'so was the biscuit; but the biscuit will be pulp by this and the religious parties not much better. And my young nephew, Alf, will have water in his works, too, I shouldn't wonder, which would be a loss. As pretty a young larcener, he was, as ever I tried, so the Judge said. I suppose you ain't got a bit of bacon-rind you could give a poor man?'

'No, we haven't,' Kay said.

'There's nobody keeps bacon-rind now,' the Rat said. 'They're too proud. Stuck-up, I call it. Yah.'

The boat drove under a low-hanging stretch of cave. There, near a stalactite, was a hole in the roof. Kay thought that he saw the evil mouth of Alf there, saying, 'Hop it, uncle.' As the boat drove under the stalactite, Kay saw that it was Alf stretching a dirty paw. The Rat sprang, caught it, swung himself to the hole and disappeared into it.

'Well, that's got rid of him,' Kay said. 'And there are the cells.'

He was wrong; it was not the prison; it was the cell containing Caroline Louisa.

'It's all right,' Kay cried, 'we are coming to get you out.'

'Try your keys, keyman,' Cole said.

The man with the nose like a broken stick, took his keys and opened the door without difficulty. 'I'm afraid you are sopping wet and half frozen,' Kay said to Caroline Louisa, as he helped her in, 'but we'll soon get you to some dry and warm things. D'you happen to know the way to the other prisons?'

'I don't indeed,' she said. 'They weren't anywhere near here.'

At this moment they heard a hail from along the

corridor: 'Boat ahoy!' Somebody away there in the darkness of the alley was clapping hands and shouting, to attract attention.

'Who are you?' Cole cried.

'The Tatchester Cathedral staff,' the Bishop's voice answered.

The boat drove on along the gallery. There, indeed, ankle-deep in the stream at the edge of the corridor, were the Bishop, the Dean, the Archdeacon, the Bishop's Chaplain, the Canons, the Minor Canons, the Precentor, the Organist, the Master Vesturer, the Bursar, the Librarian, the Chief Theologian and Peter Jones. Cole and his crew helped them on board.

'How on earth did you all get out?' Kay asked.

'Oh,' the Bishop said, 'we've been out some time. A man and a woman came down, to let out a friend of theirs, called Joe. They went away with him, but after a minute, Joe ran back with the keys and let us all out, and said, "It would be sure death to us to follow him, but that there was another way out," to which he directed us.

'We started as he told us, the caves were lit at that time. Then some terrible scoundrels, pirates evidently, wearing red aprons and sea-boots, came stamping along, led by one whom they called Rum-Chops. They said, "It's no good going that way; all the lower caves are full already, and our submarine's at the bottom of them sunk. Mizzle" (so they told us), "dead right about, or you'll be sunk, too."

'They ran on and we followed them, but all the lights went out suddenly, and we lost them. Since then we have been groping in the dark, almost at the end of our matches and our hope. Where are we, can you tell us?'

'Down in the heart of the Chester Hills,' old Cole said; 'but perhaps we'll get you out afore long. Give way, all.'

They shoved the boat on, up-stream, poling with oars and boat-hook, heaving with eager hands against the rocks.

'Where are the others?' Kay asked.

'What others?' the Dean asked.

'The Bell-ringers, the Choir-boys and at least half the Choir,' Kay said. 'Oh, and the Friends of the Cathedral, and perhaps a lot of others.'

'Shout, everybody,' Cole said. 'If they've not all been drowned, they may hear us.'

They shouted: their voices echoed and boomed among the galleries. It seemed to Kay that some other sound of voices could be heard when the echoes died a little.

'Isn't that singing?' he said.

'And what quick ears, Master Harker,' Cole said. 'Singing it is, away along there in the darkness. Heave all together, now, for they must be sorely pressed.'

They drove on against the stream: presently they heard the voices of the Bell-ringers and some of the Choir singing, 'Good King Wenceslas.' They shouted to reassure them and soon heard answering shouts. Very soon the boat was alongside the cage, where the poor fellows stood in the cold water which was already over their knees. It was pitiful to hear the piteous cries of the Choir-boys, some of whom were saying, 'Oh, if I'd only known, I'd never have cheeked my poor mother,' or, 'Oh, if I could only have my time again, I'd do what my kind master told me,' or, 'Oh, I wish I hadn't tied that tin can on the dog's tail,' or, 'Oh, if only I could get away, I'd burn my catapult and I would be good; oh, I would be good.'

'Cheer up,' Cole shouted to them. 'We'll soon get these locks open.'

But to get these locks open was not easy. It was a different kind of lock from any the keyman had known; he tried one key after another.

'No, they won't fit these locks,' he said. 'You want the Handcuff King for these.'

'Oh, please be quick, sir; please be quick,' the boys cried. 'It is up to our knees already.'

'I'm afraid it is no good,' the man with the keys said. 'I can't get these locks to work.'

'I've got keys; try these,' the Bishop said.

'And these,' the Dean said. But, no, none of the keys fitted.

'There's nothing for it,' the keyman said solemnly, 'but to compose yourselves unto a set of watery tombs.'

'A set of watery rubbish,' Cole said, heaving himself out of the boat to the door. 'Let me have a look at these locks. Why,' Cole said, 'no wonder you couldn't get them to work. They aren't locks: the doors have spring catches and not locks at all. You have only got to open them by the handle here . . . there you are. Now, come out. See that you are all out. And mind you don't swamp the boat as you get on board. Lively with you now. That's the ticket. Come, now, are you all on board?'

'Yes,' the Master Bell-ringer said. 'This is the lot of us.'

'Well,' Cole said, 'if you are all on board the lugger, we'll push off then, up-stream. These galleries are almost full to the roof now. There is not much room for us. We all will have to do what they do in the barges in the

London tunnels: all lie on our backs and push the boat forward by our boots upon the ceiling.'

All in the boat lay down upon their backs as Cole had bidden, and pushed the boat forward by getting their boots against the roof of the corridor. The sculler alone did not lie down: he bent in the hollow of the stern-sheets, heaving at his oar, which grunted in the rowlock and splashed with the blade. The Precentor kept the time for the kickers: 'One—Heave! . . . Two—Lift leg . . . Three—Boot on the roof . . . then, One—Heave!' The boat forged slowly ahead with gurglings and cluckings of water. There was a great current against them and in some places the roof was very near. Kay could see little save archings of rock, which sometimes glistened with water and were sometimes hung with stalactites. His little legs were so short that they were not much good in heaving the boat forward.

In one place, the river ran through a wide cavern, the wall of which had been painted with a procession of men leading bulls and horses.

'That was our old religion, Master Harker,' Cole said, nodding towards it. 'It was nothing like so good as the new, of course, but it was good fun in its day though, because it ended in a feast.'

'You didn't eat horses,' Kay said, 'did you?'

'Ah, didn't we,' Cole said.

After this they came into a narrow cave where the current was very strong. A sort of glimmer of light showed ahead. 'There is moonlight and there is the sluice,' Cole cried.

Kay sat up. There ahead was a silvery, shaking patch of light with a troubled roaring water pouring down in a fall. All about them the water eddied and jobbled. The boat tossed. The men, heaving with their boots, trebled their efforts, and slowly the boat plunged forward against the rush.

'We will never get up a fall like that,' the Bishop said.

'Where a salmon can go a man can go,' Cole said.

The boat drew slowly nearer against the rush of the stream. 'This is only the first half of it,' Cole said. 'There is another fall above this. But lay hold of that tumbled tree there: it seems to me to be jammed firm. We can haul ourselves up by that.'

Jammed along the length of the fall, boughs downward, was a young fir-tree. Leaning over the side, all who could caught hold of the trunk of this. Heaving all together they drove the boat into the rush and upward. Icy cold water spurted all over them in a sheet; but they hove again, held all they had won, and then hove onward. Heaving all together they drove the boat up to the top of the first fall.

There beyond them, as Cole had said, was another shorter fall. In bright moonlight, at the mouth of this upper fall, Kay saw Abner heaving on a big winch-handle which worked the sluice there. Abner was crying out:

'This thing has jammed. It ought to be wide but it's only half open. Open, will you!'

He hove and hove, then he left the winch-handle and dug at one of the cog-wheels with a knife.

'It's this cog that's jammed,' he cried. 'Open! Open!'

The boat forged forward to the foot of the second fall.

'We are in luck's way,' Cole said. 'See there is an iron railing along the fall. We can heave up by that.'

All hands seized the iron rail and drove the boat up. In the fury of his own effort Abner heard nothing of the boat's approach. Kay saw him fling off his coat and again heave upon the winch. The boat was just behind him, but he knew nothing about her.

Kay heard him cry, 'She's moving; she's moving. There she goes.' He burst into song:

> 'Wheel, Wheel, pull up the sluice;
> Sluice, Sluice, let in the stream;
> Stream, Stream, cover them deep
> So they won't sing hymns in the morning.'

'Now,' Cole said, 'heave together—heave!'

Under their enormous heave, the boat moved up in spouting, drenching jerks. She paused for one instant on the timbers of the sluice-boards—Kay distinctly felt them give way beneath the boat's weight—but the boat, under the impetus of the final heave, drove on past the astonished Abner and roaring fall, into the calm water of the lake.

Just as Kay passed Abner, something big swooped silently down and hovered just over their heads. Kay saw that it was one of the silent aeroplanes used by the gang. A light suddenly went up within its pilot-house. On the side of the car, the words 'Number Three Plane' appeared in red. Kay saw the Pouncer, the foxy-faced man and Joe leaning from the windows.

'Oh, Abner, did you really think to diddle me?' the Pouncer called.

'We've got all your jewels, Abner, ha-ha, what,' the foxy-faced man cried.

'Good-bye, Abner,' Joe called. Kay saw Joe lean further out and heave down what seemed like a bomb on Abner's head. It struck his head and exploded, but it was not a bomb: it was a two-pound bag of flour. 'Got him,' Joe said.

Then the aeroplane lifted and was away into the air.

Abner was blinded by the flour, he came too near to the sluice, slipped, clutched, gave a startled cry and fell headlong into the torrent. For one instant Kay saw his legs thus:

Then they were sucked down into the gulf and disappeared. Before any of the people in the boat could fling off coat and go in after him, there came a swift warning noise of yielding in the structure of the sluice now all sapped by the pouring of the cataract. It collapsed suddenly and utterly. With one great swirl the released water surged over it and filled its mouth. 'Forever and forever, farewell, Cassius,' Cole quoted. The boat drove out into the moonlit lake.

But oh! how the scene had changed since Kay had been there in the morning. The world was white with deep snow. Many trees were branchless or broken. Those which remained were bowed with the great clots of snow upon them.

But what was happening at the Training College? There were lights in all windows. Many men were floundering with lanterns outside the house. Men were calling. There were shouts of, 'Here's another of them, hiding in the outhouse;' 'Another pair of handcuffs for this chap, quick.' A party of men in the snow near the lake-side hailed to the boat to stop: the voice of the Inspector cried:

'Halt there, in the boat. Halt there. We have got you covered. Who are you?'

'It's the Bishop of Tatchester and all the prisoners,' the Bishop called.

'Why, is that you, Your Grace?' the Inspector answered. 'Pass the word there that the Bishop's saved. . . . And you, Your Grace, would you ask your boatman to come in towards the shore a bit.' As the boat drew in, he said, 'Well, thankful I am, Your Grace, to see you safe and sound again. Is this all your party?'

'Yes, everyone: we are all here,' the voices answered.

'Pass the word to the wireless-men,' the Inspector called, 'to report All Saved. We are in time, it seems,' he added, 'but it was a near thing. I'll tell Your Grace how it all came about.

'The Chief Constable thought we'd better act on Master Harker's information, but by that time the snow made it difficult to get here. However, what with planes and a will, we just did it.

'We have got most of these birds already, and we'll have the rest before dawn; they can't get far in this snow; and we'll have the leader, too, for all he's so clever.'

'He's gone down into the caves with the flood,' Cole Hawlings answered. 'I don't think any man will find any part of him again. Now, can we come ashore there?'

'No, don't you try it here,' the Inspector cried: 'you will never get through the snow on this side. The drifts are six feet deep between me and you; but on the other side, just opposite, by the bathing-box, it looks to me to be clearer. The hill tipped the snow just clear there. By the way, have you got Master Kay Harker among you?'

'Yes,' Kay cried, 'I am here. Have you got their submarine?'

'Oh, I am glad to see you safe, Master Harker. It's through you that all the rest are safe,' the Inspector called back. 'No, we have not got the submarine. They left her windows open and she has sunk and very nearly took the crew with her; but we have got the crew—as choice a lot as ever graced handcuffs. You trust the Law, Master Harker. Sometimes she is slow, but always she is sure. The Law's motto, Master Harker, is: "The Law never sleeps, though it knows when to close its eyes." Oh, Master Harker, my nephew's down for Christmas, and he has brought a pair of Belgian hares for you—as pretty a prize pair as ever I did see. Now, I must go to my men here, but, if you will shove your boat over there by that little bathing-box, I think you will get ashore there without being sunk in the snow.'

They gave way as well as they could with their two oars, a plank and a boat-hook. Presently, they ran the boat alongside the springboard and clambered out. The two horses whinnied and shook their manes, the two boatmen leaped on their backs and galloped away, straight up the slope of the Roman Camp. They disappeared over the rampart and were seen no more.

But indeed, now that the party had landed on the lakeside, they were amazed at the snow that had fallen in so short a time. The weight of snow had levelled all the lesser shrubs to the earth: there was no cover anywhere for so much as a rabbit. From time to time along the wood there came a melancholy cracking crash as some other bough or tree gave way under the strain. Quite close to them, in what had been thickets in the wood, the wind had driven the snow capriciously into drifts that might well have been eight or nine feet deep. Kay, who remembered the path near the water, was amazed to see it so deeply covered.

But whatever the storm had been, it had now passed over, leaving a clear sky, with a full moon shining so brightly that only the very big stars could be seen.

'It's eleven o'clock at night—after eleven,' the Bishop said. 'We'd better push on to Hope-under-Chesters and telephone from there.'

They took a few steps along the path towards Hope-under-Chesters and then realised that it might well take them all night to flounder through the drifts. No one there had ever seen such snow.

'Well, it's very disappointing,' the Bishop said. 'I am afraid that after all there is no chance of our holding our Midnight Service in any church in the Diocese.'

'Ah, I'm not so sure, Your Grace,' Cole Hawlings said. 'A travelling man, who goes up and down the world, he finds ways of doing things—or doesn't he?' he asked Kay.

'I think he does,' Kay said.

'Ah, you think he does?' Cole Hawlings said; 'I think by this and that, we needn't give up hope yet. Listen, all.'

The night was so still that they, standing there in the snow, could hear the bells of nine churches ringing for Christmas. The Precentor, who had been a curate in that district, told Kay which village each bell belonged to:

'That one,' he said, 'with the tenor bell that needs recasting, is Naunton Crucis. Old Father Goodman has rung that bell for forty-nine Christmas Eves and this is his fiftieth.'

Above the noise of the bells Kay heard the jangling of

lesser bells, or so it seemed. Then it died away so that he felt that he was mistaken, but immediately it broke out again louder than before. They were bells not ringing to any tune or time.

'They are sleigh-bells,' he said.

'Why, it's Father Christmas,' said the Precentor, 'coming with his team of reindeer.'

But it was not Father Christmas. Over the wall of the Roman Camp some lights appeared; the bells rang loud and clear. Leaping towards them, seeming hardly to brush the snow with their paws, came a magnificent team of harnessed lions drawing a long sledge driven by a lady whose eyes shone like sparks of fire. Kay saw at once that she was the Lady of the Oak Tree who had stood by Bob's shop waiting for a word from Cole Hawlings. Outside the glove of her left hand was the strange ring with the St. Andrew's Cross upon it. Kay was amazed at the beauty and strength of the lions, their gleaming eyes, and the way in which they tossed back their manes and snarled, or scuffled the snow with their pads, or showed their teeth with coughing, terrifying roars. He had never seen lions so beautiful, so powerful, nor with eyes so full of yellow flame.

'Get in, Bishop,' the lady said. 'I can take half of you in this sleigh.'

The Bishop and some of the others got into the sleigh, which seemed to be made of bright gold. It was heaped with great scarlet rugs and the furs of strange beasts. As soon as they were snugly in the sleigh under the rugs, the lady called:

'I must start before my team starts quarrelling with the other team.'

She called to the lions, who bounded forward roaring.

All the bells upon their traces and on the rim of the car jangled out clearly and seemed to Kay to strike now into a kind of tune. Kay saw them whirl round in a half-circle sending a great sheet of snow aloft, then they strode on to the night striking sparkles out of the air. Kay heard the Precentor, who was sitting with the Bishop, start singing, 'The First Noël,' but they were out of earshot in half a moment; a second sleigh drew near.

Kay had been delighted by the first sleigh, though the lions had a little scared him, but what was his delight when he saw that the second sleigh was drawn by unicorns!

'Oh,' he said, 'unicorns! And they always told me that they never existed.'

But there was no doubt about these. It was a team of eight of the most beautiful unicorns that ever stepped. In build they were something like the very best white Arab stallions, only slimmer in the barrel and even neater in the leg. They had the same proud little heads and twitching nostrils. They were all snow-white except their hoofs, which were bluish. From their brows sprouted the most exquisite white horns about two feet long, sharp as needles and glowing, Kay thought, rather like mother-of-pearl, but perhaps that was the effect of the moonlight. Their traces and harness were of silver all studded with moonstones. They were driven by a man, whose sleeves were hung with little silver chains. In his helm there were antlers; over his glove a red cross glowed upon a ring.

'Oh, it is Herne again,' Kay said. 'I do love going with Herne the Hunter.'

'Jump in, the rest of you,' Herne cried. 'There will be room for all of you.'

The sleigh was heaped with Polar bear-skins and great white fleeces from some mountain sheep. They all clambered on board and snuggled down into the fur. The driver called to his unicorns, who at once whinnied together and tossed up the snow with their hoofs. They, too, like the lions, whirled round and sent the snow flying in a cloud. Then away they went, whirling through the heaven, striking sparkles out of the air. Old Cole Hawlings touched something, all the side of the sleigh at once thrust out lighted Japanese lanterns attached to long streamers; smaller lanterns flew out from the reins of the unicorns as they sped. Cole Hawlings, who had a most beautiful voice, Kay thought, began to sing this carol:

'George took his lantern from the nail,
And lit it at the fire-a;
He said, "The snow does so assail,
I'll shut the cows in byre-a."

'Amid the snow, by byre-door,
A man and woman lay-a;
George pitied them, they were so poor,
And brought them to the hay-a.

'At midnight, while the inn kept feasts,
And trump and whistle blew-a,
George heard a trouble in the beasts,
And to the stable drew-a.

'And there within the manger-bars
A little child new-born-a,
All bright below a cross of stars,
And in his brow a thorn-a.

'The oxen lowed to see their King,
The happy donkey brayed-a,
The cocks and hens on perch did sing,
And George knelt down and prayed-a.

'And straight a knocking on the door,
And torches burning red-a,
The two great Kings with Melchior,
With robes and wine and bread-a.

'And all the night time rolled away
With angels dancing down-a;
Now praise we that dear Babe today
That bears the Cross and Crown-a.'

'Now, brothers,' Cole said, 'sing this last bit all together, will you?'

All there joined in with a will, and then made Cole sing it all again, so that they might sing the chorus after each stanza.

It was most beautiful to drive through heaven thus. The shining country spread out below them was starred by the lights in villages and towns and musical with bells ringing for Christmas. The rivers gleamed where they caught the moonlight. Sometimes big white and tawny owls came floating alongside the sleigh, so close that Kay could stretch out his hand and stroke them.

'I say,' he said, 'how beautifully your unicorns move.'

'You see, Master Kay, they hate being beaten by the lions,' Herne said.

Kay had some misgivings as to what would happen if they caught up the lions; then he thought that the drivers would probably be able to stop any fatal battle.

'There is the land you know,' Herne the Hunter said.

Leaning over the rail of the car Kay saw Condicote brightly lit; he heard a few notes from the famous Condicote bells. The unicorns were now going so fast that, a moment later, he saw the pinnacled tower of Tatchester Cathedral floodlit for the great night. In an instant he saw all the lights of Tatchester.

'Of course,' he thought, 'everybody in the city has lit a window as part of the celebration.'

The unicorns swerved suddenly, then swerved again, in a great sweep, cutting in ahead of the team of lions, who roared with rage at being passed. Dipping down, both sleighs skimmed into the snow, and galloped its feathery surface for Tatchester Gate. A delicate faint noise of bells came to them from the Tatchester parish churches.

'Ah, there, listen now,' one of the Cathedral Bell-ringers said to Kay. 'Christmas Eve, near midnight, and no bells ringing in the Cathedral, no, not one. Those are only St. Margaret's and St. Wincom's. I never thought to hear so un-Christian a silence; never.'

'There's nothing stamps a Christian town more than its bells,' Cole Hawlings said. 'And a wandering man gives heed to bells, for often in the dark night they will ring him home, who would otherwise be ate by wolves and that.'

'I could weep,' another Bell-ringer said, 'that our great Bell, Old Truepenny, of 1427, isn't throwing his tongue. He did ring in King Henry from the French Wars, Old Truepenny.'

'We might still be in time to start Old Truepenny,' the Dean said. 'It is still not a quarter to twelve; we are nearly there. The only questions are, "Can we reach the Cathedral in all this snow?" and, "Have these ruffians who kidnapped us stolen the bell-tower keys, or cut the bell-ropes?" '

'We shall soon know, sir,' Cole said. 'The snow is deep: it has been a sad storm. Wolves' Weather, as we used to say in King Harold's time.'

Now that they were over the Common, nearing the Gate, Kay could see what desolation the storm had wrought. The telegraph-posts were down; the brackets of telephone-wires had been wrenched from buildings; two old elms on the Council Piece had been uprooted; and the snow had drifted so deep at the Gate and in the High Street that no one had trodden it nor tried to drive it. The way was white unspeckt snow deserted under the lamps.

The sleighs turned up the narrow lane known as St. Margaret's Barbican; the snow scattered from their runners with a crisp, soft, slithering swish; it was so deep in that narrow lane that Kay could see into the lighted rooms on the first floors of the old houses. He saw old black beams, old men and women drinking to Christmas, or stooped over children's stockings, as they filled them with toys, neat surprise packages, Eggs of Delight, and oranges. All the narrow lane boomed and hummed with the noise of the bells of St. Margaret's Church; tremblings of music went thronging by in the air.

'Where are we going to, please?' Kay asked.

'To the Parvice St. Michael, Master Kay,' Herne said.

Now the Parvice St. Michael was a space in front of the Cathedral's North Door. It had once been a part of the Monastery: a wall still shut it from the approach to the West Door which was in the Precincts. From the Parvice there was a wicket into the Cloisters.

The sleighs sped out of St. Margaret's Lane into the

Parvice; as they entered it, the Cathedral suddenly rose up in front of them with its enormous black bulk, its windows unlit, its tower transfigured with floodlight, its ledges, mouldings and carvings all topped with snow. A man held up a lantern to check the unicorns. He came slowly past the team to the sleigh with his lantern lifted so that he might see who was there. He dragged a spade from his left hand. Kay noticed that he wore a rough dark sackcloth overall, and that other men, clad like him, were shovelling snow from the North Door. On the farther side of the wall, the scrape of shovels on stone told Kay that other workers were clearing the West Door.

'Ah, pass in, brothers, to St. Michael's Door; we've cleared the way for ye,' the man who held the lantern said.

He waved his light, and Herne moved the unicorns up the path to the Door: the shovellers stood aside as they passed and called blessings on them. They were all little men, Kay thought, with faces which looked white and tense in that dark place.

'I believe their heads are all shaven,' Kay thought. 'Are these the Monks?'

'These are the Monks of the Abbey, Master Harker,' Cole Hawlings said, 'for on such a Christmas Eve what one of them would keep away? They've all come for the glory of St. Michael's Abbey.'

Whoever they were, they had cleared a way to the door. The clergy and Bell-ringers flung aside their rugs and pressed into the porch of the dark North Door. The leader of the snow-shovellers held his lantern while the Bishop left his sleigh. Kay long remembered the thin eager faces of the Monks on both sides of the approach lit by the lantern.

'Pass in, my Lord Bishop,' some voices said.

It was strange. No one knew why the Parvice had been called Parvice St. Michael. This night, it was clear; a big statue of St. Michael stood at the entrance to the porch. There he stood, in painted armour, as though he had just been carved there.

There was someone inside the porch, working at the fuse-box, with a clutter of tools and one little inefficient electric torch.

'Mind, please,' this man said. 'You can pass in to the side.'

'Ha,' the Bishop said. 'It is Winter, the electrician. Can you give us the lights in the Cathedral?'

'Why, welcome back, my Lord Bishop,' he said. 'Welcome indeed. But as to the lights, I can't yet give you as much as one; no, not a light, Your Grace,' he said. 'No; the storm's got all the lights wrong. Whether it's these fuses or something worse I can't at the moment say.'

The clock in the central tower gave a heavy tocking whirr and rang out:

Ding dong ding dong,
Dong dong ding ding
Ding ding ding dong.

'Just a quarter of an hour,' the Dean said, 'to robe and get the bells and lights and organ going. I wonder will that snow-shoveller very kindly lend me his lantern. Oh, thank you so much. Come, then, will you please, to the Dean's Cell, where we shall know whether all the keys have been taken.'

He led the way into the end of the dark North Aisle, where he unlocked the office known as the Dean's Cell. He struck a light and lit the tapers which he sometimes used for heating sealing-wax. 'No, they've left us alone,' he said. 'Here are all the keys.'

There on the walls, neatly ticketed, and hung with plaques of wood or brass, to keep them from being easily pocketed, were all the Cathedral keys.

Some clergymen, in robes, who had been waiting outside the office, now welcomed the Dean.

'I am Jo Stalwart,' one of them said. 'We were all here ready to carry on in case of need. We are so glad that you are back. If you'll allow us, we'll go up to light the Choir.'

When they had gone, the Dean gave his other orders.

'Bell-ringers first,' the Dean said, 'Here are the keys of the Belfry. You may still have time to ring the bells in, and start a chime before midnight. Now where has my Lord Bishop gone?'

'He has gone to robe,' the Bishop's Chaplain cried. 'He promised long ago to bless the Bell-ringers in the Tower tonight before they begin to ring.'

'I was afraid, for a moment,' the Dean said, 'lest he should have been captured again. Now, Vergers, take quickly all the wax candles in the store-room and set them in the old sconces along the Nave and in the Transepts. They will at least make the darkness visible. Choir-boys, quick, to the Vestry, to robe. Anyone who has nothing to do with the service, get out candles, please, with the Vergers and help to light the doors; we must let in the people in a moment. Who are those there, please? Oh, Mr. Hawlings and Kay, it is you. Will you please very kindly take these old bronze incense tripods to the West Doors; put wax candles in them and light them, so that the people coming in may see where they are treading: oh, and open the West Doors, will you please?'

Kay had not seen him enter the Church, but when he and Cole had placed the bronze tripods near the great Entrance, lo, there was Arnold of Todi beside them. He looked perhaps madder than ever, brighter in the eye and queerer in his way.

'Ha,' he said. 'This is Feast of Nativity? You will pardon and excuse, this night, he Christmas?'

'Yes, yes,' Kay said. 'Yes, Mr. Arnold . . . Christmas dans cinq minutes.'

'Ha,' Arnold said, 'then I'm back in Anno Domini?'

'Yes, to be sure,' Cole said. 'And you must have a sup from my bottle that I brought all the way from Spain for you. And here is your Box of Delights that you have been parted from for so long.'

'No, no,' Arnold said, 'keep it, keep it. Now that I'm back in Anno Domini I'll stay there, thanky.

'But you,' he added, 'must have here a sup from my bottle that came from a temple which Alexander took; see, now, I will show.'

He produced a small glass bottle, which he opened over one of the bronze incense tripods. He poured into the cup of this a little fragrant oil from his bottle. He poured a few drops more into the second of the censers. 'Watch now,' he said.

As Kay watched, the oil burst into a bright light, which lit up that end of the Nave.

'So Alexander found it burning,' Arnold said, 'in that temple beyond the Gedrosian Waste, or one of the other Wastes. It will burn for seven hundred years, being Oil of Eternity.'

It burned now so clearly, that Kay heard the people outside the West Doors cheering. He heard cries of, 'Hurray, there go the lights. There's going to be a service after all.' Some hands pounded on the doors, as Kay and Cole turned the giant key in the lock and dragged back the bolts one by one. All Tatchester seemed to be gathered outside there, waiting to get in.

'Oh,' some were saying, 'whoever's going to take the service? Have they found the clergy?'

'No, indeed,' others said, 'nor ever will, I'm afraid.' 'No, the poor Bishop's in his grave by this.' 'I'm told the Dean's legs have been found done up in brown paper, gaiters and all, in the Brighton Waiting Room.' 'These people who go murdering are just like wolves, they stick at nothing.'

As Cole Hawlings seized one leaf of the double door, they seized the other. They swung the great doors back as far as they would go. The light from the tripods lit up a sea of faces gathered there cheering the opening of the doors.

As the cheers rose, Kay saw that a great table had been laid immediately outside the Door. This table was heaped with boxes of chocolates, bottles of sweets, dolls of all sorts and sizes, bats, balls, hoops, peg-tops, humming-tops, boxes of bricks and of soldiers, toy ships, kites, toy aeroplanes, crackers, fruits, books, papers, musical instruments and charming little mechanical toys. By this table were the three Jones girls, each dressed in white. With them was the Dog Barney, who barked with joy to see Old Cole again.

'Walk up,' little Maria was saying, 'walk up, Parents. This is the Jones' Christmas Fund, organised by Maria Jones as a token of her gratitude for having been thrice expelled from school. Every parent of a child attending this Service is entitled to one package per child.'

'Hullo, Maria,' Peter said.

'Hullo, you two. I hear they've got the scoundrels,'

Maria called. 'We had it on the wireless; but we'll talk about that later. . . . Is yours a girl or a boy, Madam?'

She and her sisters pressed packages on to all those who came thronging into the church.

At this instant, the organ sent out some spiring and quavering rumbles which passed into 'Sleepers, Wake.' Then, with a sudden burst of light, all the Cathedral lights went on, shone for one glorious instant, went out again, recovered and then burned clearly; the electrician had found out what was amiss.

Now that the West Doors were open, Kay could hear that the Cathedral bells were ringing. He stayed there, listening to them for a moment or two. Old Cole was beside him, saying, 'A happy sight: a blessed sight, Master Harker, all these coming here to sing.' Arnold of Todi went up the Nave to stare at the decorations: he seemed to Kay to be in a trance of pleasure at being certainly back in Anno Domini.

'Just two minutes more to go, Master Harker,' old Cole said.

There came the sound of many men marching to a drum-tap: a clear voice called an order. With a clink of metal and grunt of leather the band of the famous Tatshire Regiment, the Tatshire Toms, moved into position inside the church. A and B Companies of the same glorious battalion filed into place there, with the old blue and white colours, once a Spanish lady's dress, under which the survivors of the regiment had fought all one blazing summer's day in the never-to-be-forgotten wheat-field of San Luis Frontera 'against the massed might of Massena's veterans,' as the History Books said. There came an instant's silence.

Then Crash came the salute of cannon in the Barrack

Square for the stroke of midnight. In all the church towers of Tatshire men fired the bells. Organ and brass band struck up, full strength: the Vestry door curtains fell back to each side: out came the great Cathedral crosses and blessed banners, with all the Cathedral Choir and Clergy, with all voices lifted aloft in 'Come, all ye Faithful.' By this time, the triforium and clerestories, as well as every space in the Cathedral, were packed with faces: all there sang as they had never sung: the singing shook the whole building.

Somehow it seemed to Kay that it was shaking the Cathedral to pieces: all the heads came off all the bodies and moved up into the air still singing. He himself was being shaken to pieces, his own head was surely coming off, still singing, through the Cathedral roof. In fact, the Cathedral was not there, nor any of all that glorious company: no: he was in a railway carriage on a bitterly cold day: the train was stopped: he was at Condicote Station, with his pocket full of money, just home for the holidays and Caroline Louisa was waking him. 'Why, Kay,' she was saying, 'wake up, wake up. You have been sound asleep. Welcome home for the holidays. Have you had a nice dream?'

'Yes,' he said, 'I have.'